'A stunning book. A grand naval adventure of the days of sail, with mutiny, political machinations, and a scarred captain who has internal foes, including the demon of memory, to fight off as well. In an utterly authentic voice, Katie Daysh brings to life the terrifying power of the sea, and the bonds of both love and duty that tie a captain to his ship, and his men'

Damion Hunter, author of *Shadow of the Eagle*

'Katie Daysh has created an utterly unique and intriguing addition to the genre of Age of Fighting Sail fiction. Her protagonist, Captain Hiram Nightingale, is at once heroic and vulnerable, a man who is wounded in multiple ways, all perfectly believable. Daysh pulls a neat trick here, exploring issues that were certainly as real for the people of the 18th century, though rarely discussed, as they are for people today. And all the while she keeps her historical world perfectly believable and keeps the pages turning'

James Nelson, author of *The Guardship*

'A complex and compelling new naval hero sets sail!'

J. D. Davies, author of *Sailor of Liberty*

'Superb historical fiction. Profound, intricate, artful. A truly original story of forbidden love and adventure. I urge you to sail into the storm!'

A. J. West, *Sunday Times* bestselling author

Leeward

Katie Daysh works in retail but her passions are writing fiction and history, which she has an Open University degree in. Her debut novel, *Leeward*, will be followed by two other naval adventures featuring Hiram Nightingale and Arthur Courtney. She lives on the Isle of Wight.

LEEWARD

KATIE DAYSH

CANELO

First published in the United Kingdom in 2023 by Canelo

This edition published in the United Kingdom in 2023 by

Canelo
Unit 9, 5th Floor
Cargo Works, 1-2 Hatfields
London SE1 9PG
United Kingdom

A CIP catalogue record for this book is available from the British Library.

Ebook ISBN 978 1 80436 405 5
Hardback ISBN 978 1 80436 404 8
Paperback ISBN 978 1 80436 570 0

Cover design by Head Design

Cover images © Alamy

Look for more great books at www.canelo.co

Printed and bound in Great Britain by Clays Ltd, Elcograf S.p.A.

I

To my mum, dad, George, and all of my family and friends who have always supported me.

To my online friends, especially Larry, Emmarey, Emily and Wez who have been there throughout Leeward's journey.

Part I

Chapter One: The Devil's Mass

1 August 1798, Aboukir Bay, Egypt

Captain Hiram Nightingale climbed from the hot, crowded belly of the *Lion* and out into bright light. He stepped onto the quarterdeck, slipped in the frothing mixture of blood and water, and groped for the lee-rail. No one noticed. Every man rushed about to extinguish the growing fires.

Nightingale recovered himself and turned to look off the starboard bow. His stomach tightened. Remains of *Bellerophon*'s destroyed mainmast floated in the seething debris of the bay, clung to by a gang of desperate French sailors. Consumed by horrified awe, Nightingale stared up at the inflamed rage of the *Orient*. The gargantuan French flagship spat gouts of flame which licked up her ragged sails. He had to raise his head to look at her masts.

They were close, too close, not even a cable's length away.

Swallowing his dread, Nightingale staggered through the black smoke and reached the helm. In the barrage of cannonfire, one of the lanterns, hung to identify British ships, had fallen from the mizzen. A midshipman, Cleveland, was still dampening the fire. First Lieutenant Leroy Sawyer knelt with him. As Nightingale approached, Leroy stood and reached to tug the peak of his hat in salute before realising it was gone. Blood welled from a cut on his forehead, staining his sweat-soaked fair hair. The sudden encounter with his injury chilled Nightingale.

'You are hurt,' Nightingale said. He could barely hear himself.

'Below, sir!' Leroy urged. 'You should go below!'

'You are hurt!' Nightingale repeated, louder. Leroy waved a hand as if it were nothing. 'What is the damage report, Lieutenant?'

3

'The main-topmast is struck clean away, sir, and everything above the foretop. The bowsprit is only hanging on by the standing rigging and one timber, perhaps. And these fires…'

'The anchor cables are cut. Our guns are silenced for now. Attend to the fires, Mr Sawyer. There's…' *Little more we can do*, he was going to say, but it sounded too ominous.

Leroy hesitated, as if Nightingale would change his mind. Nightingale fought through those seconds, on the verge of begging Leroy to find somewhere safe.

'Be careful,' he said instead, briefly reaching out and squeezing his arm. He did not know if Leroy heard as he hurried away.

Nightingale clamped his hands into fists behind his back whilst he surveyed the bay. It was almost impossible to believe that it was nightfall. Exploding balls of light turned the waters into a fiery apocalypse, illuminated by the feverish hulk of the *Orient*. Thank God *Swiftsure* and *Alexander* had ceased firing upon her, though he could still hear the roaring of cannons further along the coast. Wood and flesh splintered at the end of each of those streaks of luminescence. At first, he had heard the individual voices.

Now it was all one devil's mass.

The *Lion* crawled through the slaughter. Nightingale had set course for the *Tonnant* and her eighty guns, but the stern anchor had been too slow to deploy and the ship faced the *Orient*. She still towered over them, even after the anchor cables had been cut to escape her.

Nightingale's nails imprinted his palm. Helplessness petrified his limbs. After the ferocity of the last hours, he could only watch the tattered sails as they caught the paltry breeze; pray that the fires had been extinguished; hope that the canvas and decks were wetted enough to bear the fury of what was coming.

Beside him, Cleveland staggered to his feet. Burn marks scored his hands from the fractured lanterns. He quickly hid them before Nightingale could send him to Dr Harrow.

'You should return to your division, Mr Cleveland,' Nightingale said. 'They'll be looking for your guidance when the guns start again.'

4

The first smile Nightingale had seen for hours crossed the boy's face. For a moment, Nightingale envied his fourteen-year-old enthusiasm. Then it vanished. Cleveland looked from Nightingale and forward, eyes widening.

'Sir...'

Nightingale turned, in time to see dazzling light streaming through the *Orient*'s stern gallery windows. Her entire quarterdeck shimmered like a mirage. In one horrible second, scything rays burst from every open space.

The *Lion* fell into silhouette. Black shadows of the crew froze.

'All hands down!' Nightingale bellowed, grabbing Cleveland, shoving him behind the helm. 'Down, down—'

He was still screaming as the *Orient*'s seams convulsed like a failing heart. A bright orange aura consumed the bay.

And the sun erupted.

The explosion kicked Nightingale in the chest. He fell to his back, instinctively rolled over, and clasped his hands over his head. The scream of 118 guns blowing to pieces tore at him, made every timber in the *Lion* bounce and shake. Angry waves, ploughing from the ripped hull of the *Orient*, lifted the ship's bows, slammed her down. The rest of the lanterns shattered around Nightingale, igniting into pockets of fire.

And then came the debris of the *Orient*. Nightingale raised his head in time to see her main-topmast pitch over in the air and impale the ocean, yards away from the *Lion*'s hull. Scraps of metal pinwheeled, slicing through the stays. Red-hot steel ripped holes in the ship's frame, tearing up rails and ladders and chunks of the helm. Nightingale ducked, but not in time to stop a raining hail of splinters gouging into his forehead.

Agony raked him. Black halos crossed his vision as thick, viscous numbness overcame his bones. He dropped into darkness, limbs like lead weights.

When he awoke, everything was silent. Somehow, he had rolled again to his back. The sky dripped down on him like a bloody scar, ragged ropes crossing the crimson, a white topsail slowly flying free. He blinked and it all turned to shade.

5

With a terrified lurch, he sat upright. His head screamed. Rivulets of blood poured down his cheeks, pooling in his collar. He blinked and blinked, trying to clear the haze, but it would not vanish. Everything blurred into an ugly spill of colour.

Trembling, he reached out and felt the broken stumps of the helm. Something warm was entangled in it. The dead weight of Cleveland slumped against the wheel; Nightingale searched, half-blind, and found a gash which had opened the boy's stomach.

He groaned, jerking backwards and staggering to his feet. He slipped on the trail of blood, caught his heel on the fallen mizzen cap. Warmth blazed at his legs as he nearly toppled into the blazing lanterns.

'Fire!' he tried to call, but his voice only croaked. 'Fire, fire...' he repeated, fumbling for something to hold on to and careening onto the deck. Orange smears shimmered across his vision. Nightingale dragged himself through the ruins of his ship. With a moan, the maintop collapsed. He could have vomited, as if every broken spar were a part of his own body. He had destroyed the proud *Lion* in this slaughter. If only he had ordered the cables cut sooner, if only they had anchored in their intended place...

Ignorant of his regret, hazy forms ran about the deck, calling to one another. Someone grabbed his arm and wrenched him to his feet, then disappeared to throw water over the blazes.

'Captain! Captain!' someone cried.

'Never mind me,' he tried to rasp.

But the voice kept shouting. Nightingale stumbled in its direction, the world rushing around him. Darkness returned and he nearly fell. Somewhere across the bay, the guns had started again. Their deep booms trembled through him. He pushed on and the voice came once more.

This time, though: 'Hiram, Hiram...'

And he knew who it was.

The agony of before became a pinprick compared to what awaited him at the foremast. Leroy had only made it that far before being struck down. Nightingale collapsed to his knees beside him. He could only see through a thin tunnel but beneath his hands, he could sense the damage. Debris pinned down Leroy's torso, spars stuck in, and as Nightingale moved his hands up, he felt worse.

'Oh God,' Nightingale hissed. He touched the splinter which had pierced Leroy's neck. With every wet gasp, blood pumped out.

'I'm going to… I'm going to take it out, Leroy. I'll staunch the blood. Find Dr Harrow.'

'No! No…' Leroy grabbed his hand. He pulled it to his chest where Nightingale could feel how weak his heart was. 'I can't… I can't see, Hiram. I'm so cold. Go below. It's not safe.'

Nightingale leant closer. 'I'm not leaving you here.'

'I can't. Please… just let me—'

Nightingale grabbed tighter. He barely realised he was weeping as he rested his head against Leroy's, cupping his damp cheek as if he could wipe away the pain. Leroy shuddered.

'I'm so sorry,' Nightingale managed.

Leroy shook his head. With his last strength, he wrapped his other hand around Nightingale's, squeezing.

'I wish it could have been different,' he whispered.

And then that strength left him. His grip loosened and he fell back against the mast, eyes closed. Nightingale could not make himself believe that he had witnessed the end of Leroy's life. He kept holding onto his hand, kept stroking his cheek, kept rasping his name urgently until his vision completely failed him.

The void opened up as the darkness swept in. There was nothing there but pain.

Hands reached for him. Voices shouted. The fires raged. 'Captain!' someone called again. Nightingale fought against them, shrieking, crying, grief sharpened by the sudden blackness. 'Captain! You have to get below! Captain!'

A cannonball screamed overhead. It was answered by the *Lion*'s guns bursting back into life.

'Captain! Captain!'

The shadows took over. Nightingale let them.

Chapter Two: Aureate

20 June 1800

Nightingale had weathered three weeks across the Atlantic without so much as a turned stomach. His head had ached at the remorseless sun, but he had become accustomed to that after years of sensitivity. Now, though, with the wind shifting in the *Maiden*'s courses and Antigua nearing, he found himself on the edge of his cot, hands pressed to his eyes. Hot shivers of nausea disturbed him as every wave rolled the cabin in slow undulations.

He had not been seasick since he was a twelve-year-old midshipman spending his first nights away from land. That was decades ago and yet the emotions were the same: crushing loneliness, nagging doubt, terror at what lay ahead.

As a child, however, he had wanted to go home. He could not do that now – not without returning to memories that hurt to reawaken.

Nightingale slowly removed his hands. They shook as if he were in the southern latitudes and not the baking heat of the tropics. Disgusted, he gripped a thin wrist to try to stop it. The trembling continued.

Damn it, he thought. *Damn it, damn it*. He had prayed this venture would stop such weakness.

'By the mark four!'

The cry from the main deck echoed through the bulkheads. Nightingale pretended that he was hiding down here to avoid the general busyness of a ship coming into port. They did not need him, a Royal Navy post-captain, judging the actions of a West Indiaman. In truth, they had performed well; the *Maiden*'s skipper, Whitehead, had been

8

very accommodating in giving him this passage, and he had only lost one spar during the crossing.

Soon, Nightingale would step back into that sphere of command, although on a much higher pedestal. If he set his feet right, a commodore's pennant might await him. Once he might have yearned for such a thing, hoisting his flag, taking responsibility for a squadron of vessels, achieving glory.

Another wave of sickness rolled over him. He breathed through it, chest constricting with every intake of air. What would people say if they knew Captain – perhaps Commodore – Nightingale was shivering and quaking like a child, close to weeping?

Angry, he rose to his feet. He tottered at the sudden change in position then, in one determined movement, flipped open the lid of his sea-chest. His clothes had been packed and repacked with neat, naval precision. Back in Portsmouth, Louisa had cast a questioning eye over the contents and asked, 'Are you certain you have everything you need?' as if ramming home the point that he would be gone for months, perhaps more, before she decided to join him.

Nightingale had delayed the inevitable all the way across the Atlantic. Atop his books and papers, spare shirts and breeches and drawers, he touched the thick deep-blue wool of his captain's dress coat. Gently, he pulled it out, shaking out the pleats and brushing the non-existent dust from the epaulettes. Gold lace trimmed the cuffs and the lapels, and anchors decorated the silver buttons. None of it looked bright or impressive in the cramped confines of the merchant ship's cabin. Nightingale rubbed at a patch of lace, realised he was deliberately obstructing his obligation, so drew the coat quickly over his arms. He had to tug at it to fit his now-thinner frame, fiddling like an awkward boy.

It was the first time he had donned it in almost two years. On the *Lion* he had never appeared on deck without it in full. That seventy-four-gun heroine was far away now, though, and he simply felt shabby. The tired, ageing man he had become should have been a stranger, yet he well recognised the pallid appearance, the drawn mouth and sallow green eyes, the curling red hair pulled sharply back into its tie. He had become a mockery of his former glory.

Stupidly, he had allowed Louisa to talk him into bringing a memento of that glory with him. It had been bundled in his frock coat and now lay upon the sheets. Nightingale eyed the unremarkable box, chewing his lip. He was not going to wear it, he told himself – but then, why had he brought it across the ocean, carrying it like a burden?

Choked with feelings he wished he could tear out, he knelt and drew shaking fingers over the latch. The lid opened and there, resting within like a body in its coffin, was the token which was soaked in so much bloodshed. Nightingale lifted it and stared, wracked with indecision, into its aureate glow. The agony it awoke was almost alluring.

'Captain Nightingale?'

A hurried knock sounded and before he could answer, the door opened. The young, beaming face of Robert Whitehead peered around.

'Captain Nightin— Oh, sir, that's it, isn't it? My father told me that you had one!'

Nightingale realised he was still holding the medal. He set it down but not before Robert barged into the room, bouncing on the balls of his feet.

'Can I see it properly, sir? Could I... could I hold it?'

Nightingale closed his mouth, which had been gaping inanely. He forced a smile.

'Of course.'

Robert, without taking his eyes from the medal, tenderly took it from Nightingale and cradled it as if it were alive. This was the inspiration that drove young boys like him out to sea: the hope of adventure and glory and some material reminder of that honour. To him, only pride should be attached to such a golden token.

'It is wonderful, sir. A real Nile medal! Did Lord Nelson give it to you himself? Did you meet him? When you fought at the Nile, what was it like? You must tell me, sir.'

Nightingale held out a hand. Robert reluctantly gave the medal back.

'Those are a lot of questions, Mr Whitehead. I'm not sure which to answer first.'

'Aren't you going to wear the medal, sir?'

Nightingale locked the box and chuckled.

'That is another question.'

'You should wear it, sir. Lord Nelson always wears his medals.'

'It is too precious for that, Mr Whitehead, and I fear I would look quite vain in front of the admiral. Come, what is it you wanted from me?'

'Oh.' Robert blinked, as if only remembering that he had come to find Nightingale. 'Father wonders if you would like to come up on deck. He would like a drink with you, seeing as we're coming into English Harbour.'

'I shall be up momentarily.'

'Can I walk with you, sir? I want to hear about the Nile, sir, and about the *Orient* exploding!'

Nightingale had no choice but to accompany the eager twelve-year-old whirlwind that was Robert Whitehead onto deck. Questions bombarded him like a cannonade. Nightingale said what the boy wanted to hear, and only once did he tell the truth – about dining with Lord Nelson in the cabin of the *Vanguard*. That, he did not say, was the last time he felt as though he belonged amongst that constellation of shining stars. Not long after, he had imploded and burnt.

'Robert!'

Captain Whitehead's booming voice echoed from the poop deck. Robert hurried over, making sure that Nightingale was still with him.

'Father,' he said, 'Captain Nightingale was telling me about the Battle of the Nile. You said that he had a medal – he let me—'

'Apologies for my son, Captain Nightingale,' Whitehead interrupted in his rough, Hull baritone. 'He can run a little wild at times. I hope he did not bother you.'

'Not at all,' Nightingale said.

'He can run up to the masthead and shout if we are about to collide with any other vessels.'

Both father and son knew that the possibility of that was minuscule, but Robert bowed his head and did as he was told. Captain Whitehead sighed. He mopped his sweat-slick forehead and took a sip from the glass he was holding.

'Apologies again, Captain Nightingale. I was going to wait to drink until you came onto deck but I can never accustom myself to this heat. And that boy... Sometimes, he presses his luck.'

Nightingale smiled thinly. He was used to boys running around his ships – children sent to sea by ambitious parents, or escaped orphans – but none had Robert's familiarity.

'Here, Captain.' Captain Whitehead motioned for his steward, lurking by the taffrail, and Nightingale found a glass being pressed into his hand. 'Have you any children, sir?'

'No.' Nightingale was surprised at such a personal question. He attempted to voice an explanation for it; none came.

'Well, when you do, sir,' Whitehead continued, 'you'll find they're more troublesome than a crew of greenhorns. My Mary didn't want Robert coming with me – perhaps I should've listened to her. But I want him to know his ships – like his father and mine. I imagine your father thought the same about you.'

'Yes.'

'Ah, now there's a fine girl. I haven't seen her before in this harbour.' Nightingale was glad for the interruption. Captain Whitehead opened his spyglass and directed it towards the approaching coast. Without the help of the instrument, Nightingale could only see the jutting curve of Antigua's English Harbour and the green rise of the hills around it. Vague shapes of ships bobbed on the calm, blue waters but which one of them Captain Whitehead was looking at, he could not tell.

'The *Prince of Wales*,' he narrated. 'She must be the new admiral's flagship. Every time we dock, there's a new commander-in-chief.'

'The yellow fever does not incite many people to linger.'

'Indeed it does not. I shall be filling sails again as soon as we unload. I wish you luck in whatever it is that you have been called to do, Captain. This place either brings you fortune or it digs your grave.'

Smiling despite the gloomy sentiment, Whitehead raised his glass and drained it. Nightingale followed, tasting the shock of the claret and swallowing with a grimace. Fortune and death occupied parallel places in his career, yet the perils of stumbling on either side had not been his concern for almost two years. As he listened idly to Captain Whitehead's reminiscences and watched the harbour approach, it all rushed back. He had much to prove – to himself, to Louisa, to the others who had convinced him to follow this new path.

Yet already he felt hollow: a captain playing make-believe in another man's uniform. Perhaps it would all come back to him. Perhaps it would not.

–

Before Nightingale had left the *Maiden* at her anchorage, Robert Whitehead had stuffed a bread roll into his hand. Nightingale had intended to eat it as he walked through English Harbour but he did not dare move the handkerchief from his nose and mouth. Sweat stuck everywhere – beneath his neckcloth and high collar, plastering his hair to his forehead. Every person – white, black, brown – gleamed hotly as the sun rose to its zenith. It beat down on the busy docklands, clustered with merchantmen and frigates and barges, choked with the sounds of hammering and sawing and men's voices competing with one another.

Nightingale kept his head down, both to avoid being accosted by folk selling their wares and to stop himself tripping on the uneven paths. A boy scurried past with a message and Nightingale stepped back, feeling an overripe orange squelch beneath his polished shoe. Stray animals and children raced to snatch the fallen fruit. He grimaced and turned, only to find himself in someone else's way. An angry voice sent him hurrying from the market towards the cramped buildings.

Straw awnings gave paltry shade to men slumped on the ground. Nightingale worried that he saw the phantom of the fever in their exhaustion until he noticed empty bottles beside them. One of the men cracked open a filmy eye and held up a threadbare hat. 'Something for a poor veteran, Captain?' he croaked.

Nightingale sped his steps, avoiding the chaos of the rest of the docks by slipping into a nearby alley and pressing on up the hill.

The white façade of a Palladian-fashion house sat on the rise, a flourish of style above the dense, practical working yard. Nightingale made his staggering way there. In the shadows of the tightly packed buildings, women lounged against the walls or sat on the laps of sailors on leave from their ships. One girl, dolled with rouge to disguise the premature lines on her face, called to Nightingale with a coquettish, 'Captain!'

He found his voice to babble an embarrassed, 'I'm married, miss,' which prompted a cackle of laughter.

It was interrupted by the sound of feet racing towards them. Raised voices reverberated through the labyrinth of alleys, accompanied by a man in a striped shirt and loose trousers dotted with blood. Nightingale hopped out of his path.

'Mr Uriah!' shouted a man somewhere up the hill. 'Follow him that way!'

An older man barrelled into the alleyway past Nightingale. He blew shrilly into a bosun's whistle then bellowed for the escapee to come back.

Nightingale stared after them for a while but knew there was nothing he could do. It was a familiar sight in any station around the globe – sailors testing their luck, creating havoc where they could. These West Indian ports, where disease and climate stoked everyone's fires, were notorious for their lax discipline.

The moment passed. Nightingale gathered himself and returned to the hill. He had boarded ships in full uniform before, yet this simple climb made his limbs ache. He removed his hat and waved it before his flushed face, and for a moment was even tempted to wrench off his coat. It was only the careful preening he had done before leaving the *Maiden* which stopped him.

Without his hat, Nightingale's eyes stung by the time he reached the port-captain's office. A headache bit at his temples. He smiled with a politeness he did not feel as he presented himself to a clerk and was guided through into an antechamber to wait. It was no better inside. The windows were sealed and the drapes were drawn. Nightingale sat, sweat dribbling between his shoulder blades. His hand came away damp as he swept it through his hair, which sprouted from its tie despite his best efforts.

Time congealed into thick molasses. Blurred by the heat, Nightingale's thoughts crept to the months ahead. Soon, he would be back upon the ocean, making his way to Trinidad. The formerly Spanish island was slowly being transferred into British governorship after its capture three years before. It would be a strange mixture of seamanship and politicking – only one of which Nightingale had any experience in. His father-in-law, Sir William Haywood, had promised to guide him, but Nightingale was uncertain whether that comforted him or not.

If he failed, many people would judge him for it – and God knew he had been judged since returning from the Nile. Louisa had been remarkably stalwart despite his ragged appearance: head half-wrapped in bandages, scars from his eye sockets to his hairline. She had nursed him through those dark months with only one comment about her own grief: 'I could have lost you, Hiram.'

Perhaps, in ways, she had.

The opening door pulled him back to the present. Nightingale stood and brushed himself down as the clerk showed him into another, equally stuffy room. A post-captain, rather than commander-in-chief Admiral Lord Seymour, sat behind a desk heaving with paperwork. He barely looked up as he finalised a letter.

'Captain Hiram Nightingale,' the man greeted. Nightingale bowed and took the moment to furiously cycle through names, miraculously landing on Captain Thomas Bridger, a colleague from Cape St Vincent. 'The winds were kind to you, then. We did not expect you for another day or two.'

'I had a good transport in the *Maiden*.'

'I noticed her in the bay, yes.' Bridger indicated for Nightingale to sit. He did, perching awkwardly. 'Lord Seymour sends his apologies. This pestilence has everyone seeing ghouls. The hospital is choked with poor devils who won't last the month. It has changed our – and your – circumstances quite dramatically.'

Nightingale frowned. He made to speak but Bridger continued.

'You came here, under Sir William Haywood's recommendation, to take command of the naval support in Trinidad. Because of certain events, it has been reconsidered. Your orders have changed.' He handed over a sealed packet to Nightingale, who took it with a bewildered glance. A thousand questions fought for dominance in his mind. 'You may read them and I shall give you further details.'

Nightingale obeyed, drawing his eyes down the neat handwriting and the set phrases, dappled with specifics about ship, place and time. He read it, then again, and again.

HMS *Ulysses*. Mutiny. The slaughter of officers. The vanishing of the vessel.

He was being pulled from Trinidad to hunt her down.

Heat crept over him – this time from the inside, making it difficult to feel anything but the warmth of his approaching dread.

'Captain Bridger,' he finally said. 'Sir, with every respect, it was Sir William's recommendation that I—'

'It was Sir William's recommendation for this too. He and your father strongly encouraged the admiral to consider you.'

The anger of his father's influence stirred in Nightingale.

'I feel obliged to say,' he intoned carefully, 'that I have no experience with mutineers.'

'It is not an experience any of us ever want, Captain.' Bridger finally lay down the pen. 'This is not something to be sniffed at, Hiram. I do not have to impress upon you the importance of it. Many have achieved greatness as frigate captains: Pellew, Parker, even Nelson began his career in these waters in command of frigates. Your *Scylla* is a fine ship – a fifth-rate, thirty-two guns plus her carronades. She is not young but she is well served and if rightly handled, a fast sailer. If Captain Carlisle had survived the fever, he would be in your position and you would be in Trinidad.'

'How many others died from the fever?'

'They were badly hit. They have only recently hauled down their yellow quarantine flag. Twenty...' he checked a ledger, '...six hands died, as well as a handful of petty officers and their second lieutenant. Lieutenant Courtney, the first officer, has been holding down affairs since the captain's death a month past, God rest the man. Courtney is a capable lieutenant but not experienced enough for this task.'

Nightingale nodded, feeling unable to do more. This commission could be a stepping-stone to great glory, the kind to erase his guilt. Yet not for many a year had Nightingale sailed so far from the watch of an admiral. A frigate captain's command could be the loneliest in the service. The higher the ascension, the further the fall.

'I'm assuming that you know the tale of Scylla, Captain, and see why, as well as her technicalities, she is so suited to the role?'

Nightingale nodded again. 'She was a great serpent who harassed Ulysses on his travels home to Ithaca. Across from her was the whirlpool, Charybdis, so Ulysses was—'

'—caught between Scylla and Charybdis, yes, Hiram, I was being droll, perhaps inappropriately so.'

'Ulysses survived her,' Nightingale said, and immediately regretted it.

'You shall join the *Scylla* today, Hiram. The stores are already coming aboard – six months' worth of supplies under the eventuality that you should need to round the Horn and enter the Pacific. They are expecting you but none of the officers know of these new orders. I recommend that you tell them before more rumour spreads and then visit the naval hospital. A boatload of survivors from the *Ulysses* arrived only yesterday.'

'How many crew shall we be facing… should we succeed?'

'That, we cannot be sure of.' Bridger picked up his pen again. 'I wish you fortune, Captain Nightingale. I trust you shall use your judgement and intuition. Sir William and your father have aided you by their recommendations.'

Nightingale did not feel the elation he knew he should have felt. His journey to the West Indies had come after a long period of debate with himself and he had barely set his feet on dry land before all of that persuasion had been overturned. He had to trust in Sir William's faith, trust in his own judgement – yet his judgement had been muddled for many a month.

He exited into the ferocious sun with the orders burning his breast. They crinkled as he left the seclusion of the port office and returned to the harbour. This time, he was barely conscious of the press of people or the work resounding along the shore. All he looked for was the *Scylla*, his new home. There were many masts splitting the sky and many painted hulls anchored on the water.

A memory of the *Lion* arose, the anticipation of joining her and then, later, in her grand cabin, his reunion with Lieutenant Leroy Sawyer: once mids together then separated by place and rank. Nightingale had climbed the ladder quicker.

And how far he had fallen, unable to save Leroy.

Nightingale breathed, feeling the old, familiar pain. He was not aware of his name being shouted until a large, fair-haired man stood up in a launch boat by the pier.

'Captain Nightingale!' he called again.

A band of bargeman craned their necks around to stare at him. They were dressed in their best blue jackets, duck trousers and sennit hats emblazoned with a ribbon saying "*Scylla*". The tall man lifted a hand. Nightingale made his way over, seeing that his chest and effects had already been delivered to the boat.

'Barty Abbott, sir,' the man greeted as hats came off in respect. 'Captain's coxswain. Steady as you go, sir.'

With hands reaching to steady him, Nightingale took a step off the pier and down into the cutter. The *Scylla*, freshly out of quarantine, awaited.

Chapter Three: The Scylla

The entire ship's company had turned out, washed and shaved, scrubbed pink and dressed in their best. The marines gleamed in red, cross-belts bright white, and with weapons shining and crashing as they saluted Nightingale. All hats immediately came off when Nightingale first set foot on the hallowed quarterdeck.

It was a time-honoured ritual; some saw it as the marriage of a captain to his new vessel. As the first pleasant surprise of the day, Nightingale noticed that she was spotlessly clean, her wales lovingly painted and not a drop of melted tar upon the deck despite the heat.

But, as he read out his commission, he let his eyes move from the page to the assemblage. White scalps emerged from beneath tied hair, bones jutted from around tired eyes. The ghost of the yellow fever still haunted the vessel.

A tall lieutenant stepped forward once he was finished. He seemed old for such an officer, somewhere north of thirty, although his ageing look could have been due to his gaunt appearance and thinning fair hair. His cheeks reddened as he saluted Nightingale.

'Lieutenant Courtney?' Nightingale asked, attributing his pallor to the stresses of Carlisle's death and his ensuing responsibilities.

'Oh.' The man cleared his throat. 'No, sir. I am Second Lieutenant Hargreaves. Lieutenant Courtney is still ashore, dealing with business.'

'I see.'

'I have sent for him, sir.'

'Thank you, Lieutenant. As Mr Courtney is not here, perhaps you could accompany me?'

'Yes, sir.'

Hargreaves lingered awkwardly. Nightingale glanced towards the waiting men.

'You may dismiss the crew by their divisions, Lieutenant Hargreaves.'

'Yes, sir.'

The glamour of the ship immediately started to fade. Lieutenant Courtney's absence was an irritating breach in protocol – as the first officer, he should have been there to greet his new captain, certainly as he had been so instrumental during this last month. But Nightingale could not dwell on it yet.

The marine sentries stood aside as he entered his new cabin. It was spacious, spanning the ship's width and painted an airy pale green. The gallery windows gaped open, letting in tiny gasps of the breeze and filtering light across the black-and-white chequered floor. It seemed to have been kept exactly as Captain Carlisle had left it, with books still on the shelves, a small watercolour sketch of a harbour at night, and even ink remaining in its pot on the writing desk. Nightingale almost expected to see the dead man's clothes hanging in the attached night-cabin.

'Has this cabin been in use?' Nightingale asked.

'Lieutenant Courtney has been using it for correspondence and administration, sir,' Hargreaves explained. When Nightingale did not vocally approve of that, he continued, 'He did not wish to be in the gunroom, sir, not after Lieutenant Pearson died.'

'But you and the midshipmen have been in your proper place in the gunroom?'

'I have only been aboard for a few days, sir – but yes. The entire ship has been cleaned, fumigated and scrubbed. It's kept the men occupied, sir.'

'Very good. Well, I shall look over the ship's logs and books then I wish to speak with the master.'

'Loom, sir.'

'Master Loom. As you were, Lieutenant Hargreaves. Please be so good as to inform me if Mr Courtney makes an appearance.'

Nightingale was left once again in isolation. Rubbing at his temples, he drew his chair to the edge of the gallery windows and tried to angle himself to catch the paltry breeze. He balanced the muster and logbooks on Carlisle's old writing desk and resisted the urge to tug the tight black stock from around his neck as he read. The books revealed the harshness of the last months: Captain Carlisle's hand started neat before wobbling, then trailing off completely in place of his clerk's. Four weeks before, Courtney's more hurried scrawl took over.

Nightingale's stomach tightened as he followed the names recorded in the muster. Many were crossed off, a brief explanation of their deaths at the hands of the fever. The disease had ripped through the compact lower berths and had only been marginally halted by the ship's anchorage. Nightingale found himself wanting to press his handkerchief over his mouth again. One hundred and eighty men, thirty-five marines, four midshipmen and two lieutenants remained, alongside the warrant officers. The only relief was that many of the crew were rated able – though whether that remained true after the dreadful malady would be tested by what lay ahead.

He saw the reality of the malaise as Josiah Loom, the *Scylla*'s sailing master, walked him around the ship. The older, stooped man insisted that the ship was well-manned and disciplined, enough to deliver three broadsides in five minutes. He narrated about each bulkhead and every beam of the vessel but between every one of those bulkheads and beams, Nightingale received his first glimpse of the crew away from their ceremonial dress. They gave the customary salutes yet he felt a strange oppression on each deck. The cleaning and sweeping went on without a single voice and even the topmen were silent as they checked the yards, canvas and rigging ready for sailing. When the noon observations were carried out, Lieutenant Hargreaves barely said a word to the midshipmen who mutely scribbled at their workings. The only pulse of energy came when food was served. Even then, as Nightingale walked past the messes, he noted many empty places.

'The bowsprit's been nicked a mite, sir,' Loom said upon the forecastle, as if that was the reason for the black atmosphere. 'Lieutenant Courtney's ensured a full repair. We're just waiting for the timber from the yard.'

'Very good, Mr Loom.' Nightingale peered over and saw nothing terrible amiss: just the same as the rest of the ship: everything in its place but something lurking beneath the surface. And there was still no sign of Lieutenant Courtney. 'Captain Carlisle obviously kept a taut ship.'

'Oh, yes, sir.' Loom removed his hat. 'He was here 'til the end. Died in his cot, he did. He said he wished to die at sea with his ship.'

'I'm sorry for your loss, Mr Loom.'

The dead man lingered everywhere. Nightingale stared at his empty cot from across the cabin, imagining the captain taking his last breaths in it. The anxiety of stepping into his shoes simmered. It was always difficult to take the helm from another man, especially one so liked. This was not what he had envisaged when leaving England. His plans had been carefully constructed and perhaps he had been foolish to place such faith in them. Nothing was ever constant on the sea.

He busied himself throughout the day, organising the administration, visiting the yard where supplies were coming aboard, setting his own possessions into place. But all of his work could not shake the orders from his mind. Later, he would have to reveal them to his officers and drop a stone into this already rippling pond.

–

Nightingale invited his primary officers to dinner that evening and from the very start, it was as morose as he had feared. Above the great cabin, the ambience of a working ship continued: the creaking of the yards as they were caught by the thin breezes; the shivering of canvas as it was hung out to dry; the constant kiss of the water against the hull. But, again, Nightingale could take no comfort in the familiar noises. He could only focus on the scraping of cutlery on plates, the shifting of the men around the table, and the slow grinding of their mouths.

He tried to engage them in idle conversation, yet each word echoed about the otherwise-dead room. Not for the first time, he hated the rigid regulation about men not speaking unless the captain addressed them. If they would just talk amongst themselves, it might not feel so damned awkward.

In between bites of the salted pork, Nightingale resorted to observing them.

His purser, John Winthrop, middle-aged and sallow, like a man who had already outgrown his skin.

Marine Lieutenant Amos Charlston, resplendent in his scarlet uniform but with sweat dribbling from his long nose. He filled the small table, broad-shouldered and solid.

The surgeon, Francis Archer, the polar opposite of Charlston – bird-like and thin, chewing every mouthful purposefully.

Yet at least they all ate what had been served to them. Lieutenant Hargreaves sat at Nightingale's right side and barely touched the meal, instead mopping up the gravy with a piece of bread and drowning it in his port. Behind him, Nightingale noticed his steward eyeing his own steward, Rylance, as if offended the man was not eating.

The only person who had spoken more than a word to Nightingale was the young midshipman, David Richmond. Very blonde and very red-cheeked, he answered Nightingale's questions about his life and about Antigua as if desperate to prove himself. The others seemed to have nothing to want to prove.

They were a diverse bunch but they were united by the ship on which they served – and by the voyage that Nightingale was now about to tell them of. He was on the cusp of it when a disturbance on deck robbed his words. Someone had just boarded and hurrying footsteps rushed to meet them. Through the skylight, Nightingale heard a strong, rural Hampshire accent not unlike those he had grown up around.

'Why was I not sent for?' it accused.

'We tried, sir,' a midshipman replied. 'Lieutenant Hargreaves sent Mr Garland.'

'Is he here now?' Then, at the affirmative, 'Good God!'

The officers avoided Nightingale's gaze. But there was no ignoring the heavy footsteps which approached the cabin, though, nor the knock at the door.

A young man entered – and a new, colder dread raced through Nightingale.

The lieutenant was red from the sun and sprinkled with a fine layer of sand, but his uniform was immaculate. Though he must have been over ten years Nightingale's junior, he stood with the easy authority of a man accustomed to his rank being obeyed – bicorne hat beneath his arm, buttons shining gold, breeches a hastily cleaned white. He was remarkably handsome, dark curls pulled back into a short tail.

But none of that was the reason for the rippled gasp which spread through the officers.

An angry black bruise circled the man's right eye and cheekbone.

'Lieutenant Arthur Courtney?' Nightingale asked.

'Yes, sir. I apologise for my lateness. I had to attend to some business ashore.'

'You are wounded.'

'It is nothing, sir.'

'You have been struck,' Nightingale rephrased.

'I am fine, sir.'

'Please, take a seat, Lieutenant. Allow Dr Archer to inspect your eye.'

Courtney hesitated but then obeyed, sitting at Nightingale's other side. Dr Archer set down his fork and made Courtney look up into the light streaming through the gallery windows. Only at the confirmation that nothing was gravely wrong did Nightingale allow the dinner to continue. Courtney, not only red from the sun now, met Nightingale's inquisitive gaze. His eyes were strikingly green but unmistakably cold. Something had happened ashore.

'You have not missed anything, Lieutenant,' Nightingale began, control over the evening wobbling. 'I was about to discuss the *Scylla*'s future. I understand that she has suffered some grievous losses and has been in quarantine for the last few weeks. Now that she is out of it, she – we are being ordered to sea.'

Courtney opened his mouth to say something but stopped himself. Nightingale continued.

'Whether you have heard or not, I'm not certain. The *Ulysses* has mutinied on the Main. We have been ordered to find her, bring her to port and to justice.'

The sound of cutlery and of chewing immediately ceased. Officers who had seemed so lifeless before suddenly found their spark, glancing at one another, back to Nightingale. Courtney shifted, his reddened cheeks losing their colour.

'Doubtless you have heard about the *Hermione* mutiny and the slaughter on her decks,' Nightingale said. 'About the murder of Captain Pigot and the officers aboard, and how the ship was given up to the Spanish in La Guaira. Captain Hamilton performed a heroic deed by recapturing the *Hermione* and returning her to the service. We shall do the same for the *Ulysses* and her crew.'

Silence echoed through the cabin. Above them, a bell rang and the midshipman of the watch shouted up to the topmen.

'As far as is understood,' Nightingale said, 'the *Ulysses* mutinied in the first week of June. Her original responsibility was to patrol the Main with the *Peregrine*, yet one night their courses diverged and she was gone by dawn. It is not certain what the mutineers plan to do with the vessel but it seems she was heading south – she may be taken into a Spanish or French port along the South American coast, or it is possible she may try to round the Horn into the Pacific. I intend to find out. A boatload of escapees arrived at the naval hospital recently. I shall talk with them tomorrow morning. Lieutenant Courtney—' The young man looked up, drawn out of the haze he had slipped into. 'You shall accompany me.'

'Yes, sir. I…'

'You may speak freely.'

'The men, sir…' He interrupted himself. 'How many are left onboard the *Ulysses*?'

'We cannot be certain of that either. The *Ulysses* is a fifth-rate like the *Scylla*. She is younger but I have been made to understand that the *Scylla* is well-manned and well-drilled.' He glanced at Loom, who nodded with less certainty than he had when touring Nightingale around the ship. 'Mutineers or not, however, it would not do to underestimate our opponents.'

'They gave up the protection of the Crown the moment they rebelled,' Charlston said in a gruff Lancashire tone.

'Indeed. That is why they shall be brought to justice.' Nightingale took a breath and looked into his half-empty glass. Just this morning, he had been shaken by these orders. Now, he had to convince his men that he believed in this voyage whole-heartedly. 'I have seen the crew today. I believe that, after this disease and the terrible situation they have been put in, this shall do them some good.'

Weighed down by the burden of what had been said, the dinner stretched for an age after that. Nightingale's own feelings clouded the evening. He couldn't deny it, sitting amongst the men whom he would share the danger with: he did not want these orders. Belligerently, he regretted agreeing to Sir William and his father's suggestions to come to the West Indies. The temptation to refuse to do more drifted into his head, formless. But he could not do that – not without losing the respect of his wife, his father-in-law, his crew and indeed, the entire Admiralty. He could not give them even more powder to fill their accusations with.

It was a relief when the men filtered out. Only one thorny matter remained.

'Lieutenant Courtney,' he said as the officer was almost at the door. 'A word?'

Courtney looked longingly out into the corridor. 'Yes, sir?'

'What business were you attending to ashore?'

'It has been dealt with, sir,' Courtney said shortly.

'Tell me, Lieutenant. I will not ask again and have you refuse.'

Courtney flushed. He stood, slightly bowed by the cabin's low ceiling, looking even stiffer with his hands clasped tightly behind his back. Nightingale waited. 'One of our men was caught stealing when midshipman Richmond accompanied a group to the town to procure stores this morning. He was rough with a merchant. I and Mr Uriah, our bosun, went to deal with him. We brought him back to the ship under arrest.'

Nightingale remembered the name "Uriah" being shouted through the town when he walked to the port-captain's office, as well as the man who had rushed past him. He rose and closed the door. 'This is a serious infraction. I do not have to remind you of the Articles and the punishments for robbery. Regardless of if it was on sea or shore, the penalty remains the same.'

'I am aware, sir.'

'Who struck you?'

Courtney did not break Nightingale's gaze, staring at him longer than was wise for a subordinate under question. 'It was not our man,' he insisted.

'Are you certain? If it was, the punishment for striking a superior officer... But you know that, Lieutenant. I shall have to call an inquiry regardless.'

'Sir—'

'I have no choice. Robbery and violence. Acting as he did onshore whilst in the service of the navy. Do you see another way to proceed?'

Courtney's mouth twitched but he did not reply. For a moment, Nightingale felt a shameful resentment towards him and his easy, handsome authority. It was gone as soon as it had appeared. Left behind was the frustration at what he now had to do.

He dismissed Courtney with the dinner churning in his stomach. The pressures of the day washed over him and he sat heavily down in his seat. Damning propriety, he tore off his stock and let out a long, wavering breath. It was not enough to be chasing a mutinous ship across the ocean. Articles of War had been broken, demanding punishment. All of his crew and officers would look to him, once word spread, to do what was right.

Just as he had begun the day, he ended it with his head in his hands, trying to convince himself he had made the correct decision.

Chapter Four: Survivors

Nightingale awoke with a splitting headache. Above him, the bell rang five times and it sounded as if the quartermaster was clanging it inside his skull. He slowly swung his legs out of the cot. He had not intended to sleep there, unable to rid himself of the idea of Carlisle's death, but the locker beneath the gallery windows had put a crick in his back. As soon as he could, he would send Rylance to buy new sheets, even a new hammock.

As if listening to his thoughts, there was a knock at the door and the young steward entered. Lighting up his freckled, round face, his polite smile was one of the first Nightingale had seen. The tray he set down was even sweeter, awash with the scent of freshly brewed coffee, and sausages and eggs just out of the galley. He stepped back and waited expectantly, eyeing Nightingale, then the food.

'Thank you, Rylance,' Nightingale said stiffly. 'How did you know I was awake?'

'Oh, I hear everything, sir. Curse of a steward.'

'I see. Well. Pass the word for Lieutenant Courtney. I wish to leave for the hospital as soon as possible.'

'Lieutenant Courtney it is, sir.'

Nightingale idly nudged his breakfast around with his fork, swilling the sausage in the fractured egg yolk. He chewed it without tasting anything. All his focus adhered to what awaited him at the hospital and, next, what he would have to do about the Article breaker. A thousand possibilities rose; he must have entangled himself too deeply in them for, by the time Courtney appeared, his coffee was stone-cold.

Despite the breakfast, his stomach still growled with anxiety as he and Courtney were rowed ashore. The bright heat made Nightingale squint under the shade of his hat. Courtney barely looked at him – he had not said a word other than their customary greeting. That curious, embarrassing resentment simmered in Nightingale again. Courtney had spilled the wretched issue of the thievery into his lap and then stepped down from the mantle of command. He no longer bore the sole responsibility for the *Scylla* and her crew.

Yet perhaps that was the heart of it. He had tripped in his final day as acting captain, watching a man break the Articles, even being struck in the heat of it. It would leave a bitter taste – and Nightingale would be a fool if he thought that Courtney would accept his place as a lieutenant with a clear mind. The advancement to post-rank was fickle but coveted, and surely Courtney had thought he was closer to it after Carlisle's death.

They walked alone through the dockyards towards the hospital. The sky hardened into a fierce blue and the sun turned remorseless. Nightingale's head throbbed with every step. His eyes would never recover, Dr Harrow had said. Fragments of the incandescent *Orient* would always scar him. The dazzling day made it worse; his vision blurred and stung at the edges. He refused to let Courtney see his weakness.

'You began to say something,' he said as they stepped out of a cart's path. 'Last evening, when I spoke about our orders, you began to talk of the men.'

'The order to sea surprised me, sir,' Courtney said.

'The *Scylla* is out of quarantine now. She has a new second lieutenant and now a new captain. No one wants her to languish in port any longer.'

'I understand that, sir. But...' He paused.

'As the *Scylla*'s commander, Lieutenant, I wish to know if there is anything that will affect her capabilities.'

'We are below complement, sir. The men can be despondent. I don't wish to speak badly of them – they've done all they can considering their situation – but the fever has sapped even those it did not infect. There's a... darkness over them.'

'As I said, Lieutenant, such a voyage may do them good. They are sailors, are they not? One cannot sail very far whilst in a harbour.'

'With respect, sir, I have suffered with them these last months. When Captain Carlisle died, it became very bleak.'

'Yes, I understand that Captain Carlisle was a well-loved man.' Nightingale did not mean to say it so sharply. He reddened and blamed the pain in his head. 'I hope I can live up to your memory of him.'

'Yes, sir.'

They smelt the naval hospital as soon as they approached it. Decay and disease bled through the doors, and Nightingale had to keep his mouth from curling when they entered and were led by an attendant through the grim aisles. The beds which were not curtained-off contained foul cases – awful enough that he wondered what the other screens hid. The large room echoed with coughing and retching. Nurses and doctors, their faces partially covered, scurried between the horrible noises, dousing foreheads in lukewarm water, changing dirtied bandages, carrying bedclothes and towels. Mostly, it was fever, but there were also the usual amputees and madmen. Nightingale kept his hand on his empty sword-belt as if it could protect him.

Their men were in a quieter corner. One of the midshipmen had died not long after landing, along with four of the hands. Yet the second lieutenant, the other mid, and three sailors remained: all the voices they had for the *Ulysses*.

The second lieutenant was a boy not much older than Mr Richmond but his sickness had aged him by a decade or so. His eyes sunk into dark craters, skin papery and pockmarked with open sores. Clumps of fair hair sat on the pillow alongside drops of dried blood. When he saw them approaching he tried to sit up, only to tremble on bruised arms. *Scurvy*, Nightingale thought.

'Lieutenant Wainwright?' Nightingale asked, taking a seat with Courtney.

'Yes, sir.'

'I am Captain Nightingale of the *Scylla*, and this is Lieutenant Courtney. We have business with the *Ulysses*.'

If it was possible, Wainwright turned even paler. 'I took no part in it, sir. I know I must go to trial, but please, I tried to stop them.'

'Hush. You are not under investigation.' *Yet*, Nightingale thought guiltily – he knew the mercilessness of the Admiralty against mutiny. 'I have been tasked with locating the *Ulysses* and bringing her to justice. Might I ask you some questions?'

'Yes, sir.'

Nightingale took a breath. 'I understand that the *Ulysses* has been out at sea for almost three months, yes?' Wainwright nodded. 'She was to sail alongside the *Peregrine* and harass French vessels along the Main. Tell me everything you can recall about the mutiny.'

Wainwright swallowed. 'I had known some of the men were not happy, sir. They were frightened of the disease, as we all are, but it was not only that. We fought at the capture of Trinidad three years ago and since then, we have seen the shore for perhaps two months in all. Such is the naval service, but many of the *Ulysses* were pressed men – a few were gained from an American merchantman. Many were not rated able. It was as though the sea knew that, sir.'

Wainwright paused with a moan. He held a hand to his bandaged chest and Nightingale saw there were lacerations along the back of it. 'I'm sorry, sir. Some of these wounds are new, some of them are old. It hurts...'

He tried to move, shifting his back up the thin pillows. Nightingale waited.

'The *Ulysses* was not my first ship,' Wainwright continued, strained. 'She was my first ship since passing for lieutenant but I've been on the water since I was a lad. Never have I known a ship so beset with dirty weather. The boys lost their heads more than once. The last time, we were in sight of a French privateer. Our topmen almost... almost disgraced themselves in front of the enemy.

'Captain Wheatley was not a weak man, sir. The men only... the men didn't believe he could stand on his own two feet. Lieutenant Davidson did most of the work, and he could be a harsh-talking fellow. Oh God, Lieutenant Davidson. I thought I had cleared the memory from my head.' Wainwright shuddered. Tears glistened in his eyes. 'I knew that some of the men called him names behind his back. They believed him to bring ill fortune to the ship – the reason we were battered by so many storms. He was who they targeted first.'

Nightingale had listened to the tale silently but now he held up his hand. 'Where was this?'

'Our course was for the waters around Saint-Domingue. We were three days west of Dominica.'

'When?'

'Early June. The seventh, I... Yes, I think it was the seventh.'

'How many took part in the insurrection?'

'There were five ringleaders, as far as I could tell, sir. The American merchant sailor, Ransome, and four of our own: Travers, Valentine, Gardner, and Nolan. Around twenty went along with them without fuss, though many tried to stay neutral. A few downright took up arms when...' Wainwright stopped as if the confession choked him.

'It's all right, Lieutenant,' Nightingale said.

'A few downright took up arms when Lieutenant Davidson was hanged.'

Nightingale felt Courtney stiffen beside him. He had felt a dim horror of such a thing as soon as Wainwright had mentioned Davidson's tyranny, but the confirmation made his bones chill.

'How many other victims were there?' he asked, hiding his reaction.

Wainwright tried to cuff his tears but they fell anyway, staining his gaunt cheeks. 'He was not a pleasant man,' he managed, 'and they hung him from the yardarm. I thought I'd be next. They took the officers one by one. It was hard to refuse once they had broken into the armoury but we – we tried, I promise you we tried, sir. They killed the purser, the gunner, the marine sergeant and lieutenant, a midshipman, and some of the hands – at least seven. I managed to run with some of the men and a couple of marines. We sneaked out when they were drunk and one of the mids cut away a launch. We were damned lucky. We passed the bodies as we sailed...'

Wainwright's voice clogged with despair. Clearly, not all of the escapees had survived.

'What was the fate of Captain Wheatley?' Nightingale asked.

'I can't be certain. They had blockaded him in the great cabin with them when we fled. I tried to reach him, but...' Wainwright shook his head. His meagre strength had drained from him during his frantic explanation, and now it was out, he sank against the pillows, repeating, 'I tried to reach him...'

'Can you estimate how many are left aboard?'

'We were below complement anyway,' Wainwright rasped. Nightingale had to lean closer. 'Perhaps one hundred and sixty.'

Such a crew could still command a fifth-rate like the *Ulysses*. 'Do you have any notion of what the mutineers plan to achieve with the *Ulysses*?'

Wainwright shook his head again. 'They wanted to sail as far from enemy ports as they could. When we left, she was on a course southwards. There are many doors along the coast that would be open to them.'

It was as Nightingale had expected, but the confirmation did nothing to ease his fears. The more he pieced it together, the closer he approached the inevitable: his own countrymen, men of the same service who had fought and died beside him at the Nile, were now his enemies.

Lethargic and ill, Wainwright pointed mutely to the charts. He indicated spots in the great blue expanse that were hundreds of miles across. The *Ulysses* could be anywhere.

As they made to leave the poor boy, Courtney lingered. Nightingale had withdrawn a few paces from him but still heard his question: 'There are women aboard, aren't there?'

Wainwright paused, then nodded. 'Two. The gunner's wife, and the master's.'

'What happened to them?'

'They were unharmed when we left.'

'You did not try to take them?'

'We could not—' Wainwright coughed and bent double. Through gasps, he managed, 'They were in the great cabin too.'

Nightingale did not ask Courtney about the bizarre question until they were outside. The other survivors repeated Wainwright's testimony, although one refused to talk, terrified of accidentally implicating himself. Nightingale's head screamed, even more with the new information, and Courtney's strange behaviour did not help.

'How did you know about the women?' he asked once they had found some shade under a palm. It was only fractionally cooler there but Courtney, almost a head taller than Nightingale, blocked some of the fierce light.

'I had my suspicions, sir,' Courtney replied carefully. 'It ain't regular, but ships do it.'

'I know that, Lieutenant. But this wasn't only a suspicion. You were confident that they had women aboard.'

'I wanted to ensure we knew who we were dealing with if it… comes to blows.'

Nightingale was not content with the explanation.

'Speaking of which, sir,' Courtney continued, 'how far exactly does our justice stretch?'

'That shall be my decision.'

'If she has been given over to the enemy, sir, then it will take more than us to deal with her. If she has foundered with that weak crew, we cannot take so many onboard the *Scylla*. If she is still afloat, do we fire upon her? Incapacitate her?'

'Lieutenant Courtney, that is not your place.' The shock at Courtney's brazen questions, tangled with Nightingale's evil headache, made his voice snap. 'You are not the sole commander of the *Scylla* any longer.'

Surprise crossed Courtney's expression, and then his cheeks glowed red.

'I have a natural concern for her and the men, sir. I want to know what we will face.'

'I do not have the gift of foresight to tell you that, Lieutenant. The same concern is mine. For now, you'll do well to help me in the questioning of your Article breaker. What he has done deserves a court martial.'

'You are going to call a court martial after what this crew have been through?'

'Lieutenant, you are treading a fine line. Do not take that tone.'

Nightingale regretted his passion as they returned to the *Scylla* and he retreated to his cabin. The bright sun had seared his eyes so much that they were streaming, so he sat in the darkest corner, dabbing at them with his handkerchief, feeling the old scars sting.

He was ashamed of himself. For a moment, he had let his personal pain interfere with his dealings with Courtney. Even if Courtney had overstepped, he should have dealt with him calmly, not snapped like a jealous child.

He was a captain again – and physical and psychological wounds did not matter anymore. The testimony of the survivors and the questioning of the Article breaker outweighed such trivia.

Chapter Five: A Worse Fate

In the manner of all naval captains, Nightingale believed in the power and the rigidity of the Articles of War. They held an almost sacred thrall onboard, and on Sundays, they could be read aloud alongside Bible passages. Nightingale had spoken them countless times. So he knew what Kieran Attrill's punishment should be.

But, with Kieran stood before him in the great cabin, and Courtney sat at his side, he was reminded painfully of where he was and what lay ahead.

'Mr Attrill, I assume that you are aware of the punishment for thievery, whether from a ship or from land?' Nightingale asked.

'Yes, sir,' Kieran said.

'Lieutenant Courtney, please read the Article that has been broken.'

Courtney glanced at him then down to the open ledger on the desk. It was important that Courtney spoke as well; Nightingale had not been the man to arrest Kieran. He was not entirely the bearer of his fate.

'Article Twenty-Nine. All robbery committed by any person in the fleet shall be punished with death, or otherwise, as a court martial, upon consideration of the circumstances.'

Kieran did not flinch. The words were law. He knew what the consequences of his actions would be.

'Lieutenant Courtney has already spoken with the victim,' Nightingale continued. 'It is beyond a doubt that, when you accompanied Mr Richmond to the shore, you stole from this merchant. It is also beyond a doubt that you ran from Lieutenant Courtney and Mr Uriah, the bosun, when pursued through the town. I happened to see you and also noted that your clothes were dotted with blood.'

Kieran shuffled. He ran the rim of his hat through his hands, rough fingers rasping.

'Lieutenant Courtney has been struck,' Nightingale said. 'That much is obvious from the state of his eye. Striking a superior officer is also a serious offence. Lieutenant Courtney, please read Article Twenty-One.'

Courtney did not respond. Nightingale turned to him and saw Kieran raise his head too.

'Lieutenant Courtney,' Nightingale repeated.

'Kieran did not strike me, sir.'

Nightingale flushed. He would speak to Courtney later. It was not his place to raise his opinion now – certainly not in front of the accused.

'Read the Article, Lieutenant, if you please.'

Courtney gritted his jaw. 'If any officer, mariner or soldier or other person in the fleet, shall strike any of his superior officers, or draw, or offer to draw, or lift up any weapon against him, being in the execution of his office, on any pretence whatsoever, every such person being convicted of any such offence, by the sentence of a court martial, shall suffer death.'

'The rest too, Lieutenant.'

'And,' Courtney continued, 'if any officer, mariner, soldier or other person in the fleet, shall presume to quarrel with any of his superior officers, being in the execution of his office, or disobey any lawful command of any of his superior officers; every such person being convicted of any such offence, by the sentence of a court martial, shall suffer death or any such other punishment, as shall, according to the nature and degree of his offence, be inflicted upon him by the sentence of a court martial.'

Nightingale nodded. 'Did you strike Lieutenant Courtney, Mr Attrill?'

'No, sir,' Kieran said instantly.

'Who was it that struck Lieutenant Courtney?'

'It was a man from the town, sir,' Kieran spoke up. 'He helped me to nab the fruit from the merchant by distracting him. When I ran,

37

he ran with me 'cos he saw Mr Richmond, sir. He gave me a place to hide until Lieutenant Courtney and Mr Uriah came to the town to find us. Then, we fought.' Kieran corrected himself. 'No, sir, he fought. He started the tussle and when Lieutenant Courtney tried to separate him from Mr Uriah, he got... He was struck. Accidentally, sir.'

'Can you attest to this, Lieutenant?'

Slowly, Courtney nodded. 'Yes, Captain.'

'What happened to this man? This additional felon?'

'He was handed over to the civil authorities. His part was not a naval matter.'

'Striking an officer of the King's Navy is most certainly a naval matter.' Nightingale turned back to Kieran who, despite his innocence in striking Courtney, still had the theft hanging over him. Nightingale drummed his fingers on the table, before realising he was doing it and stopping. 'As per the Articles, you should be punished with a court martial and then hanged. Yet I understand that these last months have been a trial for the crew. I am not a merciless man. I am giving you an opportunity to explain why you did it.'

Nightingale had thrown him a line with his mention of the past months; he hoped he would take it.

'It weren't selfish, Captain Nightingale, sir,' Kieran said. 'The fruit weren't just for us. It was for our mess, sir. One of 'em's been ill.'

'Dr Archer has reported no new men in his sickbay,' Nightingale remarked.

'No, it ain't the fever, sir, thank Christ. And it ain't anything physical. Toby'd kill me if he knew I was telling you. It's in his head, sir. He ain't been the same since his mates died.'

Nightingale had felt the black atmosphere on the ship. It would take more than fumigation and a holystone to scrape and purify a man's head.

'I see,' he said.

'I thought if we got him something, just for him, some fruit or – it didn't have to be fruit, it could've been anything. We thought it might help him.'

Nightingale mulled it over. It seemed as though it had been an act of good will that had spiralled. He could understand the desperation of the men, and he knew how easily judgement could cloud.

Yet the Articles remained.

'Your heart may have been in the right place, Mr Attrill,' he said carefully, 'but you agreed to obey the laws of the sea and of the navy when you signed on.'

'Sir.' Courtney tried to interrupt.

'However,' Nightingale said, louder, 'I have listened to your reasons and your testimony. As captain, I am granted some leeway. I do not believe further questioning is in order, not after your ordeals and not when we are so close to setting sail.'

Kieran opened his mouth to thank him. He held up a hand. 'But punishment must be observed for how you acted. You shall receive two dozen lashes and money will be taken from your pay to reimburse the merchant.'

Kieran's mouth immediately closed, the gratitude dying in his face. The lash seemed merciful – although the prolonged, humiliating pain was far greater than a short drop from the rope. Nightingale despised flogging and had more reason than most officers to feel that way. Yet what choice did he have?

When Kieran was dismissed, he rose and poured some water from the waiting carafe. It smoothed his parchment-dry throat and soothed the rising heat in his cheeks. He offered Courtney another mug but the lieutenant said, 'No, thank you, sir.'

'How is your eye, Lieutenant?'

'It is fine. A minor bruise.'

'A minor bruise which could have condemned a man to death.' He sighed. 'I don't relish doing this, you understand, but it has to be done – certainly considering what we shall be facing with the *Ulysses*.'

'Kieran is not a bad man, sir. This kind of behaviour is out of sorts for any of this crew. I shall speak to him if it would help – he grew up in the same parts as I did.'

'I should hope that two dozen lashes and a chunk taken from his pay should be a strong enough deterrent.'

'Yes, sir. It was very merciful of you.'

Courtney's tone grated him. He could not tell if there was sarcasm there. The lieutenant had been flat and resigned since Nightingale had snapped at him that morning; his shoulders were dropped and he pouted like a child. When he exited the cabin, a wall of tension was left behind – a wall Nightingale despaired of climbing. *What would you have done?* he thought bitterly. Kieran had stolen and been a near-participant in a brawl with his superiors. There was no milder way to proceed.

Yet Nightingale's frustration seethed because of his own discomfort. He feared being seen as weak by the men, and he also feared being seen as a tartar by the men. The middle ground was elusive.

And as he stood, looking out over the ship's assemblage, he thought again of Captain Pigot on the *Hermione*. Many times had he taken out the lash, and many times had he been stabbed in retaliation.

At the allotted time, the grating was rigged against the gangway. Kieran Attrill stood beside it, stripped to the waist and shivering despite the tropical heat. Nightingale read out the broken Article, followed by Kieran's sentence. The words resounded across the *Scylla*'s crowded deck and almost across to the harbour. The proximity to land made it worse. Nightingale knew that the tricked merchant was sitting atop his warehouse with a spyglass.

Over the years, Nightingale had mastered keeping his composure. He kept his jaw set and eyes firm as he gazed upon Kieran. He was a middle-aged able seaman, forecastle division, but a lifetime at sea had unsettled his years. If it hadn't been for his age written in the ship's muster (thirty-two), Nightingale could not have guessed. Pockmarks and scars covered his face and chest, the skin hard and leathery from the sun and harsh weather. He wore a long, twisted pigtail that he had tied out of the way. When he was strapped to the grating, Nightingale could see old, livid marks criss-crossing his back.

Courtney had lied. This was not Kieran's first time.

The bosun's mate's footsteps rang across the deck as he positioned himself. The long, knotted length of the cat drooped against the planks.

'Mr Lance, begin,' Nightingale ordered.

Silence, fore and aft. Then the high, scything whistle as the rope sliced through the air. It slapped sickeningly, right across Kieran's shoulder blades. He arched with a hiss.

Again. This time, the cat lashed Kieran's mid-back. A bloody mark remained when Mr Lance retreated. It spouted as he caught it once more, splashing red against the mast rings. Kieran groped for the grating, writhing against his bonds as Mr Lance delivered blow after blow. He quickly found his accuracy and speed, and over and over, welts opened and were disturbed. Nightingale made himself look – every captain had to stand by the punishments he gave out and face what he had ordered.

But it was damned barbaric. And Nightingale knew that no one saw how he had saved Kieran from a worse fate. All they saw was the cut of the rope and Kieran's convulsed, tear-streaked face.

Nightingale curled his hand into a fist behind his back. He did not miss the look Courtney gave him. Blood flew, caught the lieutenant across the cheek, and he turned away.

Nightingale could smell the metal mixed with thick, sharp sweat. In a moment, he was an eighteen-year-old again. Instead of the heat, he felt the biting chill of a Hampshire winter. The rough bark of an oak scraped against his palms and stabbed beneath his nails as he dug them into the tree trunk. Fire rained down upon his shoulders and spine. He remembered sobbing like Kieran and then snivelling and yelling until he could not breathe. The pain had seemed never-ending.

By the time Kieran's punishment had finally finished, the man's knees had buckled and he was held by only his bonds. Nightingale stared at the handiwork – the ugly, crimson lines zigzagging over Kieran's back, weeping blood and staining the deck – then looked away, remembering nights lying on his stomach, praying that the welts would heal and that no one would ever ask him why he had been lashed.

At his nod, Dr Archer hurried over and tenderly looped Kieran's loose arm about his neck. The sailor allowed himself to be walked along. Not once did he look at Nightingale.

In the painfully silent aftermath, Nightingale stepped forward and addressed the crowd. Blood still peppered the timbers.

'I don't have to remind you,' Nightingale said firmly, 'of the severity of what we shall face. I will not tolerate misdemeanour lightly. It is for the entire crew's safety that I act as I do. I understand that Captain Carlisle was a good man, so do not spoil his memory. That is all. You are dismissed.'

The men moved off in their divisions. One by one, the officers returned to their duties, but Nightingale stayed upon the poop deck. Slowly, he walked aft and perched by the taffrail. It was an awful way to begin a journey. They were not even at sea yet but blood had been spilled and the crew had doubtless formed their opinion of him. He had always considered himself a fair man. He knew just as well as any common sailor what it was like to live and breathe under a martinet.

Damn it, he thought, *I cannot be moping about it.*

Anger swirled at his weakness. He rose and realised he was not alone. Courtney lingered nearby, shining in his full dress uniform. The young man had a talent of appearing at Nightingale's side when he was at his most wretched.

'The quartermaster informs me that the last of the stores are safely aboard, sir,' he said, stiffly formal.

'Thank you, Lieutenant. I shall see him directly.'

For a moment, as he passed Courtney, he thought that he would comment about the punishments again, but Courtney stayed sensibly silent.

'Oh, and Lieutenant,' Nightingale remarked. 'You still have blood on you.'

Courtney raised a hand to his face and wiped at the streak on his cheek. He blushed and reached for a handkerchief.

Nightingale went below. Already, men cleaned the deck, water sloshing over the red stains. By the time Nightingale had finished with the quartermaster, the blood had disappeared as if it had never been there. The ship returned to its regular duties and an understated peace fell after the drama of the morning.

Whether it was true peace or simply the calm before the storm Nightingale was yet to discover.

Chapter Six: Before the Wind

25 June 1800

Dearest Louisa, Nightingale wrote, we are now three days from Antigua. The weather is fair, the sun is high and warm, and every hour, the wind has remained consistent – a blow slightly more than a breeze, enough to help us along but still allow for our t'gallants. I couldn't have asked for an easier cruise. We have kept Guadeloupe and Dominica to the west, and for a short while, we could see the curve of the archipelago through a glass – but to our east is the great expanse of the Atlantic. It has been barely a fortnight since I crossed the ocean yet it is always different as a passenger than as a commander.

Nightingale wondered about crossing that through. It was not a lie – the unmooring had been surprisingly smooth under his and Courtney's observations. Yet he painted a far more idyllic picture than he felt. And, truthfully, Louisa would not give a damn whether he had his t'gallants flying or not.

The men are still weak. Everything they do is slow. Even tacking the ship, which every seaman should be able to perform as simply as walking upright, is a drawn-out affair. I have had them practising on the guns, and Mr Loom's boast that they can fire three broadsides in five minutes was a stretch of the truth to say the least.

I wonder if I am being too harsh. The yellow fever has only recently abated, and we had some ugly business before leaving

43

Antigua. I hope it shall be forgotten with some open-water sailing. My officers have been with the crew for some time, except my second lieutenant who is another replacement for a victim of the fever. My first, Courtney, is…

Nightingale paused. Many words came to his mind to describe Courtney: passionate, assured, young, perhaps inexperienced in certain ways. He had, again, lapsed into a mute treatment of Nightingale, only speaking when addressed and to give orders. Neither of them had started on the right foot yet Nightingale did not know how to rectify that, or if, as captain, he needed to be the one to do so.

He finished the sentence with a curt, *respected*.

Perhaps you know, he continued, that I am no longer required in Trinidad. Your father was gracious in supporting me but it seems it will come to nothing. I, again, had no choice in the matter. It seems both Sir William and my own father have made it their calling to shuffle me around without asking my consent. Perhaps they think it shall help me. Regardless, I have been allowed to stop in at Trinidad for a short while on our way south. It may be good to see what might have been.

He paused again and wondered whether that was too bitter and self-pitiful. Louisa, of all people, knew about the long road which Nightingale had trod.

Yet, if all had gone well at Trinidad, he had planned to transport Louisa there too. There was still work to be done with the service in the Caribbean, and it was far from his dark memories. Perhaps it was for the best that his assignment had fallen through. He would only be running again, trying to stay ahead of the approaching shadow.

Louisa would have said that if she were with him.

I hope you have been keeping well, he wrote. It does me good to remember that you are the type of woman to always have something on her plate. I shall give your love to your father if I see him, which I may if we visit Trinidad.

I cannot promise when I shall return. I know that you understand how it is. I remain,

Your affectionate husband, Hiram Nightingale, Captain of the Scylla.

He set the pen aside and closed the letter in his journal. If they crossed a packet ship, then it would be sent. Otherwise, it would remain there. He had other letters to write – both official and private – but they could wait.

Nightingale shrugged on his uniform coat and smoothed it fastidiously, then buttoned his waistcoat and looped on his stock, which had already stiffened a little in the salt of the waves. His muscles felt the same way; almost two years off the sea had turned him into a land-creature, unused to the roll and pitch. Or perhaps he was growing old. His forty-first birthday approached and his bones reminded him of it – along with the greying of the auburn hair about his temples.

Rylance soon poked his head into the cabin. He crept on his toes, carrying a breakfast tray. He was one of the only crew members who did not have to duck under the low ceiling. 'Good morning, Rylance,' Nightingale greeted.

'Good morning, sir. You should have let me help you dress.'

'Don't fret. I should do at least something myself.'

As it turned out, he had less use than he had anticipated. Everyone was prepared when Nightingale gave the order to beat to quarters. Within minutes of the drum pounding *Heart of Oak*, Nightingale stood by the central companion-ladder of the gun deck, looking over the assembled gun crews.

Each of them crowded about their piece. Every one had a name – sobriquets like Banshee and Wailing Charlotte. Some of the men were stripped to the waist, revealing skin criss-crossed by tattoos and scars. Nightingale spotted Kieran, still recovering from his punishment and given a lighter duty, a sponger in his hand.

'Larboard battery!' Nightingale called to the left-hand side. 'You will be under the command of Lieutenant Hargreaves. And starboard battery, you will be under the command of Lieutenant Courtney. You shall each fire at the markers Mr Thomason has placed about a cable's length away from the ship. I want accuracy and speed. Our rate of fire can be the difference between victory and defeat. Do not let me mistake you for a French crew, men.'

A ripple of indignation travelled through the deck. Nightingale turned to the master gunner, Thomason. 'Mr Thomason, if you would time the larboard crews. I shall time the starboard. Whoever fires more shots in the space of five minutes shall receive an extra grog ration. That should get them working.'

It certainly did. As the second-hand reached the mark on his pocket-watch, the crews rushed to action. Thirteen cannons lined each side – the standard twelve-pounders of a fifth-rate, loaded by the extra powder Nightingale had bought out of his own pocket. At first the men had prioritised speed, but had made too many mistakes for Nightingale's scrupulous eye. Now, he saw the start of more cohesion. The old orders and the familiar actions were performed: balls loaded into muzzles along with cotton wads, guns run out to the portholes, elevations found.

The first piece roared just before the minute mark. He was warned by the lifting of a gun captain's hand, and then the cry of 'Fire!' A crash echoed down the deck and the cannon leapt back into its breech-rope. The ball splashed overside and then the second gun shouted – this time on the larboard side.

Nightingale caught Mr Thomason's subtle smile as the roaring melody began in earnest. It was a cacophony Nightingale could never describe to an outsider – almost otherworldly in its raging din. His ears sang and his throat closed around the churning gouts of smoke. Shouted orders blended into the fray, as urgent as if they had been in a true battle. In war, there would be answers to this screaming aria: other ships trying to tear apart their timbers.

He remembered the Nile – the apocalyptic scene of Aboukir Bay as the British fleet hammered the French. For a moment, he saw the burning beacon of the *Orient*, about to erupt.

He pushed the memory down.

In the time it took to step out of the present, one of the larboard crews faltered. Amongst the smoke and confusion, *Banshee's* gun

46

captain stepped back and entangled his foot in a breech-rope. Even in the din, Nightingale heard his head smack on hard steel.

'Mr Smythe!' Nightingale called to a slack-jawed midshipman. 'Fetch Dr Archer and the loblolly boy. Lieutenant Hargreaves,' for the man was still staring, 'take the gun captain's place.'

Hargreaves took over. The blasting of guns had not abated. But Banshee's crew hesitated under Hargreaves and to Nightingale's dismay, he cried, 'Shot the gun!' before pricking the touch-hole to pierce the cartridge. By the time he realised his mistake, the gun was already run out and he had to fumble between correcting himself and trying to adjust the elevation.

Hargreaves sweated. He raised a shaking hand, dipped it, pulled the hammer to full-cock, raised it again.

'Are we ready, sir?!' a fair-haired lad shouted.

'Fire!' Hargreaves cried, and yanked the line on the lock. The cannon jumped back with a scream. The young lad crumpled, yelling as the gun rolled over his maimed foot.

'Take him below!' Nightingale bellowed, just as Dr Archer and his assistant arrived, staring between the comatose gun captain and the sobbing boy. He managed to stagger up and towards the surgeon. Other gun crews watched; some helped. Hargreaves backed away from the cannon.

'Banshee, avast firing!' Nightingale ordered, yet no sooner had he spoken the words did Lieutenant Courtney switch sides and hurry into action. He threw off his coat and took Hargreaves's place, immediately ordering the men to clear out the barrel. Hargreaves opened his mouth then stopped.

'Lieu—' Nightingale started to say, but his voice disappeared beneath the guns. He no longer looked at the other crews, only Courtney's. The young lieutenant bent over the barrel and watched its elevation. Sweat stuck his dark curls to his forehead as he laboured and worked seamlessly with the other sailors. They cheered as the cannon bounded backwards and their shot landed with a crash.

Hargreaves only watched, wringing his hands.

'Five minutes!' Thomason called.

A starboard gun fired off its final round and then all fell eerily silent. Wreaths of smoke billowed down the deck, escaping out the gun ports. Nightingale cleared his throat and peered upwards through the hatchway. Mr Uriah and Mr Garland had been stationed above to watch the fall of each shot.

'Larboard, sir!' Uriah shouted. 'Quicker and more accurate!'

The larboard side cheered as the men slapped each other on the backs, grinning. Courtney joined in, gripping the gun crew's shoulders and slinging an arm around their shoulders.

'Congratulations,' Nightingale smiled. 'We'll continue at the same time in two days.'

Lieutenant Courtney approached him whilst the men were cleaning out the guns. His face was spotted with powder and his hair had wound out of its short tail. He had not donned his uniform yet so sweat glistened beneath his low collar. It was the first time Nightingale had seen him so content. Hargreaves hurried over and that pleasure died.

'You should not have taken my place, Lieutenant,' Hargreaves rushed, as if he was frightened of the words.

'The crew was down one man, Lieutenant Hargreaves,' Courtney countered. 'It was my place to help.'

'It was not your place,' Nightingale said at the same time as Hargreaves. Courtney snapped around to stare at him. 'The larboard division was under the command of Lieutenant Hargreaves. You impeded his authority.'

'Sir. Lieutenant Hargreaves was…' Courtney stopped. He had obviously not expected to be admonished. 'They did well, sir,' he said, flatter now. 'The larboard's grog ration will encourage them.'

'Indeed. Return to your station, Lieutenant. Both divisions shall clean the guns and I shall inspect them with Mr Thomason later.'

Courtney obeyed with a brief salute. Hargreaves lingered. 'It was my division, Captain,' he tried. 'He would not have done such a thing to Lieutenant Pearson.'

'Enough of that, Lieutenant Hargreaves. I shall not have this bickering. Return to your station also.'

What had begun as a promising exercise had turned sour. Once again, Courtney sat at the heart of it. Nightingale could see how he wished to be with his men, but he had broken the ladder of command and pushed Hargreaves off his rung. He did not know what to do with him.

Nightingale instead tried to take heart in the calm sea and the steadily rising breeze. He discovered that the *Scylla* sailed best on the starboard tack, with the wind abaft her beam, but gradually, she responded to their efforts to have her close-hauled. He watched the topmen as they scrambled aloft to loose the sails and noted for the first time that not a single man fumbled with the reef-points. It was smooth and fast and gave him hope that they could begin to match an enemy ship. The pride in her elegance grew, even as relations seemed to sour within her.

He wrote as much to Louisa, finding he took comfort in talking to her a thousand miles away. There was no one on the *Scylla* who he would even think of confiding in – and nor could, he as her captain. The top of the hierarchy was always lonely.

At six bells of the afternoon watch, he visited the sickbay. He ducked under the low timbers with practised ease and knocked, though he knew it was not necessary as the commander of everything from the flying jib to the stern lanterns. Five pairs of bleary eyes turned to him, then quickly lowered in respect.

Five was better than he had expected. The sickness was losing its grip on the *Scylla*, like ivy slowly being pulled off of a fine, long-standing house.

Banshee's gun captain – Gareth Taylor – slept in a hammock. Dr Archer finished taking his pulse as Nightingale walked over.

'He shall be just fine, Captain. Nothing is fractured, by some miracle.'

Next to him, Toby Warren lay on the doctor's table, eyes tightly shut. He was only young – and looked even younger with his face flushed with tears. Dr Archer rested his hands carefully on the boy's foot, examining it as he winced and gave muffled cries. The cannon had rolled over his toes and left a bright swollen bruise.

Toby raised a trembling hand to his forehead in salute.

'How are you faring, Toby?' Nightingale asked. He had had to consult the log to identify the young man's name but had vowed to learn his crew by heart. He had been surprised to learn that he was the same lad Kieran had tried to steal for.

'I'm – all right, sir – ow!' Toby bit back a sob as Archer gently turned his ankle. 'I was being stupid – I'm sorry I ruined – the exercise. It wasn't – Lieutenant Hargreaves's fault…'

Nightingale shook his head. He hadn't expected a forthright apology.

'Is it a serious injury, Doctor?' he asked.

'Well.' Archer cleared his throat. 'The gun caused significant damage. It seems that the metatarsals have been fractured.'

'Will you – cut it off?' Toby whimpered.

'Oh dear no,' Archer chuckled. 'It'll heal, but it will take many weeks. I shall splint it but it will be difficult to put weight upon it.'

'What do you recommend?' Nightingale asked.

Archer stood and smoothed down his coat. He was little, able to stand under the timbers, and Nightingale had previously thought of him as bookish and quiet – but here, in his domain, he was as much a commander as Nightingale. 'I would commonly suggest resting and not straining the injury. Ideally, he should be ashore.'

'No, sir,' Toby rushed, Devonshire accent heightened in his worry. 'No, I can't go back ashore, sir. I had trouble in English Harbour.'

'"Trouble" is a vague description, Toby.'

'I…' Toby blushed. 'I got into trouble with a girl's father, sir. And my mates are here, sir.'

Nightingale did not need to ask any more. He nodded and looked at Archer, whose eyes were twinkling.

'Well, I shan't send you ashore, Toby. We are too far away for that and I can't turn around because of a broken foot. You shall be given light duties and meanwhile, you can aid me. Can you read and write?'

Toby nodded.

'You can act as my clerk then.' Considering that the *Scylla* had had to sail without one in their haste.

'Thank you, sir.'

Toby's work placed him in the *Scylla's* waist: duties given to seamen who were not as able. His absence would be no great loss. And, as his clerk, Nightingale could keep an eye on him. He couldn't help thinking of what Kieran had said about his state of mind. He meant to surreptitiously ask him when a knock sounded on the wall. Kieran Attrill himself shuffled in. He saw Toby, then Nightingale, and ducked his head. Archer patted Toby on the shoulder and helped him into a nearby hammock.

'I'll be right with you, Kieran,' Archer said. 'Make yourself comfortable on the table.'

Nightingale stepped back as Kieran obeyed. With hesitant fingers, he unlaced his shirt and drew it over his head. Nightingale's gaze turned to Kieran's maimed back. A few days had passed since Kieran's lashing, yet the wounds remained raw and red. It seemed almost impossible that he himself had ordered that punishment. That was Captain Nightingale in his official role; he sometimes thought the man was a separate entity.

'I shall only be a few moments if you required a word with me, Captain,' Archer said as Kieran gingerly lay on his front.

'No, it's quite all right, Doctor. I should like to talk with Kieran.'

Nightingale sat as Archer worked. He made himself watch Archer pour vinegar over paper and press it onto Kieran's wounds. The seaman hissed and buried his face in the table. The lash was agony – but this treatment, to prevent infection, could be just as terrible. Nightingale's own back itched. The scars, etched over his shoulder blades and spine, would never fade.

Kieran was sweating and flushed when Archer finished. He stayed on his stomach, panting. 'Even though it might not feel it, the wounds are coming along well, Kieran,' Archer assured him. 'It won't be long until they feel like a midge's bite.'

'Thank you, Doctor,' Kieran croaked.

Nightingale waited whilst Archer put away his instruments and began his rounds of the rest of the sailors.

'You performed well today,' Nightingale said to Kieran. 'The gunnery is improving.'

'Yes, sir.'

Nightingale cleared his throat. 'Lieutenant Courtney told me that you are from the same parts as he is. Attrill is an Island name, yes?'

Kieran looked up at Nightingale's informal name for his home-place. 'Yes, sir.'

'My family used to holiday on the Isle of Wight – Yarmouth. We always ate the best fish there.'

'We were fishermen, sir. From St Lawrence.'

'I know the area.' It was a place infamous for nearby smuggling activity. Nightingale wondered if Kieran had ever been caught up in it; the poorest so often turned to such things. 'You have been lashed before,' he said.

Kieran nodded.

'What was the Article broken?' It had not been on the *Scylla*, otherwise it would have been logged.

'I disobeyed an officer, sir. He ordered the main t'gallant to be set when I thought it'd be dangerous.'

'It is not your place to disagree or agree, Kieran.'

'I know that, sir. But then the captain did away with the lieutenant's order a minute later.'

'I see.'

Nightingale thought of the *Ulysses*. He wondered what the exact point of their mutiny had been. Such a crime did not happen suddenly or lightly. Once the mutineers had acted, there was no return – they would be marked men for the rest of their lives.

'I am glad that your wounds are healing,' he said to Kieran. 'You shall be back to general duties soon.'

'Yes, sir. Can I talk to Toby? After all that to-do...'

'Yes, of course. Dr Archer believes he will heal well too.'

Outside of the sickbay and its injuries, the fresh breeze of the quarterdeck was welcome. The wind was freshening a little, shivering the canvas. Under midshipman Richmond's orders, the fore course's clew-garnets and buntlines were hauled, drawing it in. With the trimmed sail, the *Scylla* kept the wind and her course. The log was heaved and the speed and depth taken – all familiar actions that reminded

Nightingale of every other ship he had served upon. A good crew could continue without a captain's constant care and attention. He was becoming quite fond of the vessel.

Richmond saluted him. His freckles and blonde curls belonged on a boy – which Nightingale supposed he still was at fifteen, far younger than the men underneath him. But as the senior midshipman, it would not be long until his lieutenant's examination.

'All well, Mr Richmond?' Nightingale asked.

'Yes, sir.'

'What is our speed?'

'We reached six knots just now, sir.'

'Very good.'

Despite the positive news, Richmond hesitated. He kept glancing at Nightingale as if on the verge of saying something, only withheld by naval tradition.

'Is everything truly well?' Nightingale asked.

'Oh. Yes, sir. Only, I wanted to apologise.'

'Whatever for?'

'For the ordeal ashore, sir. I was in command when Kieran Attrill attempted his theft. I keep thinking that I should have done more to prevent it.'

'You acted well, Mr Richmond. You chose the right course by sending for the bosun and Lieutenant Courtney.'

'But—' Richmond cut himself off. 'Yes, sir.'

'Has Mr Attrill caused you any further trouble?'

'No, sir.'

Nightingale understood. One incident like that could shake a man's confidence in his ability and how the crew saw him. All Richmond needed was a chance to prove himself.

Satisfied that all was running smoothly, Nightingale gathered Mr Thomason for the gun inspection. Thomason was equally happy with the earlier exercise, yet as they descended to the gun deck, his smile faded. In the shadow of a companion-ladder, he paused.

Firm voices echoed aft.

'I do not need to be lectured in how to fire a cannon, Lieutenant Courtney,' Hargreaves was saying, his voice thin and almost breaking like a midshipman's. 'I seem to remember that my larboard side had a quicker and more accurate rate of fire.'

'It shall not be like that in battle,' Courtney replied with a slap of his hand on a cannon. 'One mistake and you have doomed your entire battery. You did not maintain the standard order of firing; you did not ensure pieces of cartridge were fished out after the fourth shot, and you were too hasty with your sighting.'

'You celebrated with my division, Lieutenant Courtney!'

'Larboard and starboard will not compete against each other in action. If—'

'Lieutenant Courtney!' Nightingale shouted. The two men snapped around, along with the gaggle of sailors who had been staring at them.

'Sir—' Hargreaves began, but Nightingale held up a hand.

'Lieutenant Courtney,' he said coldly, 'please accompany me to my cabin.'

When they were safely behind the doors, Nightingale turned upon Courtney and said, in as measured a tone as he could command, 'This is a ship of the King's Navy, Mr Courtney. We have an objective, the importance of which I don't need to stress again.'

Courtney's eyes flashed with a challenge – a sign that Nightingale's strike had connected. 'No, sir. I was simply instructing Lieutenant Hargreaves in the proper manner of—'

'It is not your place to do so, and certainly not in full view of the entire gun deck. It was quite enough to take his place during the exercise without humiliating him further.'

'If a lieutenant cannot keep his division in order, especially when in action, then he will soon face a stronger reprisal than anything I could deliver. It is not about the prize or jealousy, as Lieutenant Hargreaves implies. All men must know their place.'

'Precisely. You should do well to remember yours.' His curtness shut Courtney's mouth. 'Now, I shall speak to Lieutenant Hargreaves. As you embarrassed him in front of the crew, I wish for you to apologise and shake his hand before them too. Then I want you to gather the midshipmen for their lessons and join us.'

'It is not my watch, sir.'

'Is it not?' Nightingale smoothed his uniform. 'I find the din of the guns has deafened me to the watch-bell. The midshipmen, Mr Courtney. We have already made them late, and lateness cannot be tolerated in the service.'

Courtney reddened. 'Yes, sir.'

Nightingale waited for him to leave, then breathed out slowly. As the men improved, Courtney was a disappointment. After Carlisle's death, he had tasted command and the respect it brought. He still behaved as if he was acting captain, obviously assuming his good looks and affability to the crew would see him through anything. Regardless of the turmoil he had faced, he had to rein himself in.

Nightingale tried to press down his anger. He refused to lose himself to emotion like Courtney did.

Unbidden, memories of Leroy crowded in. Lieutenant Courtney was the antithesis of the man who would forever haunt Nightingale. But he still reminded Nightingale of Leroy in some cruel, mocking way: two officers at a point in their career which could make or break them.

It was an added thorn in the tangle Nightingale already felt himself in.

Chapter Seven: Baptism of Fire

'Sail off the larboard bow! Sail off the larboard bow!'

The shout resounded from the topmen stationed on the yardarms. Nightingale heard it, even below in his cabin, and hurried up through the hatch, tugging on his coat. The day was clear, yet he could not see any vessel from the deck. Lieutenant Courtney, on watch and leaning against the gunwales, peered through his spyglass. 'Two masts, sir,' he said. 'A brig – and with stuns'ls sails flying, it looks. Can't make out the colours.'

Nightingale took the glass. He tried to wipe the smear from the lens before realising it was his own damaged vision. *Goddamn it all*, he thought. 'We'll go aloft, Lieutenant,' he said.

Courtney nodded.

'I can go, sir,' Richmond piped up. Nightingale hadn't even realised he was on deck as he was not on duty. The boy had his collar undone, without his necktie.

'Stay here, David. You have the deck.'

Richmond flushed.

Nightingale had loved climbing the rigging as a child. Up there, above the close order of the ship, he was free – just him and the wide horizon. He wasn't a child anymore, though, and he often chose to send his officers up instead. But he had given the order now and he refused to back down in front of Lieutenant Courtney.

He cast off his coat and swung onto the mainmast shrouds. It was deceptively easy to begin with, finding the ratlines with his hands and feet. But soon, he was leaning backwards, the futtock shrouds tilting steeply over the churning sea. Then, with a push, he was feeling for the yard, clambering up and over. Topmen greeted him with their knuckles to foreheads and Nightingale grimaced, feeling ridiculous. He lay almost flat as he hauled himself onto the thin spar.

Lieutenant Courtney easily beat him to the crosstrees. He gripped a backstay, legs braced, already training his spyglass over the ocean.

'You should watch your footing at your age, sir,' he said.

Nightingale was too breathless to feel offended.

He rasped, 'I am forty, Lieutenant; I am not decrepit. May I have your glass?'

The unknown vessel was a brig, for certain. Her extended fore- and main-topmast stunsails, white splotches in the sun, made her appear to be flying. That extra canvas would drive the ship quickly.

'Spanish colours,' Courtney said when Nightingale failed to make out the pennant. 'Her name's the *Fénix*.'

Nightingale's primary orders were to find the *Ulysses* – yet any enemy ship was a potential prize for the King's Navy. And a Spanish ship, sailing the same supposed route as the *Ulysses*, could hold valuable information.

They had the weather gage, the brig was smaller, and the conditions were fine.

But Nightingale did not know if the men were ready.

'General chase,' he ordered, and the die was cast.

The *Fénix* was fast, elegantly cresting the waves with white foam fluttering along her sides. Nightingale watched her blurred image from the quarterdeck and Courtney told him that she had eighteen guns, standard for a ship of her size. Nightingale did not have to calculate to see the advantage the *Scylla* had.

The gap between them grew smaller as the *Scylla* unfurled her own stunsails and let loose upper t'gallants and royals. Nightingale imagined what that must look like to the *Fénix* – another bird of prey spreading its wings behind her.

Within the hour, she came in range of the bow-chasers – which meant that they were also within range of the enemy ship's stern guns. Lieutenant Courtney glanced at him, itching for the order.

'We will beat to quarters,' Nightingale said.

The bosun's whistle piped and the drums sounded their rhythmic tattoo. The familiar motions before action swept through the *Scylla* – stations cleared, guns run out, partitions struck down. Nightingale hurried below. His cabin had become part of the sweep of the gun deck now and cannons marred the chequerboard floor. Through the open portholes, blue water rushed by. They would overhaul the *Fénix* if they were not careful.

He tried to loop on his sword-belt. His hands shook terribly. For a moment, his composure wobbled. This would be his first action since the Nile.

'I've got you, sir,' said a voice, and Rylance appeared. He effort-lessly dressed Nightingale, smiling encouragingly. Nightingale only felt nauseous.

A sudden splash in the ocean cast out all other thoughts. The *Fénix* had fired her first shot.

Some of the hands were jeering the enemy when he returned to the deck. Nightingale called for silence, just as the next ball soared abreast of the *Scylla* and bounced harmlessly into the waves. The *Fénix* was smaller, less powerful; a fight would cost her men. But the shots fell again.

Nightingale knew that he risked spars and yards by engaging her – and so soon into their voyage. All this, and more, raced through his head. And yet he weighed it all, as he had done a thousand times before, and responded.

The bow-chasers boomed: the first shot Nightingale had fired in anger since the Nile. It scored the stern gallery of the *Fénix* and blasted a shower of splinters. A cheer rose from the crew. Suddenly, Nightingale became aware of everything: the spray of the sea as it leapt over the lee-rail, the racing breeze as it streamed down the deck, the scrape of the metal as the fearsome carronades were re-shotted. He gave the orders on instinct, only strange in his mouth for a second, and then no more.

Cannonballs soared over the ocean. Nightingale looked ahead, saw the *Fénix*'s fore-topsail flapping dangerously, about to tear. They had no choice but to trim the canvas, forcing her further in range. Barty gripped the helm as he turned it two points, bringing the *Scylla*'s starboard broadside to bear. The ship was close enough to see the men on the *Fénix*'s deck. Nightingale's equivalent – a Spanish captain dressed in red and blue – stood upon the quarterdeck, watching the frigate tearing down upon them. He was brave. But his best option was to fly the white flag.

It never came.

Smoke swirled as the *Scylla* unleashed her gun deck. The first shots fell short, but then the gun captains found their elevation. A hole exploded in the *Fénix*'s hull and sent a porthole-lid flying. Nightingale gripped a backstay as the simultaneous firing of three cannons shook the timbers. Below, Richmond's voice encouraged the men.

'Where is Lieutenant Hargreaves?' Nightingale suddenly asked.

'I don't know, sir,' Courtney said. 'He should be here. I shall—'

A six-pound ball scouring the rigging interrupted him. It caught on the shrouds and tore a great snag before hurtling over the port side. Topmen disentangled themselves from the ragged ropes and then clung to their positions as the next ball cleaved the crossjacks from the foremast. Nightingale weighed the cost. Still enough, still enough.

A sudden gust screamed through the canvas. The yards jerked around.

'Reef topsails!' Nightingale called. They were almost too close. Faces of the crew peered through the *Fénix*'s gun ports, emerging between the gouts of flame and whirling smoke. 'Grappling hooks and boarding pikes!' he cried, and did not miss the surprise in Courtney's eyes.

'We are to board her, sir?' he asked. 'If they have any sense, they shall surrender whilst we are this close.'

Red flashed amongst the fog as the marines took their positions. Nightingale grasped Lieutenant Charlston's solid arm. 'I want you to command the boarding party,' he ordered. 'We shall take them at the waist. I will engage their captain.'

Charlston nodded, florid face burning crimson.

'I shall – I can accompany you, sir,' Courtney prompted.

59

'Yes, Lieutenant. Lieutenant Hargreaves and Mr Richmond can man the gun deck.'

'Lieutenant Hargreaves?'

'Damn it, Lieutenant, you cannot be in two places at once!'

His outburst was soon forgotten as weapons were handed amongst the men: cutlasses and axes and pistols. Nightingale felt for his own flintlock and sword. He stared at the opposite crew as they tried to chop at the hooks and ropes and wondered which man he would have to gun down. He had no time to think of the coldness he felt for it.

At such close quarters, the *Scylla*'s shots smashed into the *Fénix*'s timbers. She fired two to the *Fénix*'s one but still the Spanish ship kept fighting, pennant flying. As the *Scylla*'s gunwales loomed over her, Nightingale looked down the length of the connecting ropes at the red-stained deck. Blood swilled and frothed out of the scuppers.

He gripped the rail and lurched forward when the hulls collided. Yardarms and rigging tangled. 'Boarders!' Nightingale cried through the smoke. 'Away!'

Charlston yelled and his aggression rippled through the men. Bodies swarmed around Nightingale, pressing him onto the gunwale. He was one of them now, never mind the epaulettes on his shoulders and the gold lace on his cuffs. Sword aloft, he vaulted the rail onto the quarterdeck where a crowd of hands and limbs met him, jostling and writhing. He struck blindly, blade snagging fabric and flesh. The excitement of the fight coursed through him as he shoved men out of the way. Blood and sweat and metal stung his nostrils.

'*Scylla*! *Scylla*!' the crew cried, and his heart swelled proudly.

A sword-hilt cracked down on his shoulder. He turned, slashed, and felt blood splatter his sleeve. Another body dropped against him. He kicked it to the side.

Musket shots rained from the *Scylla*'s maintop in a hail of invisible darts that dropped men all around Nightingale. He heard the whistle and puncture of the bullets, the crack of wood as they missed their mark, and everywhere, the cries of men. The chaos, the slaughter, the loss – the same as on the *Lion* – swamped him.

Insensible emotion raged in Nightingale. He stabbed his sword at a charging man and twisted it out of his stomach. As he fell, Nightingale caught sight of the helm. The finely dressed captain stood there, his uniform blackened with smoke.

Their eyes met. The Spaniard ran for a hatchway.

Nightingale leapt over a prostrate body and chased him. Amongst the individual clashing and flaring battles, he saw Courtney, hair spilling from its bindings, yelling as he brandished his blade in one hand and used the fist of the other. He span, punched a *Fénix* man and sent him sprawling with a knee to the groin.

Nightingale turned and raced for the hatchway. Sailors waited in the gun deck below, wreathed in acrid fog. Boarding pikes clashed as Nightingale and his men forced their way through. To the stern, a grenade suddenly exploded and they all tumbled.

Ears ringing, Nightingale attempted to stagger to his feet. He had fallen on top of an old, one-eyed man who caught him about the wrist and tried to bite at his arm. Nightingale drove his elbow into the man's nose and he went limp.

He forced himself up, the blood of the *Fénix* and *Scylla* crews pooling beneath him, steaming in the heat. The guns had fallen silent but their crews still fought around them. Charlston's burly form blocked the light coming through the hatch as he and his marines barrelled down the companion-ladder. The brig's men did not stand a chance. Disciplined, steady fire split their resistance.

Nightingale ploughed astern, eyes watering, throat spasming at the smells and heat. Find the captain, he thought, and this would all be over. Staring around at the primal brawling, Nightingale knew the man should have just surrendered.

Would he have surrendered? Would he have put his crew through that dishonour?

He dealt with the men by the stern cabin and wrestled with the locked door. Someone raced up beside him and slammed an axe into the wood. Courtney, splattered with blood and powder, hacked at the latch until it burst open. Together, they broke into the cabin.

The Spanish captain stood behind his desk, pistol in a white-knuckled hand. He aimed it at Courtney and Nightingale, moving it between the two. Nightingale stepped in front of Courtney. His heart throbbed in his chest. With great effort, he croaked, '*Capitán*. Please surrender your ship.'

The captain stared. He looked about Nightingale's age, unshaven, eyes ringed with shadows. Dark, sweat-drenched hair plastered against his slashed forehead. His hand shook as he listened to the slaughter beyond his cabin.

He lowered the pistol.

'Please,' he said in heavily accented English. 'I surrender.'

Nightingale nodded. In a wave, the weariness swept over him.

It had only taken minutes.

The ship was theirs.

Chapter Eight: Butcher's Bill

The wound on Nightingale's shoulder burnt. What he had thought was a blow from a sword-hilt turned out to be from a hammer blow and when he returned to the *Scylla*, blood clotted his lapels. He stood in the mess of his cabin – guns run out and still smoking, chests overturned, even a stray ball rolled beside the stern locker – and gently peeled off his coat. A nasty bruise ringed his collarbone. He touched it gingerly and swore.

For a sharp action, though, they had emerged relatively unscathed. Dr Archer's butcher's bill was short: a few fractures and breaks from falling down hatchways, a handful of burns from the grenade which had exploded, and three deaths. Nightingale regretted he had been yet to learn their names. But the Scyllas had performed well – better than he had anticipated.

The *Fénix* was now their prize. If they could keep her afloat, her price would be divided amongst the crew. Winthrop, the purser, was already at work with his calculations. As captain, Nightingale would gain the highest share. But even the minute bonus for the regular seamen would please them. The *Fénix* was a fine ship, perhaps fine enough to be brought into the service.

The capture of the *Fénix* meant the orphanage of her former crew. The Spaniards would be kept under armed watch and forced to sail her into their enemy's port. Who should command that prize crew was another matter.

With a sigh, Nightingale sagged against the locker. He wanted nothing more than to turn in. He carefully pulled off his shirt to peer at a laceration at the centre of his bruise. What a brave fool he had been to lead the boarding party with Lieutenant Charlston. Charlston was young and strong. Nightingale's body reminded him that he was not.

Movement behind him marked Lieutenant Courtney's entrance. Nightingale stiffened and instinctively ensured his back was turned away. But he was too late to hide the flogging scars from Courtney. The lieutenant stared, opened his mouth, then closed it again. He diplomatically looked away to Nightingale's bloodied shoulder.

'Do you need me to find Dr Archer?'

'No,' Nightingale said brusquely, pulling on his shirt. 'He has enough on his plate. I'm well. Where is Rylance?'

The little steward, who seemed to be constantly in earshot, hurried in. He had a pistol strapped to his chest and when he smiled, Nightingale saw that two of his teeth had been knocked out. 'Sir?'

'Can you fetch me my dress coat, Rylance?'

'Yes, sir.'

Nightingale straightened. Courtney lingered awkwardly, Nightingale thought it was due to what he had just seen before realising he expected a word about the action. The Scyllas's work had been admirable but the bad taste that followed every battle seared Nightingale's mouth. He still felt the resistance of his sword as he tugged it free of the crewman's stomach and the break of the old man's nose beneath his elbow. It would fade with time, as all the other deaths had. Yet now he just felt loose and hazy, in the purgatory between a battle and its aftermath.

'Is the captain aboard?' he asked.

Courtney's shoulders sank at the neglected praise.

'Yes, sir. That's what I came to tell you. Lieutenant Charlston is bringing him down with his lieutenant.'

Nightingale was glad when Rylance returned quicker than the Spaniards. Rylance helped him into his dress coat, careful not to jar his injury.

'I've brushed it down as much as I can, sir, but—'

'It'll do, Rylance.'

Nightingale turned to Courtney. The lieutenant was as dishevelled as Nightingale felt, but at least Nightingale attempted to disguise it.

Courtney's free dark curls stuck to his face, which was coated with powder-burns and sweat.

'You should tidy yourself, Lieutenant. We are representing the service to these prisoners.'

'We already have a victory, sir.'

'The victory does not end here. Neaten your coat and hair at least.'

Courtney reluctantly obeyed, scraping his hair back into a tighter tie. He rubbed his dirty hands across his face and smeared the powder to the edges. When he had removed his coat and donned it again, Nightingale sighed and conceded, 'It'll do. You do not speak Spanish, do you?'

'Not a word, sir.'

'My grasp of Spanish extends only to ship-boarding and I never could pick up enough French. Are there any amongst the crew who know the language?'

'Lieutenant Hargreaves has family in Portugal, sir.'

'That is not the same. Where is Lieutenant Hargreaves?'

'He was on the gun deck during the fight, sir, as you ordered.' Courtney paused as if wanting to say more about Hargreaves. Their mute tension had not vanished since the affair with the cannons. 'Toby Warren speaks Spanish.'

'Toby?'

'He's lived in the West Indies for a while. I think he learnt some Spanish to impress a woman.'

'Ah. Well, pass the word for him.'

Toby was not far. He had protected the powder magazine during the battle but had come forward to congratulate his mates. He hobbled into the cabin on his crutch and tried to salute Nightingale. Nightingale urged him to sit down before he broke something else.

When Lieutenant Charlston entered, he filled the cabin with his broad shoulders and blood-red coat – which made the trailing Spanish captain look even smaller. A short while ago, he had been resplendent on his deck. Now, he wore an expression that showed he knew he had been conquered: eyes down, face pallid, shrivelled beneath his gilded uniform. Tufts of lank, dark hair sprouted beneath his cocked hat and his moustache drooped over a thin mouth.

His lieutenant, an extraordinarily handsome man, followed. There remained a flash of resistance in him as he stared between Nightingale and Courtney. Auburn ringlets bounced as he removed his hat and sharply bowed. Nightingale found himself comparing him to Courtney – not the same English beauty, but something darker and colder.

He pressed down such thoughts.

'I am Captain Nightingale,' he said, extending a hand. The captain took it with a small nod. 'This is my first lieutenant, Courtney.'

'Ramirez,' the Spaniard replied. 'And Lieutenant Allende.'

They sat around Nightingale's desk, hastily pulled back into place by Rylance. 'My clerk can converse in some Spanish,' Nightingale started. 'He will help us reach an understanding.'

'I can also speak some English, Captain,' Allende interjected.

'I am sure you realise the position you are now in. The *Fénix* will become property of the British Crown, and you, your officers, and your men shall become prisoners. I will assign a prize crew of my men to sail the *Fénix* into Bridgetown and as recompense, shall be taking some of yours into our service. I assume you have your papers with you?'

Allende and Toby translated the words. Ramirez stayed silent amongst the chatter, only making noise as he rustled the paperwork in his breast pocket. Nightingale glanced over the *Fénix*'s muster logs and ship inventory and handed them to Courtney. 'Capitán Ramirez, you shall stay as our prisoner onboard the *Scylla*. We shall deliver you to Trinidad. Lieutenant Allende, shall you stay with your captain or rejoin your ship?'

'I stay with my captain, sir,' Allende replied immediately.

Nightingale nodded, admiring his loyalty. He wondered what it would be like to receive that again.

'Now, I have some other questions for you, *Capitán*,' he said, chest constricting. 'They may seem unconventional. But I would be grateful for any information you might have.'

He looked to Toby as he translated, using the gap as a space to clear his thoughts. The *Ulysses* was never far from them. He knew that, one day, he would have to take the *Ulysses* as he'd taken the *Fénix*. It would not be the enemy cut down, then. It would be his own countrymen. 'We are searching for a vessel,' he said carefully. 'She is named the *Ulysses* – from the same class as this *Scylla*, indistinguishable from a distance, I have been told. She was last—'

But Nightingale did not have to continue. At the mention of the name, Ramirez drew up, shoulders tightening. He glanced to Allende.

'Do you know her?' Nightingale pressed.

'She hailed us,' Ramirez said, Toby translating.

'You have seen her? Where was this?'

Ramirez hesitated.

'Please, sir, I have treated you well. This ship may be dangerous to all nations.'

Ramirez sighed. 'It was about two weeks ago,' he said slowly. 'I can find you the exact date if needed. We were east of Grenada when she gave chase. She flew British colours but as soon as we were within range, she hauled them down. We had not even fired a shot at her, and she was the one to give chase, so we knew something was wrong. A man shouted to us from the quarterdeck. I could tell he was not the captain. He was dressed in a seaman's clothes: loose trousers and a simple shirt. He said he wanted to talk.'

Ramirez shuddered in remembrance. 'I thought it was a ruse. As soon as I saw the ship, I felt something about it, as though something terrible had happened. But we allowed the man to come across. He brought another man who I knew was the true captain. The captain was bruised and beaten and the first man guided him around as if telling him how to act. He was an American, this man. I recognised the strange accent.

'He wanted us to support him down the coast of South America and asked for advice about how to disguise the ship as a Spanish or French vessel. I couldn't give him that advice. I am not… that is not my place to make such a decision. But I agreed to support him. I could not turn away a ship which swore allegiance against Britain.'

Nightingale had feared such a thing. The Caribbean and surrounding coasts teemed with enemy activity. Every island held a place in a huge patchwork of global influence – each settlement under a tapestry of flags. And the vessels were symbols of that nationhood, carrying the colours of their homes and acting by their laws. For the crew to haul down the British colours as an act of amity was near-treason by itself.

'The decision did not sit pleasantly with me,' Ramirez continued. He looked genuinely aggrieved, face drawn, eyes downcast. 'But I had to act. Our Spanish vessels are blockaded in Cadiz by your fleets, Captain. The seas grow smaller and smaller for Spain. Once, our flags could be seen everywhere. Now, we are a forgotten partner of another empire, and the enemy of one more. Another ship – another chance to spit in the eye of Britain – could be a small portion in reclaiming our names.'

Nightingale ignored the platitudes. 'Where was the *Ulysses* heading?'

'They were not precise. I'm not certain they knew themselves. They wished to take on more stores first. Having the captain alive was a way to give an air of legitimacy to any port they entered.'

A mutinous ship, sailing without a clear course, brave enough to hail enemy ships and ask for aid: it was a keg surrounded by loose powder. Any stray spark could rupture it – and Nightingale was no longer sure who would set it off.

'What happened to the *Ulysses*?' he asked.

'We lost her in a storm. I was glad of it. I could tell my men were not comfortable with her sailing so close. *Oro maldito.*'

Nightingale frowned as Toby translated. 'Are you sure that's what he said?' Nightingale asked.

'*Oro maldito,*' Ramirez repeated.

'Cursed gold.'

Nightingale glanced at Courtney who looked just as bewildered. Surprisingly, amusement crossed Ramirez's face. His lips twitched and he chuckled. 'You were tasked with finding the *Ulysses*, yes?' Ramirez asked. 'You were not aware what was onboard?'

Nightingale did not need to reply. Ramirez continued to speak but Toby hesitated in his translation.

'What did he say, Toby?'

'I-I do not want to insult you, Captain.'

'Tell me.'

'He asked why you were not told. He asked if your superiors do not trust you.'

Nightingale gritted his jaw.

'Ask him whether he took any of the gold.' That would be an equivalent insult, maligning Ramirez's honour in taking the handout of a mutineer.

'I did not want it,' Ramirez replied with some satisfaction. 'Even after the American sailor tried to bribe us with it. He did not say why it was onboard. That ship and all her men were tainted with blood.'

Nightingale had taken on six months' worth of stores in the case of rounding the Horn into the Pacific. Almost two hundred men, brow-beaten and harassed by their lieutenant, fearful of the yellow fever, battle-weary, would dive on the chance of gold and fortune; they would go anywhere. Nightingale felt a surge of anger and humiliation that he had not been told.

'When I saw your ship, Captain,' Ramirez continued, 'I thought that you were the *Ulysses*. Then I feared you were a reprisal against us. I had to fight. Our honour drains by the day.'

Nightingale shifted, only half-listening. Perhaps, as Ramirez said, they truly did not believe in him. Perhaps they had seen him for what he truly was.

Courtney noticed his pause. He leant forward, hands grasped together on the table. 'Did you see the rest of the crew?' he asked. 'How many were there? What was their condition?'

'I only talked with the American sailor and the captain. The crew remained behind on the *Ulysses* and we saw them aloft and on the deck. I cannot say how they fared. They behaved like normal men – which is even more grotesque, knowing what they had done.'

'Did you spy any women?'

Ramirez frowned. 'Women aboard your ship? Sailors?'

'No. She's a—' Courtney quickly reformed his words. 'We believe there is a gunner's wife and master's wife aboard. We naturally fear for their safety.'

'I cannot answer this either. I saw no women. Though if what you say is true, I fear for them also.'

There was much to fear. Every time Nightingale thought he had untangled a knot, more appeared. He was glad when Ramirez and Allende left the cabin. The two Spanish officers would remain on the ship for now, until they could be delivered to the proper authorities in Trinidad. Nightingale could not wait; he already wanted them out of his hands.

'Toby,' he said. Toby turned to him, pallor touching his cheeks. 'I don't want a word of this beyond the cabin.'

'N-no, sir.'

'Return to your station.'

Courtney had not looked up. He rubbed at his cut knuckles, making them bleed again. 'You were not told about the gold,' he said – not a question but a fact.

'No.'

'Why should they have gold onboard? Their cruise was to protect trade and harass any privateers and enemy vessels. Do you think they found a treasure ship?'

It wasn't likely. Treasure ships – the kind a man could have made a fortune out of decades before – were rare. 'As I said – no one else beyond this cabin should know,' he said. 'Not until I'm clearer about what is happening.'

Courtney for once did not disagree.

'Why did they not tell you?' he asked, echoing Ramirez's doubts.

Nightingale could not answer. 'You asked about the women again,' he said instead.

Courtney nodded.

'Who are they? You know one of them, don't you?'

'No, sir. I was only… aware of them.'

'I cannot tolerate any further secrets, Lieutenant Courtney. If you know something about that crew, please tell me.'

'I do not.' Courtney kept picking at his wound, peeling off the reddened skin. Nightingale knew that bluntly ordering him would

70

not crack his defences; such a treatment had not answered so far and it would not answer now he was so surly.

'I wish to pick good men for the *Fénix* prize crew,' he continued, adhering to his responsibilities. 'They have to be capable, trustworthy seamen. At the same time, we cannot lose too many skilled hands from the *Scylla*. I shall send Sergeant Norris across to keep order.' He paused. 'Lieutenant Hargreaves will command.'

Courtney finally raised his head. Nightingale saw the collision of resentment and anger on his face – the bitter sting of being passed over again.

'I do not want to send away my first lieutenant, not when the situation is so fraught. Lieutenant Hargreaves needs a chance to prove himself after being brought onboard so recently. After the ordeal with the gunnery...'

'Lieutenant Hargreaves will refuse, sir.'

Nightingale frowned at the bold certainty. 'Lieutenant Hargreaves shall not be in a position to refuse or accept. I am ordering him to take command.'

'Midshipman Richmond would be willing, sir. He knows his navigation and sailing and you shall need a stronger character to maintain control of the *Fénix*.'

'This is not up for debate, Lieutenant. I do not enjoy your repeated attempts at questioning me – or Lieutenant Hargreaves. Pass the word to him. And for God's sake, stop irritating that cut.'

Before Nightingale realised what he was doing, he slapped a hand on Courtney's bare wrist. Courtney froze at the sudden touch. Nightingale quickly withdrew his hand.

'I shall fetch Lieutenant Hargreaves,' Courtney rushed, and then he was gone.

Nightingale closed his aching eyes. A whirlpool raged around him – if it did not suck him down, then the darker seas beyond might. He should not have believed this voyage would help him. He fought against a current he could not swim through.

He thought of the *Ulysses*. He thought of Captain Wheatley, pushed along by the American sailor, Ransome. He thought of the gold. The lies. Louisa, far back in Portsmouth. The mysterious women onboard the *Ulysses*. The burning scars on his back. Leroy, at the bottom of Aboukir Bay where they had buried him.

Lieutenant Hargreaves did not arrive in the cabin. Word reached Nightingale that he was in the sickbay, and when he visited, Hargreaves nursed a glistening, bloody cut on his forehead.

'It was a splinter, sir,' he said, expression like a cowed dog. 'My head is raging. Dr Archer wishes to keep an eye on me.'

The lieutenant turned even paler when Nightingale mentioned the *Fénix* prize crew. In the end, Nightingale knew it was no use pressing the matter. He found Richmond, suggested the command and the midshipman smiled so widely he nearly burst at the seams. 'Do not give them any slack, David,' Nightingale warned.

'No, sir. I'll whip them into shape as good as any English crew.'

That night, during the second dog watch, Nightingale stood upon the deck. The shadows of a companion-ladder shielded him from the crew. Midshipman Richmond was gone, waved off and wished fortune by his fellows and taking a handful of good men with him.

On the forecastle, those off watch sang and danced. The sound of their tambourines and pipes drifted along the deck and out across the water. A clear, bright voice sang 'Don't Forget your Old Shipmate' to the stars, accompanied by the resident musician, Ashley Marlin. Courtney was nowhere to be seen.

Nightingale turned to gaze leeward. He could vaguely see the twinkling stern lanterns of the *Fénix*. Nightingale wished them well.

He wished them all well.

Chapter Nine: Pyrrhic

20 October 1798, Portsmouth

The chill of an approaching winter drifted over the waves. Nightingale felt it the moment they entered the Channel. Though land masses merged into blocks of colour and shade, he knew well the homely approach: past Plymouth and Portland and the Isle of Wight, to sail into the final harbour of Portsmouth. He could smell the tar and timber and hemp, and hear the clatters and shouts of the busy docks.

Home again. He had not seen it in over two years. Even then, it had been a brief visit before embarking for Portugal and the fleet. He doubted much had changed.

'Nearly ashore, Hiram,' a voice said beside him. Captain Lovett had insisted on accompanying Nightingale, as if he didn't trust him to find his way. Lovett swayed with every pull of the oars, thick legs crammed against the wales. 'Ah! Fortune has smiled on us. You have a fine welcoming party. She must have received the message.'

Nightingale squinted against the bright sun. Washed-up seaweed replaced the scent of the timber and tar. A gathering of formless dark figures stood on the shingly beach. One of them must have been Louisa. She raised a hand then pulled it back to grasp the streaming tail of her bonnet.

Oars came up and Lovett took Nightingale's arm, helping him out of the small boat and guiding him up the uneven shore. Louisa took her first steps towards him. Closer, Nightingale saw how pale she looked: circles beneath her blue eyes, little stray curls of black hair against her fine white throat. She was wearing an undecorated cobalt gown with a cloak slung around her shoulders – a plain façade, so as not to draw attention to them.

A small smile touched her lips. It was always a shock to see how beautiful she was – a cruel, ironic twist.

'Thank you, Captain Lovett,' she said as her servants hurried to fetch Nightingale's sea-chest and effects. 'You are very kind to bring him ashore.'

'With pleasure, Mrs Nightingale.' Lovett swept off his hat at the sight of Louisa. Nightingale did the same and revealed the mass of bandages wrapped around his head. For two weeks after the battle, he had been utterly blind with both wounds and linen. Many had been removed but it remained bad enough that a rare flicker of surprise crossed Louisa's face.

'Are you well?' she asked softly.

Nightingale nodded.

'Come, I have a carriage waiting.'

They walked up through the gates onto the first steady ground Nightingale had felt in months. The surface was too solid beneath the soles of his shoes. He focused on his feet, setting one in front of the other and hoping he did not fall. His eyes stung in the grey winter light so, like a child, he reached out and took Louisa's arm. She had been advancing too far ahead of him but she paused and laid a hand over his cold fingers.

A few men and women had assembled near the harbour. Nightingale did not want to look up at their murmuring voices and curious shuffles towards him. The arrival of a naval officer in Portsmouth should not have been a novelty – but he had underestimated the force of English feeling after the Nile.

Nightingale had pushed that battle away, resigned to only remember it through his scars. It rushed back when someone shouted, 'Huzzah for Captain Nightingale! Huzzah for the Nile!'

The excitement of the audience bubbled over. He felt a swarm of hands, reaching out to shake his, grasping his arms, thumping his shoulders. Smiling faces faded in and out of his blurred vision. He found himself passed between congratulations, each one more avid than the last: officers who had served under him, men who were once midshipmen, captains who had not been with the fleet, and their wives and sisters and children beaming and bowing their heads politely. His tongue dried in his mouth. He could not push a single word out of it, nor did he have the time between the well wishes. His head throbbed, his stomach churned. For a moment, he thought he was going to collapse.

And then he was being pulled into the carriage.

Louisa slammed shut the door. The wheels moved and the sound of the crowd died away.

Louisa smoothed down her skirt and folded her gloved hands on her lap. Her jaw was tight, lips a thin pink line.

'You have their hearts,' she said.

'It would seem.'

She sighed. Every minute away from the harbour seemed to relax her shoulders and uncurl her fingers. 'I read of the victory. The French fleet destroyed at anchor. Your Lord Nelson has a gift for bold moves. I should have thought the praise would sit well with you. Father has been celebrating and said that the Commons is in a hysteria.'

Nightingale said nothing.

'I did not think Lord Nelson required such close emulation,' she continued. 'I almost expected to see an empty sleeve.'

A flicker of worry touched her fine features. Louisa was the mistress of her own feelings – able to beat them into submission and lock them in a place that only she knew. It was flattering to see such concern. Nightingale knew the terror of families and loved ones as their sons and fathers, and husbands and brothers went off to war. Louisa had always been so stoic about it and he had contented himself with the idea that she was able to return to her own life and ambitions whilst he was gone. Her love was always a surprising thing.

'Is it too terrible?' she asked, softer now.

'The doctors said I was fortunate not to lose an eye.'

'Well, fortune has a way of finding you, Hiram.'

She fell quiet as they rolled through the familiar streets. Nightingale saw the shadowy form of the Royal Garrison Church, the tall spires of the cathedral, the red-bricked grammar school. They were places he had known for many years yet now they looked like hollow masks.

All his previous connections had been severed and he was left with the outer shell. No more did he remember his first shy days as a midshipman; no more did he remember coming home to tell the news of his promotion to lieutenant; no more did he remember his wedding day to Louisa. It had all been washed away by the salt.

'There are some fellows who wish to dine with you at the George tonight,' Louisa said. 'Captain Ermine visited me earlier this morning as soon as he knew you were due to return. I said you should be happy to accept. I did not expect to see you in this way.'

Nightingale's stomach sank. 'I do not wish to see them.'

'They were anxious to hear from you.' But when Nightingale did not respond – only continued to stare out the window – she nodded and said, 'I shall send a message to them saying that you are too weary to attend.'

To his relief, they travelled home, busy streets giving way to green, open country. Riders pulled off the narrow paths and raised their hats as they passed. They recognised Louisa before they saw Nightingale and she smiled politely. Nightingale felt guilty for tipping the balance she maintained over her life.

She had been busy with the house whilst he had been away. New trellis arches, weaved with azaleas, vaulted over the entrance path. Fresh flower beds carpeted the garden, surrounding an unfamiliar stone fountain and waterlily-fringed pond. Haywood Hall itself had the beginnings of a new extension which the old greenhouse had been knocked down for. The house had been handed down through the Haywood generations – more Louisa's than Nightingale's.

'Father thinks of making it his second place of business,' Louisa explained, confirming Nightingale's musings about the expenses. This could not solely be from his prize money. 'He grows tired of travelling so often between here and Bath and London and Bristol to visit my brother at the shipyard. He has been a true bee recently, and I have been at his side, alongside dealing with the household. I suppose you did not receive word of Trinidad? General Abercromby took it. Picton has been made Governor General.'

Nightingale had not known. He did not question Louisa or her father's decisions, though she watched him closely as if expecting an argument. When none came, she knocked on the carriage door and grasped the groom's hand as he helped her out. Nightingale leant on him gratefully and then accepted Louisa's arm. She laid gloved fingers on his elbow. 'It is good to have you home, Hiram,' she said. 'You understand that you simply shocked me. I do not mean to offend or seem so vexed.'

'Of course, my dear.'

'I fear I shall not be a very proficient nurse.'

He smiled wanly. 'I fear I shall not be a very acceptable patient.'

Louisa laughed.

Finally home, Nightingale realised how weary he was. The weight of the past months collapsed on him and it was all he could do to sit uselessly in his armchair as his valet unpacked his effects. He turned in immediately afterwards, despite the sun still trying to peek through the drapes. Louisa came in once, whispered she was returning to town and he nodded without a word. He fell between reality and dream – fire raining down from the heavens, igniting the debris upon black waters, the entire world exploding with light. He woke a dozen times, eyes blurred and head pounding. His room was too still, the bed fixed to a floor which should have been tilting on a constant sea.

He rose, walked down to the new pond, threw a handful of bread for the carp and tried to drink a mug of tea and eat some plain scones. He felt listless and hollow – the world too quiet, the day too bright. The bottom of his world had been cut away and the pieces had drifted into dust.

That evening, he sat, silent, before the fire. A lamb pie, specially decorated with anchors, remained on his plate, untouched. Above him, the oil eyes of his father and Louisa's watched. There was a portrait of himself next to them, dressed in the gilded uniform of a post-captain, the hulk of a French vessel burning in the background. He looked so much younger, red hair tied back, freckled skin, and green eyes shining with determination.

'We should commission another,' a voice said. He had not heard Louisa enter. She shed her coat, bringing the cold smell of the outdoors. 'Perhaps a portrait together. Here – your fellows at the George wished for me to give you this.'

Nightingale frowned as she handed him a wrapped parcel. His name was written on a note attached to the bow alongside warm regards. He put it aside and opened the covering. Inside was a round, glass object, mounted on a polished wooden base. Within the transparent orb lay a perfect carved rendering of the *Lion*. He recognised the lofty heights of her masts and the clean chequer paint on her hull. She sailed under full, snowy-white canvas which floated softly as Nightingale turned the ship. The carvers had even captured her slight way of leaning to the stern.

'The *Lion*,' Louisa said in approval. 'It is beautiful.'

Nightingale nodded. He could feel his throat constricting, unwanted memories simmering to the surface. He put it aside.

'Upon the mantelpiece?' Louisa asked.

'No. I shall have it in my study.'

But, as he set it down upon his window sill that night, it was as though that weight upon him suddenly found physical form. He nearly dropped the gift, so much did his hands tremble. He had gained a grand victory upon that ship. But he had nearly destroyed her. And upon her decks, Leroy had breathed his last.

Tears, long held back, rushed to his eyes. Louisa entered, saw the model and delivered the fatal strike with her, 'You are home now, Hiram.'

His façade shattered. On his knees and with his face buried in her skirt, he wept and wept, inconsolable.

Chapter Ten: The Tempest

6 July 1800

On the surface, life on the *Scylla* continued in the same, defined way as on all warships. Though work was continual, each new day officially started at noon when the angle of the sun would be taken, the log updated, and eight bells struck. The watches cycled around in their regular periods: decks were swabbed, sails patched and washed, guns cleaned, the bilge pumped. At quarters, Nightingale rigorously ran out the cannons, pleased when each gun crew became faster and more accurate and efficient. Lieutenant Hargreaves, despite Courtney's obsessive eye, made no further mistakes.

Those not on duty rested below or sewed up the frequent tears in clothing. Meals were marked by the bosun's piping at noon and during the dog-watches, always provoking a stampede of running feet. All the while, men took their places aloft and in the tops, looking for the phantom of the *Ulysses*. Reaching a respectable ten knots in the rising winds, they made good progress. Graced with weather she excelled in, the *Scylla* maintained her steady attitude, settling into her favourite starboard tack and allowing them to often sail full-and-by.

It was a familiar routine which Nightingale preferred to the hazy, loose days onshore. On the sea, he was the commander of a small, compact piece of time and space, always aware of where things and people would be.

Yet the surface could hide so many depths.

Ramirez and Allende remained their prisoners. They were guarded, separated from the crew as much as possible in the ship's bowels, but Nightingale frequently invited them to dinner. He introduced them to his officers and quickly quelled any impoliteness. Ramirez's knowledge about the *Ulysses*'s cargo pricked continually at his mind. It was best to keep the man content.

And Nightingale found he enjoyed their company. His country battled Spain, and he thought nothing of maiming and capturing Spanish ships and harassing their trade, but the people held no blame. The two officers at his table were still men, united by their careers upon the sea and their devotion to its fickleness. Nightingale sat with them and, despite the foreign colours of their uniform and accented English, saw two people embroiled in the same long conflict.

So he understood the weariness in Ramirez's face. The Spanish captain had boarded the *Scylla* already looking like a beaten hound. The further the days stretched on, away from his crew and ship, the more sallow his skin became and the more the shadows ringed his eyes. Nightingale visited him once with Dr Archer. He wished to rule out disease before accepting the inevitable.

'There is nothing physically wrong with him,' Archer said in the privacy of his sickbay. 'He is under a black spell. The loss of a ship and his honour is as wounding as any mortal injury.'

Nightingale nodded. He had thought the same – and in the doctor's assessment, saw one more link between himself and Ramirez. The *Lion*, the *Fénix*... Both of them almost lost.

'Can anything be done?'

'He is our prisoner, sir. Unless that changes, I can see no improvement.'

Allende did not follow his captain into the blackness, perhaps due to his greater proficiency with the English language. Though the Scyllas hailed from each corner of the world, from East to West Indies and everywhere in between, their common tongue was English. A diplomat's son from Cordoba, Allende was accustomed to it – enough to speak up at dinner. He preferred to tread safe ground and comment on the *Fénix*. She stayed within sight, although making better way before them through Mr Richmond's skilled repair and command.

'Her crew are proud of her,' Allende said over a glass of Madeira one evening. 'Many of them have served commissions on her since they were young. They know her well.'

On other nights, he was invited to the gunroom – a step down from the rigid formality of Nightingale's great cabin. Nightingale hesitated to allow it but did not wish to offend. Lieutenant Courtney willingly made the arrangements. Since capturing the *Fénix*, Nightingale had barely spoken to the lieutenant, other than in regards to the ship. A weight hung between them. It could have been because of anything – but the cold truth was that they now shared a common, forbidden knowledge about the gold.

That – and the scars Courtney had seen upon his back.

Even as he remained in purgatory with Courtney, Nightingale managed to commit the crew to memory. Sundays called for a thorough inspection of men, berths, decks, and stores. Along with accompanying Dr Archer around his sickbay, and frequently perusing the muster with Toby, he remembered division by division, and gun crew by gun crew. So much that during the gunnery practice, he could refer to men by name and not by position. No more would die anonymously.

It was apt, then, that Kieran Attrill's wounds improved as the days passed. Nightingale watched again as Dr Archer dressed them and was pleased to see that the angry red had faded a little. But Kieran did not speak beyond one-word answers anymore. Nightingale resorted to observing in silence, hoping his mere presence was enough to allay any ideas of Kieran's that he did not care. On the contrary, he feared he cared too much, reminded of the scars upon his own back.

Four days after the *Fénix* action, another cry of, 'Sail ho!' resounded from the top. Nightingale hurried from the great cabin to find Cecil Smythe, the midshipman on watch, half-leaning over the gunwale into the chains. He grasped him and pulled him back to safety as a wave rushed along the side. The boy seemed unaware of the danger, though, cheeks ruddy.

'I can just see the signal, sir,' he gabbled. 'She has post for us.'

'She' turned out to be the *Racehorse*, a nimble little brig which gave some light relief with letters from home. Once they had been handed out amongst the men, Nightingale returned to his cabin and broke the seal on his own post. He laid aside the messages from creditors and insurance agents and, as always, opened Louisa's first. Her sturdy, clear writing relieved him. She told him about the house and its new adornments: the greenhouse only recently finished, the lawn about to be trimmed into a maze. Nightingale knew she only fussed about the manor when she was nervous and, for a while, he couldn't tell the reason. She mentioned meetings with friends and neighbours. His heart squeezed when she said how Lucy Sawyer, Leroy's sister, had visited, wearing her brother's Nile medal.

And then he found the kernel of Louisa's worries. It was not her father, as he had wondered. Sir William was already in Trinidad to aid in its transfer into British governance.

It was his own father.

Nightingale's blood ran cold as he read how Admiral Nightingale had considered journeying across the Atlantic. By the time of Louisa's writing, he had not – but her letter was dated to over a month before.

Nightingale did not have the strength to deal with him. He sat alone at night and, in the darkness, boyish feelings crept in. His head was tangled enough without his father reaching in and scrambling it more. And he would, of course he would, if he was there. Nightingale had never travelled the path his father wished for.

As if Ramirez felt the dark shadow, he worsened. Allende translated his words to any of the crew curious enough to see him up close, like an animal in its cage. The words "Jonah" and "curse" ripped through the decks. In a few days, the *Ulysses* turned from a ship made of wood and rope and canvas to a wicked, almost mythical monster. Ramirez used his helplessness as if it were a weapon.

Eventually, Nightingale banned anyone from visiting Ramirez. He only went to him with Toby, wanting his trusted clerk, not Allende, to translate his words. 'You shall be in Trinidad soon,' Nightingale insisted. 'You shall get the help you need.'

'My only help shall be at the end of a noose,' the captain spat.

'I have treated you well – and this is how you repay me? By stirring unrest amongst my men?'

'You shall put them through more. Perhaps this time, you shall go down with them.'

That grey afternoon, Nightingale left him in his imprisonment in steerage. He felt the *Scylla* pitching a little as he climbed up, sensing the difference in the timbers and the wind freshening in the sails. He was about to return to the deck when music drifted to him. It was not the raucous piping of the men or the clatter of dancing bare feet. Someone skilfully plucked a guitar. As it reached the end of its refrain, a fine, strong voice took over.

Oh the wind was foul, and the sea ran high
Leave her Johnny, leave her
She shipped it green, and none went by
And it's time for us to leave her

Nightingale felt himself drawn closer. Something about that voice sparked memories. Leroy Sawyer, in the wardroom, singing to his fellow officers. Nightingale watching with a distant smile on his face. The lieutenant catching his eye and bowing his head, hand over his heart.

Leave her Johnny, leave her
Oh, leave her Johnny, leave her
For the voyage is long and the winds don't blow
And it's time for us to leave her

Nightingale looked into the gunroom. Dr Archer and midshipman Burrows watched Courtney, who stood at the head of the table, smiling beatifically as he sang for them. Beside him, Allende had a guitar on his lap, fingers stroking the strings.

The walls ached around him. Nightingale felt as though he had stepped into a world where he didn't belong. Courtney seemed a different person, face flushed with joy, his voice light and beautiful. Waves of loneliness crashed over Nightingale. It was impossible, he had thought, to feel such emptiness along with such agony but again and again, for almost two years, it had recurred. He wanted Leroy with him – Leroy Sawyer and the *Lion*, not this crew.

Across the gunroom, his eyes connected with Courtney's. The lieutenant's words died in his throat. A sharp bolt cut through Nightingale, forcing tears to cloud his vision. He looked away.

A crack of thunder saved Nightingale from the humiliation of his other officers seeing him. Within a second, a wave lashed alongside the *Scylla*, tilting the deck and buckling Nightingale's legs. Allende's guitar fell to the ground with an ugly twang.

Above, running feet scampered across the timbers with the bosun and Smythe calling out orders. Courtney, still lacing his cloak, hurried from the gunroom and grasped Nightingale's arm. It throbbed from where he had crushed it against the bulkhead when falling. For a moment, lightning illuminated the deck from an open hatchway and showed Courtney's pale face.

But all anger at Courtney and Allende was doused by the breaking storm. Nightingale rushed with Courtney up through the ladders onto the main deck just as a fierce gust of wind streamed across the *Scylla*. It nearly knocked him off his feet. He grabbed for the shrouds, feeling how they sang and shivered beneath his palm. Through the mesh of rigging, the sky closed like a fist, black clouds racing to strangle the remaining fragments of blue. Shadows, as deep as night, scythed over the ship's yards.

There was still too much aloft. The storm would tear through the sails like paper.

'Bring down t'gallant masts and sails!' he ordered. 'Close reef topsails! Furl the mainsail! Mr Uriah – ensure all hands are on deck!'

The bosun's pipe whistled, barely cutting through the din, to bring all men to their duties.

Smythe ran across the deck. He looked so young, cheeks vividly red beneath the freckles, like a boy playing in the rain. His eyes sparkled with anticipation.

'I was going to give the order, sir,' he insisted. 'It came up so quickly. We were running at eight knots – I had only just written it on the log when Mr Abbott pointed out the sky.'

'You did well, Smythe. Come with me.'

Nightingale hurried to the quarterdeck and leant over the windward side. The gust blew hot and cold as it cut across the cresting waves and sent spray over the rail. The surface whipped up like a green canvas tipped with flecks of white paint. To Nightingale's alarm, the clouds grew thicker and blacker. A cloak of darkness surrounded the ship – and they travelled in the very eye of it.

Aloft, the topmen scrambled to set the preventer braces and bring the sails in. The rigging leapt and tautened as they leant over the yards, tying the points as quickly as humanly possible, but Nightingale could still hear the wind lashing against the canvas. His coat flapped about his legs, hair tangling around his mouth. The wind came from aft: a small mercy. If they were fortunate, they could run before it.

With a tear, the fore-t'gallant sail billowed free. It snapped in the wind before flying southwards. The empty spar it left creaked and swayed whilst a group of topmen clung to the bouncing yard. Without the balance of the canvas, it wrenched around, nearly throwing them into the sea far below.

Courtney ran to the foot of the foremast.

'Lieutenant!' Nightingale shouted, but the officer was already clambering aloft. As nimble as a boy, he raced to help set the stay-sails.

Nightingale turned away – in time to receive a face of rain. It was as though a dam had broken. Hot streams soaked him through in seconds. With the sudden deluge, the sea pulsated, flogged into a frenzy; troughs deepened and the crests rose. Nightingale looked along the deck and realised the bow was dipping into the foaming white water. Men out on the jib-boom clung to the stays as they fought to keep above the surface.

The waves rolled angrily under the *Scylla*'s keel and frothed about her quivering frame. She was being ripped back and forth like a toy.

Nightingale ran to the helm. Barty struggled to hold onto it so Nightingale gripped the spokes with him. The wild soul of the ship shook and bucked.

'A short squall!' Nightingale yelled. 'It can't last at this power for long!'

Barty didn't reply.

With his hands on the wheel, Nightingale liked to believe he had command. But the forces of nature – a sailor's bane and blessing – cast them along so that the *Scylla* soared down into the pit of a surge and then raced out the other side. Each time it got more violent until even Nightingale's stomach lurched.

Stay-sails bloomed into sight. He looked up at the masts, at the rigid rigging and yards which should have been perpendicular but were tilting further and further, and could almost count off the degrees by the second. Courtney gripped the foretop cap, drenched as he stared out over the water.

Nightingale saw what he was staring at.

Ice froze his limbs.

The shadow of a gargantuan wave fell across the sea. It raced towards them, trimmed with foaming white. Nightingale gazed up, higher than the foremast. At the wave's peak, lightning struck and illuminated the grey tendril of a water-spout spiralling down from the clouds.

He had no choice.

'Two points starboard!' he shouted, and he and Barty wrenched at the helm, straining and slipping as the rudder resisted. Another pair of hands joined them as Lieutenant Hargreaves appeared, head still bandaged. Between them, they brought the *Scylla* head-on to the giant wave. It loomed, rising like a mountain, the ship's bowsprit tilting to meet it, stay-sails convulsing. 'All hands, brace!' Nightingale screamed.

He clung to the wheel as the ship pitched backwards and the bows arched into the wave. A cry ran along the deck which lifted and lifted, men scrambling for ropes as they were forced onto the slope of the water. Streams rushed along the timbers. For a moment, they faced the black sky and the great heights of the masts vaulted directly over Nightingale's head.

With a shriek, the *Scylla* crested. Nightingale took a breath and coughed out mouthfuls of the spray. To larboard, the water-spout cascaded past them, throwing up whirling mist.

'Captain!' someone called. Nightingale wiped streams of the deluge from his eyes to see a topman pointing to Courtney, who jabbed a finger to starboard.

Nightingale followed Courtney's indication across the pinnacle of the wave. A mass of mountainous waves surrounded them, crashing and breaking and turning the world into a boiling green wilderness. Lightning illuminated pockets of water and there – to starboard, the shadowy form of a ship.

The *Fénix*.

She was listing dreadfully, battered by the sea.

The *Scylla* descended and blotted the view. Like a bucking horse, she went down only to rise again, beaten between the waves. Nightingale desperately stared at the horizon. If it weren't for Courtney's pointing, he would have thought the *Fénix* was a mirage. He attempted to piece together the brief glimpse – if she had been listing, if it had been a trick of the weather, if his injured eyes had deceived him, if she had been moving at all.

Courtney slipped on the slick deck as he staggered to his side. Nightingale grabbed his arm. 'She's nearer than she should be!' Courtney called through the hail. 'Richmond must have been caught out by the storm too!'

'Keep your eye out for the *Fénix*!' Nightingale shouted at him, so close he could feel the water whipping off Courtney's hair. 'Lieutenant Hargreaves, did you see her?'

'Just a glimpse, sir!' Hargreaves replied.

'She was listing. She is in danger.' Nightingale regretted saying it, as if it might not have been true before but now his words had condemned her.

A wave ran aft of the *Scylla*, raising her stern, pushing Nightingale against the helm. The sails billowed as the wind wailed along the deck and the ship screamed her protest. Nightingale prayed for the rudder and then the swell continued along the keel. They rose, the sky rushing past them again.

There she was. The *Fénix*. She was heeling over, for certain; the hull showed above the waterline, the streaks of her paint giving way to the fouled bottom. There was no use in hailing her. Richmond needed to heave things overboard – needed to right the balance of the ship – needed to draw in more sails. He should have known all of that. Why was he not—

The sky sparked with tremendous light. A tapestry of lightning shot across the black clouds.

One fork struck the *Fénix*'s main peak.

Fire raced down the mast. Splinters flew off in every direction. Mast-rings and metal blocks illuminated with a fantastical glow. In a second, the main-topmast collapsed and plummeted to the deck. It brought with it a roaring inferno.

The *Fénix* ignited.

Nightingale watched silently. He didn't realise they were descending the other side of the wave until the *Fénix* vanished from sight.

Courtney turned to him, eyes wide, mouth open.

'We can't avert our course in this wind!' Nightingale shouted.

'The fire will reach the powder store!'

'Midshipman Richmond is a capable man!'

Boy. He was a boy.

Nightingale could not breathe – not only from the furious weather and the water lashing the deck. He clung to the helm like a lifeline. Begged the tempest to cease so he could aid them.

Black smoke bled over the horizon. Nightingale saw the *Orient* once more: the seething conflagration of that ship, exploding in a hailstorm of fire and debris. It was her again. Again and again and again.

Nightingale barely heard the orders coming from his mouth anymore, barely felt the lashing rain. He retreated into the cold heart of a captain but felt the aching soul of the ship beneath his feet and hands.

But even as he prayed for their own survival, he looked east and saw the glow of the fire and the stream of the smoke.

Chapter Eleven: From the Ashes

After the wailing of the tempest, the grey sky seemed too empty, the waves too calm. Aside from the splashing oars and the creaking pinnace, cold silence shrouded the sea. Nightingale's pulse beat in his ears. He clasped his hands between his knees and dug indents into his palms with his nails. His jaw ached as he trained his eyes ahead, but he allowed only this as an indication of his fear. Everything else he pushed down.

Behind, the *Scylla* rested hove-to with shortened sails. With every stroke of the boat's oars, she retreated. Courtney watched them over the rails, and for a time, Nightingale had heard his voice. Now, it was gone.

Ahead, the hulk of the *Fénix* smouldered. Mere hours ago, she had been a fine brig, manned by a crew of almost one hundred. The storm had ripped her guts over the water, barrels and planks and cordage floating in a halo of debris. A gun carriage bobbed past, followed by a sea-chest and a spar which may have once been part of the foremast. Nightingale glimpsed two initials carved onto the chest – perhaps belonging to a man sinking to the seabed.

The *Fénix*'s bow tilted into the water; the surface already reached her gun ports and swilled around the peeling paint. The hole in the deck from the fallen main-topmast gaped at the sky, guzzling the salty brine. In the chaos of what had followed, the remaining mast had cracked too and now it leant at a dangerous angle over the forecastle. Rigging hung limp and useless, sails fluttering like old, stained sheets.

Mercifully, the rain had dampened the worst of the fires. The ghost of the inferno still remained, though – black scars tarnished everything aft of the torn main chains and smoke wound into the sky.

89

Nightingale could not see any movement on deck.

Beside him, Captain Ramirez gave a small moan. He had insisted on coming and Nightingale had relented, though he knew the man's spirit was already cracked. Tears ran silently down his cheeks.

Nightingale had the boatsmen pull as close to the charred ship as they dared. The men lay on their oars and Nightingale stepped under the shadow of the vessel. She was very low in the water; her main deck was almost in jumping distance. He gently reached out and placed his palm against her warm, dark side.

'We must work quickly,' he said, repeating the orders he had given before leaving the *Scylla*. 'This ship will not be afloat for much longer. Search the areas you can reach. Leave the areas you cannot. Any survivors well enough to travel will be placed in Mr Thomason's cutter.'

He looked over his crew: men hand-picked for their strength. 'Obi,' he said to the black starbowline man at the stern. 'Take your men forward and I shall take mine aft. Do not enter the lower decks if they are obstructed. Captain Ramirez, please stay with me.'

One by one, they climbed over the side. Nightingale's heart throbbed in his throat – not only for their own safety but for the men who could be trapped. He imagined their hope at hearing the Scyllas's voices. Such light would be dashed when they realised they could not be reached.

Nightingale set his feet down on the deck. It tilted, sloshing water about his shoes. With careful, measured steps, he went aft over the broken main deck. Spars had toppled and crushed anything in their way; holes littered where obstacles had crashed and slid around in the wild seas; some things still burnt. Nightingale heaved debris over the side and heard it sizzle in the cold water.

From this higher vantage point, he could look down upon the wreckage. Shadows flitted back and forth between the fragments: tiger sharks, drawn by the scent of blood. They circled the bodies, some unrecognisable amongst shreds of blackened clothing. A red-coated torso drifted past: Sergeant Norris, floating towards the waiting creatures.

The firestorm of the *Orient* – the aftermath of torn limbs and burnt corpses – flared in Nightingale's mind.

He turned back to the ship, shuddering.

'Jones,' he said to the tall Yorkshireman nearby. 'See if those hatches can be opened. Shout down to any survivors.'

The hatches had been battened down during the storm but remains of the mast now covered them. It would take remarkable strength to get them up. The best chance for those on the lower decks would be to escape out the gun ports – if they could reach them.

Fallen men leant against the gunwales or crouched in the shelter of the ladders. To Nightingale's relief, some still breathed. No matter British or Spanish, any well enough were laid in the cutter, weeping over their broken limbs and twisted bodies. Not many could be taken.

Nightingale tried to remember the names as they found Scyllas. Jim Rayner, Ashley Marlin, Graham Worthe… No sign of Richmond.

'Captain!' Obi's voice suddenly echoed from the foremast. Nightingale turned, saw the man waving at him and hurried over the deck. To starboard, the yards listed further over with a groan.

Obi crouched over a prostrate body. A tangle of braces and halliards covered the wounded sailor. Chunks of a spar crushed his right leg. Nightingale thought of Leroy, choking on his own blood as the wooden spike burrowed deep into his throat. His stomach twisted.

'David,' he breathed, dropping to his knees. Together, he and Obi shifted the debris. Richmond's chest still moved but his limb was twisted and an ugly gash split open his forehead.

'He's alive, sir,' Obi said.

'Can you carry him?'

'Without a drop of sweat, sir.' Despite his brawny strength, Obi was as gentle as a nursemaid when he lifted Richmond. Nightingale supported the midshipman's leg but at the sudden movement, his eyes sprang open. He gasped in panicked sips before moaning and fainting with the pain.

'Into the cutter. Quickly, Obi,' Nightingale urged.

Richmond had to be the last. As they lifted him over the side, the remains of the mainmast toppled. By some miracle, it fell to port, away from the boats – but the balance was ruined. Nightingale felt the *Fénix* surrender to the waves, water spilling further into the open gun ports and holes. He hurried to rejoin his men.

Only to realise Captain Ramirez was still on the deck.

'*Capitán!*' he called. 'We have to return to the *Scylla*. This ship will not last.'

At first, he didn't think Ramirez understood him. He lingered with glazed eyes, leaning with the broken rhythm of the ship.

'*Capitán!*' Nightingale repeated. 'We must leave!'

'No.' Ramirez turned to face him. He reached out, laid his hand on the stump of the mast and ran his fingers lovingly down it. 'I stay with the ship.'

'Don't be ridiculous, man! You cannot be saved if you stay here!'

'I stay with the ship.'

Something cracked deep below the water. Slowly, the *Fénix* cleaved in half. Nightingale looked desperately at the pieces, beginning to drift apart, then back at Ramirez.

'We have to leave, sir!' Barty called from the pinnace. 'If we're here when the ship goes down, we'll go down with her!'

'Please,' Ramirez insisted. 'I stay with the ship.'

Nightingale shook his head. No words would come. Tears gathered in his eyes.

He swung his legs over the gunwales and clambered down into the waiting pinnace. 'Out oars,' he croaked. 'Give way starboard.'

He barely remembered the pull back to the *Scylla*. The men rowed as if possessed, heaving against the current as the *Fénix* was claimed by the brine. He did not watch her go down – did not watch Ramirez's last moments as the water took him. The spot would become one more unmarked grave for the sons of the sea. Ships would sail over it, never knowing that, fathoms below, skeletons rested as an eternal reminder of how fickle all of their fates were.

Men raced to help when they reached the *Scylla*. The wounded were tenderly passed up and Dr Archer immediately ferried them below. Fourteen had been saved. Fourteen out of a crew of more than a hundred.

Nightingale could not conjure any emotion, as if his mind was protecting him from the pain. He only stared numbly at the procession of the injured.

Lieutenant Allende, who had been under marine guard on deck, shoved through the crew to look frantically at the wounded.

'Ramirez?' he urged Nightingale. 'Where is my captain?'

'He chose to stay with the ship.'

'What?'

Nightingale did not repeat himself. He watched the truth sink in and saw the minutiae of Allende's reaction: the bewilderment, the grief, the fury, the realisation that he now commanded the sparse *Fénix* crew. Allende took a step back, breathed. Then all of those reactions emerged in one fierce, 'Damn you.'

Courtney lingered close enough to hear. He stepped forward to intervene but Nightingale extended a hand to stop him.

'Lieutenant Charlston,' he directed the marine officer. 'Take Señor Allende below.'

Allende struggled but then succumbed to his torment. He wept silently, entire body trembling. Nightingale watched, angry at how much he surrendered to his emotions, angry at how much he could not.

'Captain,' Courtney's voice said.

Nightingale ignored him and headed for the safety of below-decks. He heard Courtney follow and prayed he would stop, but the man kept approaching like a looming shadow.

'Captain Ramirez made his own bed,' Courtney offered. 'It was his decision to go across and to stay with the—'

'Do not tell me what is right and wrong,' Nightingale snapped, freezing in his hurried steps. 'Only be grateful that you are not in command now.'

He regretted it as soon as it left his mouth. It was an awful thing to say – and only came from a place of distress. But it was in the air now and he could not take it back any more than he could raise the *Fénix*.

He tried to walk away. Courtney again followed.

'Is that what you think I wish for, sir?' Courtney asked. Somehow, they made it to the great cabin and its relative privacy. Nightingale reached for the door but Courtney was quicker. He closed it with a bang. 'Do you think I want command?' he breathed harshly.

'Do you not?' Nightingale knew he should not pull tighter at this rope but the words still poured. 'You wished for command of the prize crew. You held the *Scylla* after Carlisle's death. You berated Lieutenant Hargreaves as if you were his superior, and you question my actions. I am not so old as to misunderstand the ambitions of young men. I cannot blame you. Young officers always look further up the ladder and around those above them on the rungs. You only see the world as something to take from and never think about what it shall—'

He paused, realising what he was saying. Suddenly, he was not speaking to Courtney anymore but to a youthful version of himself. His anger wasn't really directed at the lieutenant; it never had been. It was a fear of what he had been and what the world had taken from him once he had achieved greatness.

' what it shall cost,' he finished, the fight dying in his voice.

Courtney shook his head. He had not heard his hesitation. Seething passion pulsed behind those green eyes as he tried to determine the borders of this infringement.

'Captain Carlisle was good to me, sir,' Courtney said coldly. 'I know that chances for promotion are scarce. I do not have connections. I do not have money. My father is not an admiral. He was a cooper and a tailor and a butcher and a fisherman and anything the town wished for him. And he was a bastard in birth as well as nature.

'I ran away from home when I was thirteen. I knew nobody on the sea but I did my duty, I learnt everything I needed to. I was a lieutenant at twenty. When I was posted here, I wondered what the point of it all was. This is a disease-ridden, ugly place, when the wars are being fought so far away. And when Captain Carlisle died, I had to take his command. One hundred and eighty scared, ill men. I did not complain, I did my duty as I always have done.

'Captain Carlisle was…' Courtney's voice hitched. 'He intended to write a letter of recommendation for me. He intended to help my promotion to post. He died before he got the chance. Do I wish for command? Yes. Of course I do – but I wish for it through the proper channels. Not off of the back of a dead captain. Perhaps I am a bloody fool to think that way and because of it, I never will advance. But I am not an ignorant young man, sir. I never have been. Have me flogged for saying so, I don't give a damn.'

Nightingale stood in silence. Courtney was shaking, as if those words had stewed inside of him for so long and now he was empty. He averted his eyes – which he had not torn from Nightingale's face throughout his speech – and lowered his head.

Nightingale tried to digest what he had said. He had never thought of himself as fortunate. Life had constantly played cruel tricks on him. His father was not a blessing and nor was his wealth. Glory was not the noble cause some dreamt it to be.

But Nightingale had always accepted his lot and taken his suffering without resistance. He had never heard such an open word spoken against the ways of the world – certainly not from a subordinate.

'I…' he began. 'I did not think of any of that.'

To Nightingale's shock, he saw tears in Courtney's eyes. Courtney tried to cuff them away but one still fell.

Shame, sorrow at the loss of so many men, remorse at his lapse of judgement, bubbled in Nightingale. He reached into his pocket and offered a handkerchief to Courtney.

'I was once an ambitious young man too, Lieutenant,' he said carefully. 'When I said that, I was thinking of myself. There is enough in this world to make men weep. I did not mean to be another cause.'

Courtney shook his head. 'I was not honest with you, sir. About the *Ulysses*.' He paused with a shuddering breath. 'My sister. She is on that ship.'

'Your sister?' That was why Courtney had been so concerned about the women onboard the *Ulysses* – why he had asked Wainwright and then Ramirez about their safety.

'She is the master's wife,' Courtney explained. 'It is through my judgement that she is on the ship. We ran away from home together. She stayed with our aunt and uncle but when I was sent out here, I convinced her to come. Jane. My Jane.'

'You should have informed me.' But his previous resentment towards Courtney had faded.

'I was afraid I would be stripped of the commission on the *Scylla*. I was afraid my ability to make decisions would be questioned.'

His admission cut too close to home. How many nights had Nightingale weathered, terrified of his judgement after Leroy had died? It was still there, simmering under every decision he took and every order he gave.

'Arthur.' Nightingale didn't realise he had said his name until it came from his lips. Courtney blinked, surprised. All of that petulant defiance had vanished from his face. He looked like a man who had been battling through a storm his whole life. Nightingale had misjudged him and was as much to blame for this crippling tension as he was. 'I need every good hand aboard that I can muster. You know this crew well, and have kept this ship taut and trim better than many could have done. What is more...' He sighed. 'We will find the *Ulysses*. I swear it. We will find her.'

Courtney nodded. 'Yes, sir,' he muttered, then louder.

To the east, the *Fénix* slowly sank beneath the waves. Aboard the *Scylla*, wounded continued to be taken below, their injuries and fears soothed. Some would not survive. But the sails still had to be set and the course still had to be travelled.

Nightingale stood on deck later that night, watching the moon's crystal-white glow on the calm sea. He kept his eyes on the horizon, knowing Trinidad neared with every mile. The *Ulysses* lurked there too. One veil had been pulled from her but the falling of one barrier only revealed more. Danger remained in every shred of her canvas and in every timber of her frame.

He knew that this was only the very beginning.

Chapter Twelve: Posthumous

15 December 1798, Portsmouth

'Well, Hiram. I believe there has been improvement since the last time I saw you. I cannot identify so much swelling and upset around your eyes. How is the sensitivity? Have there been any further migraines?'

At last, Nightingale was able to turn away from the bright light of the winter noon. He blinked the tears from his eyes, stinging from where Dr Harrow had made him keep them so open. The way he flinched and drew the curtains a little should have answered the question.

'There have been two more bad attacks,' Louisa answered for him. She had been sitting upon the couch, watching eagerly throughout the examination. 'But we have only had to resort to opium in those instances. The baths and the rest seem to have worked.'

'I would say so too, Mrs Nightingale.' Dr Harrow gathered his bag and finished off the last sips of his tea. 'This is not a wound that is easily treatable or simple to recover from. It is not in the manner of an arm or leg where it can simply be strapped up. Remarkable that such an important organ as the eyes can be so very delicate. My recommendation is to maintain the treatments I have already suggested and to adhere to this same behaviour. Have you tried any form of eyewear?'

'No,' Nightingale said.

'Once,' Louisa corrected. 'But the constant removal of them, to then wear them again, seemed to do more harm. It seemed to prompt one of the migraines.'

'I see. Have you a quizzing glass?' Dr Harrow continued.

'I have,' Louisa replied. 'We shall try that as an intermittent measure, though I am not quite sure it is part of a standard uniform.'

Dr Harrow smiled at her attempt at lightness. Nightingale hated her mention of the service and hated even more why she did it – to convince them all that everything would return to normality soon.

'Aside from the pain, Hiram,' Dr Harrow said, 'is everything else well? How have you been?'

Nightingale could imagine the smile dying on Louisa's face. He plastered a thin one upon his.

'I have been fine.'

The examination over, Louisa accompanied Dr Harrow to the door. Nightingale did not watch him go. He rose quickly when he was alone, vanished out of the side door and up the stairwell to his study. All of the curtains had been thrown open to let in the rare sun. Nightingale hated its reappearance – not only for the uncomfortable brightness but for what it meant. For weeks, he had used the dull weather as an excuse for his solitude, locked up in the house. He had not even travelled with Louisa to Bristol to visit her father or fulfilled the long-awaited promise to see his comrades at the George Inn.

The manor was safe and familiar.

Yet, now, he had an obligation to complete.

Louisa paused as he descended the stairs again, coat buttoned, hat upon his head with its eye-shade. 'You have no engagements with anyone today, Hiram,' she said as if he ever had in these last months.

'I have some business.'

She glanced at the box beneath his arm. 'I can take it,' she offered. 'Tell me where.'

'No.' He touched her elbow and guided her away from the door. 'You have done enough for me. I shall be fine.'

'Hiram.' Up close, Nightingale detected a hint of weariness in the lines around her mouth and the pallor about her eyes. He knew that was because of him. 'You are not well,' she whispered. 'You may tell Dr Harrow that all is fine, but you cannot lie to me.'

'I have been here for too long. I shall be no more than a few hours.'

'At least tell me where you are going.'

'Lieutenant Sawyer's family invited me to their house.' It was a small lie. There had been no such invitation. 'It is on Milton Road, if you have concerns.'

'I know where it is.' She still hesitated – but she had been the one to try to convince Nightingale to visit Bristol with her. She wanted him to brave the outdoors again. 'I shall wait for you here.'

'Do not stop your business on my account. I shan't be long.'

He felt her eyes on him as he climbed into the waiting carriage. He did not look back as it drove away.

Gradually, the open countryside gave way to the wide city streets. Pockets of snow and frost clung to the grass and the branches of the trees. Nightingale drew the brim of his hat further down, shielding himself from the low afternoon sun. His mind faded away as he watched the daily business of the townspeople. The normality still seemed strange. Men and women walked to and fro, bundled in coats and mufflers. Children sold refreshments on the corners or called out the news. A grocer arranged his display at the frontage of his shop. By the cathedral, a carriage awaited a bride and groom. This was the Portsmouth he had forgotten after so long on the waves. It was unsettling to think that all of this continued even when he was battling with cannon and pistol shot.

'We are here, sir,' his driver suddenly said.

Nightingale had drifted too far into his thoughts. He climbed out of the carriage to see Leroy Sawyer's house. The front garden was exactly as he remembered it, with its fragrant honeysuckle and snowdrops growing alongside the quaint pond. The cycles of the years had turned enough so that he was again here when these particular flowers were blooming. He tightened his grip around his box and took a deep breath.

Movement shuffled behind the windows and then the door sprang open. A young girl raced down the garden path, fair hair flying out of her bonnet.

'Captain Nightingale!' she cried, and leapt into his arms. Nightingale laughed, spinning her around. She giggled, clinging to his coat, but within seconds, he could feel her damp tears against his neck.

'I didn't know you were visiting, sir,' she gasped as he set her back down. Her cheeks were rosy-red and puffy with her sudden weeping. A faltering smile struggled to stay on her mouth.

'You are so much taller than when I last saw you,' Nightingale said. She nearly reached his shoulders. 'Fourteen already!'

She nodded, sniffing. 'Yes, Captain.'

'Come now, Lucy. What have I told you? You are not one of my crew. It is "Hiram".'

'Yes, Mr Nightingale.'

'Lucy Sawyer! What the devil are you doing?' A female voice echoed out of the house. A woman in her older years appeared at the door, carrying a cloth. The anger vanished from her face as she saw Nightingale. The cloth fell from her hand. 'Hiram...'

Nightingale swept off his hat. 'Mrs Sawyer.'

Within minutes, he sat in the Sawyers's small parlour, a cup of steaming tea in his hands. Mrs Josephine Sawyer fussed around, straightening the blankets over the armchairs and putting more and more sugar and lemon and biscuits upon the table on little plates. She only stopped when her husband emerged from upstairs. Nightingale rose to his feet and found his hand grasped in a strong, almost painful grip.

'All of England has been talking about the victory at the Nile,' Edward Sawyer announced. 'It was a noble thing. Napoleon's fleet destroyed along with his hopes of conquering Egypt! I have not stopped thinking about the *Orient* – what that must have been to experience.'

Nightingale sat back down, ignoring the tightness in his stomach. 'Nelson is an extraordinary man,' he said.

'Admiral Nelson and his band of brothers. Surely you stand amongst their number now. Every captain who fought—'

'Edward,' Josephine muttered, laying a hand on his arm. Edward blanched and took a seat by the fire. Husband and wife fell into silence. The joy at seeing Nightingale seemed to wane as the reason for his visit dawned. This was not a time to discuss his fortune and success.

'I wished to visit you and pay my condolences,' Nightingale said softly. 'I apologise that I was not able to do it sooner. Affairs tied me to the house and to other business.'

'I won't hear any apologies, Hiram,' Edward said. 'You have done enough for our family.'

'No. It is your family who has done the good deeds. Your son—' Nightingale took another breath and felt it ache in his chest. 'Your son was an exceptionally brave man. I could not have commanded half as taut a ship without his aid. It was my honour to know him and serve alongside him.'

Once upon a time, they had truly been equals. Nightingale had not always been Leroy Sawyer's superior officer. They had been mids on the *Strabo*: Nightingale, sixteen years old and painfully shy, and Leroy, an intelligent and eager thirteen-year-old. They had grown together, finding their way around the peculiarities and dangers of the service. Nightingale had passed for lieutenant before Leroy, but his dear friend had not been far behind. They had served three perfect years together before different commissions separated them – only for Leroy to duck into the great cabin of the *Lion* more than a decade later, assigned to Nightingale's command.

Nightingale still remembered the smile on Leroy's face: the exhilaration at serving on a ship of the line, and under his long-time friend.

Nightingale cleared his throat. 'He was a brilliant officer,' he continued. 'I wished to tell you how courageous he was during the battle, and—', *at the end*, '—when he was wounded.'

Edward nodded his thanks, wet-eyed. Josephine touched his hand. 'It is comforting to know that you were there with him, Hiram,' she said.

'I wanted to honour him. I would have brought him home to be buried but I could not. So, I...' He set the box he had brought down on the table. The lid had been carved and painted with a beautiful ship under full sail, crystal-blue waves streaming past her hull. It was not the *Lion*, but the *Strabo* – a memory of his and Leroy's first vessel. 'As soon as I heard of the scheme to honour the Nile combatants, I wrote to Admiral Nelson and his prize agent, Alexander Davison. It was not expected that the deceased should receive such an accolade, but I… I thought it was fitting.'

He pushed the box over to Leroy's parents. His throat tightened as Edward opened it and brought out the contents.

The gleam of the silver medal caught the sunlight. Nightingale had already memorised the design: the elegant figure of Peace on one side, the curving line of the fleet passing Aboukir Bay on the other. Each captain and lieutenant had been gifted the award. Nightingale's own medal was tucked away at the bottom of his sea-chest.

He was prouder of the one now cradled in Josephine Sawyer's hands. She stroked the rounded edges, fingers trailing the inscriptions that honoured the British ships and their fortune. Silent tears fell down her cheeks.

'You are very kind, Hiram,' Edward managed to say.

'It is the least I could do. Your son — Leroy — he deserved it.'

It was bitter recompense. A piece of silver would not bring Leroy home. Nightingale would have traded all the medals in the world for that. Each time he thought of his own it turned his stomach. Every fragment hid how close he had been to losing the *Lion* and how Leroy had been the price paid for victory.

But Josephine Sawyer reached over and took his hands, squeezing them. Nightingale blinked, feeling his eyes sting.

'Leroy thought the world of you, Hiram,' she said. 'Every time he wrote to us, he praised you as a commander and as a friend. I believe he was never so happy as when he served alongside you. You should find comfort in that. I certainly do.'

'I shall. I…' Nightingale swallowed and lowered his head, taking a desperate moment to clear the tears from his vision. When he looked up again, all he could say was, 'He was very dear to me.'

Nothing he said — nothing he did — seemed to equal what he felt for Leroy. He tried to find solace in being around the people who were closest to Leroy, who could understand his grief, but emptiness still pulsed inside of him. Something festered in that void — something he was slowly realising, with every piece of his heart that chipped away.

The weight was too much to bear. And so he departed the Sawyers earlier than intended, whilst Lucy Sawyer admired her brother's medal, her mother and father at her side. Nightingale kept that final image in his head. These seagoing families never knew if their loved one would return, or if during the next voyage, the ocean would finally claim them.

Who did he have? He had no brothers or sisters. He barely saw his mother – she was separated from his father and from England, living in Porto. The only family who waited for him to come home was Louisa. She cared for him like a sibling, like a friend, but they were as different as ocean and sky. He could not give her what people expected of them – not a family, not a child, not the love of a husband, not even his honesty. He did not deserve her affection or her patience.

Nightingale sat alone in the carriage. He felt his breath shudder. He knew he could not make Louisa happy, just as she could not make him. But Leroy...

I believe he was never so happy as when he served alongside you.

Nightingale had known the truth for many years. It had been a feeling which had crystallised into certainty as soon as he and Leroy had reunited on the *Lion*. Leroy's beaming smile, his bravery, his kindness, how they had realised each other's thoughts without even saying a word.

And Leroy had responded. He had stayed awake long into the nights with him, discussing tactics, talking of home and what he wished for. He had been devoted to him, had obeyed every order, had accompanied him to every service dinner, had never gone ashore when he could have. He had once jested that he would never serve under another commander.

Oh God, Nightingale thought with agony. *God, I loved him. I loved him. I loved him.*

But of course, Nightingale had never told him. How could he? The direction of his love was condemned – by the law, by the Articles he upheld on his ships. He had had men flogged for breaching that code, all the while knowing the feelings he harboured. It was torment to think that, perhaps, Leroy had felt the same. What might have been if he had been honest – if someone else had known and understood.

Nightingale's stomach roiled. Perhaps Louisa had been correct – perhaps he should not have left the house. The barriers he had constructed inside of himself were tall and hardy – never had he allowed them to erode. Some things were best kept under lock and key.

He wanted to weep, but that would unleash the turmoil behind the walls. He tried to tell himself what he always did: for a man like him, there could be nothing more.

So he smiled at Louisa when she came to the door at home. She looked him over and held back.

'How were the Sawyers?' she asked.

'They were well. It was good to be out.'

That was all. He retreated back behind the walls, comfortable in his seclusion and denial.

Chapter Thirteen: Port of Spain

10 July 1800, Port of Spain, Trinidad

When the *Scylla*'s anchor finally dropped in Port of Spain's harbour, Nightingale could almost feel the ship breathe a sigh of relief. The tension loosened from her sails and the yards ceased their groans. After the tempest, which had torn canvas and snapped spars, the crew had patched her up as best as they could. Long, agonising hours had been spent in the bilges, pumping out water, shifting her ballast, continually repairing the rudder – but she still crawled like a wounded animal to her berth. He felt cruel to push her to the limit of her endurance.

Nightingale had not slept more than a couple of hours each night. In the early mornings, before the West Indian sun seared the energy from his body, he returned to his report. He knew he had performed his duty: he had followed proper procedures for installing a prize crew on the *Fénix*, he had sent her to the nearest British harbour, and when she had been damaged in the storm he had tried to salvage what he could from her wreck.

Yet men had died. A ship had been lost – and with her, a Spanish captain, a valuable prisoner.

No matter what he wrote, his formal report sounded hollow. Families across the world would mourn the sailors. His meagre role was to bury them at sea and then write them as numbers alongside the *Fénix*'s lost cargo. Time and time again, he struck words, crumpled the paper, tried again. It always ended with his head in his hands, losing the will as the sun blazed through the great cabin.

As they moored in Port of Spain, he watched the return of civilisation unfold. Hills, stripped of their greenery, surrounded the small city. Clusters of homes jostled for space along the span of the harbour. Smoke billowed, dust clouded, voices raised even across the water. Dense throngs of people occupied the waterfront – faces of every colour, but always under the eyes of red-coated soldiers. Nightingale tried to keep his gaze from straying too far. Gallows, as much a deterrent as the troops, lined the port. Prisoners and slaves, some little more than bones, swayed in the breeze.

Nightingale prayed the *Scylla*'s repairs would not take too long.

Ordnance officials clustered aboard. They assessed everything still standing and some things that were not. Lieutenant Hargreaves and the carpenter, Parry, guided them around and, by the looks on their faces, Nightingale could tell his prayers were not going to be answered.

Surrounded by his officers, he sat in the great cabin and said, heart heavy, 'I have been informed that repairs will take at least five days.'

'Five days lost behind the *Ulysses*,' Courtney remarked, staring down at the table.

'Is there nothing that can be done?' Hargreaves asked meekly.

'It cannot be helped,' Nightingale sighed. 'We were due to stop in at Trinidad for a small period anyway. The prisoners shall be delivered to Governor Picton and the wounded shall go to the hospital.'

Lieutenant Allende had not emerged from his place in steerage since the storm. Nightingale had not clapped him in irons – the young man had done that himself, binding his spirit in a cold prison of grief. All the amity he had shown to Courtney and the officers before had vanished. With every furious stare from him, Nightingale felt as though he was the one who had killed Captain Ramirez. He pushed the insults aside. If the lieutenant wished to stew and spit, then so be it.

His main concern, other than the *Scylla* herself, lay with the wounded. Eight Spanish sailors remained alive in the sickbay, and six Scyllas, including Mr Richmond. Nightingale spent long hours at his bedside, holding his hand through the fevers and assuring him when Dr Archer had to amputate his leg. The boy wept and shouted around his gag as the saw cut into bone. Nightingale felt the grinding as if it were inside of him.

Yet he survived.

'Plucky little sod, aren't you?' Courtney said with a laugh when Richmond at last sat up in bed. The lieutenant had wiped tears from his cheeks and for the first time, he and Nightingale had shared a smile.

Now, Richmond was taken ashore, hobbling down the gangplank with his arm around Obi's neck. The rest of the British wounded went with him – some were carried, some were able to walk. Nightingale took one last look at Allende as the Spanish wounded were rounded up too. He didn't wish for him to die, but the decision of Allende's fate was not his.

He was glad for it.

Later that afternoon, a boat pulled alongside the *Scylla* and a messenger came aboard. Toby hobbled into the cabin and Nightingale bid him to sit as he took the note. But before he could open it, the gloomy look on Toby's face had to be addressed.

'Is anything amiss, Toby?' Nightingale asked.

'No, sir,' Toby murmured, only to then blurt, 'Do I really have to go ashore tonight, sir? Begging your pardon and all...'

Nightingale was touched by what Toby was not saying. He had acted well as his clerk, a marked improvement from the boy Kieran had stolen for. 'I do not wish for you to come to any more harm,' he replied. 'One broken foot is quite enough.'

'Yes, sir.'

Nightingale heard the unspoken 'but' in that mutter. 'When we return to Trinidad with the *Ulysses*,' he said, 'I shall check in on you, if only to ensure that disgruntled father hasn't found you.'

'Sorry, sir. I... I forgot you knew about him.'

Nightingale smiled and opened the missive. He scanned it and sighed.

'I wish for you to come ashore with me,' he said to Courtney when he called him and Hargreaves to his cabin. 'I have been invited to the governor's house for dinner. Picton shall be there with other officials. We are representing the ship.'

Courtney, who had braved the yellow fever and the boarding of the *Fénix*, turned pale. 'I have never dined with men like that before.'

'They are like other men,' Nightingale said, before realising it wasn't quite true. Not to an unconnected, rural man like Courtney. 'It will only be a short evening. There are things I want to know about the *Ulysses*. My father-in-law has travelled out to aid the governor and he might be able to help us.'

'The men, sir...'

'Lieutenant Hargreaves shall stay and keep an eye on them. We've had to weather a lot, I know, so I'll allow some to go ashore. Only under Lieutenant Charlston's watch, though – I am not adding the pox and paralytic drunkenness to our list of grievances.'

Courtney said nothing. Hargreaves glanced at him and tried, 'I am willing to go ashore with you, Captain. If Lieutenant Courtney has his... doubts.'

Nightingale waited for the argument from Courtney but for once, the man did not rise to Hargreaves.

'Thank you, Michael, but it would be remiss of me not to bring my First along. Lieutenant Courtney, I'll have Rylance brush down your best uniform.'

Having been paraded out in Antigua, Nightingale's own uniform was in a tolerable state. He donned it, opened the box which contained his Nile medal – then promptly shut it with the token still inside.

Courtney sat quietly beside him as they were rowed ashore that evening. Rylance had performed an exquisite job with his dress uniform, considering it had been stuffed at the bottom of a sea-chest for months on end. The young man shone in beautiful blues and golds, black stock preened to perfection, white breeches spotless, shoes and buckles polished. He had even managed to tame his dense, dark curls beneath his bicorne hat. As they approached the harbour, Nightingale turned to him and saw how he gripped his ceremonial sword as if throttling it.

'We are not going to battle, Lieutenant,' he commented.

'Oh.' Courtney released his hold, only to grab on again.

Feeling an urge to relax him, if only so he did not embarrass them both, Nightingale said, 'My original orders were to command a squadron here, in the anticipation of smoothing the transition between

Spanish and British power. I received the commission on the *Scylla* when I set foot in Antigua. I suppose another man has taken my job here.'

'Why were your orders changed, sir?'

'That is not something us officers often question – not aloud, anyway.' He paused. 'My father and Sir William Haywood, my father-in-law, recommended me for the position – in both instances.'

Courtney nodded. Since his confession about his past and his link to the *Ulysses*, he had begun to mellow – as had Nightingale's own frustration with him. Yet something still nagged him.

'Lieutenant Hargreaves is older than you, yes?' Nightingale asked.

'By about a decade, yes, sir. I am twenty-five. He is thirty-five if he's a day. Begging your pardon, sir.'

Courtney must have thought of him as positively ancient. 'You have never served with him before?'

'No. I'd not heard of his name at all in Antigua before he came aboard.'

Nightingale both wanted to ask the next question and did not. It was not proper to ask his officers about the state of affairs in the gunroom or between ranks. To his surprise, Courtney heard the unvoiced question.

'I do not think he resents that he is older but junior to me, sir,' he said. 'That is not his manner.'

Between Hargreaves's eagerness to come ashore and his disinclination to command the prize crew, Nightingale was uncertain how to think of him. He set that aside as they reached land and climbed into a waiting carriage.

Travelling through the town and into the hills, he tried to imagine what might have happened if he had taken command in Trinidad. For the first time, relief in having received the *Scylla* spread through him. Everywhere he looked, he could see the influence of the Caribbean's most lucrative trade: slaves owned by his countrymen outnumbered the European faces. He did not want to be embroiled in that.

The carriage halted at a grand, white-washed residence adorned with columns, sitting in the midst of a plain which had been levelled for gardens and pathways. Construction still occurred to the sound of hammers and saws, even as the sun lowered to the horizon. All of this was a stamp of Europe upon a far-flung island. He thought he should feel proud.

But he saw the disdain on Courtney's face – and again, did not know what he, himself, truly felt.

They were shepherded into the mansion and through corridors in the midst of renovation. Neither of them spoke, but the sound of men's voices grew louder. As they reached the source – a small parlour wreathed in cigar smoke – the five men there broke into laughter at the end of a joke, so much that they did not notice the two new arrivals.

Nightingale glanced at Courtney, suddenly glad for his presence.

'Hiram,' a voice suddenly said. A man in his later years parted from the company and strode across to grasp Nightingale's hand. It had been a while since Nightingale had seen him but Sir William Haywood left an impression on everyone he encountered. Tall, with dark eyes as piercing as a hawk and a face which would not have been misplaced on a Roman senator, he was dressed immaculately: a black coat with a dash of emerald, the colours his daughter loved.

'Sir William,' Nightingale greeted with a polite bow.

'Just "William" will suffice, Captain. Thank you for attending. Come, I shall introduce you.'

Sir William had not even looked at Courtney, but he trailed along after Nightingale. All eyes pierced them.

'Captain Hiram Nightingale,' Sir William announced, steering Nightingale into the fray. 'You probably do not know these men, Captain. Governor-General Thomas Picton.' Another imposing, steely-eyed man with greying hair. 'Captain Henry Harrison and his lieutenant, Isaac Matthews.' A pinched, blonde man in a post-captain's finery, escorted by a younger officer who was already ruddy-cheeked from the port. 'And Cornelius, Lord Fairholme.'

Nightingale's throat tightened as he saw the younger man. He knew the name but had not expected Lord Fairholme to appear in the West Indies. He was whispered to have a finger in every pie, enough that he could continually lick off the sweet filling. His presence confirmed

Nightingale's suspicions that more lurked beneath the surface of this voyage. Fairholme gave a boyish, coy smile and lowered his grey eyes, putting a ringed hand to his fine azure coat.

'I am honoured to meet you,' Nightingale said by rote. 'This, uh, is my first lieutenant, Arthur Courtney.'

Courtney did not know what to do. He bowed, made a leg, and saluted, nearly knocking off his hat. 'Your servant, sir,' he mumbled.

Nightingale grimaced.

They were saved by a servant arriving at the door to announce that supper was served. The men slowly filtered out and Nightingale followed until Sir William touched his elbow. He pulled him aside, out of earshot.

'Governor Picton received your Spanish prisoners,' he said quietly. 'We know about the *Fénix*.'

Nightingale nodded sombrely. 'There was little that I could do. It was a lightning strike that—'

'Yes, yes, the Spanish officer — what was his name? Allende, he informed us. But others shall make the judgement.'

'What judgement?'

Sir William drew a breath. 'Although the *Fénix* never reached the shore, and so was never assessed by the prize court, she was still under your command and, by extension, the Crown. Men died, Hiram. Your senior midshipman is in hospital. Questions must be asked.'

The room shifted. Nightingale had known — how could he not have? — but to hear it spoken was another matter. And from the mouth of someone he trusted and respected, speaking as though he was already condemned...

'Hiram,' Sir William continued, 'it is a standard procedure. We must follow it.'

'Yes, I... I understand.' Nightingale swallowed. Movement in the corridor distracted him, and he was relieved to see Courtney lingering. 'My lieutenant is waiting for me,' he rushed. 'We should attend the dinner.'

Sir William nodded: the picture of composure. Both he and his daughter had mastered what Nightingale could not. When he joined

Courtney, he must have been ashen for Courtney asked in low tones, 'Are you all right, sir? Is something wrong?'

Nightingale nodded, intending to answer the first question but unwittingly answering the second too. Was he all right? He didn't know. When was the last time he had been able to answer in the affirmative?

He forced a smile. 'I shall be fine once I've eaten something,' he replied.

Side by side, they walked into the dining room. The heavy cigar smoke mimicked the boarding of an enemy ship. Nightingale could only wonder where the next blow would come from.

They were positioned around a long, mahogany table in the middle of a wide space, curiously austere in the ongoing construction. Large windows looked down over the bay, turning purple and pink as the sun set. Two women joined them – Jennifer Sandham, Captain Harrison's sweetheart, and her sister, Tabitha, who turned so red around Courtney that Fairholme relinquished his seat for her to sit beside him. Nightingale found Sir William at his side. The man said nothing to him as the meal was brought out.

Mercifully, no one else decided to say anything else to him either. Nightingale stayed comfortably in the shadows of the aristocracy for much of the dinner, content for the focus to be elsewhere. He chewed slowly and deliberately on the venison, smiling when looked at and raising his glass when prompted by the rest. Conversations bounced back and forth over the Atlantic – opinions of Pitt's London government, then to Picton's schemes to improve the roads of his island despite the small garrison, back to the state of their home counties in England.

Not for the first time, Nightingale felt as though he were looking in from the outside. He fell into inner thoughts – the *Fénix*, the battered *Scylla*, the *Ulysses* far ahead. How harsh would his judgement be? Surely they could not call a formal court martial when time was so pressed already. The very thought made Nightingale's blood turn cold. Captains were unfortunate if they witnessed such a trial, let alone if they were the subject.

His thoughts shattered when he took a bite of venison and nearly broke his back tooth. Wincing, he extracted the shot and placed it at the side of his china plate. Across from him, Captain Harrison laughed.

'That is considered fortunate, Captain Nightingale!' he announced – which drew all eyes to them. 'Perhaps not for the red brocket that was shot, mind you.'

Nightingale smiled and sipped at his port, surreptitiously running his tongue over the molar. It would be ridiculous to survive countless skirmishes and retain all his teeth, only to chip one at dinner.

'I've heard that Captain Nightingale is famed for his fortune,' Harrison continued. 'Not everyone possesses a Nile medal.'

Nightingale's smile turned into a grimace. He had wondered when that topic would awaken.

'Where is your medal, Captain? God forbid, it's not lost?'

'No.' Nightingale slowly set down his glass. 'I clean forgot to wear it tonight. I apologise.'

Harrison raised an eyebrow. 'You are too modest, Captain Nightingale. I was not there, but it almost feels as though I was after all the tales I have heard – the tales and the poems and the accolades. It would be an honour to hear the truth of it from someone who saw the *Orient* erupt.'

'I—'

'Oh, I'm sure Captain Nightingale is tired of constantly regaling people of his history.' Lord Fairholme was Nightingale's unlikely rescuer. He was leaning back in his chair like a bored child, that boyish smile on his face. Soft grey eyes pierced Nightingale. 'I am more interested in his connections out here. Did you all know Sir William and the captain are related?'

'Not by blood, my lord,' Nightingale replied.

'But by marriage. I know Lou in passing.'

Nightingale felt Sir William's gaze shift over him. He smiled, mimicking Fairholme's innocuous expression and trying not to show how much his use of "Lou", not "Louisa", needled him. 'She is a very industrious woman.'

'Very beautiful.'

'Yes.' He shifted, knowing he stood on unsteady ground. He hated the thought of accidentally maligning Louisa before her father and these people. 'We had planned to move our lot out here to Trinidad,' he said carefully. 'Sir William graciously schooled me in the position I would receive – that has now been given to Captain Harrison. Louisa is very settled in England, though. She is… industrious,' he repeated.

'Sir William was telling me of her house,' Lord Fairholme continued. *Our house*, Nightingale thought. 'I shall have to visit one day and see for myself all her industry.'

Nightingale nodded noncommittally. He tried to return to his venison but the wave of attention stuck to him. Another of Picton's guests, a florid and balding man named Wendell, turned to him with a smile as wide as his belt. 'You should still consider moving out to the islands, Captain,' he urged. 'By the grace of English industry and ambition, our country's finances have not been upset even by these long wars. These markets keep the empire afloat. You shall have to visit the Glades, Captain, and I will surely be able to convince you.'

Sir William cleared his throat and set down his glass with a thump. 'I shall, uh, see if my ship can spare me,' Nightingale said, with no intention of doing so.

'You are a planter?' Courtney finally spoke up. Wendell's gaze shifted along from Nightingale, seeming surprised that there was a man next to him. Courtney had been even more silent than Nightingale throughout the meal.

'Whatever your stance on it,' Wendell said, looking briefly at Sir William, 'it is one of the foundations of the empire that you serve, Lieutenant. Its lucrative nature cannot be denied.'

'Hiram's father would certainly support you both, Wendell,' Fairholme remarked with an amused grin.

Nightingale gritted his teeth. Admiral Nightingale was far away but still had a talent for winding his way into conversation. *God*, Nightingale thought, *I hope he is still far away*. 'Lieutenant Courtney,' he announced, 'played an important role in the search for the *Hermione*.'

Courtney opened his mouth, glancing down. Without realising, Nightingale had slapped his hand on Courtney's knee when addressing him. He was clutching it so tightly that he could feel his kneecap digging into his palm. He removed his hand with a blush at his slip in decorum. 'I… yes,' Courtney managed.

'Is that true?' Captain Harrison leant forward, head cocked. 'I thought that the *Surprise* was alone when she cut out the *Hermione* from Puerto Cabello.'

'She was,' Courtney replied. 'But the *Scylla* – our ship under Captain Carlisle – he's, ah, he's dead now – supported her in her journey down to Aruba. It was not such an important role. Captain Hamilton and his Surprises were the leading force.'

'Extraordinary.' Harrison immediately dismissed Courtney's modesty. 'This was only last year, yes?'

'Yes, sir.'

A vague silence fell. Nightingale looked around at the guests, wondering how many knew about the *Ulysses* and his orders. They bore an eerie similarity to Captain Hamilton's. Perhaps a year from now, someone else would sit around a table and mutter 'extraordinary' about his capture of the *Ulysses*.

'So, Captain Nightingale,' Harrison pressed again, 'I hear it has been a while since you were at sea. You were wounded at the Nile, yes? Like Lord Nelson himself! I do hope you recovered well.'

'I…' Nightingale's words stuck in his throat. The fleeting relief at shifting the attention drained with a wave of cold nausea rolled over him. 'I, um…'

'Captain Hamilton was a remarkable leader,' Courtney said suddenly. Nightingale turned to him, as did Harrison. 'I remember when the *Surprise* was in the gulf of Venezuela. Her orders were to wait for the *Hermione* to set sail, and take her on the open sea, but the days went by and the *Hermione* did not adhere to the timetable that we reckoned on. Captain Hamilton eventually cut her out, as you know. But before that, a sail was spotted. If that vessel could be seen by the *Surprise* then she could see the *Surprise*. There was a fear that she would spread the message back to the Spanish. So, Captain Hamilton…'

Courtney's words emerged in a tumble. Amused smiles spread over the guests' faces. Nightingale eased as their focuses moved again from him and to the lieutenant. Harrison and Matthews poked and prodded Courtney for more detail, and even Tabitha spoke up. Courtney was as red as the port when he was done – but by that time, the meal had wound to its end. Harrison announced, 'Another drink with you, Lieutenant Courtney!' and they filtered into the parlour.

The men and women separated. Courtney was guided into the fray, flushed with the spirits which constantly flowed into his glass. Nightingale walked to the windows. Idle chat rose like a fog around him; he could only think of the *Scylla*, and imagined disaster, even though he could see her from the mansion's vantage point on the hill.

Nightingale flipped open his pocket-watch. Almost eleven o'clock.

A touch on his elbow interrupted him. Sir William appeared and pressed another glass of port into his hand. 'Do not tell me you are considering Wendell's business proposition,' he said in low tones.

Nightingale frowned. Which part of the conversation had that been?

'His ideas about the Glades? No. It hadn't even crossed my mind.'

'Good,' Sir William said forcefully, then tried to hide his vehemence through a sip of his drink. 'You know how I, and Louisa, feel about that.'

Nightingale reddened. 'I am not my father.'

'Oh, I know that, Hiram. There are too many admirals out here already. I know what he had his eye on.'

'Did he follow you out here?'

'Your father? He intended to. I don't know if he did.'

Nightingale wrestled with the fear which rose in him. 'My father has money enough,' he said meekly, and wondered why he was bothering to defend Admiral Nightingale.

'Forgive me, Hiram, but he is the kind of man to always search for more.'

Nightingale decided to say nothing else. He walked on thin ice already. Louisa and her father occupied staunch positions in the ebbing and flowing cause of abolitionism – the polar opposite to his father. He resented being tarred with the same brush, but each time he tried to voice it, the denial caught.

Sir William, seeing Nightingale would not bite his bait, drifted back amongst the guests. Nightingale seethed at his distrust. Perhaps he had been naive to think Sir William would help him with anything.

He realised he was curling his fist hard enough to hurt behind his back. The sight of Courtney approaching made him relax it. The smile fixed on Courtney's face echoed similar sentiments to his discomfort.

'Give me five minutes, sir,' Courtney said quietly, 'and I can have Mr Smythe run up to tell us the ship is on fire.'

'I'm not sure they would believe that.'

'I can create a small, contained fire in the maintop.'

'I am sorely tempted.' The tension within bubbled out in a laugh. Courtney's taut smile turned genuine, his green eyes sparkling. Perhaps helped by the drink and the new surroundings, the lieutenant's guard had dropped. Nightingale hoped it would outlast the night.

Rising laughter and a ripple of applause interrupted them. Jennifer Sandham stepped forward, fanned out her skirts, and sat down at the piano. The room quietened, attention on the young lady, and she began to play a sweet, soulful melody. Her fingers were light and skilled on the keys, a pleasant change from the busy voices.

When the first refrain finished, Jennifer jovially beckoned to Harrison. He laughed and adamantly shook his head. 'I cannot sing,' he declared.

Jennifer looked around for another partner. The men stepped away, amused. 'Lieutenant Courtney?' she asked, turning and giving a dazzling smile.

Courtney blushed. 'Oh, I—'

'Come on, Lieutenant,' Harrison urged, as if throwing down a gauntlet for his lady. To his side, Tabitha clapped and giggled.

Courtney glanced to Nightingale but he could offer no defence. The lieutenant sighed and walked to the piano to a smattering of more applause. He stood awkwardly and gave a thin smile.

'Do you know it?' Jennifer asked.

Courtney nodded. He shifted and drummed his fingers on the piano's lid.

Then he opened his mouth and began to sing.

Silence fell around Nightingale. Courtney's strong, crisp voice flowed through it, burrowing into places he had locked up for years. He tried to shove down the surge of emotion – but his heart swelled, pushing into his throat. He clutched at his glass, the smile wobbling on his face.

As he sang, Courtney turned, caught his eye. For a moment, Nightingale thought he saw Leroy. Time condensed, with only Courtney's voice to set the pace. He could have been on the *Lion*, years back, before his life fell to ruin. What was he doing here? They were going to condemn him and judge him for his failings once more.

He shouldn't have come, shouldn't have agreed to this mad attempt to right his past mistakes.

Cold, stark terror struck Nightingale like an iron fist. He couldn't do this again. Couldn't open up this side of himself.

Applause rang through Nightingale's ears. He blinked, looked around, surprised that there were others still in the room.

Courtney bowed, sweeping off his hat dramatically and bowing to Tabitha as she nearly hopped up and down. Jennifer rose from her seat and curtseyed, before Captain Harrison took her aside, squeezing her hands and grinning.

'He has a very fine voice.'

Lord Fairholme had somehow appeared next to Nightingale. He clapped politely but there was a look in his face that Nightingale did not like. His gaze did not leave Courtney.

Nightingale swallowed. 'He does.'

'Tabitha informs me that he is the most handsome man in the Caribbean.' Fairholme smiled. 'Can he ride?'

'I… I'm not sure.'

'It does not seem like a pastime for a man of his background. But—' Fairholme finally looked away from Courtney and turned those striking eyes upon Nightingale. 'If he would like, he can join us at the stables tomorrow morning.'

'Us?'

'You and I, Hiram.'

'I have business with my—'

'I shan't take no for an answer.' Fairholme laid an elegant, gloved hand on Nightingale's sleeve. 'You shall want to attend.'

'Why should I want to...' Fairholme squeezed his arm, making Nightingale pause. 'Yes. Yes, my lord.'

Finally, the event wound to a close and Nightingale was able to make his excuses. They tried to keep Courtney for a round of cards but Courtney saw his face and refused. As quickly as he could, Nightingale returned to the night air. Farewells followed them back down the hill. He looked back once, raised his hat politely at the guests, then sped his steps.

Even as midnight approached, repairs resounded on the *Scylla*: men clung to the spars to patch up timbers and caulk seams. It was a far more familiar din than the port-soaked conversations of the governor's house but even so, Nightingale knew he would not sleep. He would feel it sorely in the morning. Only Fairholme's sly look of promise stopped him from refusing the appointment.

He and Courtney stood upon the deck. Courtney lingered, waiting to be dismissed after the long evening, but Nightingale stopped him with a small, 'Arthur?'

'Yes, sir?'

'Thank you for tonight.'

'I was invited, sir.'

'That's not what I meant.'

Courtney smiled. He had drawn the focus away when the attention became too heavy, and he knew it. 'You're my captain, sir,' he said. It was an outward recognition of rank that should not have moved Nightingale as it did.

'Indeed. Good night, Lieutenant.'

'Good night, sir.'

Nightingale watched him go, smiling as the lieutenant unwound the tight stock from his throat and loosened his golden buttons.

He entered his cabin again, stripped out of his dress uniform, and finally lay down on his cot. The tangled events of the night clogged his head. He tried to concentrate on the gentle, rhythmic bobbing of the *Scylla* but each thought competed for attention. In the end, he called for Dr Archer. It was only with a tincture of laudanum that sleep washed over him in a deep, rolling current.

Chapter Fourteen: A Mercy

That dreary day in October 1778 would forever mark Nightingale. The passing years gave him no distance from the pain; he still felt the bitter wind, the cold air, and the drops of rain that seeped down his collar into his coat. They continually awoke the fresh, raw scars across his spine.

But still, he gritted his teeth and pretended it did not hurt.

Bodies pressed tightly around him, all assembled under the shadows of the gallows. Nightingale did not care about the men and women and children in the audience – only the firm hand that gripped his shoulder. Ringed fingers dug into his flesh, forcing him to stay still and watch. Admiral Laurence Nightingale, dressed in an immaculately brushed black civilian coat, loomed over him as much as the swinging noose.

'You are fortunate, Hiram.' The words his father spoke still echoed in his nightmares. 'This could have been your neck.'

Nightingale did not reply. He had not said a word to his father since he had been cut down from the oak tree, his back pouring blood. He vowed he would never speak to him again, but he knew he would – knew he would go crawling back, yearning for the approval of the man who had ordered his punishment.

Tom ascended the stage. A second passed between Nightingale laying his eyes upon him and the noose being looped around his throat. He could not save him, could not do anything.

Admiral Nightingale's nails sank in through his jacket. 'I helped you, Hiram,' he insisted in a harsh whisper. 'Watch him. Watch him and be thankful that I dealt with you myself.'

Tom cried as his crime was spoken for all to hear. The stable-boy, only eighteen, could not deny it – not the firm accusation of such a powerful member of the community as Admiral Nightingale. He could only sob, eyes turned heavenwards, lips moving in pleas for mercy.

Sickness rose in Nightingale. His knees weakened. His father held him up.

As Nightingale nearly fell, the trapdoor snapped open. Tom's body jolted, the noose tightening. His feet dangled and kicked. He choked and frothed at the mouth.

Then he stilled.

'Each time you feel those scars,' Admiral Nightingale hissed, 'remember that they are a mercy.'

Nightingale awoke, wrenched from laudanum-infused depths. He rolled over, panicked and blinded by the bright haze of the cabin. In a spasm, he reached out until he could feel a firm bulkhead. Through the night, he had managed to twist and kick the sheets from the cot, and now, hot air rushed over his clammy skin.

Port and venison and thick puddings churned in his stomach. He rose, groped his way to the seat of ease, and vomited. Long, painful minutes passed as he crouched there, head throbbing, organs twisting with the shades of his dream.

When the nausea finally lifted, he closed his eyes and forced himself to focus on his breath. In his mind, he pictured a ship under full canvas, billowing in a fresh breeze. One by one, he named the yards and sails and rigging, from the skyscraper down to the belaying pins. His images tangled – one moment he saw the *Lion*, one moment he saw the *Scylla*.

A knock on the outer cabin door made him groan. On trembling legs, he rose to his feet and greeted Rylance in his nightshirt. Rylance stared at his obviously green face.

'I have your breakfast, sir,' the little steward said, nervously holding up the tray. 'Would you like me to take it away?'

'No. No, it is quite all right. I shall dress and have it. It's only a passing sickness.'

'Yes, sir. Uh... Mr Parry has a report on the repairs. He sends his compliments and wonders if you would like to see it?'

'I shall have Lieutenant Courtney accompany him to see the repairs. He can report back to me.'

'Yes, sir.'

In his uniform again and with a hesitantly eaten egg and slice of bacon in his stomach, Nightingale felt a little more human. Courtney's report cheered him only a little. It wasn't as terrible as to need to careen the ship over to patch up the keel, but the rudder still needed a seeing-to; the bowsprit Courtney had replaced a few months ago was shedding its timber; the lower decks had been beaten about, not to mention the torn canvas and nicked yards.

But, at four bells of the forenoon watch, that was all set aside by a messenger from the town. Nightingale did not need to hear the missive. With a spyglass, he could see Lord Fairholme on the dockside, accompanied by a servant and two geldings. The man waved as he noticed Nightingale and then indicated the horses.

'Pass the word for Lieutenant Courtney,' Nightingale reluctantly ordered.

Not only Courtney appeared, but Hargreaves too. Both of them stared across at the lord, now sweeping his hat in the air like a distress signal.

'We have been invited by Lord Fairholme for a ride,' Nightingale said.

'All of us, sir?' Hargreaves asked.

'Not you, Lieutenant Hargreaves,' Nightingale sighed. Perhaps he should simply send him anyway; it was not the first time the man had tried to come ashore. 'Lieutenant Courtney and I. I meant to inform you last night, Lieutenant.'

Courtney opened his mouth.

'I do not wish to any more than you, Lieutenant,' Nightingale admitted. 'But Lord Fairholme was very insistent. You heard Mr Parry this morning – the ship will not fall apart. It would be unwise to refuse.'

For the second time in as many days, Nightingale left Hargreaves in command of the *Scylla*. Hoping his nausea would not attack him again, he sat in the gig and ascended onto the pier where Fairholme waited. He was hardly dressed for riding, in a deep green tailed coat, brocaded waistcoat and breeches rather than trousers. But he gave a dazzling smile, laying his hand to his chest. 'I'm pleased to see you, Captain, Lieutenant,' he said.

'This is a very kind invitation, my lord,' Nightingale said, 'but I cannot bear to be apart from my ship for too long. I imagine disaster calling.'

Fairholme laughed. 'Can you ride, Lieutenant?' he asked Courtney. 'Yes, my lord.'

'There is no shame in being unable to, Lieutenant,' Nightingale said, but Courtney stuck his boot upon a stirrup and effortlessly settled into the saddle. Fairholme laughed again, and Nightingale wondered if that was at his expense, or in surprise at Courtney.

It had been a while since Nightingale had ridden. One of Sir William's wedding presents had been a fine golden thoroughbred named Midas, and Nightingale had enjoyed riding through the heaths north of Portsmouth. Yet it had taken a long while for them to become accustomed to one another. Louisa was a better rider, often watching the Hampshire hunts with her glass and skilfully following the chase.

Nightingale still managed to keep pace with Fairholme and Courtney as they navigated the uneven streets. Once they left the hectic Port of Spain, it was easier, riding along the St Ann's River into the wilderness which hugged the city's edge. Lush cedars and calabash trees crowded the paths but there were fewer people to avoid.

Some areas had been cleared for Picton's development plans whilst others grew free with tall grasses and prickly bushes. The cries and songs of potoos and shrikes and other things Nightingale could not identify rang through the canopies, accompanied by rustling as animals scampered over the ground. He lost count of how many times he had veer for an ambling peccary.

Courtney rode as if he was born to it. On a few occasions, he overhauled Nightingale and had to slow down.

'I am surprised at you, Lieutenant,' Fairholme said. 'You did not strike me as the kind of man to know how to ride.'

'I was our family's messenger, my lord. My father did more or less everything in Ryde, where I'm from. We borrowed the horses – sometimes they were as wild as sin.'

Fairholme smiled. 'You are full of surprises.'

As they rode, Fairholme talked about the food grown on the island and its natural bounties. He reached into a tree and plucked off three ripe mangoes, throwing two back to Nightingale and Courtney.

'The highest bounty, of course,' Fairholme said just as easily, 'is from the plantations. I hear Jeremy Wendell gave you a proposition, Hiram.'

'He did,' Nightingale said tersely. 'I cannot accept.'

'I thought not. His Glades plantation is a few miles over the Laventille hills. Prime spot, so close to the port.'

They climbed that rolling ridge, the sun brightening with the height. The horses did not even sweat, obviously used to this exertion, but Nightingale could feel perspiration sticking to his uniform coat and nausea threatening. He squinted as he looked down to the growing sprawl of the town. They had advanced further than expected, and as always, the far distance blurred into a mass of shade and colour.

Upon the brow of the hill, Fairholme reined his horse in and beckoned Nightingale and Courtney closer. Nightingale peered into the valley below, seeing another clump of colours until his eyes adjusted somewhat. Long stalks of sugarcane dominated the landscape, broken by a mass of buildings: mills and processing houses and rudimentary shacks. Further back, a grand manor sat amongst neat, trimmed gardens. Nightingale felt fortunate that his vision was not sharp enough to see the army of slaves who would be attending those fields.

'Jeremy Wendell's Glades?' he asked.

'Indeed. He is proud, almost absurdly so, if I can say that – and I am no great lover of the abolitionists.' Fairholme glanced at Nightingale, pausing meaningfully as if to bait Nightingale. 'Part of me,' he remarked when Nightingale remained silent, 'is surprised that your father-in-law was permitted to come out here, after he made such vocal talk against the trade a few years past. I remember he was one of Wilberforce's favourites.'

'He was.'

'The movement has waned a little now but I wager it shall return. The uprising in Saint-Domingue has certainly raised a few eyebrows.'

Courtney, who had been peering through his glass, stowed it away with a sour expression. 'The uprising in Saint-Domingue is not the first,' he said.

'Indeed not. But it is the first slave rebellion to evict their masters – us and France, and soon, perhaps Spain if General Louverture presses the conflict westwards into Santo Domingo.'

'Louverture is in allegiance with the French,' Nightingale remarked, then doubted himself. The situation in Saint-Domingue shifted by the day. 'Is he not?'

'Nominally, yes. But do you think such a man would concede power so willingly? War has already broken between him and his lieutenants.'

'It is barbaric,' Courtney suddenly said.

'Are you talking of Louverture's violence, Lieutenant, or the trade itself?' Fairholme asked with a knowing smile.

'All war is barbaric, my lord, but it is often necessary. I know I—' Courtney paused, obviously trying to describe the unsteady line on which he trod. 'My father was a foul man,' he finally said. 'We were not wealthy so we were often hungry, and *he* was always angry. That doesn't excuse what he did to us – the violence he made our lives hell with. Both my mother and father worsened, so my sister and I ran away. I wager they both died, drunk. God knows I would have risen up and killed my father if I had been brave enough.'

Nightingale stared at Courtney, surprised at such a bold admission. In an instant, he understood his fierce desire to find the *Ulysses*, not only for justice's sake, but for Jane, again thrown amongst men's violence.

'You do not speak like any lieutenant I have known,' Fairholme said.

'Thank you, my lord.'

'I'm not sure that I meant it as a compliment. Come.'

He tugged the reins and led the way along the ridge. The plantation remained in sight, and occasionally, voices drifted up from the valley – the distant drone of singing, now and then cut off by a sharp shout and the crack of a whip through the hot morning.

They rode higher through the trees until a green meadow fell away beside them and a rocky outcrop rose ahead. It was to that vantage point that Fairholme took Nightingale, keeping Courtney at the bottom with his servant. Nightingale turned back to look for Courtney's reaction but he was remarkably obedient that day, and only nodded.

The outcrop watched over the bunched town and the harbour where hazy shadows of ships dotted the swathe of blue. Fairholme pointed southwards to what resembled a pile of jagged sticks but which Nightingale knew was a forest of masts. 'Do you see that vessel there?' Fairholme asked.

Nightingale squinted. 'Which one do you mean, my lord?'

'That one, the third rate with her sails drying.' He kept pointing but offered no spyglass. 'That is Captain Harrison's *Actium*. No pennant on the tail yet, but perhaps in a week or so...'

Nightingale could not distinguish the ship, yet he knew the implications of a pennant: it was what he might have had if his orders had not been changed.

'Captain Harrison may be made a commodore in his capacity as commander of this flotilla,' Fairholme continued. 'Pending the results of the next few days.'

'Sir William informed me that there would be questions asked about the *Fénix*,' Nightingale said stiffly.

'I wager he did not tell you all.' Fairholme raised a fine eyebrow. 'What do you suppose Captain Harrison's role may transform into if they find you incapable of continuing?'

That implication had floated, formless, in Nightingale's mind ever since Sir William's warning. There were a hundred reasons he could be cast aside – but which ones could be seen, and which ones came solely from his own doubt he did not know. Therein lay the true problem of it.

He could no longer tell the one from the other.

'You have embarrassed Sir William,' Fairholme said. 'You were his choice for the command of the *Scylla*. It was a mercy from him, a lifeline thrown to a drowning man, if I have to give my honest opinion.

There were other men who could have been recommended – your young lieutenant, for example – but he was adamant about you. He said you could be… suitably discreet.'

'Why exactly should I need to be discreet?' Nightingale asked.

Fairholme looked into his eyes. Nightingale felt like a rat facing a viper. 'I pressed them to tell you what was onboard the *Ulysses*,' Fairholme sneered. 'If you were the one to be chosen, then you should at least know the full details.'

'I heard about the gold from a Spaniard,' Nightingale said, surprised at the coldness in his voice. 'My own enemy told me more, and seemed very amused to do so.'

'Yes, I visited Lieutenant Allende at the gaol and he told me his poor captain was bribed by it, almost. The lieutenant will be safe, don't fret – he'll be exchanged for a prisoner of ours. The rest of the *Fénix* crew who survive, I'm not sure.'

'Why is the *Ulysses* hauling gold?' Nightingale asked, not expecting an answer.

But Fairholme sighed. 'I mentioned the Saint-Domingue rebellion,' he said, quieter now. 'General Louverture has already butted heads with one lieutenant, Rigaud. There are many others who wish to take power, and allegiances constantly twist and turn. As is so often with revolutions, chaos is descending and more lives are being lost by the day. You are aware that Britain was thrust out of Saint-Domingue two years past?'

Nightingale nodded.

'Treaties were made with Louverture, ensuring his promise that he would not foment any more slave rebellions in our colonies. He promised this if we withdrew. So we did. Yet word is filtering through various ears that the French wish to establish firmer control on the island, and we know how fickle the French are. We worry that they will try to re-establish slavery, after vowing not to. And if that were to happen…'

Nightingale made the connections. A French betrayal like that would ignite further violence. There could be no promises of anything then.

'The gold was insurance?' he asked. 'Another bribe to persuade Louverture to submit?'

Fairholme inclined his head. 'There are other ways to control, other than invasion.'

'I should have known it was about money.'

'Isn't it always?' Fairholme looked down the hill at Courtney. He was getting restless, tugging at his tight neckcloth. 'Your lieutenant should be careful what he says about the trade. There are many people who would consider it treasonous to speak against it when it provides us such revenue.'

'I have heard the arguments before.'

'I am sure you have.' Fairholme laughed and turned back to the fine landscape around them. 'Come now, we are being waited for.'

Nightingale wanted to ask more but it would be folly to needle Fairholme beyond what he was willing to say. He spent the rest of the ride in silence. All the threads of the tapestry were in place now, yet he did not like the picture they formed. What he had thought was a simple image now refracted and swarmed with colours he hadn't even known were present. His position remained the same: hunt down the *Ulysses*, and let the politicians and spy-masters like Fairholme sort through the aftermath. But he could not truly separate himself from that chaos, could he?

And it would be the decision of those same politicians and spy-masters if he retained his command, or if Captain Harrison inherited the quagmire.

One more thing ate at him. Once they returned to the port, under the shadow of the *Scylla* again, he beckoned Fairholme aside and asked, quietly, 'Why did you tell me everything you did?'

Fairholme chuckled. 'We are men of the world, Hiram. There are not many like us. Call me sentimental but I like to look after my own.'

He touched Nightingale's shoulder and squeezed. Nightingale opened his mouth to deny it but found he couldn't.

Fairholme's smile burnt into Nightingale's mind as he disappeared back into the crowd. Nightingale still felt the grip on his shoulder. He thought of his father, standing beside him and making him watch as

Tom was hanged. Each time someone tried to help him, they called it a mercy.

Nightingale was beginning to doubt the meaning of the word.

He was beginning to doubt everything.

Chapter Fifteen: Swansong

Nightingale stood on the dockside, squinting through the searing sun despite the sunshade above his eyes. Lord Fairholme had offered him a parasol but he would have felt ridiculous with that over his shoulder. Fortunately, he did not have to look far for the *Scylla*. Through his glass, she towered into the crystal-blue sky, all her masts and yards repaired. Men scrambled aloft to dab the last drops of tar and paint on the timber, and though she was naked with all the intact sails close-reefed, she looked healthier. Soon the new canvas would go aloft, but for now deck hands washed and stitched it.

A gang of able seamen, under the direction of Mr Parry, had wrapped themselves in cordage and hung upside down beneath the bowsprit. They had struck off the entire jib-boom in the last day and were ensuring the seams were tight on the new spar. Rigging swayed loose, soon to be lashed back into its blocks.

With fortune, they would be away sooner than anticipated.

If he retained the command.

'Captain Nightingale!'

A loud voice interrupted his thoughts. He lowered the glass to see Captain Harrison striding through the gathered crowd, Tabitha Sandham on his arm. He tipped his hat at the ordnance officials, watching the progress on the *Scylla* as eagerly Nightingale was, and then, unexpectedly, grasped Nightingale's hand. He smiled broadly, blue eyes twinkling.

'She's coming along capitally,' Harrison said. 'I heard she went through quite a knock. One wouldn't know.'

Nightingale doffed his hat to Tabitha and she smiled shyly, though her eyes then turned to the *Scylla*. Nightingale knew who she looked for.

'I hope we might beat the estimated five days for the repair,' Nightingale said, touched by the compliment towards his ship. 'Mr Parry knows her intimately.'

'Married to the ship, eh?' Harrison chuckled. 'I have a few officers on the *Actium* like that too. You should visit one day. I would be happy to give you the grand tour.'

'Thank you, sir, but I must visit the hospital soon. I've had worrying news about one of my men.'

'Oh, I am sorry to hear so. Shall I accompany you?'

'It is not a sight for a young lady,' Nightingale said with a deferential smile at Tabitha.

'I should like to see it if it is a naval matter,' Tabitha replied.

'Miss Sandham is becoming quite knowledgeable about the service,' Harrison praised. 'She can name a foremast's rigging and sails better than some of my midshipmen, God bless them.'

'If I am to be an officer's wife, Captain, I would like to know what he speaks of.'

'I'm sure, ma'am,' Nightingale said. 'Yet even I do not want to see what might await me at the hospital, and I have served for almost thirty years.' He gave a meaningful look to Harrison, who seemed to understand with a small nod.

'I shall leave you with your sister, Tabby. I'll return as soon as I am finished with Captain Nightingale and we can continue our walk.'

'Oh, I do not want to interrupt you,' Nightingale tried, but soon he was walking up to the military hospital with Harrison. Harrison, barely out of breath, kept speaking of the *Scylla* as they climbed the hill. Nightingale answered as best he could, though he did not want to talk. It was frustrating that Harrison's *Actium* could not do the *Scylla*'s mission – she was larger and not as fast. The *Scylla* would continue, and only the *Scylla*.

The hospital, a relatively new addition, shone in the bright sun – and as everything on the island, it was surrounded by red-coated soldiers. Dr Archer, who had requested Nightingale's presence, waited in the gardens.

'Captain Harrison, this is our doctor, Francis Archer,' Nightingale introduced. 'Dr Archer, Captain Harrison.'

Harrison shook Archer's hand with the same firm grip he had shaken Nightingale's. 'Henry, please,' Harrison insisted.

They passed the marines, who saluted Captain Harrison, then Nightingale. Inside, the eye-watering stench immediately struck Nightingale in the throat: an acrid conflagration of blood and disease and rotten wounds, peppered with cures and powders. He could never accustom himself to this scent. In battle, it was expected – the hot claw of smoke and gunmetal mixed with the injuries. But walking into the all-pervading, cloying rankness turned his stomach.

'Mr Richmond has been in and out of fever over the last day,' Archer said. He had not winced or crinkled his nose, used to this atmosphere. 'I have barely left his side. I thought that I had dealt with the wound after the amputation of his leg. Yet it appears I missed something – the injury is festering again. You shall see.'

Richmond's youth had been scoured away like a holystone on a deck. He lay on thin sheets that were damp with sweat and his skin glistened in the dusty sunlight coming through the high windows. Nightingale tried not to react.

'Hello, David,' he said softly, taking a seat.

'Captain,' Richmond fought to say. 'You are – you're still here.'

'Ssh, yes, the repairs are ongoing. Don't fret about that. Dr Archer tells me you are unwell.'

Richmond nodded. His eyes washed with tears, dribbling down his cheeks and staining the pillow.

'Hush,' Nightingale cooed, finding the boy's hand and squeezing it. 'Hush now, you know Dr Archer's prowess. He'll have you dancing before you know it.'

'May I show the captain your wound, David?' Dr Archer asked.

Richmond nodded again, incapable of more.

Cautiously, Dr Archer pulled back the sheet. Nightingale smelt the wound before he saw it. The stump of his right leg was turning a purple-black shade, his veins pulsing angry and dark. The neat cut Archer had made was ragged like the edges of a frayed shirt.

'My God,' Captain Harrison whispered.

'I believe there is more splinter material in the thigh,' Archer explained. 'It must be buried deep, near to the bone. I should have been more thorough.'

'We had a man onboard the *Actium*,' Harrison commented. 'Took a ball to the leg and it cleaved straight off at the knee. Our surgeon neatened the wound but the lad got sicker and died only a few days afterwards. The ball had forced shattered timber into the limb and it was too late to do anything more.'

Richmond's eyes widened. Nightingale felt him grip his hand. He glared at Harrison.

'I'm sorry, I-I was only giving an example,' Harrison sputtered.

'What can you do, Francis?' Nightingale asked Archer.

'I shall have to amputate again. The limb will have to come off up to the groin.'

'Not again,' Richmond moaned. 'I can't do it again, sir.'

'It is the only way, David,' Nightingale soothed. 'And I shall be right here at your side.'

Richmond stared between the three men for a while as if one of them would relent. But this amputation was the most merciful thing to do; he had no hope if they let the wound rot away. Finally, he sniffed and took a rough, quivering breath. 'All right. If you think it is the only way, Captain.'

'Good lad.'

Dr Archer insisted on performing the surgery, rather than submit to the doctors at the hospital. Richmond almost crushed Nightingale's fingers as the saw dug in. Nightingale could sense the other patients staring in horror and fascination as more and more of Richmond's muscle was cut away. For a few blessed moments, Richmond faded, the pain too much. Then his muffled screams returned and he sank his teeth hard enough into the gag to almost splinter it.

Blood dripped down onto Nightingale's shoes but he did not want to move and upset Richmond. It was Captain Harrison who left eventually, giving a quiet moan and striding outside. 'I'm not going anywhere, David,' Nightingale insisted. 'You're nearly there. Nearly there, I promise you.'

At last the severing finished and Dr Archer worked quickly to cauterise the wound. One more tight squeeze on Nightingale's sore hand and Richmond dropped into a troubled slumber. It was done. Nightingale finally breathed.

'I shall need to keep him here,' Dr Archer said, laying aside his tools and wiping his bloodied hands on his gown. 'I have hope for him, but then I did the first time as well.'

'We can pray,' Nightingale replied.

'He shall not be in any sense well enough to rejoin the crew before the *Scylla* sails.'

Nightingale had already assumed that, but for now, it was only important that Richmond was safe. He looked down at him once more, brushed a lock of sweat-drenched hair out of his eyes, and then left him in Archer's capable hands.

He found Harrison outside. The blonde captain looked almost as pale as his hair, rubbing his hands and pacing over the dry grass. 'My apologies, Captain Nightingale,' he said. 'I have been at sea all my damn life, yet I've never been able to accustom myself to amputations. I feel I spooked your poor boy by talking about my seaman.'

Nightingale shook his head. 'There is no need to apologise. I have sat by many men who have been treated and it never becomes any easier.'

'You have a strong stomach, man.' Harrison righted himself, tugging down his waistcoat and straightening his neckcloth. 'I trust that your midshipman shall recover?'

'Dr Archer is not entirely positive. I shall have to write to his family... whatever happens.' He sighed, mind ticking over about the voids in the *Scylla*'s crew. 'We are fortunate that we did not lose too many crewmen in the storm. My marine lieutenant Charlston is filling the gaps from the town. God only knows what their condition will be.'

Harrison laughed, though Nightingale had been serious. The colour returned to his cheeks the further they walked from the hospital. 'I may not be able to help you, Hiram, but I can offer you some relief. I wish I had asked before the hospital. I would like to invite you to dine on the *Actium* tonight. Your Lieutenant Courtney has made quite an impression on Tabitha.'

'Truly?' Nightingale asked, as if he did not know.

'Oh, yes. They have met a handful of times over the past couple of days. I apologise, I would have thought Lieutenant Courtney had spoken of her. I do hope that does not say what he thinks of her.' Harrison laughed again – it was starting to grate on Nightingale.

'I...' Nightingale forced a smile. 'I am sure he meant nothing by it. My lieutenant can be a private type. I shall ask him if he is willing to accept the invite, but I should certainly attend.'

Nightingale's smile dropped as soon as he left Harrison. He had known Courtney had spent time away from the ship and had permitted him to do so. But it did not cool his frustration. Courtney should not make connections on the island when they had such a task ahead. If Nightingale lost command then at least Courtney should stay. Hot-headed or not, Nightingale could see the respect the crew had for him.

Courtney's actions were only a veneer to his irritation, though. Why had Harrison come along to the hospital with him? Why had he taken such an interest in the repairs? Was he simply being friendly, acting as one captain to another, or was there more?

In his frustration, Nightingale allowed himself to think the worst: Harrison had been sizing up the ship and the crew in case he gained command.

With that thought, Nightingale hailed a boat and made the journey out to the *Scylla*. She was still his – for now. And he would be damned if he did not leave her in the best state attainable.

So, he took care, as he came aboard, not to tread or trip on any of the cordage and canvas spread across the main deck. The men sang as they scrubbed and cleaned and sewed whilst forward, over the bow, hammering echoed with the figurehead's re-carving. Mr Smythe, the mid on watch, stood by the main chains, out of the way but close enough to keep an eye on the crew. He saluted Nightingale as he made a path over.

'Mr Smythe, your watch came around quickly,' Nightingale commented. He had not realised how long he had been at the hospital. 'Do you know where I can find Lieutenant Courtney?'

'He's in the gunroom, sir. Lieutenant Charlston came aboard with some fellows from the town and he's going through their names.'

'Thank you, Mr Smythe.'

'Mind how you go, sir.'

Nightingale climbed down into the remarkably empty decks. Courtney sat in the gunroom, paperwork before him. Two midshipmen – Finley, the youngest, and Burrows – hunched over their journals, scribbling in the dim light and telling their families about their adventures so far from home. Before Nightingale could approach, Finley looked up and asked, 'Lieutenant Courtney, how do you spell venereal?'

Burrows tried to suppress a cackle. Courtney frowned. 'I don't think you should be writing home to your parents about that, Mr Finley. Enough of that noise, Mr Burrows.'

Finley reddened, turning almost scarlet as he saw Nightingale.

'Mr Finley, Mr Burrows,' Nightingale said, 'perhaps you could work on your journals in the orlop. I'll check them later.'

To a chorus of garbled 'Yes, sir's', Finley and Burrows hurried from the gunroom. Nightingale sat opposite Courtney on the low bench. 'Venereal?' he asked.

'Lieutenant Charlston had issues with a handful of waist-gunners in the town. I reckon Dr Archer will have to administer his blue pill.'

Nightingale sighed – but that was the risk of the shore: a place for crewmen to spend their money in whatever way left their pockets first. Sometimes, he felt as though he was the only man in the world who was not pulled by those temptations. 'I'll have words if it becomes any worse,' he decided. 'Speaking of which, I have just come from the hospital. David Richmond is still ailing. Dr Archer had to amputate the rest of his leg. He hopes that will sate his fever but it's clear that he won't be joining us for the journey ahead.'

'Damn.' Courtney ran a hand through his hair. It looked more unkempt than unusual, as if he had not bothered to tame it. Even the tropical sun had not touched his skin. 'That poor kid,' he sighed. 'Begging your pardon, sir, but the *Fénix* seemed to do more harm than good.'

'We lost capable men. These are our replacements?' He glanced over the papers.

'Eight men. All healthy and six with experience on the water. Although I'm not entirely convinced one isn't an escaped slave.'

'Well, he would not be the only man onboard with that history.'

'The Jeremy Wendells of the island would not be happy,' Courtney said with a slight curl of the lip. 'Is that what Lord Fairholme spoke to you about on the hill the other morning? I wager he was not happy with my attitudes.'

'He said that you should mind who you speak to with those words.'

Courtney huffed. 'Do you agree with him, sir?'

'How so?'

'Do you think it would be wise to keep my mouth shut – about Saint-Domingue and the slaves? I'm not an idiot, I saw how it made him itch.'

Nightingale did not owe Courtney the explanation. Since leaving Antigua, he had been needled by what he had thought was Courtney's restlessness in his place of the hierarchy. But more and more, he saw that Courtney was not the true enemy. He had, at least, by revealing his connection to Jane and the *Ulysses*, told Nightingale the truth – which was more than he could say for others.

'I shall not admonish you for what you said,' Nightingale said honestly. 'I have rarely met a man who is so unashamed of his background or his views. But there is a delicate balance with the *Ulysses*. Men like Lord Fairholme have a stake in her.'

'The gold?' Courtney latched onto the meaning immediately. 'Did he tell you why she is hauling gold?'

A splinter had come loose on the mess table. Nightingale eyed it, was half-tempted to rip it out, but he worried it would disturb a deeper chunk of the wood than he thought. 'There are other ways to control Saint-Domingue than invasion,' he said.

'A bribe,' Courtney stated, without question. 'Damn their eyes.'

'I'm only telling you this so you can keep your nose clean,' Nightingale said, but realised that was not the full reason; the desire to share what he knew with someone was stronger than he had anticipated. 'This is not knowledge that Lord Fairholme wishes to be made public.'

'I imagine.'

Courtney fell silent. Nightingale continued to look down the list of names. 'I received another invitation today,' he said. 'Captain Harrison accompanied me to the hospital and suggested we dine onboard the *Actium* tonight. He told me that Tabitha Sandham would be attending.'

Courtney, who had been rereading the list, looked up. Colour touched his cheeks. Nightingale had not expected that reaction. It quelled his former desire to want to advise Courtney against such connections.

'It isn't anything like that, sir,' Courtney babbled. 'She is a sweet girl, but I have my duties.'

'Many officers are married.'

Courtney's eyes widened. 'She has not spoken of marriage. I have accompanied her on a handful of walks, that's all. I should stay aboard the *Scylla* tonight, sir.' He paused and returned to the paperwork. His eyes scanned the same page again and again but Nightingale could tell he was not absorbing it. Finally, Courtney asked, 'Is your wife Sir William's daughter?'

'Yes.'

'How did you meet her?'

Nightingale drummed his fingers on his leg before he realised he was doing it and stopped. He did not owe Courtney this story either, yet he said, 'My father and hers knew one another. They suggested we marry and so we did. The eighteenth of September, 1783.'

It had been around a fortnight after the end of the American rebellion: the fierce conflicts that Nightingale had spilled his first blood in. Sir William and his father had hoped that, with the peace, Nightingale would return home to start a family. Wars had broken out again in that decade – and provided years' worth of excuses for husband and wife.

'I nearly married a girl when I turned eighteen,' Courtney said. He was picking at that splinter on the table. 'I had just been made a lieutenant and she was a poor lass in Gibraltar. In the end, we did not. Sometimes, I wish I did – her brother was a wicked bastard and I wanted to take her away from him. I don't know what became of her. The next time I was shipped to Gibraltar, she was gone. I hope she ran away.'

Nightingale stared at that splinter. 'Did you love her?' he asked.

Courtney paused. 'Perhaps. I only wanted her to be safe, just like Jane. That is why Jane came west with me.' He breathed out. 'I cannot bear the thought of her alone on the *Ulysses* amongst those animals.'

'Jane has her husband aboard,' Nightingale tried. 'In the same way that you would have protected your girl in Gibraltar.'

'I hope that is the case. Shall you tell Sir William and Lord Fairholme about her – about my connection to her?'

'No.' Nightingale again thought, adamantly, how Courtney should stay onboard the *Scylla*, no matter what happened. 'Why should they need to know?'

'Thank you, sir. I worry if they know, they shall question my judgement. I want to get her away as soon as I can, and then help her to forget about all of this.'

'She is fortunate to have you looking out for her.'

Courtney smiled, but the spark soon vanished again. 'I have still lost her,' he said, and the splinter finally came loose.

Nightingale thought of Courtney's words as he sat in the great cabin throughout the stifling afternoon. He wished to strip down to his shirt-sleeves, but the new men were being brought before him one by one and he wanted them to see him in his full uniform. They were as Courtney had said – healthy and strong, the youngest being eighteen and the oldest in his early fifties. He talked to them individually then bid them to put their marks on the rolls.

No matter the background, no matter the colour, no matter the age, there was brotherhood in joining a crew. Each man was as part of the ship as Nightingale and his officers. The most unlikely bonds could grow, the most curious points of similarity.

In Courtney's admissions, Nightingale saw something of himself – not only the eager young man he used to be but a deeper, more personal note. Courtney was wracked by the guilt he felt at losing Jane. Nightingale understood that, knew well the pain of a loved one slipping away as a consequence of his decisions.

And so, the *Ulysses* was the best chance for both of them – an opportunity to right the balance again, to save those who could still be saved.

Not for the first time, the depth of his need to retain the *Scylla* struck him.

Nightingale hoped Courtney had changed his mind about the invitation to the *Actium*. He would have enjoyed showing a united front to Harrison – a captain and lieutenant who knew their ship and crew, which Harrison would struggle to break into if he received command. Yet Nightingale had left Lieutenant Hargreaves in command too often and, with new men aboard, the face of the first lieutenant, if not the captain, would be needed.

He and Hargreaves were rowed across the harbour. Nightingale kept turning back to the smooth lines of his elegant fifth-rate, absurdly proud of their progress. To stop the impulses, he asked Hargreaves, 'How is your wound now, Lieutenant?'

Hargreaves, bedecked in his finest uniform, which somehow looked ill-fitting on his gangly frame, frowned. 'My wound?'

'The head wound. From the *Fénix*.'

'Oh. It healed well, sir.' He swallowed and rubbed at where the cut had been. 'Is Lord Fairholme going to be here tonight?'

I bloody hope not, Nightingale thought. 'No. I do not think so.'

'He is quite impressive,' Hargreaves said vaguely.

When they stepped onto the *Actium*, Harrison beamed. He marched across the spacious deck – wider and so much higher than the *Scylla*'s – and grasped Nightingale's hand. Dizzying introductions passed him by: Harrison's first lieutenant, his second lieutenant, his third lieutenant, surgeon, master, three midshipmen, and then the women – Jennifer and Tabitha Sandham. Tabitha was dressed for the opera, fine auburn hair curled into immaculate ringlets, diamonds glittering at her throat, gown a vivid blue and gold. She curtseyed politely to Nightingale but he did not miss her surreptitious glance over his shoulder. Her face fell as she saw Hargreaves.

'My first lieutenant could not attend,' he apologised to Harrison. 'Business on the *Scylla*. This is my second lieutenant, Michael Hargreaves.'

'Pleased to meet you, Lieutenant Hargreaves,' Harrison said. 'Shame about Courtney. He was a fine singer. I had hoped we would receive another song from him.'

Harrison ushered them below and it did not take long for Nightingale to regret accepting the invitation. His stomach was still tender from the past days so he could not appreciate the tottering, four-decked sea-pie and the assortment of rich broths. The entertainment – a pet monkey which had been trained to tie knots – became less charming by the fourth time it nearly tipped over Nightingale's Madeira. So many people jostled around the table, even in the larger cabin, that Nightingale struggled to hear or be heard. Moreover, Lieutenant Hargreaves made a poor companion, unable to tell many stories of his past when prompted, only returning to the same incident at Groix again and again.

And always, a bass-note throbbed. This ship could have been Nightingale's, and he could have filled Harrison's shoes. He tried to imagine himself, with Louisa at his side, living under Governor Picton's sharp eye. Nightingale watched Harrison, a few years younger, gesticulating with one hand, weaving his fingers between Jennifer's with the other. He was in the midst of an anecdote that Nightingale could not quite decipher, but everyone around him nodded and laughed. Harrison was the kind of man he should be. The kind of man his father would be happy to have as a son.

Yet he had no desire for it. Not like this.

Later that evening, as the cook emerged again with the figgy-dowdy and treacle tarts, another midshipman appeared and knocked quietly on the cabin door. 'Did you smell the sugar, Mr Jewell?' Harrison teased.

Mr Jewell blushed and stepped into the room. 'Pardon me, sir, but a message has come. It is for Captain Nightingale.'

Nightingale felt his Madeira burn his throat. He slowly put down his glass as eyes swivelled to him.

'Please, Captain,' Harrison said genially. 'You are my guest. Receive your message.'

Nightingale followed Mr Jewell out onto the deck. The note he was handed was only small but his heart skipped as he opened it and saw Picton's seal and Sir William's neat, copperplate handwriting.

He read it, then read it again, and again as he thought of the excuses he could give Harrison.

It was a summons to the governor's house the next morning.

Ensuring his hands were no longer shaking, he pocketed the note and looked across to the *Scylla*. The regret at leaving crested over him. These had been two hours he could not claw back. Tomorrow, he would have to fight for her.

Once, he had seen his career as a performance, wanting all eyes to witness it, believing himself was unworthy if they did not. Now, he knew that that performer's stage was rotten and fickle.

He was tired of performing. For his father. For Sir William. For men like Lord Fairholme. For the entire world.

Chapter Sixteen: The Puppeteers

17 March 1799, Portsmouth

With an absent mind, Nightingale tapped the end of his pen against his lips and cast his eye over the letter. The phrasing still set his teeth on edge. At turns, it was too sweet and sycophantic – at others, far too understated. Evidently, he had forgotten how to achieve the delicate balance in writing to senior officers.

His pen hovered over the paragraphs, near to scrubbing everything out. He doubted John Jervis – the Earl of St Vincent, recently promoted to Admiral of the White – remembered him. Nightingale had been one of a whole sky of stellar commanders under Jervis, and the *Lion* had been a single vessel of the fleet at the battle which had won Jervis his title.

Still, Louisa had suggested this letter of congratulations for St Vincent's promotion. As though she could see further into Nightingale's future than he could, she had urged him not to sever his ties with the navy. Though the *Lion* was being repaired under a new captain, he retained his rank. One day, Louisa said, he might wish to put his foot back in those waters.

Nightingale stared at the model of the *Lion* as he mused. St Vincent had been a fine commander, if severe with discipline. He had ensured each and every one of his captains followed that line, certainly after the mutinies at Spithead and the Nore curdled terror throughout the fleet's officers. Nightingale thanked God that no man had spoken up on the *Lion*. But he had watched men hanging from the yardarm on other vessels and wondered if he could give that order. Mutiny was a thorn, one which Nightingale hated as much as any captain.

With each hanging, he had only seen Tom. And the scars on his back had itched and burnt in his guilt.

'Hiram?'

Louisa stood in the doorway of his study. He had not heard her approach. She wore a different dress to the one she had donned that morning, shining in emerald green.

'I'm sorry, my dear, I was trying to get my phrasing right. I hoped it would come back to me.'

Louisa did not smile.

'My father is here,' she said.

'Oh. I shall be down in a moment.'

'He has your father with him as well.'

Nightingale paused. That warm itch spread across his back again.

'Shall I tell him he is not welcome?' Louisa asked.

'He knows that already,' Nightingale said coldly. 'It would not deter him.'

Nightingale set down his pen and stood, brushing down his waistcoat. Louisa laid a hand on his arm and guided him out of the study. The major works for the house had been completed but Nightingale could still hear the banging of hammers. He realised it was his pulse rising in his throat. He had not seen his father since returning from the Nile.

For a moment, he considered lying that his eyes were hurting too much, even though they slowly improved.

'Would you like to rest?' Louisa whispered as they descended the stairs.

'No. It is better to have it done with.'

Nightingale could hear him in the parlour. His voice chipped away at the careful defences Nightingale had made, reducing him once more to a frightened little boy. Even before Tom, his father had never treated him with any love.

Nightingale stepped into the parlour. Sir William, bedecked in a simple coat, turned and smiled at him – but Nightingale trained his eyes on his father. He no longer wore his admiral's finery nor sailed. No one could wrench his title away from him, though.

'Good afternoon,' Nightingale greeted thinly. 'I trust you are both well.'

'Very well, yes,' Sir William said. 'You have more colour than the last time we met.'

'Hiram has been a better patient than I expected,' Louisa jested, squeezing his elbow. 'Dr Harrow believes it is all uphill now.'

'I recall a splinter almost giving me a similar fate,' Admiral Nightingale commented. 'An inch more and it may have gone clean through my right eye.'

This was not a splinter, Nightingale thought. *An entire ship exploded not two cables in front of me.*

'Yes,' he said. 'Well, a little sacrifice is expected in the service. Should I send for some tea?'

'No, thank you, Hiram,' Sir William replied. 'We wished to speak to you only briefly before I travel back to Bristol with your father. We have a proposition for the entire family.'

Nightingale sat beside Louisa, though his father and Sir William remained standing at the mantelpiece, as if they were schoolmasters surveying their students. Louisa gently slipped her hand into Nightingale's and he squeezed it gratefully.

'I am sure you have followed the developments in the Caribbean,' Sir William began, continuing before Nightingale could answer. 'General Abercromby recently took Trinidad from Spain and Thomas Picton has been installed as the military governor. Further north, the rebels of Saint-Domingue have reversed our fortunes and cast us out. Over the last years, Britain has been fighting in Belize, Grenada, and pushing to retain command in her current colonies.'

'I'm aware,' Nightingale said, wanting to reach the point.

'There is ample opportunity out there,' his father remarked.

Nightingale wondered if he was going to expand or leave the implication hanging. Neither his father nor Sir William offered more. 'Are you suggesting that I look for a command in the Caribbean?' he asked.

'It is an option,' Sir William pressed. 'I have contacts out there, as does your father. Hyde Parker commands the Jamaica Station, and

Hugh Seymour is tipped to take the Leewards from Harvey. Both men are fond of you or your father – and I know of many potential open doors over the islands. Bureaucracy stretches wherever Britain extends her hand.'

'It is a world away.'

'You do not speak like a man who has freely sailed the seas for over two decades,' Admiral Nightingale commented with a wry quirk of his brow. 'We have both served to ensure nowhere is far from this country's grasp.'

Nightingale ignored the platitude. 'I know my wife said my health is improving, but I am in no fit state to travel to the West Indies. The Leeward, Windward and Jamaica stations are notorious for their death tolls to the fever.'

'Governor Picton is always looking for capable men to populate Trinidad.' Sir William tried for something more specific. 'And with the recent uprisings, many colonies fear a repeat.'

'That is not a position for me,' Nightingale insisted. 'I have some experience in those waters, yes, but not in politics. And I have served in the Mediterranean for many years.'

An uncomfortable silence fell. Had they truly thought he would accept instantly? This suggestion, so out of the blue, reeked of ulterior motives. He wondered why his father and Sir William – two men on opposite ends of politics and interests – were united in it.

'What is your interest in the Caribbean, Father?' he asked. 'You have not been stationed out there since the American revolt.'

'My interests are manifold. I believe that your successes could benefit us all.'

Nightingale fought the urge to laugh. He had learnt very young how to detect his father's lies. He realised precisely what his interest in the Caribbean was – not the protection of Britain or the defence of her colonies, but how much money could line his pockets. Since retiring, that had been his new quest. Glory had been attained, and where to go from there but a more material legacy? Sir William had the influence his father coveted but Nightingale was surprised Sir William, the rigid favourite of Wilberforce, did not see his father's roving eye.

Or perhaps he did – and the true motive was to cart Nightingale out of the picture.

Seeing his hesitation, Sir William glanced at Admiral Nightingale and tried to smooth his words. 'It is our concern to help you, Hiram. We are only thinking of your name and reputation.'

His name – which was linked to Sir William's. Whose reputation was at stake here?

'Hiram has a medal from the Nile,' Louisa said suddenly. 'He has fought Britain's enemies for more than half of his life. Does that not count for anything?'

'A name that is not constantly polished will soon turn to rust,' Admiral Nightingale sighed.

'Returning to the service may benefit you, Hiram,' Sir William continued, drawing Nightingale's thinly veiled frustration back to him. 'The longer that you spend within these walls, the more that they will trap you.'

'You cannot allow your wife to make your decisions for you,' Admiral Nightingale tutted.

Louisa's nails dug into Nightingale's knuckles. He felt her shift, as if she wanted to rise and stand face to face with his father. Even Sir William glanced away in shame – but he did not oppose the statement. 'Hiram has not been well,' Louisa began.

'It is all right, my dear.' Nightingale laid a hand on her arm, feeling how tense the muscle was. 'So instead of allowing my wife to make my decisions,' he said slowly, 'you wish to make them for me instead?'

'Hiram,' Sir William tried.

'I apologise, but I am in no way to be discussing these matters. This is the wrong time. I cannot leave my home, or Louisa.'

'She would be willing to travel with you,' Sir William suggested.

'Father,' Louisa said firmly. 'I said I may. We discussed this.'

Nightingale frowned. 'Where was I during these discussions?'

'Hiram, it has been a matter my father and I have talked of in pieces over the last years, ever since the tide began to turn in our favour under Wilberforce. Yet we have never settled on anything definite. I did not know this was what was going to be said today.'

Nightingale felt the surge of anger roll over him as she tenderly stroked his fingers. His emotion did not know who, or what, to focus on. He could not accuse her – not the woman who had cared for him these last months. She had not once spoken of his reputation, or hers – only, genuinely, of his health.

'I appreciate your journey out here,' Nightingale said carefully, not trusting his words. 'It is a kind thing to do – and I confess that it has taken me a while to become accustomed to the land again. But to rush out onto the sea again… It would benefit no one, and I fear it would lead to more danger.'

It was the most Nightingale had said about his condition in months, skating on the surface of the turmoil that lay beneath his scarred face and damaged eyes. He barely knew or trusted himself anymore. Certainly not enough to stand on a deck as a captain again.

That was what lurked underneath his reluctance to accept and his inability to write his letter. He no longer felt in control.

It was best that Sir William and his father left. When Nightingale's own words fell on deaf ears, Louisa tried herself. Nightingale appreciated her effort, as he appreciated everything else she had done for him, but it added weight to his father's words: that he allowed his wife to stand on ground he should have defended himself. In the end, she tactfully mentioned his eyes and how any more excitement might prompt a migraine.

Nightingale sat like a lost child whilst she herded them towards the door. He only breathed out when he heard it rattle in its frame as Louisa closed it.

She returned, rubbing her hands together, playing with her wedding ring. Her cheeks were flushed, jaw tight. 'I had no idea that he was going to spring that upon you, Hiram,' she rushed. 'To bring your father as well is unlike him. I know they do not see eye to eye.'

'I don't think anyone sees eye to eye with my father.'

'I at least believe that my own father was trying to be helpful. He has discussed it before with me, and he appears genuine.'

'And I am grateful for that,' Nightingale insisted. 'But my father making himself known… The only reason he would consider the Caribbean is for wealth.'

'My father would not allow that – not after the campaigns he ran against the trade.'

'Then why do they pursue the same idea? Why use me as their puppet? My reputation! Christ almighty, it's not my reputation they care about.' Nightingale put a hand to his head, feeling the first pulses of a raging migraine. 'This is what my father excels at. He manhandled me into the navy when I was twelve. I had no choice – he did not even put me on his ship, just one captained by a friend. He wanted to use me a pawn – out of his sight, but performing his wishes.'

He realised he had spat the words out. It was hard to swallow the bitter taste in his mouth these days. Stewing inside these walls had seemed the safe option, but his body was rebelling against him. He had imprisoned himself – and the longer he stayed, the harder it would be to find the key.

Damn it. Perhaps there was truth in what Sir William said,

He wanted to weep, or scream. He trembled, hands over his eyes, before feeling gentle fingers glance through his hair. 'You have been successful, Hiram,' Louisa said. 'That fortune has been in your own right, not your father's. And you are improving. Not only in Dr Harrow's estimations but in yourself. Do not let them shove you backwards. You must cast aside this hold your father still has over you.'

Nightingale pushed her hand away and rose to his feet. All hope of his bettering health drained. In its place was the old shame and grief and anger. 'You know what he is. You know what he has done to me.'

'My father is not the same as yours,' Louisa insisted. 'He would not allow such treatment.'

'He should not be the one to allow or disallow such treatment!' he shouted. 'I shall be the one to decide what it is I accept or do not! Why is it that no one listens to a word I say?'

He tried to escape the room but Louisa bravely snatched him by the arm. A servant had appeared in the doorway at Nightingale's outburst, and she snapped at him to leave. 'Then tell me what it is you want, Hiram,' she pleaded. 'Be honest with me, and I shall stand on the same ground as you. If you do not want to go, then do not go. But don't close the door on me. I am your wife! I am your friend.'

Nightingale did not look at her. He stared at the clock which ticked on and on. He had one foot in the past – terrified of his father and the scars he had made – and one foot in the future: an inevitable future that already felt written for him. 'I cannot,' he said. 'I cannot have what it is I want, and be honest at the same time.'

He untangled himself from her grip and marched from the room. The letter to St Vincent remained on the desk in his study. He grasped it and tore it in half, throwing each scrap to the floor. A childish, ugly satisfaction lifted him for a second before dropping him back into the mire. He collapsed into his chair and hid his face from the model of the *Lion*, as if the shades of his former crew could see him acting like this.

He had hated the navy in the beginning, and hated his father for putting him there. But the years had turned, he had climbed the ladder and felt as though he had gained some control and worth in his life.

But there was a reverse to all of the medals and accolades he had gained.

Leroy had died in his arms during the greatest battle Nightingale had ever witnessed. He had been unable to keep him safe and he could not ever leave that guilt behind. If he were to take another command, who could guarantee that it would not reoccur?

All he was certain of was that staying here was killing him. And perhaps out there – that would kill him too.

Nightingale had to decide which was the lesser of the two evils.

Chapter Seventeen: The Hangman's Noose

13 July 1800, Port of Spain, Trinidad

Nightingale rose early and left the *Scylla* before the forenoon watch could begin. At that time of morning, the sun was not quite so blistering but his tired eyes still ached. He took care on the uneven streets and the rough ground, not wanting to arrive at the governor's house flushed or with a stained uniform. Perhaps he should have hailed a carriage but he wished to be completely alone: a final few moments to settle his thoughts.

With every chiming of the ship's bell, he had woken, plagued by another accusation they might heap upon him. He had told no one of his true destination when leaving the ship, only that he was meeting with Governor Picton.

The gardens of the governor's house were nearly empty. Two sentries guarded the gates and they allowed him to pass without question. No one said a word to him until he was taken through to a small parlour and told to wait to be called. He smiled thinly and perched on the edge of a seat with his hat on his knees. A drop of sweat wound down his nose and wet the gold lace on his sleeve. He hastily wiped it away.

Paintings lined the walls of the room. Nightingale recognised the battles they depicted – the Battle of the Saintes, the Glorious First of June, Quiberon Bay: all British victories. He had been on deck during the Glorious First of June, could still hear the screaming of the guns as they raked the French ships off Ushant. The oil colours hid the fact that for days afterwards, both sides had suffered dreadfully. Disobedience and misunderstood orders had nearly cost the British fleet.

He wondered what all of his service had been for. Always, something lay below the burnished, glorious colours.

He stewed in his doubts until a young staff officer appeared in the doorway. 'Captain Hiram Nightingale?' he asked, as if he could be anyone different. 'The board is ready for you.'

He entered the same hall he had eaten in not a few days previously. The table had been turned, broadening the wide space and making Nightingale's footsteps echo off the walls. It was a long walk. His eyes would not focus on the men waiting for him – he only saw a line of drab coats, broken by shining epaulettes which caught the sun. Nightingale kept his gaze above the panel's heads, but the closer he approached, the more he wanted to know who would be wringing his neck.

Severe, ice-blue eyes stared straight through him.

His footsteps faltered. The fierce heat immediately turned to winter. It took all of his strength to keep moving.

Admiral Nightingale, in his uniform again, sat at table next to Governor Picton. At first, Nightingale prayed he was an illusion – he could not be here, so far from home. But it was him, as it had always been: the man looming over Nightingale, pulling his strings, making him do whatever he wanted. The same death-like gaze, the same glittering medals, the same thin, weathered face and slicked, silver hair.

Nightingale looked away, terrified. This was not the time to let it show. There were other men at the table: two post-captains, Sir William and Lord Fairholme, as well as Picton. These were not the proper regulations, he thought in his panic. More members of the service should be in attendance to pass judgement. This was not a place for politicians, or men who were his relations.

He swallowed as he finally stopped. He stood as if he was before the king, hat tucked under his arm, back straight, head held aloft, though he could feel his knees trembling. Eyes clawed silently over him. One of the post-captains coughed. Papers shuffled.

'Thank you for such a prompt arrival, Captain,' Lord Fairholme said in the same lazy, calm voice as ever. 'We realise that this isn't regular – but you agree that haste is important, considering the circumstances.'

'We mean to say that we do not ignore the fact that proceedings require a broader presence in the panel,' Sir William clarified. 'But with the need to return to sea as soon as the *Scylla* is ready, a decision has to be made.'

Nightingale said nothing.

'Do you understand, Captain?' Sir William prompted, and he realised he had to try to speak.

'I understand,' he managed through an impossibly tight throat.

'Do you also understand why we have called you, Captain?'

'I do.'

'Questions must always be asked when a ship of the King's Navy is lost.' Admiral Nightingale finally spoke, resting his chin on his curled fingers. It was a look Nightingale remembered from his youth, hurrying into his father's study to ask him for something. The answer, without fail, was in the negative. 'Though the *Fénix* never reached shore and thus, was never condemned by the court, she became property of the Crown as soon as she was taken as a prize. The Articles of War explicitly state that no goods or money can be stripped from a prize until official judgement. You held responsibility for her and her stores – and she was lost at sea.'

Nightingale took a breath. He squeezed his hat so tightly that he doubted the dent could ever be removed.

'I behaved as well as I could in my capacity,' he said, desperately concentrating on each word. 'The Spanish captain and his first lieutenant were taken onboard the *Scylla* and held as prisoners. I assigned a prize crew under Mr Midshipman Richmond to sail the *Fénix* into Bridgetown. No stores were removed from the *Fénix* – she was repaired as securely as possible. When the storm—'

'Why did you engage her in battle?' Admiral Nightingale interrupted.

'She… she was a Spanish vessel. My orders—'

'Your orders were to search for the *Ulysses* and bring her to justice.'

'Sir, I understand that her size may not be considered worthy to battle for, but I made a decision. I believed she could be a valuable source of information about the *Ulysses*. She was, sir. Captain Ramirez was forthcoming about the *Ulysses*.'

Admiral Nightingale brushed off the accusation as if it were dust on his uniform. 'You were saying about the storm, Captain.'

'Yes.' Nightingale tried to regain himself. 'It came from the south-west – a sudden black squall. I have experienced such weather but rarely that abrupt. We hauled in canvas to only storm- and stay-sails, and we tacked so we ran before the wind.'

'The *Scylla* is still under repair.'

'I believe that she was relatively unscathed considering the squall's strength. The bowsprit became damaged, the rudder was nicked, and—'

'Yes, we have the ordnance reports for the damage,' Admiral Nightingale said dismissively. 'Following the storm, you opted to return to the *Fénix*.'

Nightingale frowned. 'Of course. I had men on the ship. I prayed that some survived. A lightning strike had ignited her, and Mr Richmond acted quickly and admirably to extinguish the fires before they reached the powder store, but with canvas alight and so much other damage, they were at the storm's mercy. A wave struck the *Fénix* broadside and the effects were irreparable without a harbour.'

'If Mr Richmond was not ailing, he would be examined too. When he does recover, questions will still be asked.'

'He has lost a limb. He was fortunate to survive.'

'Precisely. Did you believe he was ready for the command?'

'Yes. Without a doubt.'

'Why did Lieutenant Courtney and Lieutenant Hargreaves remain on the *Scylla*?'

Nightingale paused. 'I…' he said, and wondered what excuse would come. 'I needed Lieutenant Courtney onboard the *Scylla*. With the high-ranking Spanish prisoners, I thought it best to have senior officers present. And Lieutenant Hargreaves was wounded during the action with the *Fénix*.'

'You also had Lieutenant Charlston, your marine officer, aboard to keep order. Instead, you sent a fifteen-year-old boy to command a crew which included Spanish prisoners.'

'I did.' Nightingale swallowed past the rising dread. 'All of my officers are capable. I cannot fault them for how they acted during the storm or during the rescue attempts from the *Fénix*. And you well know, sir, that boys at sea are young, but they grow quickly.'

His father fell silent for a moment, and all Nightingale could hear was the scratching of the clerk's pen, writing down his responses. Barely anyone else had questioned Nightingale; they were making his father interrogate him.

'The *Fénix* is not the first ship that you have lost, Captain,' Admiral Nightingale finally said.

The words struck Nightingale like splinters. 'I do not see how that is relevant,' he rasped.

'We are not here only to discuss your actions, Captain,' Admiral Nightingale said. 'Many things cross a man's mind before he takes a step or says a word or makes a decision. It is the concern of the panel that perhaps your decision-making capabilities have been... marred.'

'Say it plainly,' Nightingale spat, suddenly not caring about his poise. Silence followed.

'Hiram.' Sir William returned. 'I understand my suggestion prompted your position here in the Caribbean. I could tell that you had doubts about Trinidad – so when the *Ulysses* incident occurred, I recommended you as the man to lead the hunt. I believed it would help you, truly I did. You were wounded terribly at the Nile, and with the near-loss of the *Lion*, this was always intended as a means of your improvement. Doubtless you have performed in a manner which you believe is apt, but... Is there something you wish to say, Captain?'

Nightingale realised he was shaking his head, chewing on the inside of his lip. Heat pulsed in his cheeks. Fury and humiliation, long pushed down, raced to the surface. Sir William had spelt out his illness for everyone to hear. They already had their excuses to be rid of him.

He had thought awful things about his crew, about Courtney – believing they would distrust him, believing the lieutenant was on the hunt for glory and for his own downfall. He realised now that that had all been implanted by these men, pushing him all the time, turning him against himself and his companions whilst blinding him to the fact that they were the ones hurting him.

'Please, Captain, say what you will,' Admiral Nightingale prodded.

'You brought me into this position,' Nightingale said coldly. 'You brought me into it without telling me the full extent of what I would face. Perhaps I had my doubts in the beginning, but I behaved as I should have behaved. I stand by my decisions. I fail to see how I could have acted in any other manner. You placed me here, you withheld information, and now you condemn me for it.'

'Hiram, think of these accusations—'

'Lord Fairholme told me that you made the decision not to inform me about the gold onboard the *Ulysses*.'

Fairholme blinked and inclined his head. 'I believe he should have been told,' he said smoothly. Admiral Nightingale's lip curled in disgust.

'If you were informed, Hiram,' Sir William insisted, 'then we feared word would spread and a similar occurrence would have plagued the *Scylla*.'

Nightingale looked down, hands curling to fists. When he was half-sure he could control his voice again, he raised his head and stepped forward to the table. 'You believed I would not be able to control my crew,' he said in low tones. 'Did you ever believe I would succeed? Why even put me in this position in the first place? Say it plainly, if you are going to say it. You think I am hysterical.' With a surge of defiance, he grasped his hat and placed it firmly upon his head. 'Ask me all the questions you wish, but do not pretend to listen to my answers. Do not pretend the decision is not already made.'

'Hiram,' Sir William pleaded.

Nightingale turned and marched from the room. With every forceful step, he knew he trampled on his hope of keeping the *Scylla*. He wished it were not so, but there was nothing he could do against these men. They could try to mould him into whatever form they wished yet his heart remained the same.

And he was tired of pretending it was not.

'Captain Nightingale!' the staff officer cried at the door but he kept walking, out of the parlour and through the hallways into the gardens. He almost expected the marines to stop him. They let him through into the blazing sun and onto the long, winding path which led to the harbour.

Nightingale did not know where to go. He walked and walked, vision hazy, until footsteps raced to catch up with him. He thought it was the staff officer again, perhaps Sir William or Lord Fairholme, so he sped his pace, not turning.

'Sir! Captain!' Courtney's strained voice, out of breath, calling for him.

Nightingale stopped dead. At the same moment, Courtney reached him and grasped him about the arm. He realised what he had done, tried to pull away, but Nightingale already had his wrist in his grip.

'They brought my father, damn their eyes,' Nightingale spat. 'My own father to condemn me! He is retired. Why is he here?'

'I don't understand,' Courtney rushed, his eyes wide and fearful, darting over Nightingale's face. 'I was told to attend the governor's house and answer questions. What have they done?'

'Nothing they did not plan for. Go. Go and answer their questions honestly.'

'What are they asking? It sounded as though they planned a court martial.'

'The *Fénix* was lost. I lost her.'

Nightingale pulled away. More than a year ago, Louisa had said he was recovering. That was not true; all he had done was push his fears and grief down, waiting for the moment they would spill over again like boiling pitch. Courtney must have thought he was mad, standing there, tears teetering dangerously in his eyes.

'Be honest with them,' Nightingale said. 'They will throw me aside but they won't do the same for you. You have to find Jane.'

'Captain.'

But Nightingale was already walking away. He hurried back down the track which led to the town, the scent of the sea cutting like a knife through the hot noon. Before he knew it, he had reached the harbour and there was the *Scylla*. He looked away, turned sharply through the streets, and retreated to the safety of a darkened alleyway.

There, as he wobbled on the edge of his composure, he realised how far he had fallen. He had been terrified of returning to the sea, terrified of making the same mistakes. He had failed himself, had failed Louisa, had failed Leroy and his family. He had been so close to righting the wrongs of the *Lion*.

Now, it was all cruelly out of reach.

–

Later that morning, the staff officer from the governor's house found him as he meandered in a purgatory. He had the kindness to look apologetic as he directed Nightingale to the inn which Sir William had paid for him to stay in whilst decisions were made. Nightingale did not want to go, but he had no choice.

For hours, he sat in the common room of the inn, only moving when his sea-chest and effects were brought from the *Scylla* by a morose Rylance. The rest of the time he watched people drink and eat and gamble. Every opening of the door brought in fresh miasmas of fish and tar and sun-baked wood. Voices in a mix of languages shouted from the kitchen and a poor young girl would hurry out to meet the latest patron. Mugs clinked and wobbled in her hand, plates of food clattered onto tables, wooden chair legs scraped over the stone floor.

Nightingale was intensely aware of everything – each scent clogged his throat; each sound tapped an irritating cadence along his spine; each taste burnt his tongue.

He was grateful that no one joined him. He hid himself in the corner, alone at a small table and away from the window where he might be tempted to gaze at the *Scylla*. A bottle of untouched rum stood before him. If he reached the bottom of the drink or not, it would not sway the fermenting decisions in the governor's house. He swore to meet whatever verdict with dignity. They could take the command away from him, but he would not wilt and crumble.

Would he?

Yet, when he heard that voice again, everything he had tried to ignore during these last hours crashed over him.

'Hiram,' his father said. 'Here you are.'

Nightingale raised his head and realised that darkness had fallen outside. His father and Sir William stood beside the table. Neither of them betrayed anything on their faces. They only looked down at him in silent judgement. 'I am not having this conversation here,' Nightingale said, standing.

'Very well.'

There was no denial that a conversation was to be had.

They followed him quietly up the narrow stairwell to his room. It was a simple arrangement: a small living space with an adjoined bedchamber. With the door shut and his back to it, he felt confined, but he did not want to move another step towards the men. 'You are here to tell me that a decision has been made,' he said steadily.

Sir William inclined his head, a mockery of politeness after they had thrown him to the lions.

'Did you truly think you would retain your command after your childish outburst?' Admiral Nightingale asked.

There it was. Nightingale had expected it. But to hear it aloud wrenched the last fickle hope away; the deck collapsed in rotten, worm-eaten splinters beneath his feet. He looked away, curled his hands into fists as emotion coursed through him, then crossed his arms tightly over his fluttering chest.

He was not sure what he was going to say, but he did not expect to spit, 'Why are you here?' at his father.

'I am here, Hiram,' Admiral Nightingale replied, 'to ensure that you do not embarrass yourself further, or fall into trouble.'

Sir William glanced at the taller man, his lips in a thin, stern line. 'You have been through a tough patch, Hiram. This is no condemnation of your skills as a captain, but—'

'It is,' Nightingale snapped. 'Please be honest with me.'

'I am being honest with you. It is true that we were not honest before about the gold and the original orders of the *Ulysses*. Perhaps, as Lord Fairholme says, we were wrong to withhold that information. Now I say that perhaps I was wrong to suggest this voyage for you entirely. I recommended you for the Trinidad post as I intended to travel out here and join Governor Picton. You would have performed well, but then the *Ulysses* incident occurred… I thought that would be beneficial for you also. I was mistaken.'

'And now you deny me the command before I embarrass you and Admiral Nightingale any further. The blame shall fall on me, and not you.'

'This is not a matter of blame, Hiram—'

Nightingale laughed, hearing how strangled and helpless it sounded as soon as it left his mouth. 'Of course it is. Someone must always be blamed. I am a simple target.' He shook his head. 'You cannot take this command from me – not without a formal and orderly court martial. My orders are from Admiral Seymour at the Leeward Islands Station. They are addressed to me, and the *Scylla* is my vessel.'

'Once the *Ulysses* is brought to justice, a full and formal court martial shall be held,' Sir William said. 'Until then, it is wisest to allow Captain Harrison to command the *Scylla*. The position shall be offered to him tonight and the ship shall sail the instant repairs are complete.'

'And I am supposed to simply watch her sail away? The command you recommended me for? The command I have obeyed my orders to the letter in?'

'Sacrifice is always necessary in the service,' Admiral Nightingale said dismissively. 'This is about more than your position, Hiram.'

Hot swirls of anger constricted Nightingale's throat. He tried to think of an escape – a letter he could write, a contact he could unleash all his accusations at – but the extent of his influence stood in this room: Sir William and Admiral Nightingale, two men who had never seen eye to eye but now were united in their schemes against him. Whatever he said or penned, they could counteract and countermand ten times over.

'You must understand our position,' Sir William insisted. 'I fear for you, Hiram. I fear for Louisa. I do not wish for her to be a widow if you… unduly endanger yourself.'

'You married me to her.'

'To help you.' His father spoke again. 'What would have been said about you without her, Hiram?'

'I love her.'

'As do I,' Sir William pressed, voice tight and genuinely impassioned. 'That is why I wish for her to remain unharmed by your actions or any talk about you. Return to England, recover, then address your options.'

'I was trying to recover!' Nightingale did not intend to shout but now his voice had raised a pitch, he could not quieten it. 'I was wounded! I nearly lost my ship! I lost my crew! I lost...'

Leroy's name would not come to his lips. It felt like sacrilege to speak about him in front of his father and Sir William. Only once – *only once* – had he spoken about him to Louisa.

The fight sapped from Nightingale at his memory, as if the gun had blown and the powder leaked out, useless. He looked away, stricken with that old guilt and grief. He had fantasised that the *Scylla* could patch over those tears, could give him something to feel proud of again.

'Precisely,' Admiral Nightingale said darkly. He sounded as if he was right at his ear. 'You lost too much. Sir William is correct about one aspect: we believed this voyage could benefit you. But he is wrong about another: it *is* your fault that you no longer have command. Not Sir William's, and not mine. You cannot release the past.'

'Why do you think that is?' Nightingale snarled. 'I have it etched on my back.'

Sir William frowned. *Oh*, Nightingale thought, *that is one thing my father hasn't mentioned*. The cold fury that crossed Admiral Nightingale's face dredged up a surge of spite.

'They were a mercy,' his father said, regardless of Sir William. 'I saved you from a far worse fate. By dealing out the punishment myself, it meant our name was untarnished.'

'And how is our name now, Father?'

He did not reply.

'I want you to leave,' Nightingale breathed, opening the door. 'You have said your piece. I do not want to see you until this is over.'

Sir William opened his mouth to speak then quickly shut it. He nodded, donned his hat, and walked to the door.

'I'm sorry, Hiram,' he whispered, and no more.

Admiral Nightingale towered over him as he brushed past. In the confines of the door, he stopped, and hissed, 'You should be careful, Hiram. Everyone shall know about you.'

'Get out,' he spat.

He did not intend to watch them disappear down the long corridor. He wanted to close the door on this awful day and force his thoughts and emotions back into place.

But another figure moved – and there in the middle of the hall was Lieutenant Courtney. Sir William raised his hat politely. Admiral Nightingale gave a glare which should have unmanned him. 'I am here to see my captain,' Courtney said without a quiver.

'He may not be your captain much longer, lad.'

'Until I hear differently, he will remain so.'

Nightingale allowed Courtney inside. He still wore his best uniform, although it was slightly rumpled and had drops of tar down the right sleeve.

'I apologise, sir, I went from the governor's house to the ship and then here as soon as Master Loom returned. He was the last one questioned.'

'I don't give a damn about the uniform, Lieutenant.'

Nightingale reached the seat just before his knees buckled. He leant against the table and rested his head in his hand. He was going to weep, he knew it – it was only a matter of when.

Courtney's footsteps approached then stopped as he sank into the opposite chair. 'I was honest with them, as you said, sir,' he said. 'I told them how there was nothing more we could have done.'

'The decision has already been made, Arthur. The *Scylla* shall be offered to Captain Harrison.'

Courtney took a moment to digest that. His mouth curled as if it tasted foul. 'I hate this meddling. The *Fénix* was not officially condemned by the court. How can anyone be blamed for a bloody lightning strike?'

Nightingale's heart swelled at Courtney's genuine anger. 'It is not only the *Fénix*,' he admitted, grief pushing away his defences like water overflowing a dam. 'There are other reasons.'

'Then what other reasons are there? I don't understand any of this.'

Courtney had been honest with him – he had admitted about Jane, about the girl from Gibraltar, about his terrible father. Nightingale's honesty only came from despair; he had always seen it as something to be ashamed of.

'I nearly lost the *Lion* at the Nile,' he said slowly, still not looking at Courtney. 'I lost so many of my crew. I lost... I lost people I cared for.'

'I thought that you had a medal from the Nile.'

'I do. Hateful thing.' It felt bitterly satisfying to say it aloud. 'I told you that Sir William and my father suggested me for the *Scylla*'s command. They thought it would help me, after the Nile, but they truly only care about their own names. I thought that – if we saved the crew on the *Ulysses*, it would – I could alleviate what happened to Leroy.'

'Who is Leroy?'

'My, ah, my first lieutenant from the *Lion*. We knew each other as mids. He died. At the Nile. I had a medal made for him.' The tears filled his eyes, threatening to fall. Nightingale heard the shake in his voice. 'I went to his family, I apologised to them, I promised that I would help them. I only – I didn't know how to. He was my – he was my friend. He told me that he would never serve under another man. He was right. I failed him and his family.'

'Captain.'

Nightingale was sharing too much, but he no longer cared. He was going to lose his command and his chance at redemption. He was not sure he could face this again, not even if future ships would take him. This was his end, spelt out for him – at the hands of his father, once more.

'Captain.'

This time, Nightingale looked up. Courtney leant on the table, brave enough not to look embarrassed by Nightingale's childish behaviour.

'What did your father mean when he said that everyone shall know about you?'

Such a question should not come from a junior officer. He should have made Courtney leave. Both of them were already overstepping. Yet now, Nightingale desperately wanted someone on his side, desperately wanted a friend.

'My father…' Nightingale began, and it did not feel real to say it aloud to someone who was not Louisa, '…had me flogged when I was eighteen.'

Courtney paled. He frowned, opened his mouth, closed it, swallowed.

'What?!' he said. 'What reason could there be for a midshipman to be flogged? By his – by his own father?'

A tear finally escaped, wetting Nightingale's cheek. He tasted salt as more fell.

'The other man was hanged for the same offence,' he said brokenly.

It had been his father who had found him and Tom. Tom, the stable-boy who had promised that nothing terrible would happen, leaning in to brush his mouth over Nightingale's cheek, down to his lips. Nightingale had wanted so ardently to believe him, wanted so ardently to be honest with himself and happy.

It had all ended when Tom's neck snapped in the noose.

His father desired to keep the knowledge within the family. He said it was a mercy, that he had saved his son from the same fate – and that if anyone knew, the entire family would collapse. It had been more than twenty years ago. But Nightingale had never once gone a day without thinking of it. And to stand on deck, giving the very same orders his father had ruined his life with, brought it to the fore again.

He did not dare look at Courtney. He could not raise his head from his hands where he cried in shame and despair. Perhaps it had been his fault. There were only two people he had ever been drawn to before now – and both had died as he watched.

Long, awful silence stretched. Nightingale could feel the cogs of his life turning, leading up to this moment. How had he thought anything would be different? Eventually, all the defences he had built would crumble and he would be left upon the bare hill, not a barrier or lie to protect him.

'Captain,' Courtney voiced, and it was pathetic to hear the title addressed to him. 'I am sorry.'

Nightingale shook his head. 'You can tell them all; I don't give a damn anymore. I shall lose this command, as I lost the *Lion*. There is little more they can do to me, or I to myself.'

'Sir, I don't—' Courtney sighed. 'I shall not breathe a word. You did not tell them about Jane.'

'You are a good man, Arthur. Too good.' Nightingale looked up, the tears blurring his vision, sticking to his lashes. He tried to wipe the dampness from his cheeks. Courtney handed over his handkerchief. 'I should apologise. I spoke some harsh words to you before. You are not an arrogant young man. I misjudged you.'

'No. I should apologise, sir. I overstepped. I needed to hear the things you said to me.'

Nightingale admired Courtney for his tenacity. He felt wretched to sit there, weeping in front his lieutenant. He consoled himself in how Courtney could complete the voyage for both of them, and perhaps rise up the ladder that he had been pushed down so often. Other men had to overhaul Nightingale, as it had always been in the service. He had taken Courtney's role when he had gained the *Scylla*, and now the watch changed to another man.

Courtney left him later, laying a gentle hand on his shoulder. They had sat in horrid silence for what felt like hours.

He gained fragments of sleep. He laid his head on the pillow, faded into dreamless shadows, then rose to pace around the small room. The *Scylla*'s masts split the sky outside the window. She was unchanged, uncaring about how she had a new captain. It would be the same with the *Lion*, leagues away on the Mediterranean station. Two vessels... two assemblages of wood and canvas that he had poured too much hope into, attached too much meaning to.

In the painful, early hours, Nightingale searched through his seachest and pulled out the box at the bottom of it. He held his breath, looked once more at the medal, then snapped it closed.

Alone, he walked along the harbour under the shadows of the ships. No one looked his way, no one questioned him. On a spit reaching out into deeper water, he paused. The waves rolled before him, beyond the island, shrouded with a thin layer of mist.

He grasped the box firmly in his hand.

And then threw it as far as he could out into the sea.

Chapter Eighteen: Patroclus

23 February 1800, Portsmouth, England

The journey to the Sawyers's house always passed in the blink of an eye. Nightingale would sit, his head full of what he had practised to say, and soon, it would be time to speak it aloud. The journey home, however, lasted an age. In the carriage, he suffered in the aftermath of the encounter, wondering if he'd said the right things, stewing in the possible repercussions.

Now, for the first time, he thought he had chosen the correct path.

In truth, he knew the Sawyers had no part in his decision. This was a weight that should have been solely upon his shoulders. But his father and Sir William had ensured it was not that way. In the months since they had proposed a command to him, their hands had constantly steered his thoughts. He had spent his entire life obeying orders, but this was different – he could not even see the helm.

But, before he disappeared into the mist, he had one chance to lay his fingers upon the course.

Josephine and Edward Sawyer frowned at him when he told them what he would do. How did a position in Trinidad relate to their son? Nightingale tried to explain, though the reason was selfish and fringed with feelings he could not articulate. The hope of escape and redemption was something he kept trying to grasp, only for it to fall through his fingers like sand.

They swore they did not blame him for Leroy's death. Nightingale did not need to hear that. He only needed to feel it inside of himself.

After what felt like hours sitting in the carriage confines, Haywood Hall and its gardens opened up before him. He made the familiar journey up the path where the fountain was now complete and the lawns were being tended with the allotments in full plenty. It had been a year and a half since his return from the Nile, and he had watched the house expand under Louisa's care. A pane of glass always separated him from it. This was his home, but until this past stretch of months, he had only spent brief periods here – a few weeks at most before he sailed, abandoning it again for a ship.

Curious lightness danced in his chest as he entered and climbed the stairs to his rooms. Perhaps it was a sense of finally letting go, of returning to a world he knew at sea. Or perhaps it was a feeling of being able to do no more. His path was before him and there was nothing else but to travel it.

The door to his study was slightly ajar. He glanced at the model of the *Lion*, still in its place, the glass shining in the evening light. A letter he had been composing was open on his desk. He had tucked it away before leaving that morning.

He walked through into his bedroom. Louisa perched on the end of his bed, wearing a simple azure day gown, her black hair unbound, and with another note on her lap. She did not even flinch at Nightingale finding her there. Long had it been since she had come to his bedroom.

'It is official then,' she said carefully. 'You are to leave for Trinidad.'

Nightingale removed his coat and hat. 'We have discussed it,' he replied without emotion. 'You knew that I was to leave.'

'Yes.' Louisa gently set aside the note. Nightingale wanted to see what it was but he didn't wish to look suspicious. 'I only want to know that you are doing it for the right reasons.'

'What are the "right reasons"?'

'You tell me, Hiram.'

He tried to decipher if she sounded angry or not. She was calm, unsmiling, and, as always, maintaining a careful façade. 'I am acting as our fathers suggested,' he offered. 'They believe it is best if I... return to my feet. I can see their reasoning.'

'Can you?'

'Yes.' Nightingale sighed. He had not moved from the door, but stood against it, arms crossed. He realised it looked too defensive so put his hands behind his back, squeezing them out of sight. 'You suggested yourself that I should keep my connections to the service. It will have been two years this August since I stepped upon a deck.'

'Our fathers and I have suggested similar things, yes. But do you wish to return?'

Yes. That was the obvious answer. But perhaps it was yes with a caveat. His reasons were not the same as his father's or Sir William's. 'I do.'

'Tell me why. I know it is not for reputation or fortune. And you have been recovering here. I can see an improvement in you and—'

'I need to.'

Louisa opened her mouth to respond, then seemed to decide better. She looked at the note, picked it up and handed it to Nightingale. He tried not to take it too hastily. It was the letter he had composed to Alexander Davison about Leroy's Nile medal.

'I thought you knew that I asked for this,' Nightingale said, his voice as light as he could make it.

'You have just returned from the Sawyers's house.'

'Yes. They are my friends.'

'Am I not your friend?'

'My dear, you are my wife.' He looked back up at her. In the time it had taken for him to glance at the letter, her eyes had filled with tears. One fell down her cheek and dropped upon her skirt. He went cold with surprise, and all he managed was, 'Why do you weep?'

Louisa licked her lips, biting at the bottom one as she tried to stop it wobbling. 'My father,' she began. 'When I was a young girl, he did not like me reading. He did not think it was right for my sex. But I was as stubborn as a mule even from a small age. I changed his mind – he knew he could not stop me anyhow. I read anything I could lay my hands on. Shakespeare, Spenser, Defoe, I even learnt as much French as I could to handle Voltaire. My favourite was Homer.'

Nightingale could feel an icy draft winding over him, slowly growing. He stayed as still as he could, as if any movement would fracture the glassy tension between them.

'I found the *Iliad* again the other week,' Louisa continued. 'The wars of Troy, the sacrifice of Iphigenia, the death of Patroclus and

Achilles' vengeance over his dead lover. It has never made me weep before.'

Nightingale stayed silent. He could feel the thundering of his heart. The nausea churning in his gut. The shaking of his knees.

Louisa looked up at him, eyes swimming with tears. 'Did you love him?' she asked.

He could play ignorant and question who she was talking about. He could deny it all and keep this part of himself locked up as it had always been. He could act indignant, even angry.

But he only nodded, and whispered, 'I did.'

Louisa breathed out, as if a weight had suddenly lifted from her chest. Her shoulders sank and she wiped the remnants of the tears from her face with shaking hands.

'I do love you,' Nightingale insisted. 'I did not at the start, but I – I have come to admire you and respect you and... yes, love you.'

'But not as you loved him.'

Nightingale swallowed past a tightening throat. He felt his knees buckle and had no choice but to slump down on the edge of the bed. The world felt hazy and dreamlike – distant and yet so close. So, so close.

'I'm sorry,' he whispered.

'No,' Louisa said forcefully. 'No, don't say that. I am not sorry, and neither should you be. I believe that this arrangement has suited us both. If I were married to a man who forced children upon me, who wished for affection and intimacy, I would lose my mind. I wish for none of that, so I have never asked you for it. You have allowed me to be as I am, and I have – I *will* – allow you to be as you are. We were married to fulfil expectations. I think that we have always known that neither one of us fulfils any expectations on the inside.'

Nightingale shook his head. 'No,' he managed.

'I knew it,' Louisa breathed. 'I knew it when I saw the scars on your back and you told me who commanded the lash. I wondered why, what Article you must have broken. Why they should flog a midshipman... Perhaps I always knew.'

They sat in silence for a long while – a warm, honest silence with nothing more that needed to be said. Nightingale trusted her not to tell, as much as she trusted him not to force anything upon her that she did not want. This had always been their way – a way that broke with tradition and acceptance, but had always settled into place: something that Sir William and Admiral Nightingale could never have schemed for when they paired them.

It was comforting to know that within the confines of their orders, there was still some freedom to move. It was what he intended to do in Trinidad.

Eventually, Louisa shifted. Darkness had fallen outside. Nightingale had his head against her bare shoulder and she gently guided it away. She tucked the note into his fist and closed her hand around his.

'Go and avenge your Patroclus,' she said. 'I shall not ever stand in your way.'

Chapter Nineteen: Ship of Theseus

14 July 1800, Port of Spain, Trinidad

The inn had a small walled courtyard at its rear. A single orange tree grew in the corner and its ripe fruit hung within picking distance. Sheltering from the blazing sun, Nightingale plucked a fruit off a branch and carefully cut it open. The young serving girl had offered him tea but it was already too warm for that. He sipped at his water and nibbled at the soft flesh of the orange.

Once again, he tried to imagine himself living in this town. He disliked the climate and the heat. He could barely sleep or concentrate with the chattering noise from the harbour. And that was without mentioning the slave industries that touched everything on the island.

He wondered if Louisa would like the island any more than he did. Sir William had said she would be willing to move her lot out here, but Nightingale could not see it. He pictured himself living alone, aiding Sir William, becoming a politician like he was, perhaps.

The images existed for seconds before fluttering away. Sir William and the administration did not wish for his presence. After Captain Harrison dealt with the *Ulysses*, the man would return to his post and the *Scylla* would be without a commander again. Nightingale doubted he would be offered the position. The only fragment of hope was that Courtney might receive his promotion.

Nightingale supposed England was the only place for him now.

An hour might have passed, perhaps less, when a footfall on the stone path disturbed him. He opened his eyes and came face to face with Lord Fairholme, dressed in dark velvet gaudiness and leather riding boots. Wisps of curled red ringlets bounced as he swept off his cocked hat. Nightingale took a moment to recover from the shock, but he did not have long to regain his composure when a figure moved behind Lord Fairholme and Captain Harrison also entered the courtyard.

A bitter, cruel idea rose in Nightingale to dismiss Harrison and leave the inn without a word. He would like to see the look on Lord Fairholme's face.

Instead, he rose to his feet and smoothed down his waistcoat. In civilian dress, he felt shabby compared to Captain Harrison's naval finery.

'Lord Fairholme. Captain Harrison,' he said, words coming by rote. 'Congratulations on attaining command of the *Scylla*. She is a fine ship and she has a fine crew. I know you shall do well.'

Harrison smiled thinly.

'Perhaps we should sit,' Lord Fairholme suggested.

Fairholme stretched out his legs as they sat at the small table, and clicked his fingers to get the maid's attention. She brought more water which he sipped with a sigh. 'Ah, I barely slept a wink last night,' he announced airily. 'I was up at all hours with your father and Sir William. I really don't know how they are working together, almost amiably.'

'Well.' Nightingale chewed the inside of his mouth, then decided it looked petulant. 'I have seen them in a new light these past few days.'

'I think we all have.' Fairholme smiled. 'This has been such a tiresome business. I understand that the *Scylla* had to come into harbour for repairs, but your father and Sir William have stretched it out like some Drury Lane drama.'

Nightingale frowned. 'I thought the panel agreed that something had to be done about the *Fénix*.'

'Yes, but not to this melodramatic extent. As soon as your father stuck his oar in the water, the whole thing became like the bloody whirlpool of Charybdis. Even I did not know he was going to appear.'

'He thinks he has his reasons.'

'Certainly he does. Everyone here has their reasons for acting as they do. My role is to ensure that none of them affect the bigger picture.'

'And that is?'

'The *Ulysses* and her cargo, of course.' Fairholme sighed and brought out a fan from the inside of his embroidered coat. 'Christ, this heat will kill me. I never wished to come out here. My place is from afar – chilled lemon juice and paperwork whilst others boil in the sun. But as I'm here, I have to do what is best.'

'This is more important than a captain's jostling for position,' Nightingale said carefully. 'I am certain that Captain Harrison will do what you require.'

Harrison glanced at Fairholme. He set down his glass, which he had not drunk from, only cradled awkwardly in his hands.

'Hiram,' Harrison said. 'I refused the command.'

The world shifted. For a moment, all the heat dropped before returning in a rush down Nightingale's spine. He thought of the hours he had spent stewing in his ire and anxiety. He thought of the insults his father had given him. He thought of the debacle of the sham court martial.

'What?' he managed.

'I want no part of it,' Harrison said slowly. 'My place is here in Trinidad. Jennifer took months of convincing to come out here – she would slaughter me if I left her so early in the position. And I...' Harrison cleared his throat. 'I was with you when you visited your young Richmond. They are your men, and for the voyage ahead, you shall need all the loyalty and cohesion. I do not have that with them.'

Nightingale stared between them as if they played some cruel joke on him. Anger flared, stoked by his bewilderment. Not twenty-four hours ago, he had been ripped from the *Scylla*'s helm. Sir William and his father had implied he was sick in his mind. And now Lord Fairholme dismissed all of that as easily as he waved his fan.

'Sentimentality is not the only reason here, Hiram,' Fairholme continued. 'You also have a very persuasive first lieutenant.'

'Lieutenant Courtney?' Nightingale croaked.

'He arrived at the same time as Captain Harrison last night – uninvited, I might add. He revealed information that had slipped by me. Apparently, he has a sister onboard the *Ulysses*. He claimed that he could negotiate with her when the *Ulysses* is found. He made a good case for being an invaluable asset onboard the *Scylla*.'

Courtney had been terrified of anyone discovering about Jane. Nightingale had promised not to reveal that information – and so he hadn't. For Courtney to suddenly do so now was a bold and perilous step. But he failed to see how that could retain him his command.

Fairholme smiled, reading his expressions. 'He is remarkably loyal, Hiram. He refused to serve under any other commander. You must be doing something correctly, as Captain Harrison implies.'

Leroy had said the same thing, years ago – and Nightingale had told Courtney so. He had torn himself apart at the terror of being so honest with Courtney. That uncertainty blended with his regret at thinking so badly of Courtney throughout the first leg of their voyage. All he could conjure to say was, 'What does this mean?'

'It means that your orders are unchanged,' Fairholme confirmed. 'You shall retain command of the *Scylla* and search out the *Ulysses*. You shall recover the gold and bring her to port for justice.'

'I should be congratulating you, Hiram, not you congratulating me,' Harrison remarked.

'There is nothing to congratulate,' Fairholme snapped tartly. 'For now, this debate has not occurred. But when you return, you shall still face questioning, Hiram. And, needless to say, Admiral Nightingale is not pleased about this change.'

The decisions had finally been wrenched from Admiral Nightingale's hands. But were they in his own? Nightingale cleared his throat. 'I understand.'

'Now, Captain Harrison,' Fairholme said. 'Return to your post. There is work to be done by all of us.'

Harrison left with a bow. Nightingale felt guilty for disliking him – they were both two men pulled around by others, small threads in a constantly changing tapestry. Nightingale knew he should feel relieved that he was now back where he wished, but he could not. He watched Harrison go, mind reeling, then turned to Fairholme when the lord laid an elegant hand on his sleeve.

'You must understand, Hiram,' Fairholme said. 'Though your lieutenant and Captain Harrison were helpful in bolstering my suggestions, the final decision rested with me.'

'Why?' he asked, voice barely disguising his frustration. 'Why put me through this? If you were going to speak up, why allow my father and Sir William to humiliate me? To make me think I had lost command… I *did* lose command.'

Fairholme squeezed his arm. 'You should be grateful, Hiram. I did not know that it would rise to this extent. I was as astonished as you were to hear Captain Harrison would be offered command.'

'My father shall try to defame you.'

To Nightingale's surprise, Fairholme laughed. 'He has tried already. I have spent an entire night and morning being called a meddling molly. But there is very little he can do. One rock he throws at me and I can bring down an avalanche. And Sir William would not dare.' Fairholme smiled. 'I should like to talk with you when this is all over, Hiram. I believe we can come to some arrangement over what I have helped you with.'

Nightingale knew that he was indebted to Fairholme. He had been indebted to him as soon as he had told him about the gold on the *Ulysses*. That had been a little line he had thrown into the pond, bait masquerading as helpful feed. Nightingale did not respond. He didn't need to.

'The *Ulysses* has been seen again,' Fairholme continued casually. 'I hear that she was off Salvador on the tenth. I would suggest you make port along the Brazilian coast and do some probing. Your Lieutenant Hargreaves speaks fluent Portuguese. I have already spoken to him and mentioned how his talents might be useful.'

'You spoke to him? Did you tell him that I had lost command, or perhaps told him I had regained it before even I knew?'

Fairholme smiled. He did not reply, only rose and brushed down his elegant coat. 'I was very impressed by your lieutenant, by the way. Not Lieutenant Hargreaves, although with polishing, the man might mature. Lieutenant Courtney. He spoke well – certainly in front of men such as your father and Sir William. I cannot decide if it was courageous or stupid.'

'He is very capable,' Nightingale said stiffly.

'I am sure. Just as your wife, dear Lou, is. But I am certain I can guess whose company you would rather enjoy.'

Nightingale's throat tightened. He had half-assumed such a thing of Fairholme but had thought it too scandalous to even be spoken aloud. He opened his mouth inanely, closed it when not even a denial would come to his lips.

'Do not look so shocked, Hiram. I am not scandalised by such a preference. I have known for a long while. When Louisa spoke of the Nile and your injuries, she declined to mention one detail: the loss of Lieutenant Leroy Sawyer, whom you served with for years. Such an omission spoke volumes. I always wondered what kind of husband Louisa Haywood, the chaste and untouchable, would take.'

'Do not,' Nightingale rasped, 'speak about my wife that way.'

Fairholme laughed again. 'I hope you do not think so lowly of me to assume that I will tell. But I am eager to speak to you about what a man who hides such secrets could do for me. Now, though, I do not wish to keep you from your orders. Farewell and *adieu*, until we meet again.'

As quickly as he had approached, Fairholme left. Nightingale watched him, sauntering away leisurely as if he had the world in his hand, bowing politely to the young serving girl. Nightingale knew that he could not trust him. And he also knew that he had moved from the grip of his father straight into the fist of a man far more powerful.

But, whatever occurred, that same powerful man had set him back aboard the *Scylla*.

And, at last, despite everything, she was waiting.

–

The repairs finished in the early afternoon. The last timber was set into place, the final inch of water pumped from the bilge, the remaining holes stitched up in the canvas. Nightingale raised his spyglass to his eye as he was rowed across the harbour. The *Scylla* had not been re-patched enough to call her a new beast, but she still looked virginal in the noon sun. Fresh licks of paint decorated her hull, and even the fearsome female figurehead had been garnished with colour, her writhing tail a vivid blue, her spear gleaming gold.

She was ready. And with his back to Trinidad, Nightingale knew he had to be too.

The bosun's pipe wailed as he approached the starboard side. His boatsmen, who had escorted him dressed in their finest uniform, laid down their oars and guided him forward. As he had done many times before, Nightingale climbed aboard.

The marines' arms clashed as they stood to attention. Nightingale's eyes drew to them, bright red coats and scrubbed white cross-belts, muskets at their sides. Then he looked around – at the entire ship's company who had turned out in their best. All hats were off, faces shaved and washed, clothing pressed and stitched. It was as it had been on his first day aboard. Not even a month had passed since then.

The officers stood to the side. Lieutenant Hargreaves nodded to him and then Nightingale's eyes shifted to Courtney. He wore the serious, placid expression of an officer showing off his ship and men, but a small smile pulled at his lips.

'Welcome aboard, sir,' Courtney said, holding his hat to his chest. 'All crew are accounted for, sir – present and sober.'

'Very good, Lieutenant. They look remarkable. But it might be best if they change into their working clothes. As soon as we have the tide, we shall bid farewell to Trinidad.'

'Of course, sir.'

Nightingale returned to the great cabin. It had only been a day or so since he had stood in it, but it seemed an age. He took a moment to look at the green-painted bulkheads, the wide, picturesque gallery windows, Captain Carlisle's watercolour of a harbour at night. Everything was the same.

'Sir?' A quiet knock soon came on the door. Lieutenant Courtney stood there, still in his best uniform.

'Come in, Arthur, if you please.'

'No, sir, I don't want to intrude. I only wished to say something quickly, if I may.'

'Of course.'

Courtney glanced down the deck behind him. 'The men don't know, sir. I had it spread through Kieran and the petty officers that you were called to the island for some administrative purpose, on account of knowing Sir William. None of them know that Captain Harrison was offered the captaincy.'

Nightingale smiled. 'Very good, Lieutenant. I appreciate that.'

'Some of them think you're related to the king now, sir. I'm not sure how that came about. A few of them see a "sir" and assume he's at court.'

Nightingale laughed. 'Thank you, Arthur,' he said, honestly, genuinely.

'For what, sir?'

'You know what. Thank you.'

Courtney lowered his head and nodded before leaving Nightingale to his thoughts.

For a while, Nightingale indulged himself and listened to the old world coming back to him: running feet, the shrill bosun's whistle, the bell for the change of watch. Except it wasn't the same old world that he knew. The parts were all identical, yet their spirit was different, a prism throwing off new light. He did not act for his father anymore, or Sir William, or even for the sake of British justice.

He acted for himself, and for the innocents still onboard the *Ulysses*.

One final odyssey.

Part II

Chapter Twenty: Odyssey

21 July 1800

'Whilst we were moored in Trinidad,' Captain Nightingale said, 'I received new intelligence. Eleven days ago, the *Ulysses* was seen off of Salvador.'

Nightingale picked up a paperweight and placed it upon the map of Brazil. His papers covered the great cabin's table, each one showing South America in greater detail. Fronds of lettering sprouted from the inked land, an intricate mass of ports and cities decorating the shoreline. Written in bold black, Salvador was nestled in the Bay of All Saints on the Brazilian east coast.

In the sepia void of the surrounding Atlantic Ocean, the paperweight representing the *Scylla* sat off Paramaribo – a distance of some one and a half thousand miles. He looked between the two, wishing it could be as easy as nudging the *Scylla* closer.

'The *Fénix* encountered the *Ulysses* off Grenada.' Another marker, north of their current position, was set down, separated by a gap of just over three weeks. 'Judging by her course – off Dominica where she mutinied, down to Grenada, and now here at Salvador – it is evident she is going south.'

That was a brazenly obvious point to make, but it was the only concrete evidence they had and Nightingale wished to make it clear. Across the table, Lieutenant Courtney's eyes scanned across the known positions then dropped further down the map. 'There are plenty of enemy ports,' he said, just as Nightingale started to say the same thing. 'Apologies.'

'No, please, Lieutenant. We are all working with the same handful of clues here.'

'There are plenty of enemy ports,' Courtney repeated now he had permission. 'But they have already passed Spanish Venezuela and French Guiana. Suriname is under British occupation and Brazil is Portuguese.'

Nightingale nodded. 'Before we left English Harbour, we were instructed to take on six months' worth of supplies – in case the *Ulysses* rounded the Horn.'

'Could she do that – a ship of mutineers?' Hargreaves looked up, fair eyebrows raised. Nightingale had felt discomfited around him since Fairholme had mentioned their conversation. He was unsure whether the lieutenant knew about Nightingale's almost-dismissal or not, and he did not want to raise the matter.

'Lieutenant Wainwright from the *Ulysses* said there was still a substantial crew left onboard. Many were not rated able but I don't think we should underestimate them. The *Ulysses* is still a fifth-rate frigate like the *Scylla* and, captained and crewed well, yes, she could reach the Horn. Captained and crewed well or… with desperation, at least.'

Nightingale stared at the paperweight representing the *Ulysses*, wondering, not for the first time, what was happening on the ship in that precise moment. Fear and desperation prompted men to do improbable things.

'However,' he continued, 'her orders when leaving Antigua were to patrol the Main with the *Peregrine*. It was never intended that she would leave the Caribbean. We can therefore assume that, if she were to round the Horn, she would need further supplies. Even with a reduced crew.'

'She may have stopped in Venezuela or French Guiana,' Courtney suggested.

'She mutinied off Dominica,' Nightingale said. 'If I were a mutineer, I would wish to remove myself as far as possible from the point of mutiny. I would not stop for supplies so close to the hunting ground.'

'The *Hermione* sailed to La Guaira after she mutinied. That was Venezuela.'

Once, Nightingale might have been irritated at Courtney's questions – just as he had been when he asked about the fate of the *Ulysses*, back outside the hospital in Antigua. But he had learnt to appreciate Courtney's way of speaking, even if others may not have.

'Indeed.' Nightingale nodded. 'Captain Ramirez mentioned the mutineers intended to gather supplies – and that was after he encountered the *Ulysses*. But we cannot truly know where. We simply have to assume she is going further and further south.'

'The Pacific is not for the faint of heart, sir.' Master Loom spoke up. He had been sitting back, listening, nodding sagely. 'They must be truly desperate if they wish to brave that ocean.'

Nightingale glanced to Courtney. In the cabin, only they knew about the *Ulysses*'s cargo. 'The *Ulysses* carries valuable assets,' Nightingale said, breaking that secrecy without a pang of regret. 'I believe that word spread through the crew about this and further spurred them to mutiny. The cruel treatment from the officers was the final nail in the coffin.'

'Valuable assets, sir?' Loom asked with a frown.

'She carried gold. Around two thousand guineas' worth.'

Nightingale expected a reaction. For long moments, there was only silence. Loom stared at him, then Courtney, then Hargreaves, who looked down at the inky paper, thin face paling.

'Good Lord,' Loom finally breathed.

'So, yes, I think that answers the question of whether they'd be willing to brave the Pacific. I don't think this is about courage, though. This is a ship of mostly pressed men, led by a disenchanted American. This is about taking back what they feel they are owed, or... sheer despair.'

Even on the static and neatly colour-washed charts, Cape Horn looked ferocious. Nightingale had rounded it twice – as a midshipman, then as a young lieutenant. He had no wish to repeat the experience of mammoth waves and biblically fierce winds.

'Brazil,' he continued, 'as Lieutenant Courtney says, is under Portuguese control. Portugal is being pulled to and fro like a ragdoll. France is putting pressure on Spain to sway her neighbour into abandoning her long-standing alliance with Britain. She is neutral for now – uneasy and troubled, but neutral. A mutineers' ship trying to enter their harbours would be a thorn in their side.'

'No one wants that ship,' Courtney said. 'The *Hermione* nearly caused a hundred diplomatic incidents.'

'Yet considering her last sighting was off the Brazilian coast, we should make contacts there. Lieutenant Hargreaves, I believe you speak Portuguese?'

'Yes, sir.' Hargreaves looked up, as if surprised to be addressed again. 'I was born in Portugal. My mother has family there.'

'Excellent. Our course shall be Salvador. If we hear nothing, then we make for Rio de Janeiro. These port cities shall have many eyes.'

Talk of intelligence and backstage knowledge faded into logistics. Nightingale tried to reduce the long voyage into a series of manageable legs, thinking of the practicalities in a very impractical venture. It was not the lengthiest course he had ever sailed – not by many miles – but it seemed one of the most impossible.

They were searching for a speck in a fathomless expanse of blue.

When Loom and Hargreaves had gone, Rylance cleared away the paperwork and the plates and cups. From his lips, Nightingale knew word would spread of the *Scylla*'s destination.

Courtney rose to go too but Nightingale held up a hand. 'Rylance, another tea for Lieutenant Courtney and me, if you please.'

'What do you think, Arthur?' Nightingale asked when the tea was steaming in his hands again. Rylance had made enough for him now to know precisely how much sugar to drop in. He sipped it and regretted that such a sour subject had to spoil the sweetness.

'Surely it doesn't matter what I think,' Courtney said.

Nightingale stayed silent, long enough for Courtney to sigh, as if he were a student prompted by a schoolmaster.

'The *Ulysses* has a few weeks on us, at least,' Courtney conceded. 'She could be anywhere along the Brazilian coastline – anywhere along the entire South American coastline.'

'I know. But we were tasked with finding her – and I will chase her around the Horn if it comes to it.'

Courtney nodded. 'Yes. It is only… The closer we get, the more I think about Jane. And what I might have to see if – when – we find the *Ulysses*. We've already lost men, and with David in the hospital still…'

Nightingale had regretted leaving Richmond, but he had ensured he had the best doctor whom Archer recommended. The last time he had seen Richmond, he had been sitting up in a wheeled carriage, colour slowly returning to his cheeks.

'When we find the *Ulysses*,' Nightingale repeated. 'I wish to keep as many men alive as I can. They will be arrested and delivered back to the courts. But yes, there will be bloodshed. I do not have to tell you that, as an officer in the King's Navy.'

'Of course.'

'It is possible that we shall take the *Ulysses* at sea. It is also possible that we shall take her in a harbour and have to cut her out. Like the *Hermione*, her colours may have changed. Whatever eventuality arises, I want the men to be prepared. Starting from now, we shall stage mock-boardings over each side of the *Scylla*. I want small-arms practice in the mornings along with our usual gunnery. And it may be worth throwing a sail overboard, when it is calm, to allow the men to practise their swimming. There is no use in a man drowning before we even reach the *Ulysses*.'

'Yes, sir.'

'If the *Ulysses* does not strike her colours to us, you and I shall lead the boarding party. Once she is ours, I shall entrust her to you. You shall command the prize crew.'

Courtney's eyes sparkled. 'Thank you, sir.'

'You have more than earned it. And, if you conduct yourself well, then I shall finish that letter of recommendation that Captain Carlisle began. Perhaps we began on an unstable footing, but I believe that you are a very capable officer – certainly after what you came from.'

Redness spread over Courtney's fine cheeks. He lowered his head in a polite bow. 'Thank you, sir.'

'You do not need to thank me. That will be all, Arthur, thank you.'

Courtney rose and was nearly at the door when he suddenly paused, as if deciding upon something. He turned back, hand upon the latch. 'Sir, if I may?'

'Go ahead, Arthur.'

'I truly meant what I said when I walked into the governor's house and spoke to your father and Sir William and Governor Picton. It was not simply pig-headedness or brashness. I did not wish to serve under another commander. Perhaps that is vain, but I know that we both have our reasons for wishing to find the *Ulysses*.'

Nightingale nodded. Courtney stayed for a moment longer, seemingly working up to say more – then with a soft, 'Good afternoon, sir,' he vanished back up the companion-way. Nightingale's smile lingered.

He had thought Courtney was the antithesis of Leroy. They were not outwardly similar, and they pursued their ambitions in different ways, but they had the same determination and loyalty. Perhaps Nightingale could help Courtney as he'd been unable to help Leroy.

For now, the waves rolled past the *Scylla*. He contented himself with thinking that each one brought them closer to their target. Soon, a new horizon would break – and perhaps the *Ulysses* would emerge, returning to the world.

Chapter Twenty-One: The Midnight Bell

25 July 1800

Nightingale had hoped for stars but in the blackness, he was glad for the challenge. Clouds veiled the crescent moon and blotted the lights of the heavens. He looked to his side and could barely see Kieran Attrill, a foot away from him. The man was shrouded in dark clothing, fair pigtail tucked up inside his blackened sennit hat; not a scrap of light material could be made out. It was only when he sensed Nightingale's eyes on him that he turned and there was a flash of his pale face. Nightingale put a finger to his own lips.

The muffled, soft kiss of the oars rippled through the waters, driving the crew further into the darkness. Nightingale, with his hand on the tiller, hardly wanted to breathe and disturb their concentration. Everything had conformed to his scheme so far. He had planned it meticulously, but he was not a fool; weather and error and nature could never be truly accounted for. Three boats moved on this, the starboard side, and three boats, under Courtney, to larboard. The oars of the leftmost launch grew quieter as it pulled around to the ship's stern. Soon, the boat to his right would divert further towards the bows whilst his own aimed for the waist.

Nightingale felt instinctively for the flintlock in his belt and the cutlass strapped to his side. To his surprise, his palm came away wet with perspiration. He wiped it on his cloak.

The vessel's shadow rose high above the black waters. For a moment, a sliver of moonlight scythed downward and caressed her topmasts. Without her sails set, she looked eerily desolate, but looks could deceive; she still had fire in her belly without her canvas. As if to prove him right, the lunar illumination glinted off a waiting carronade. Chills ran down Nightingale's spine: the awe which never went away, even after twenty-eight years at sea.

Rylance, near the boat's waist, mistimed a stroke and the oar sounded deafening. 'Easy,' Nightingale whispered to a hissed, 'Sorry, Captain.'

The ship's starboard battery roared into life. A flash, blindingly bright in the darkness, and a searing whistle split the silence. In the light, Nightingale saw his division duck. The water splashed fifty or so yards behind him, swiftly followed by another scream as the next cannon fired. Closer. In the barrage, ten pairs of terrified eyes turned back to him.

'What are you looking at me for?' he shouted, no need for quietness now. 'Pull!'

The red coats of the marines shone as they hurried to the ship's waist. Nightingale's boatmen gripped their oars and doubled their urgency, straining with each stroke. The pop of muskets echoed above their heads. Nightingale stared at the looming gunwales, alight with bursting fireworks. He tried to see – tried to hear – if the larboard side faced the same display but could not decipher anything in the flashing lights.

To the stern, the leftmost boat thumped against the hull.

Smythe shouted, 'Up, men! Climb, climb! To your positions!'

Within seconds, Nightingale's launch nudged the ship just under the ladder and in the coruscating confusion, he found his way to the bow and groped for the first slat. The little boat rocked as oars were downed and the tether lashed to the ship whilst men grabbed their weapons, pistols and dirks glinting. A night breeze wound beneath Nightingale's clothes, but he still sweated.

'For the *Scylla*! For the *Scylla*!' he cried, and began to climb.

The men roared as they followed. Some tailed him up the ladder, but others gripped on to curving timbers on the hull and clambered past the gun ports. The cannons had fallen silent, yet the muskets made Nightingale's ears ring. They aimed down at them now, next to pikes jabbing down the sides. To his right, Kieran grabbed hold of one and yanked it, dragging a yelling crewman over into the water.

Nightingale kept climbing. He knew his uniform made him a target so he had covered it with a cloak – but now it kept tangling around his feet. He took the risk and threw it into the boat below.

The *Scylla*'s name was being screamed by the division at the stern. The first of Nightingale's men vaulted the sides, raising their weapons like bludgeons. Nightingale stared up, gripped the final slats of the ladder and hauled himself over the rail.

A mass of crew greeted him, each one jostling to throw the boarders back into the sea. Pushing, shoving, strong bodies collided – every angle covered, barely able to tell who was friend and who foe. Across, Courtney's division leapt over the larboard side. Courtney raised his cutlass in the air, hair loose, looking like a pirate of old.

'Scyllas, with me!' Courtney shouted, and threw himself into the fray.

Weapons clattered. Men yelled. The whole ship raged and wailed.

Nightingale fumbled for his whistle. Two men gripped his arms, but he pushed them away and blew as hard as he could. The shrill bosun's call ripped above the din.

And like a wave rolling back, the fight stopped.

Nightingale caught his breath. Through the mess, Lieutenant Hargreaves emerged. His face was flushed and eyes sparkling: more animated than he had been in days. Nightingale grabbed him by the hand, unable to stop the smile reaching his mouth.

'That was a good show, Lieutenant,' Nightingale said. 'Exactly what I was aiming for. I think Mr Thomason took the men quite by surprise.'

Hargreaves nodded. Before the exercise, Nightingale had taken both him and Mr Thomason, the master gunner, aside and given them secret instructions. They were to open fire on both the starboard and larboard divisions, emptying cannons without cartridges and muskets without shot around the men. He had hoped the surprise would reflect the confusion awaiting them with the *Ulysses*. They could not, for all love, expect a clean approach to the ship, no matter where she was.

Behind him, a sopping wet marine clambered over the side. Kieran gave him a hand over the rail and muttered, 'Sorry, nipper. Didn't mean to throw you all the way in.'

Though it had all been a show, it was remarkable how the crew could turn from savages and back to men in such a short time. Nightingale knew it would be different with the *Ulysses*. That was one thing he could not imitate.

Lieutenant Courtney caught his eye through the dissipating smoke. Nightingale pushed his way over. 'How did your division fare, Lieutenant?' he asked.

Courtney, as wild as he had been mere minutes ago, retreated into the formality of a naval officer. The fire left his gaze and he reached to tie back his unbound hair again. 'They fared well, sir. The boat which headed to the bows arrived a mite earlier than intended but they had the good sense to hide beneath the bowsprit and wait.'

'And the cannonfire?'

'A little shock, sir, but they kept their heads.'

'Good. I'm pleased to hear it.'

Dismissed, Courtney returned to the gunroom. Though the men had performed well, there was much that remained to be done: sails to be set, guns to be cleaned, logs to be updated by the officers. Nightingale had had to keep one division from their rest, and they would have to stay awake now to stop the regular cycle of work becoming upset. Smythe, now the senior midshipman in Richmond's absence, was one of those sailors, but he was still telling his mates what he had done. Nightingale caught his breath – still tight after clambering the *Scylla* – and walked over to gently remind him of his duty, only to be interrupted by a cry from the masthead.

'Sail to port!' a topman yelled. 'Sail to port!'

The men left on deck immediately abandoned their work to peer in the same direction. Smythe, remembering his obligation, hurried to the binnacle and returned to Nightingale with a spyglass.

The sea was as black as pitch. No stars reflected in the depths so all the world resembled a shadow without form or end – but on what would be the horizon, lights flickered. They swayed in the movement of a vessel, slowly approaching. Nightingale could not make out her colours and certainly not her name.

For a moment, he dared to think it was her – the *Ulysses* – and the order to beat to quarters itched at his throat.

'Barty!' he called, knowing the coxswain was on watch. 'Lay us alongside her.'

'Yes, sir!'

Still tense and excited from the mock-boarding, the men hurried to their usual positions whilst the quartermaster, Marley, and his mates tidied the deck. They set the *Scylla* onto the starboard tack as easily as always but it felt like a long process. Nightingale kept to the windward side of the quarterdeck, mindful that he had not ordered the marines below.

'The weapons are to go away too, sir?' Marley asked.

'No. Not yet.'

Nightingale paced and paced, and with each turn, he tried the spyglass again. He felt no relief when he finally saw the unknown vessel's British pennant; the sight was tempered by the discovery that she was a fifth-rate, like them. Remarkably like them. It was not unheard-of for ships to run up false colours. Again and again, the idea to beat to quarters crossed his mind.

But then, leaning into the main chains, own glass in his hand, Hargreaves called out. 'I don't believe it, sir! It's the *Peregrine*!'

Nightingale looked again. With his blurred vision, he could just make out a 'P' and a 'G'. 'I don't believe it,' he echoed.

The *Peregrine*: the vessel the *Ulysses* had accompanied on the Main before the mutiny. She was meant to be in the Caribbean. But here she was before them, their paths slowly converging.

Nightingale ran up the signal inviting the *Peregrine*'s captain to repair aboard. He waited for the acknowledgement, almost expecting a trap, but then the reply came and a small launch cast off from the frigate. By now, Courtney had returned to the deck, drawn by the furore. He took Hargreaves's place at Nightingale's side, and under Nightingale's orders, directed the marines for the customary salute for the *Peregrine* captain's arrival.

The man climbed effortlessly up the side, arriving on deck and sweeping off his hat to reveal reddish curls. His face was pinched, worn, but he smiled. 'I am Captain Sallis,' he greeted in an accent touched by Scottish parentage. 'I was beginning to think there was no other sail on this ocean. When I heard gunfire, it astonished me more than the second coming of Christ would.'

'Welcome aboard the *Scylla*, sir. I am Captain Nightingale. Please, come below if you have the time.'

Sallis's face had changed at the ship's name. His smile stayed yet it became more rigid, his eyes losing their green sheen. 'Of course,' he replied by rote.

Rylance served them coffee in the privacy of the great cabin. Courtney did not have to accompany them, but he chose to anyway – and as Courtney came, so did Hargreaves. Sallis sat between them and Nightingale, chair scraped back and almost at the edge of his seat.

'As I say, when I heard shots across the water,' Sallis said, 'I wondered if my ears deceived me. We've seen nary a soul for weeks.'

'Boarding and gunnery practice,' Nightingale replied. 'We have an uncommon journey ahead of us.'

'I could tell by the faces on deck. They watched me like hawks. And I recognised the name of your command. I assume that is why you have invited me here?'

Nightingale smiled. 'You were the last vessel of the King's Navy to see the *Ulysses*. I have been tasked with finding her and bringing her to justice.'

'It was a long couple of months ago that her men rose up in mutiny.'

'I'm aware.'

'I do not envy you, Captain. That ship had a black shadow attached to it. You feel it with some vessels – like a spirit haunts her and is constantly trying to pull her down to the depths. She dragged a foul wake.'

Nightingale nodded patiently. 'I have been told that she had more than her fair share of dirty weather and rough seas. She accompanied you, yes? Along the Main to search out French and Spanish privateers?'

'Yes. Well, no. The *Peregrine* was not my command then. The captain she was under – he resigned his commission not long ago.'

'Why?' Nightingale frowned.

Sallis looked down, mouth in a sombre, thin line. 'As you say, the *Peregrine* was the last vessel of the King's Navy to see the *Ulysses*.

The captain was within sight of her when she mutinied. Near enough to see the stern lanterns aglow. By morning, she was gone. They didn't have a clue what had happened – not until they ran into the bodies.'

Nightingale said nothing. There were not many words to sympathise with, nor express the horror of finding the victims of cold-blooded murder floating in the sea. This was not war. This was a fellow man turning on his own.

'My lieutenant was there when they hauled some of the dead aboard. He said it was like a scene from the Theatre of Pompey. The amount of stab wounds... They had heard about such things, of course – from the *Hermione* only a few years ago. It is different to see it yourself. They wanted to identify the victims but it was almost impossible after weeks in the salt water and the disfigurements. Some of them had a few distinguishing tattoos or marks but that is all.'

From the end of the table, Courtney leant in. 'Did your lieutenant ever say what distinguishing tattoos he found?'

'Ah...' Sallis closed his eyes, thinking back.

'A swallow on a wrist?'

Nightingale turned to Courtney. Worry creased Courtney's brows as he chewed on the inside of his lip.

'Yes,' Sallis finally said. 'Yes, I think that was one of them.'

'Oh God,' Courtney breathed.

'I am sorry. A mate of yours?'

'My...my brother-in-law.'

Nightingale's heart clenched for Courtney. The death of his brother-in-law meant Jane was alone...if she was still alive. 'How many bodies were found?' he asked.

'Not many, I believe. They were fortunate to find the ones that they did. Not long after that, they became even more fortunate, if that is the right word. The *Peregrine* found the survivors in their little jolly-boat. Never has a vessel been more inappropriately named. Those poor things. Injuries and scurvy already setting in.'

Nightingale remembered Lieutenant Wainwright in the hospital at Antigua – his sallow, paper-thin skin and the sunken holes of his eyes. The *Peregrine* had returned the survivors to the station not long before Nightingale gained command of the *Scylla*.

'It is awful to think that they were the lucky ones,' Sallis said with a shake of his head. 'They escaped that ship. I dread to think what else occurred onboard, what else might still be occurring. A part of me is glad for not standing in your shoes, Captain Nightingale, if you'll forgive me. But another part of me would have been happy to search for that cursed ship. I would hang every one of those mutineers from the yardarm.

'But the poor captain of the *Peregrine* suffered dreadfully on that return journey to Antigua. The guilt ate him alive – for not being able to save the crew, for not realising what was happening onboard within sight. There was a terrible uproar about it, questions into his conduct and the state of his mind. It made him worse. So the *Peregrine* was stuck for weeks. I was eventually given command, and we were sent away from the Leeward Islands Station – out here, en route to the Suriname blockade.'

The fate of the previous *Peregrine* captain sounded remarkably familiar. Nightingale nodded, pretending he did not know exactly how it felt.

'Well,' he said, 'it is my job to find her now. Her last sighting was off Salvador. I do not suppose there has been any other word of her whereabouts?'

Sallis shook his head. 'As I say, you are the first sail I have seen in at least a fortnight. I apologise that I could not be of more use.'

'No, don't apologise, Captain. You have been a help to us. I wish you fortune in Suriname.'

Sallis nodded in gratitude and, once they were back on deck, he accepted Nightingale's hand.

'God help you, Captain Nightingale,' he said. 'May you find her and salvage what is left.'

The *Peregrine* slowly sailed away. Nightingale stayed on deck and watched. The excitement of the boarding billowed away like the wind suddenly changing. The noises faded into the regular running of feet, the aching of the cordage, the slapping of the canvas: all normal life, but tinged with a note of foreboding.

Perhaps it was only his own thoughts clouding the ship. The crew acted as ordered, no matter what new revelation came their way.

Nightingale's job was to face the bad tidings and steer the men in spite of any doubts and flaws.

He slept little for the rest of the night, awakening continually to the *Scylla* rocking softly. The waves lifted her in rhythmic pulses, starboard then larboard rising in angles that must have been trivial judging by the gradual shiver of his lantern in its fixings, but it made Nightingale think of peril. Eventually, he came on deck and had the lead-line thrown. There was no bottom to the reel, not yet. The water passed in cream-topped flows and the yards were braced trimly. Nothing was amiss.

Yet, when the bells for the morning watch sounded, Nightingale had long given up on sleep, so he retrieved the charts. Salvador and its state, Bahia, were surrounded by perilous coral reefs and sand bars and inlets, the water depth fluctuating dramatically. There were numerous places a ship could hide, numerous variations to a plan.

If they had to cut the *Ulysses* out of a port, they would need speed and stealth. With Loom, Nightingale poured over the lists of his men, changing his mind over and over about which division to assign them to. From barely being able to distinguish between the forecastle men and the men of the afterguard, Nightingale now prided himself in reeling off their names and strengths. The nimblest men could take the stern, the most powerful and intimidating could surge up the sides. Nightingale would lead the starboard division himself and Courtney would lead the larboard.

It was a risk, but Nightingale wanted to be seen amongst them. This was a task for them all now; they would either all share in the glory or the defeat.

The day passed with fair weather and a blue sky. As with every day since leaving Trinidad, barring Sunday, Nightingale had the guns run out and conducted small arms practice on the main deck. The gunnery had improved drastically – enough that the men could knock some of the fire out of the mutineers if they met them at sea.

Adhering to usual form, Nightingale invited both Courtney and Hargreaves for dinner in the evening. They arrived from the gunroom, Hargreaves in his best uniform and Courtney in some semblance of his. Rylance served beef and gravy, fresh from the resupply in Port of

Spain, and quietly they ate and drank. Nightingale must have drifted into his thoughts, exhausted from a sleepless night and still in the midst of muddled schemes, for suddenly he was pulled from a haze by Hargreaves's voice.

'I'm sorry, Michael, I didn't quite catch that,' Nightingale said, ashamed.

'I only mentioned that I was sorry to hear how Lieutenant Courtney's brother-in-law was on the *Ulysses.*'

Courtney, on Nightingale's right, nodded whilst taking a slow bite of his beef.

'What was his position?' Hargreaves asked.

'He was the master,' Courtney replied, and then, bitterly, 'An obvious victim if the mutineers were killing those with authority and experience.'

'The captain may still be alive,' Hargreaves said, but must have realised how useless that sounded so lowered his head with reddened cheeks. 'I am sorry for your sister. I pray she is well.'

He uttered it in such a mumble that for a moment, Nightingale thought he had misheard. When the words connected, he glanced at Courtney, who had abruptly ceased chewing. Hargreaves looked up at the silence. Realisation crossed his face, his mouth opening, his brow furrowing.

'How do you know about Jane Courtney?' Nightingale asked, the fog of the day suddenly clearing.

'I...' Hargreaves coughed. He set down his glass and squeezed his fingers together. 'Lord Fairholme... He visited me before we left Trinidad and he mentioned it to me. I did not think it was... He only spoke to me about the situation in Salvador and how I could speak Portuguese.'

'Why would Lord Fairholme speak to you? About Jane?' Courtney spoke up.

'I know Lord Fairholme spoke to Lieutenant Hargreaves, Arthur,' Nightingale said, hoping to curb the sharpness in Courtney's tone. 'But I did not expect Jane to be mentioned.'

'I'm sorry, I didn't realise it was not common knowledge,' Hargreaves stammered, bright red.

'We would prefer to keep it that way.'

Hargreaves nodded with a quiet, 'Yes, sir.'

They tried to return to the food but Nightingale could see that Courtney was not in the same room as them anymore. He knew he would be thinking of Jane. Nightingale had spent a long while thinking of her too; he did not know what she looked like but he imagined Louisa, on the deck of the *Ulysses*, fine emerald gown in tatters and elegant black hair unbound. Even just the image turned his stomach. For Courtney and his sister, it might be a reality.

'Sir,' Hargreaves said again. 'If I may?'

'Yes, Michael?'

'What does this mean for the mutineers? Surely the most important priority is still the gold.'

'The most important priority,' Nightingale replied, almost tersely, 'is that the mutineers are brought to justice, and those who can be saved are rescued.'

'And Jane Courtney?'

Courtney scoffed. He set his knife and fork down and pushed the plate away with a look of disgust.

'I am asking for clarity,' Hargreaves insisted. 'If she is a mutineer, then shall she be treated with the same laws and punishment? All the mutineers have given up protection. They have taken unlawful possession of the ship and its cargo.'

'Lieutenant Hargreaves,' Nightingale said before Courtney could respond. 'That is not your place. We are to retrieve the mutineers and bring them to justice, saving the ship if it is possible. All else is impersonal.'

'Impersonal, sir?' Courtney asked.

'But all those who are to be protected shall be protected,' Nightingale added firmly.

'We do not know what has happened to any of them,' Hargreaves continued to say. 'Tacit acceptance of a mutiny is near enough to mutiny itself.'

Courtney rose. He seemed to fill the cabin for a moment, blocking the swinging lantern and towering over Hargreaves. Nightingale began to stand to stop whatever he planned but Courtney only took a breath and tugged down his waistcoat. 'Captain Nightingale,' he said through gritted teeth. 'May I be permitted to retire?'

Nightingale nodded.

The cabin door closed behind Courtney with a bang. Nightingale closed his eyes, fatigue creeping up on him. He was half-aware of a quiet knock outside and Rylance's head poking into the room. 'Can I be of assistance, sir?' he asked.

'Yes, Rylance, actually you can. Please clear this away. I believe we have all quite lost our appetite.'

'My apolo—' Hargreaves started, but Nightingale held up a hand. 'Back to your duties, Lieutenant. That will be all for tonight.'

Rylance kept his head down as he shuffled around the room and out with the cutlery and plates and half-finished food. Nightingale sat in silence until he was gone. What else had Fairholme told Hargreaves behind his back? The lack of knowledge, the feeling of still being twisted and turned in this web, made his skin itch. Not only was he unaware of what had happened behind him, but before him as well. As blunt as Hargreaves had been, he was correct that the treatment of the *Ulysses* mutineers would be a complex thing, certainly with potential innocents aboard – and now the gold, too.

Nightingale sighed and wiped at his weary eyes. He glanced at his night cabin but then, finally alone again, he once more brought out the charts and lists. It was so clinical and cold to see the names and locations printed in ink before him. He knew that emotions and opinions and real lives could adapt any plan in ways he could not expect.

He only hoped that, in the end, they could unite together.

Chapter Twenty-Two: Ships in the Night

3 August 1800

Dear Louisa, Nightingale wrote, all the while listening to the sounds of the gulls outside the gallery windows.

> *It has been a fortnight since leaving Port of Spain, and I can barely find fault with the crew. It is as if being away from them for even that short time in Trinidad has made me fonder and has made them work like devils. Truly, we have only been on our voyage since June — not even two months have passed — but I can feel their eagerness as much as my own. The gunnery and hand-to-hand drills have improved, and any of that laxness which they began the journey with has vanished.*
>
> *I suppose you will hear of the events that happened in Trinidad. Perhaps I should have heeded you a little closer when you asked me if I travelled to the Caribbean for the correct reasons. I asked you what they were, and to be frank, I was not sure I knew myself. It took me a long while to find the answer to your question. It is thanks to my father and yours that I became more certain: a begrudging thanks that comes with the caveat that...*

Nightingale paused, wondering if he was ready to set words to the feeling.

> *...I do not wish to associate with my father any longer, he wrote decisively. There is nothing I can do to sever the blood ties, but I shall not allow him to hang over me. It might be impolitic to mention that to you, yet you know me as well as any other;*

sometimes, I think you know me better than I know myself. I should have carved the man out of my life long, long ago.

As for Sir William, I believe he had the better intentions, as you will no doubt hear from him yourself. He seemed genuinely aggrieved to treat me as he did. Nevertheless, he did, and I thought that you should know.

I cannot mention our exact position to you now, my dear, but it may still be a while until this voyage is done. I had meant to write sooner and longer; other matters have been pressing.

Nightingale found himself on the verge of writing about the discontent between Courtney and Hargreaves. They had barely said a word to each other after the disastrous dinner. But, just as he could not find the words to help them, he could not write them down to Louisa.

He tapped his pen against his mouth, about to continue when a sudden din echoed above. Footsteps raced and someone knocked excitedly on the cabin door.

'Come in,' Nightingale called, tidying away his correspondence – just as the door sprang open and the youngest midshipman, Finley, tumbled in. He was bright red and grinning, nearly bouncing on the balls of his feet. 'Where is the fire, Mr Finley?'

'We've raised Salvador, sir. There's boats pulling out to meet us.'

'There *are* boats, Mr Finley. Don't make me correct you again.'

But Nightingale smiled and followed him up on deck. Courtney was there with Hargreaves, directing the men as they hauled in canvas. The coast of Salvador suddenly loomed: a long, rocky arm of land curving backwards and into the sheltered Bay of All Saints. Huddles of vessels waited at the entrance. Some faced the land, some faced the ocean. Nightingale scanned them through the spyglass and counted two sloops and one medium-sized frigate.

He thought of what he had said about Portugal's troubled neutrality in the war. Had a decision been made whilst the *Scylla* had been at sea? Were the boats now coming to meet him full of enemies or allies?

'Sir.' Hargreaves appeared at his side. 'I must speak with you.'

'This instant, Michael?'

'Yes, sir.'

With one last glance at the boats and the defended coast, Nightingale led Hargreaves back down into the cabin. He did not miss Courtney's eyes on them.

Hargreaves shut the door behind him, then hesitated, fiddling with the lining of his coat.

'Is something the matter, Lieutenant? There are men coming to meet us.'

Hargreaves looked up at the skylight and then quickly pulled a roll of paper from his inner pocket. 'These,' he said, handing them to Nightingale, 'are my directives from Lord Fairholme. I am to make contact with a man in Salvador and discuss the *Ulysses*.'

Nightingale opened up the roll and glanced down at the neat handwriting. He frowned. 'This is the goal for all of us. Why do you have particular instructions?'

Hargreaves wrung his hands. 'Lord Fairholme knows the contact in question. He has worked with him before.'

Nightingale mulled it over. He looked again at the directives, signed by Lord Fairholme, and then back up at Hargreaves. It took him too long to connect it all – perhaps because he did not want to.

'When did he put you onboard my ship?'

'In Antigua,' Hargreaves said. 'As soon as the mutiny on the *Ulysses* was known or… there around. Lord Fairholme knew of the cargo aboard. I replaced the lieutenant of the *Scylla* who died of the fever.'

Nightingale's head muddled the dates as he tried to match them. How had Fairholme known? That was a ridiculous question – the lord knew everything.

'You had met Lord Fairholme before? You did not meet for the first time in Trinidad when he spoke to you about Salvador?'

Hargreaves shook his head. 'I am here to protect the cargo onboard the *Ulysses*, sir.'

'I see.' *An agent in naval intelligence!* Nightingale thought. It could not be possible of Lieutenant Hargreaves, who was still standing there, playing with his coat buttons, barely meeting his gaze. But that must have been a façade – a bloody good one.

'With your permission, sir,' Hargreaves said, 'I shall talk to the officials once they board. I'll inform them we are here for a short victualling stay. It is best to keep the *Ulysses* voyage under wraps, with the current climate.'

'Yes, I — yes, of course.' Damn Lord Fairholme for springing this trap upon him. 'I shall arrange a party of marines for you and a handful of trusted men to gather the supplies. If it is your intention to go ashore.'

Hargreaves nodded.

Back on deck, they watched the boats approach. When Nightingale had written to Louisa, he had felt confident that he was gaining a measure of control over the ship and her crew. Now, Lord Fairholme's web again ensnared him, in ways he had not even anticipated.

He stood by Courtney, a man he was pleased to finally understand, as the boats arrived. An officer of the Portuguese navy boarded, his emerald coat with its red facings gleaming in the sun. He swept off his plumed hat and politely saluted the quarterdeck. The officials who accompanied him wore dour, serious expressions. Nightingale extended a hand to the officer, smiling despite the rising anxiety.

'Welcome to Salvador,' the man greeted in heavily accented English. 'I am Lieutenant Nazario.'

'Captain Nightingale of the *Scylla*. My lieutenants Courtney and Hargreaves. He shall conduct our discussions.'

Hargreaves immediately stepped forward and addressed Nazario in rapid-fire Portuguese. The officer nodded, the officials gathering around him in a small huddle.

'We shall go to the cabin?' Nightingale suggested.

They returned again to the companion-way leading to the cabin, but before they could descend, Nightingale turned to Courtney and said, 'Stay on deck, Arthur. I need your eyes along the coast and it is your watch. The fore course could be tied tighter.'

Courtney did not look up at the sail. Instead, he eyed Hargreaves, still talking with Nazario.

'Yes, sir,' he said shortly, and walked away. Nightingale listened to him yelling at the topmen as he led the Portuguese officials into his cabin. Courtney had always been distant towards Hargreaves, even hostile. Had he known or suspected something?

Nightingale stifled the feelings as he sat at the table. Rylance, ever on hand, came hurrying in with coffee and tea. He handed them out with an admiring glance at Nazario's gorgeous red hat feather and gold-buttoned uniform. Nightingale caught his eye, glanced at the door meaningfully and he scurried out.

Nightingale wished he could direct the ensuing conversation as well as he could direct Rylance. Since his youth, he had been around people who spoke many different languages, but nothing adhered in his mind. He could utter a few halting phrases in French, a little Spanish, and no Portuguese. His father's tactic of dealing with foreign-speaking enemies had little to do with learning their language.

He looked between Hargreaves, reeling off answers and explanations, and the officials. They read and reread the ship's papers, feeding questions to Nazario. Finally, Hargreaves turned to Nightingale and nodded.

'They are happy for us to gather supplies,' he said simply.

'It shall only be a short stay,' Nightingale insisted.

With the delegation gone again, Nightingale returned to Hargreaves's real task. He took him aside on the deck and asked, quietly, 'How long do you require to find your man in Salvador?'

'Not long,' Hargreaves replied and, with a glance at the hourglass. 'I shall be back by the first dog watch.'

'Ensure you are,' Nightingale ordered brusquely, unable to help his tone. 'Sergeant Jennings and a group of marines shall accompany you to the town whilst the other men resupply. As I said to Lieutenant Nazario, I hope for this to be a short stay.'

With the wind rising, stirring up higher waves, Hargreaves and the men went ashore. Nightingale watched him, head aching in a way it had not since leaving Trinidad. Courtney looked at him but the imperviousness of the captain on his quarterdeck saved Nightingale from any questions.

He pictured Lieutenant Hargreaves and Lord Fairholme in Trinidad, scheming to put him back onboard the *Scylla* under Hargreaves's watchful eye. He felt like their puppet – straight from his father and Sir William's hands into theirs.

For the next two hours, the *Scylla* went about the motions of a mooring ship. Nightingale paced with Parry, Winthrop and Loom, formulating lists of items to be added to the *Scylla*'s stores. When ready, the assigned groups of men ferried supplies back and forth and at one point, someone returned with a girl and her friends. The ensuing debate between Smythe on one side, trying not to look at the women's barely covered bodies, and forecastle men Coleman and Jones on the other, gave Nightingale the distraction he needed. Courtney and the bosun intervened, dragged Coleman and Jones back aboard and sent the ladies ashore, not without an earful of Portuguese.

'I shall deal with Coleman and Jones, sir,' Courtney promised.

By the time the ordeal was over and the men were swabbing the head, the afternoon watch had come around. Nightingale had been unable to sit and wait for Hargreaves so had been perusing the charts in between visits to the hold and pantry where petty officers dealt with the stores. On the sun-drenched deck, Courtney stood by the binnacle, not looking towards the town, but out around the bay into the open blue. He did not notice Nightingale approach and jumped a little as he stopped beside him.

'Everything as it should be, Lieutenant?' Nightingale asked.

'Yes, sir.' Courtney recovered himself quickly.

'I don't believe we need to update our speed and course when we are stationary.' He indicated the log-board. Courtney reddened.

'No, sir. I was—'

'We shan't be here long,' Nightingale interrupted, sympathising with his floundering. 'Lieutenant Hargreaves promised to return by the first dog watch. If he is not, I will lead the party to find him myself. I want to be gone from here.'

The captain's desire to always move, to always adhere to his course, itched inside of him – but it was more than simply duty to a career; loyalty to his crew was every bit as urgent. 'I have been thinking,' he continued, 'about what shall happen with Jane. I am willing to help her, if that is one of your concerns.'

'One of many,' Courtney sighed.

'I shall give her whatever aid is required,' Nightingale said adamantly, 'whether that is a passage back to England, protection, shelter... And whatever I cannot give, my wife is a very remarkable woman. She – *we* – have a house full of empty rooms. If she wished to stay, wished for companionship, Louisa and I would be honoured to help.'

Courtney frowned. A plague of emotions crossed his face, never settling.

'Why are you offering this?'

'I have always helped the families of my officers. I was one of the first visitors after Leroy's young sister, Lucy, was born, and his family remain my close friends. Your Jane's position is different, but my orders are to find the *Ulysses* and bring her crew to justice. That justice involves aiding any innocent passengers.'

'I don't—' Courtney took a breath. 'I don't know what state she will be in. Her husband is – was – a good man. He would not have taken part in the mutiny. Perhaps that is why they killed him. And Jane... She would not have gone against him, no matter what Lieutenant Hargreaves implies.'

Nightingale said nothing, only watched Courtney twist his hands together.

'They had not been married long,' he continued. 'I introduced them only a year or so ago. Jane had good friends in Antigua, where she worked as a seamstress. But I always worried about how lonely she must have been when I was away, and about her welfare too – not only the fever, but the idea of a young woman alone. She always said she was well, but I wanted to be certain she was. Especially as I convinced her to come out here.

'Bill was on the *Nereid* – I knew him from when I was a midshipman. I brought them together. He was older but they were good companions. He looked after her. When the yellow fever struck the *Scylla* and I had to quarantine aboard, he kept her safe and calm ashore. I could not stop her when she chose to accompany Bill on the *Ulysses*. Nor would I have. Now, I wish I had.'

'No one could have known, Arthur,' Nightingale soothed. 'None of this sits on your shoulders.'

'She's so young,' Courtney breathed in agony. 'She turned twenty just before Captain Carlisle died.'

'Young women have remarkable fortitude. Lucy is, well, she would be sixteen now. She always wears the medal I had made for her brother, and if she were a boy, I would have no doubt that she would have been a good midshipman. I often think it is a shame that some women cannot join us in the navy. My wife would run a taut ship.'

To his surprise, Courtney laughed. With his laughter, some of the shadows lifted from his brow. He unclasped his hands and brushed at the salt spray which had whipped up onto his sleeve. Nightingale smiled and without thinking, laid his palm upon Courtney's arm. It was a soft, inconsequential touch, but he felt a jolt as if he had been struck with the bosun's starting cane. Courtney did nothing to move him.

'Boats to starboard!'

The cry suddenly broke through. Nightingale shifted away and hurried to the side, Courtney behind. Across the harbour, the launch returned, manoeuvring across the waves. They had grown choppier this last hour, the wind increasing. Nightingale looked for Hargreaves but could not see him.

Barty had accompanied the lieutenant hours before, dropping him at the Cathedral Basilica. The large coxswain now climbed aboard, flushed and breathless, fair hair damp with sweat.

'Hargreaves?' Nightingale asked.

Barty caught his breath. 'I'm sorry, sir. Had to pull like the devil across that harbour, what with the waves getting big. And Mr Hargreaves, sir, he wanted us to get back to youse as soon as possible.'

Nightingale felt a spark of relief that the lieutenant was unharmed. 'Where is he?'

'He sends you his compliments and requests you to go to him, sir. He's at the plaza – near Church Francesco, or something. Says he's got something to show you.'

'Of course.'

'I can go, sir,' Courtney offered, coming forward.

'No, you stay put, Arthur.'

'I can accompany you, sir.'

Nightingale paused, halfway to the waiting boat. Courtney was serious, imploring. Barty took one glance at them and sensibly hurried to prepare the launch again. 'I will be only a turn of the glass,' Nightingale promised.

'He is—' Courtney lowered his voice, 'one of Lord Fairholme's, isn't he?'

A slow chill crept over Nightingale's skin. For a moment, he wondered how Courtney had known and he hadn't. Perhaps he really had been blind, too convinced in his relief at regaining the *Scylla*. The spectre of Lord Fairholme loomed again; he had given him that command, had extended one hand – but Nightingale could not see the other.

Courtney took advantage of his silence and tried to follow him to the boat.

'No, you stay here, Lieutenant,' Nightingale ordered. 'I cannot have three senior officers off the ship. You have the deck. If there is trouble, fire both of the bow-chasers, five seconds apart.'

Courtney hesitated. Then, at last, replied, 'Yes, sir.'

The pull across the harbour was a tough slog, the waves rolling past them, sometimes bursting over the bows. Nightingale felt one of those rare sensations of gratitude in reaching dry land. Shadowed by a handful of Charlston's marines, he made his way through the commercial district. Houses sat alongside colonial government buildings. People milled through the wide streets, selling, trading, gazing suspiciously at the British men.

Nightingale averted his gaze. He could not stop thinking of Courtney and Hargreaves. The worrying idea that he did not trust Hargreaves formed. Hargreaves was still his lieutenant and, regardless of Fairholme, Nightingale was the lord of the *Scylla*. Fairholme had a long arm but it could not be so long as to turn his helm or strike his sails. He would deal with him when he returned to land, and not before. Now, he had to not play favourites, could not allow bias to sway him to Courtney and abandon Hargreaves.

He schooled his face into something placid when they finally reached Hargreaves. He waited in the shadows of an arcade off the main plaza, overlooked by the intricate sandstone towers of the Church of São Francisco. There were many windows and balconies surrounding them. Many places to hide.

Hargreaves greeted him with a small nod as the bells chimed. He ushered him close, and then, in a low rush, said, 'They were not only here for supplies. Apparently, they were battered something dreadful by a storm. They came to Salvador for repairs.'

'Repairs?' Nightingale asked.

'Yes. They were here for just over three weeks.'

'Good God.'

'They only left around seven days ago,' Hargreaves clarified.

Mixed emotions simmered in Nightingale's chest: hope at abruptly being so much closer to their target than expected; concern at being so near that they could taste their wake; and anger at their delay in Trinidad.

'If we hadn't had that whole affair, we would have nearly had them,' he commented bitterly.

'Their American came to the town,' Hargreaves continued. 'He had Captain Wheatley with him, behaving as though nothing was wrong. He was their way of making sure no one smoked their crimes. The American introduced himself as a man from Loyalist stock and said he was Lieutenant Davidson.'

'Davidson was hanged by the mutineers,' Nightingale said, frowning.

Hargreaves nodded. 'Yes, evidently Ransome, the mutiny leader, in disguise. He wore the dead officer's uniform, and he was accompanied by another lieutenant, Wainwright.'

'He is dying in a hospital in Antigua.' If he was not dead already.

'Then, it must have been another mutineer – Valentine, perhaps. But this other man was English, tall and broad, with a thick West Country accent, and he and Ransome had a few loud disagreements.'

'Did nobody see past them?' Nightingale asked. 'We already knew that the *Ulysses* was a mutineers' ship when they arrived at the start of July. I had my orders to find the *Ulysses* at the end of June.'

'That news did not reach Salvador for a while. And by the time it did...' Hargreaves sighed. 'Portugal is not on one side of this war or the other. This mutiny is a rebellion against the British Crown, against a king's ship. Taking action could have been interpreted as a statement of loyalty. Salvador suffered in wealth when the colonial administration was moved to Rio de Janeiro. Perhaps they feared reprisals. But now, by not raising a hand, they worry about the news spilling out – that a rebel ship was sat in their harbour for weeks and nothing was done.'

The *Ulysses* had been fortunate – and that fortune had cost the *Scylla*. 'Was anything more seen of them other than for their repairs?'

'Ransome and his lieutenant came to the land often. They went to the brothels and taverns and even to the whipping post in the Pelourinho where slaves are punished. Ransome also frequented the blacksmith. He paid to have a sword made, topped with an eagle. It cost him an arm and a leg. And he paid for it with this.'

Hargreaves reached into his pocket and extracted a small cloth bag. He carefully opened the drawstring and set one coin down into Nightingale's open palm. Nightingale felt his breath catch as he turned it over. He had seen many like this – the polished surface, the obverse of King George III, the reverse of the spade-shaped shield – but here was what Captain Ramirez had called 'cursed gold'.

The silence loomed; the sound of the plaza drifted away. He felt Ransome in that one guinea – both of their hands had touched this thing: the hunter and the hunted. In that moment, Nightingale was not sure who was who.

'That is not all,' Hargreaves finally said. 'You should see something else.'

–

Nightingale squeezed himself into the dark, damp space beneath the jetty. He clenched his hand onto his sword hilt, spasmodically chewing the inside of his mouth. A hunched form lay at his feet. When Hargreaves pulled back the tarpaulin, a wave of nausea churned through Nightingale's stomach.

For a long, terrible moment, he could not tear his eyes away. The image before him burnt into his vision. He had seen death before – death on decks slippery with blood; anonymous death that snuffed a man's light as quickly as blinking; agonising, slow death that eventually felt like a mercy – but this inhuman, sudden acquaintance with it knocked out his wits.

The man – if that was what it was – was broken over a stinking pile of seaweed and spindrift. Much of him was gone. There remained a deformed, twisted face, a mottled neck and bloated abdomen, then one arm and half of a leg. Time and tide had ravaged him. The sharks had done the rest.

Nightingale clenched his teeth, tasting the rotten smell. 'Who is it?' he managed.

Hargreaves bent down and, with a flinch, picked up the corpse's remaining arm between his fingers. He lifted it and brushed off a coating of black sand. Marred skin was revealed.

'This,' he said, showing Nightingale a faded tattoo of a bald eagle in flight, 'is our American friend, Ransome.'

Chapter Twenty-Three: Messina

Ransome was dead.

When he had died, and how, Nightingale did not know. It must have been some time ago for the water to rot him and the sharks to devour him. Perhaps it had been when the *Ulysses* was in Salvador. She might have waited in the harbour, murder and bloodshed weeping over her decks.

The more he thought of it, the more some new, awful truth occurred to him. Wainwright and Ramirez had implied the same thing: if it was not a curse on the *Ulysses*'s timbers and canvas, then it was retribution for what they had done.

And yet Nightingale knew enough about man's evil to know that this was not the work of phantoms. Fathers and brothers and sons and friends could be cruel. It was no demon who had hanged Tom, no sprite who had killed Leroy. Savagery and war existed in the heart of every man; it was the way of the world. Give out power so freely, without checks, without balances, and the hand that grasped it would soon turn into a bloody fist.

Ransome had thought he had power. When he had led the murder of Lieutenant Davidson and the *Ulysses*'s officers, perhaps it had given him a sense of vengeance. He had been pressed against his will into the service of a king his people had raised arms against. That service had shown him no mercy. Nightingale imagined word spreading of the gold. Even if they had not known its purpose, the temptation would have been the final burning fuse on the powder-keg.

But something had changed. The lawless freedom had grown unwieldy, a rudderless ship tossed and beaten in the waves. Hargreaves spoke of Valentine and his tension with Ransome. The right-hand man could have struck: Brutus turning against Caesar.

Unbidden, Nightingale's thoughts wound back to his father. He had risen against him, though it had taken all these years. If he had been brave enough to do so before, would he have raised his hand in mutiny against his father's thrall?

Nightingale would have been foolish to say that he did not understand why they had mutinied. Yet he could never condone it.

There was more now too. A mutiny against a mutineer.

So the cycle might continue if the *Ulysses* was not found.

Nightingale spent long hours with Courtney, Hargreaves and Loom. He even invited the midshipmen in to the cabin, testing their studies and chart-reading. The long Brazilian coast stretched away to the west, a jagged line rimmed with islands, reefs and narrow channels. Nightingale fought with the desire to drive the *Scylla* under full sail, imagining the *Ulysses* just over the horizon, a short run away. But he could not be so reckless, not when the log was heaved at such fluctuating depths, and not when the *Ulysses* could be hiding in the coves and bays.

Nightingale kept a frequent vigil on the windward side of the deck, seeing phantoms of white canvas in the low clouds and hearing shots when it was only the shivering and cracking of cordage. Obsessed with the thought of being so close, he practised the gunnery and boarding until the divisions had the actions down to a fine art. Nightingale shifted the members of the boats so he was fully satisfied with them – then restrained himself from dabbling anymore in their organisation.

It was hard to admit it – but there was nothing more he could do other than keep an eye on the winds and waters. It was a chase now, and only one would be the victor.

'I never really knew what the *Scylla* was named for,' Courtney said one evening in the gunroom. It was a rare occasion where Nightingale had been invited into the world of the junior officers. 'I thought it was the name of some island that we English colonised centuries ago.'

Across the table, Hargreaves paused with a fork of sea-pie almost at his mouth. He said nothing.

'It is from Homer,' Nightingale explained, fearing Hargreaves would think Courtney uneducated for such a question. 'Scylla was a sea monster faced by the Greek hero, Odysseus, or Ulysses as he was called by the Romans. She had six heads and for every ship that passed her, she would eat one sailor for each head. The Greeks later believed she was near the Strait of Messina and close to her was a great whirlpool, Charybdis. To navigate around them, Circe – the sorceress whom Odysseus had lived with for a year before – instructed him to sail close to Scylla and so avoid the maelstrom.'

'And the sailors were eaten?' Courtney asked.

'Yes.'

'Then it was not very sound advice.'

'The alternative,' Hargreaves said, 'was to lose the entire ship in Charybdis. Circe had him choose the lesser of the two evils.'

'This Circe was well-versed in nautical matters?' Courtney jested, but there was a tone of malice there that Nightingale did not like.

'She knew the area well,' Nightingale said. 'She was a trickster at first to Odysseus and his crew but she proved helpful and she became Odysseus's lover.'

'She acted in their interest,' Hargreaves said quietly.

Courtney opened his mouth to say more, but Nightingale did not enjoy the tension that had grown around Hargreaves. He quickly moved on, trying to find neutral ground in Hargreaves's childhood: where he grew up, if he remembered anything of Portugal. Short, one-word answers were the norm from Hargreaves. Nightingale could find nothing at fault with him on the surface – he served his watches well, he commanded his division better now – but he never did anything more than his duty, as if he was frightened of setting one toe over the line.

And below the surface... Nightingale could not do anything around the second lieutenant without thinking of Fairholme. He desperately wanted to ask about his connection with the lord, exactly what he knew, what his plans were, if Fairholme had sprung the employment upon Hargreaves as he had done to Nightingale. But Hargreaves – shy, awkward Hargreaves – remained mute and Nightingale could not, for all love, demand he break his secrecy.

In the wooden pyramid of his ship, Nightingale teetered at the top, the capstone who was supposed to keep the structure together – but truthfully he could not see what was below. And he could not simply climb down and question it, otherwise those blocks would fall out of place.

The only outlet he could find was in his letters to Louisa. They became a controlled feed of his worries, as if he slowly opened the locks on a canal and allowed the water to drip out. He wondered again and again, on the page, what Lord Fairholme wanted from him. It was not sheer magnanimity that had set him back on the *Scylla*.

Perhaps he was the Circe in this odyssey: the sorceress, the trickster.

At the end of another long day, where the decks seemed to pulse with warm blood and the ropes gleamed from sweating palms, Night-ingale sat alone with a glass of Madeira. He toyed with the idea of reprimanding both Courtney and Hargreaves for their behaviour. But what behaviour had that been? The odd comment? Glances on deck? Nightingale worried that his own bias clouded his treatment. Damn this sniping and damn the events in Trinidad. The most important consideration was the *Ulysses*.

And yet he knew what had tipped the balance on that mutinous ship: friction between officers, friction between men and crew.

Nightingale looked into the amber liquid and swilled it around the edges. His mind felt the same, going around and around in a vicious cycle that he had never broken.

He stared until a sudden shift of light glittered through the cabin.

Nightingale rose from his writing desk and looked out the open gallery windows. The *Scylla*'s wake frothed in bright, azure tones, illuminating shadows split by glittering pinpricks.

Voices rose from above. Nightingale pulled on his uniform coat and hurried from the cabin, ascending through close, lantern-lit gloom and emerging into a night aglow with hues of shining blue.

Abandoning their duties, most of the men had flocked to the sides, staring down into the glowing water. The radiance reached up the hull, reflecting off the newly painted timbers which shimmered as a wave broke over them. Above, the masts gleamed, almost as if they were ablaze. The awed faces of the topmen peered down from the yards like spectres. Only the roll of the sea and the creaking of the ropes broke the reverent hush.

The crew parted as Nightingale passed through. The sea resembled the night sky, nautical constellations that burst and reformed.

'Have you seen anything like this before?' he asked Courtney, who had accompanied him.

'No, sir.'

Nightingale beckoned Loom over from the waist. He was the oldest officer on the ship, and had over a decade more experience than Nightingale.

'Thousands and thousands of tiny creatures, sir,' he explained. 'Their bodies glow like fireflies.'

Despite the natural explanation, Nightingale still heard some of the men muttering. He caught the words, 'They're the devil's lights'.

He was about to scold them when he noticed the horizon. Far ahead, he thought he could see a break in the lights. He blinked to try to clear the blur from his vision but it didn't shift. With his glass, he peered at the glow, which seemed to rise above the amorphous black line of the sea.

'Masthead!' he called. 'Five points to starboard, what do you see?'

'It's hazy as a battlefield, sir! But I can see lights. They look like lanterns, sir!'

Lanterns, and gradually, the ringing of a ship's bell.

–

They hove-to in the lee of the *Senhora da Graça*. She was a small brig, but in the claustrophobia of the shining lights, she looked twice her size. The blue glow shimmered off her beams and caught on her cordage. The more Nightingale stared at her, the more ragged she appeared: her jib hung loose, the shrouds like threads in embroidery that a woman had abandoned. When her skipper came to the quarter-deck, Nightingale could not tell how old he was. The luminescence turned his expression into a jagged patchwork.

The reaction of the *Senhora*'s crew was clearer. They shied away from the gunwales, looking up at the towering masts of the *Scylla*. The frigate was wreathed in moonlight, scattered through the prism of the blue radiance. What a sight they must look – savages in a strange, tinted mist.

At his side, Lieutenant Hargreaves called across the water to the Portuguese captain. The captain answered in a rough shout that echoed across the otherwise silent waves.

'He says he's seen nothing like this before,' Hargreaves translated. 'Not until now, when the lights have appeared every night in the fog.'

'Ask him about the *Ulysses*,' Nightingale prompted.

More shouting and the Portuguese captain started gesticulating towards the horizon.

'He says that nature has turned against them,' Hargreaves explained with a frown. 'There are these lights, and before that… They have been in a fog-bank these last five days.'

'Fog?'

'He says it came over them suddenly and they had no choice but to sail through it. It went on and on for days, and they could not navigate. They emerged out of it to this glow. They're only trying to get home to Ilhéus.'

'The ship,' Nightingale urged again. 'The *Ulysses*. Ask him about her.'

Hargreaves spoke once more. The Portuguese captain shook his head. And then paused as if remembering something.

'In the fog,' Hargreaves said after the man had finished. 'Three days in, they saw something in the fog. At first they thought it was an illusion. But then they kept seeing lights glinting in the darkness, and a shadow passing through the mist. This ship… it acted strangely, going back and forth on its course and performing strange manoeuvres. They saw it a dozen times.'

'*Fantasma*!' the Portuguese captain shouted.

Nightingale glanced to Courtney. He knew that the same thought was going around the lieutenant's head. 'It's her,' Nightingale said.

Courtney nodded.

'It's the *Ulysses*.'

The *Senhora* and her crew seemed glad to be away, setting sails quickly again and turning their helm for home. Their courses diverged – the *Senhora* heading to the safety of the shore, and the *Scylla*'s bowsprit sweeping towards the unknown horizon. They cut a void through the blue glow. Men still lingered at the gunwales, staring into the lights as though captured by sirens, but a sharp order from Nightingale separated them.

He descended into his cabin, chest tightening. The Portuguese captain might have called the *Ulysses* a phantom, but, in the vastness of the ocean, she may as well have now been their neighbour.

Hargreaves followed him, closely accompanied by Courtney. The door shut and Hargreaves asked, 'What is our plan, sir?'

Nightingale stopped at his desk, touching the wood as if it could bring them luck. 'We follow her,' he said.

'Into the fog? Sir?'

'I see nowhere else to go.'

Hargreaves opened his mouth, then quickly shut it.

'We cannot simply wait for her to come to us,' Courtney remarked, a needle against Hargreaves.

'In the fog, we have no advantage,' Hargreaves retaliated. 'This sea is a maze of reefs and atolls and hidden sandbars. If we cannot see, we cannot navigate around them. What use would it be if we became wrecked within her range? These ships are evenly matched.'

'An even chance is all we need.'

'An even chance does not privilege victory. We have to ensure that she does not escape. The ship has to be brought to port for justice, and the gold recovered.'

'Which shall not happen if we do not follow her,' Courtney pointed out. The lieutenant had turned his attention to Hargreaves, as if they had forgotten Nightingale's presence. Nightingale sighed, wearied by the hardship of the past days and the thrill of suddenly being so close to their goal. He opened his mouth to interrupt but his officers had not finished.

'Have you ever sailed in fog before, Lieutenant Courtney?' Hargreaves asked.

'Yes. Off Gibraltar. When my captain was incapacitated, no less. Have you ever seen the Rock of Gibraltar suddenly looming above you out of the fog? How many voyages have you truly been on, Lieutenant Hargreaves?'

'Mr Courtney,' Nightingale warned.

'Enough, Lieutenant, to know that if you lost sight of the Rock of Gibraltar, then how shall we see the *Ulysses*?'

'We're all frightened here, Lieutenant,' Courtney said coldly, 'but this service is not about individuals.'

Hargreaves's eyes flashed with anger. 'What are you accusing me of?' he spat. 'I am only trying to warn of the dangers, and you are questioning my—'

'Questioning your courage and intent, yes, Mr Hargreaves. Who are you truly here for?'

'That is enough!' Nightingale slammed his fist down on the desk. It upended a pot of ink and made both men jump. 'This is not a damned debating society! Mr Courtney, Mr Hargreaves, we follow the *Ulysses* into the fog, and that is final. And I don't want to hear any harsh words between you. You are men, not children. I will not have infighting onboard this ship. I do not need to remind you of what occurred onboard the *Ulysses*!'

A fierce blush rose into Courtney's cheeks. Hargreaves glanced away.

'Now, return to your duties. Both of you shall be on watch as we enter the fog-bank. And one of you pass the word for Master Loom. He knows these waters and speaks sense. Go, now.'

Courtney skulked towards the door, followed by Hargreaves. The second lieutenant lingered for a while but at one glance from Nightingale, he too vanished from the cabin. Nightingale let out a breath and sank down into his chair behind the desk. Frustrated, he glanced at the overturned ink pot and began to mop it with his handkerchief. As if by magic, Rylance appeared at the door and hurried in with a rag. Without a word, he tried to clean the black liquid before it stained the wood.

But slowly, the ink spread and engulfed the ocean – just as the fog did outside the ship.

Chapter Twenty-Four: Dead Reckoning

Slowly, like stars flickering into life, the lanterns were lit. At first, Nightingale had been able to see at least two cables ahead of the light lashed to the bowsprit, but then the fog enveloped the main deck, consuming the glow until it was a struggle to even see the lantern ten paces away. The men of the forecastle disappeared, followed by the topmen and anyone above the main yard.

Just four hours that had taken after they had entered the bank – only four hours, with a long distance still ahead of them.

Nightingale wrapped his boat-cloak around him as he and Loom scoured the sea-charts. Their last known position had been forty miles off of Santa Cruz Cabrália. Soon he had expected to see the landmark of Monte Pascoal rising above the horizon to the west. Now, there was nothing. Not a star in the sky – not even the sun or moon – to guide by.

The sails shivered, all set, white shadows that were interrupted as a man crossed the yards. Nightingale wanted to use as much canvas as he could but the breeze was dying. Barty, at the helm, kept a close control on the course. Leeway was their issue, though; they would make more in these low speeds and that could scupper their known position.

As if on cue, Smythe, at the lee-rail, shouted, 'Turn!' and the master's mate upended the hourglass. Smythe counted off the knots on the line as it ran aft, and Nightingale cast his eye between him and the charts. The thirty seconds dragged on and on, but finally, the mate cried, 'Stop!'

'Two knots, sir,' Smythe reported.

It had been dropping steadily. Loom, knelt on the deck with the logs and instruments, noted it down for the hour of six. Four bells in the morning watch chimed. There were still six hours until the day officially began at noon, but this was no regular day. Loom and Nightingale and the lieutenants had all the information they could gain: wind speed, headway, fathom depth, and course, which Nightingale relayed to Barty by the hour. The only thing they lacked was the celestial measurements.

And that was the difference between knowing precisely where they were – and dead reckoning.

Nightingale remembered what the *Senhora* captain had said about the *Ulysses*. Somewhere ahead, she travelled in circles, tracing and retracing her course. It was easy for a man to lose his head in such dense fog. All that could be seen was the close confines of the ship and then, beyond, a mass of clouds with no fixed points and no horizon. It was like sailing in another world.

By the mainmast, Lieutenant Hargreaves peered skywards, trying to glimpse some heavenly body. Courtney was avoiding him, standing close to Nightingale on the quarterdeck. 'Is this like Gibraltar?' Nightingale asked, if only to break the deathly silence.

Courtney gave a thin smile. 'With a girl to rescue and all,' he remarked.

'We'll find her,' Nightingale insisted.

He nursed that thought as the hours turned, saying it over and over as if its repetition would lead to fruition. The bells rang every thirty minutes; the log was heaved; measurements taken; information updated, and, at every opportunity, the lead-line was thrown to determine the water depth. Hargreaves's worry of hidden dangers had yet to haunt them as the seas remained comfortingly deep – and when they reeled in the line, there was only white sand, no coral or shingle yet.

At noon, dinner was served and Nightingale smelt the usual pork and pea soup. The volume of the crew rose from the lower decks, and when the grog was served, Ashley Marlin's flute echoed across the otherwise quiet waters. Courtney and Hargreaves seemed to compete for who would go below first, not wanting to eat together, but the naval routine soon bested them and Nightingale was left with Loom on deck.

With the afternoon struggling on and the watches changing, he stayed on deck. Light airs around them could not even be called that anymore. Nightingale sighed, drumming his fingers on the almost stationery helm where Barty's mate glanced at him.

'We shall have to lower the boats and drop the kedge anchor,' he said, realising he had not spoken for a long while.

Loom, who had employed a different midshipman each hour to teach them their trickier navigation, looked up with Burrows. 'Yes, sir. See if we can't make some movement.'

'I should have done it hours ago.'

But he had not, fearful that the men would lose their strength hauling in the anchor on the capstan. The *Ulysses* could have appeared at any moment. They would need all of their fortitude for her.

During the second dog watch, they lowered the boats. Nightingale assigned men to them, knowing they would be glad to leave the turgid *Scylla* for a while. He watched them fan out ahead of the bow until the fog consumed them – then it was only the cables stretching out in their wakes, connected to the vanishing kedge anchors. Those anchors would be dropped, the men would return, and the capstan would be turned to haul the *Scylla* up to the kedge. It would be laborious, but those were one-hundred-fathom lines; they would make good progress.

Yet, now, for the first time since leaving Salvador, the *Scylla* remained still, lonely in the world of mist. Nightingale felt impatience itch at his skin. His only consolation was that the *Ulysses* would be experiencing these dead calms too. They were two lame ducks in the middle of a huge pond.

By his estimates, they now neared Espírito Santo. The heavy fog took on a different quality as darkness fell. There were still no stars, no moon, to help guide them. The only lights came from the lanterns and their reflection off the smooth waters. All orders were given with a hushed urgency – no bawling or crying like usual, just deadened voices to ensure no noise was missed outside the ship. With their eyes gone, sound was the next best aid.

By the main chains, Smythe once again threw the lead-line, a practice he had taken to with a skill that made Nightingale proud. The sounding line dropped, was retrieved, and he rushed over to whisper, 'Sixty fathoms, sir, and a sandy bottom,' to Courtney.

Courtney, back on watch, noted it down.

'How long have we been in this fog, Lieutenant?' Nightingale asked.

'Almost seventeen hours, sir.'

Nightingale checked his pocket-watch and was surprised at the lateness of the time. He had supervised the log ever since coming on deck but had only connected it with the ship's speed and course, not his own well-being. He had been awake since the night before and had not eaten more than a saucer of cold meat and later, pudding. 'Perhaps I should send for Rylance.'

Within minutes, the steward appeared with a plate and a mug of coffee in his hand. He tried to salute Courtney and Nightingale and had to scramble to hold on to the food. Courtney hurried forward to stop it ruining the sanctity of the deck. 'Perhaps below, Rylance?' he suggested.

Rylance lingered, looking between the lieutenant and Nightingale.

'The weather hasn't changed, sir,' Courtney continued. 'The barometer has not fallen or risen.'

'I'm aware, Lieutenant,' Nightingale replied, before realising that Courtney was again prompting him to go below. He reddened at his and Rylance's care. 'Shall you be all right?'

'I shall try, sir.' Courtney smiled.

Rylance accompanied him to the cabin. Suddenly out of the cool air and into the relative warmth of his own space, the fatigue caught up with his body. He sat down at his desk and stretched out his legs as Rylance fussily put his food and drink before him. 'It's all right, Rylance,' he said, easing the plate away from the map on the table. 'I can take it from here.'

Rylance left him and, as soon as the door had closed, Nightingale sighed and rubbed wearily at his face. If only he could do as he had wished before and move the paperweights on his chart – the *Ulysses* and the *Scylla* – so they were alongside each other, as easily as that.

Picking at his late meal with an absent mind, Nightingale returned to that map. The ink from earlier had stained it. He again tried to rub at it, only to realise where it had flooded.

A mass of coral ahead drew closer and closer. And the *Ulysses* was leading them right towards it.

-

The fog was in his lungs. Nightingale breathed it in, sensed the acrid taste of fire on his tongue. He coughed and heard it rattle through the mist. He mustn't do that – he mustn't give the *Ulysses* anything to locate them by.

Blindly, he searched for his handkerchief but could not find it. A hand came out of nowhere and pressed the fabric between his fingers. Nightingale spluttered again, trying to get the memory of the blazing *Orient* out of his mouth.

Perhaps it would always be there, rising to the surface when he least expected it.

'You should go below, sir.' Leroy was beside him, palm pressed around his clenched fist. The dead lieutenant was still smiling, even though a terrible red scar ringed his throat. Nightingale could not remember a time when Leroy was not smiling. He squeezed Nightingale's hand softly and tossed a lock of fair hair out of his eyes. 'She'll appear whether you're on deck or not, Captain. You have to look after yourself for what's ahead.'

'I can't,' Nightingale rasped, though he wasn't sure anything emerged from his dry lips. 'I want to be here when we first see her. She's the French flagship. We'll be able to see her from miles off.'

Leroy chuckled. In the second that Nightingale had looked away from him, he had changed. Now, he was Lieutenant Courtney. His fair hair was jet-black and in wild curls, eyes green and hard. The scar had vanished but Nightingale knew that didn't mean Courtney was зafc.

'You're thinking of the *Orient*, sir,' Courtney said plainly. 'This isn't the *Orient* or the *Lion*. We're hunting the *Ulysses*.'

'It's all the *Orient* and the *Lion*,' Nightingale managed. He rubbed his sore eyes, not believing he was on the *Scylla*. Wreathed in this smoke, she could be the same as that wounded ship of his past.

'What are they doing down there?' he asked.

'Oh, down there?' Courtney looked the same way as he did – along by the forecastle where two figures stood in silhouette against the fog. 'That's Lieutenant Hargreaves and Lord Fairholme. They want—'

But Courtney's words were muffled by a sudden roaring coming from leeward. It sounded like the world ending – water rushing, waves and waves colliding with each other in a furious war. Gunfire tore the fog to shreds.

'What did you say?!' Nightingale shouted. Courtney leant closer, mouth moving but no sound emerging. The apocalypse raging to the east only became louder. Behind Courtney, Nightingale could see the skeletal forms of masts reaching through the separating mist. He stared up at them as they approached, still yelling, 'What did you say?! What did you say?!'

The *Ulysses*, wreathed in fire, towered over the *Scylla*. Like a spear, the bowsprit tilted down to slice the deck in half. Nightingale stared, helpless, even as Courtney grabbed his arm, pulled him close, and screamed, 'I said – they want the gold!'

Nightingale jerked awake. Courtney's voice echoed in his ears. He slowly blinked, haze falling from his eyes and revealing the span of his cabin. He spasmodically reached out a hand and blindly knocked over a mug. It smashed on the floor.

The noise chased away the last of his dreams. He rubbed at his face, stretching out his back. It ached like hell. Somehow, he had fallen asleep over his desk, arms resting over the pile of maps and charts, cheek pressed against his logbook. The dividers rested beside his hand. Christ, how had he managed to sleep?

He tenderly sat up, blanket dropping from around his shoulders. He could not remember having one around him before. The last thing he could remember was the *Ulysses*, floating above them, about to crush the ship into splinters.

Nightingale groaned and went to light a lantern. A quick glance at his pocket-watch showed it was early morning.

'Oh, sir!' Rylance cried as he appeared. 'I'm glad you're awake, didn't want to disturb you. Let me get you another mug of coffee.'

'Thank you, Rylance. What…' He cleared his throat. 'I didn't mean to sleep for so long. Thank you for the blanket.'

'Oh, that wasn't me, sir. Lieutenant Courtney came to see you during the first watch but he had nothing important enough to wake you with.'

'I see.' Nightingale reddened – both at the idea of Courtney seeing him asleep and at the officer's kindness. 'Well, if you would be so good as to pass the word for Lieutenant Courtney, I shall see if he has anything more important now.'

As he waited for the lieutenant, his mind, unbidden, dwelt on Courtney and Hargreaves. He had not dealt well with the tension between them. The *Ulysses* was his sole focus and yet, as the depths of his vision told, he could not untangle Courtney or Hargreaves from that vessel. Every man was bound up in it.

'They want the gold!' Courtney had screamed. It was preposterous. But could that be why Courtney was worried? Could that be some reflection of Nightingale's own thoughts? Spitefully, he wished he had never been told about the *Ulysses*'s cargo – or, rather, that it had never been set onboard in the first instance. Perhaps he was too idealistic, too naive, still. Corruption and deceit were everywhere; Nightingale simply did not like it so close to him. Too many had suffered for it.

Courtney arrived looking almost as tired as he felt, eyes ringed with dark circles, skin pallid.

'Good morning, Lieutenant,' Nightingale said. 'How do we fare?'

'We've made progress with the kedge anchors, sir, but the fog has not thinned. It is Lieutenant Hargreaves's watch still, sir. I can fetch him if you need?'

'No, it's all right, Lieutenant, I'll be on deck shortly.' Nightingale paused. 'How is Lieutenant Hargreaves?'

'Quiet, sir, but getting on.' At Nightingale's silence, Courtney continued, 'I believe he has questions about the coming assault on the *Ulysses* and his position on the *Scylla* when we board her. Now we are nearing her…' He twisted his hands behind his back. 'Am I still to command the larboard division?'

'Of course. That has been what we practised.'

'Thank you, sir.'

Nightingale nodded. He had rarely been alone with the lieutenant since the affairs in Trinidad. The reminder of what Nightingale had told him hung between them, only dampened by the current concerns of the *Ulysses* and Lieutenant Hargreaves.

'You knew of Lieutenant Hargreaves,' Nightingale said.

Courtney looked down. 'I had my suspicions – after Lord Fairholme spoke with him in Trinidad.'

'Do any of the other men know?'

'No.'

'I should like to keep it that way. And please leave any reprimands to me. I have told you before about speaking to him as if you are his superior officer. Lord Fairholme's business is with me.'

It was not entirely true. Nightingale's business was the ship's business – but he wanted to keep Fairholme's attention on him and not allow it to infect the rest.

'Yes, sir,' Courtney said, and then, unable to leave the subject of Fairholme alone, 'It is not Lieutenant Hargreaves I don't trust, sir. It is who he represents.'

'Lieutenant, I—' Nightingale's words died as there was a sudden rumble to starboard. He rose, shrugging off the blanket. Courtney followed him as he threw open a window.

'Sir?'

'Hush.'

At first, Nightingale thought it was thunder. And then it struck again.

'That's cannonfire,' he breathed.

'A twelve-pounder, like ours,' Courtney added.

They looked at each other for a single moment before Nightingale hurried for the companion-ladder.

'Masthead!' Nightingale shouted as soon as he reached the fog-shrouded deck. 'Can you see anything?'

'No, sir!' came a voice from an invisible topman. 'There was a flash and then nothing! But the boats are coming in, sir!'

It seemed to take an age, punctuated by the further sounds of gunfire. In the fog, Nightingale could not work out exactly where it was coming from, nor how far away it was. He held his breath, counting the seconds. *Come now, hurry*, he urged the boats, listening for the oars.

Eventually, the silhouette of Obi's cutter emerged. They pulled like madmen, Obi's strong voice encouraging them on. As they clambered the side, Nightingale greeted them and Marley handed out a mug of grog to Obi, then the boatsmen.

'We heard cannonfire,' Nightingale said simply.

Obi nodded and finally found his words. 'We saw the ship, sir. It was like a shadow in the fog, so we... we couldn't see the colours, only that it was a frigate. We tried to ignore it, until it fired straight at us. The ball went short but each one – there were four in all – came closer. And in the flashes we saw it proper, sir.'

Nightingale's breath stuck in his throat. 'And?'

'It was the *Ulysses*, sir. Kieran said he'd seen her in English Harbour a dozen times.'

Nightingale turned to Kieran. 'Are you certain it was her?' he asked.

'Without a doubt, Captain, sir.'

Nightingale looked up as if he could suddenly see her through the fog. She was there. And the first interaction had not been friendly, as they had known it wouldn't be.

He nodded to no one but himself. 'Ship the capstan bars,' he ordered. 'Another haul.'

The operation – a cumbersome and draining job – was done to the sound of running feet and Ashley Marlin's flute. Nippers were attached to the thick messenger cable which ran around and around the capstan, lashing the anchor's hawser tight. As a smaller frigate, the *Scylla* did not have the massive multiple capstans of larger vessels, but she still had two mighty wooden machines on the upper and gun deck. Nightingale gathered the strongest men and, as the flute wailed 'Randy Dandy Oh', they turned the bars.

Nightingale listened, and waited.

The *Scylla* moved slowly. With the dead wind, it was nothing but the strength of the men and the anchor cables tugging them through the water. Frustration stirred in Nightingale's chest. Again and again, he looked for the invisible horizon, thinking he could see shadows in the unbroken fog. Every time, it turned out to be a mirage.

But it gave him hope. The flute echoed across the sea; there was no need for silence now. The *Ulysses* knew they were here. Perhaps she was marooned in the calm too. He wondered if they would have the sense to try to warp her out of the stillness. He could not underestimate their seafaring, but he clung to the idea that their sensibility had broken down with the order onboard. They were so close.

Close enough that the *Ulysses* could wear and appear suddenly through the fog, or cut their anchor cables. He shook the thought away.

The bells rang as each thirty minutes passed. Smythe kept heaving the log and taking soundings. There was little change in their steady speed, yet the ongoing hours showed they were making progress. The men at the capstan swapped to a new group. Some of the officers joined too: Loom and Courtney each took a handle and pushed with the regular seamen.

Ashley Marlin, atop the capstan drum, span on it for hours but he showed no signs of being dizzy – not until he stepped off and nearly tripped into the belaying pins. Kieran picked him up and said, 'Not long now. We're at eighty fathoms along, at least.'

Kieran was right. They were drawing nearer to the end of the line. Slivers of the morning, the fragment of the sun, began to emerge in the sky. Six bells of the morning watch rang out: seven o'clock. Nightingale was too coiled up to feel any fatigue. He raised his eyes and realised he could see the light, clearer now. For the first time, the ghost of a breeze kissed his skin.

Gradually, inch by inch, they approached the bedded anchor. By that time, the sails were shivering. A long-forgotten wind stirred. The minutes ticked on. Beyond the bowsprit, a succession of holes was being torn in the tapestry of the mist. It was slow going, the fog resisting the pulls. But it was enough.

In a void, the hint of a rose-pink sky.

A shadow marred the rising morning.

It was her – it had to be; it was as if they were looking into a mirror at a far, far distance.

Courtney, who had returned to his side, lowered the spyglass he had put to his eye. He looked at Nightingale and nodded. 'As sure as night follows day, sir.'

Nightingale took a breath. Again he thought he tasted ash, the phantoms of the *Orient* and the *Lion* imprinted on each lung. He sighed them out and gripped a backstay, an old action for good fortune. On cue, the wind rose a point. He looked up, felt the moment all around him: the breeze on his face, the sturdy cordage at his palm.

'General chase,' he ordered.

And once again, the die was cast.

Chapter Twenty-Five: The Ulysses

Nightingale's heart lifted with the return of the *Scylla*'s vigour. The wind rose and scoured the fog, allowing the royals to be set. Topmen shouted and sang whilst they shook out the final reefs and the yards creaked as they pulled against the canvas. Above, a blue sky emerged through the shades of the dawn's pink. It was perfect; Nightingale could not have asked for better after the days spent in the mist-filled confusion.

And there, on their larboard quarter, floated a reflection of themselves. Nightingale could see the whiteness of the *Ulysses*'s sails – as much as possible aloft as she tried to cut through the remaining patches of fog. Yet in the last hour, the distance between them had closed.

With every watch-bell, Nightingale hurried into the bows to get just those few yards nearer to her. He raised his spyglass, strained through the hazy vision, and made her out, almost like a model in the lens. He saw only superficial damage from the storm that had sent her into Salvador: a jagged spar on the mizzen topsail yard, making the braces hang strangely, and chips along the rudder.

Her ensign was missing, though, no colours flying from her stern.

Perhaps she thought she could still escape. But on that vessel were murderers and mutineers, shoulder-to-shoulder with innocents, and Nightingale would have never let them go. He knew, standing on the forecastle and obsessively eyeing her canvas and trim, that he would have chased her anywhere: around the Horn, into the Pacific, to those islands in the middle of the ocean.

For the first time, with the wind shivering and the waves kissing along the hull, he felt free. This was what had kept him at sea for so long: liberty from his background and all its expectations. On the deck, there was no Admiral Nightingale. No Lord Fairholme. No Sir William.

He turned to Courtney. A smile pulled at the corners of the lieutenant's mouth as he saw Nightingale's expression. 'We'll have her by sundown,' Nightingale said, touching Courtney's arm.

In the main chains once again, Smythe threw the lead and when it had run out, he called, 'Five knots, sir!'

Their speed increased with the wind and the banishment of the fog. Time raced by, the opposite to the lethargic fugue of the last hours. Noon arrived and accurate measurements were finally taken of the newly arrived sun. Loom had done well; Alcobaça was just astern of them with Caravelas fifty miles to the west.

Despite the chase, after noon observations, the drum beat out to signal the crew's meal. Galley fires had been lit in preparation for what Nightingale thought would be their last hot food in a while. He made do with a slice of ham and egg which Rylance again hurried up to the deck.

The sea charts arrived soon after. Loom's face was dark. He set the paper down and jabbed at a point south of their position.

'I know,' Nightingale said simply.

'We're running right towards it.'

'I know.'

'If *we* know of it, then the *Ulysses* knows of it.'

Nightingale said nothing. Loom looked at him and the charts and then out at the *Ulysses*. 'It is a risk,' he said, not an admonishment but a warning. 'We did not practise for that.'

'If we can avoid it, we will. But I am following her course. It all rests on her new captain's seamanship.'

'Yes, sir.'

The watches changed and those off duty scurried below to clean and polish their weapons. Garland operated the grindstone and man after man went to sharpen his blade. All that could be done before the order for battle was done. Nightingale had the men aloft reduce the sails by one more reef. It would be a matter of timing. He could not impede their movement, but for what was ahead, they needed to be prepared.

'Thirty fathoms, sir!' Smythe cried, and then, 'Twenty-five!', 'Twenty!' as they made more and more progress.

At four bells of the afternoon watch, she was closer, though Nightingale could see that she had not reduced sail at all. Packets of fog drifted to the east, but she evaded them or dipped into them to then emerge seconds later. Nightingale weighed it up, then weighed it again with every minute that passed; that was what it took now, assessments and reassessments, over and over.

They were catching her – never too much to overhaul her, but it was enough.

He knew he could not delay the order. He turned to Courtney, nodded, and said, 'We shall beat to quarters.'

A flicker of hesitation crossed the lieutenant's face. Then he nodded back. 'We shall beat to quarters!' he shouted across the deck, and the drum rolled.

All hands hurried to their duties, regardless of watches. Gun crews assembled and ran out the cannons, the wheels scraping on the wood. Partitions came down so the action could sweep from stem to stern. The armoury opened for the rest of the weapons to be handed out. Fire-buckets were placed, sand poured to prevent slipping in blood, powder-monkeys scampered to their positions. All this done in a matter of minutes – no time, but enough for the gap to close more; Nightingale could now read '*Ulysses*' without a glass.

Lieutenant Hargreaves hurried up to the con.

'I want you on the gun deck, Lieutenant,' Nightingale ordered. 'Lieutenant Courtney and I will lead the two boarding divisions. Ensure every man on the boarding party has a scrap of fabric tied about his arm – it'll be close quarters and I don't want any melee between our own men. When we board, you shall have the *Scylla*. Give the *Ulysses* enough fire to cover our backs, but do not damage her unnecessarily.'

'Sir—'

'Your place is on the *Scylla*, Lieutenant.' Nightingale moved a discreet few steps away from Courtney. Hargreaves followed. 'Tell me where the gold is stowed on the *Ulysses*.'

'They may have moved it, sir.'

'Where was it originally?'

Hargreaves paused. For a moment, Nightingale thought he was going to refuse to tell him. Then, 'It is in a false panel in the great cabin. Three steps from the door, in the ceiling. It seems to lead to the upper deck, but it goes nowhere. Only a small void.'

'Thank you, Lieutenant. As soon as we have the *Ulysses*, you will come across. I shall leave the matters in your hands – yours and mine.'

Hargreaves nodded with an obedient, 'Yes, sir,' but Nightingale saw the frustration in his eyes as he saluted and ran below-decks.

The instant he had gone, a flash and a crack split the afternoon. The *Ulysses*'s stern-chaser opened its mouth, sending a ball whipping towards them. It fell short. But it was the final confirmation Nightingale needed. Nonsensically, he'd believed they might have made a mistake, and that the British vessel ahead of them would heave-to and surrender.

The burst of their guns, without even a flag flying, told him everything.

Two more balls danced across the water before falling with resounding splashes. The spray leapt around the *Scylla*'s bowsprit. The men commanding the bow-chasers – an honoured job that could be reserved for the captain and his first lieutenant – ducked from the water and were ribbed by the midshipman, Burrows, at their side. They made up for it when firing the next shot. It scoured along the *Ulysses*'s taffrail, sending a hail of splinters over the poop deck. A cheer rang out which Nightingale quickly silenced.

Beside him, Courtney rubbed his hands together, white-knuckled as he clenched his fingers.

'Jane will be all right,' Nightingale said. 'If she's sensible, she will be below-decks. I've escorted diplomats and their wives across the Mediterranean before – they've never come to harm in the hold during battle.'

'Yes, sir,' Courtney said quietly.

'Arthur, I need you. You need to be alert.'

Courtney nodded. 'Yes, sir.'

Ahead, the *Ulysses*'s stern-chasers grew louder as they neared. She had turned half a point to starboard, trying to bring a hint of her broadside to bear, but she was fighting against the wind. Even with near-full sail, she could not bend nature to her will. And by doing so, she had ruined her guns' trajectory and targeting. The stern-chasers drifted out of line with the *Scylla*, the balls flying diagonally across her bows.

But the *Scylla*, the wind on her side, could now aim as she pleased, either at her cordage or hull.

The *Scylla*'s shot tore through the *Ulysses*'s mizzen topsail, taking out a tangle of backstays. The next bounced over the gunwale and ate a chunk out of a companion-ladder. Nightingale watched, throat tight. They could still surrender and stop all of this. But the halliards remained empty of all signals.

And then, from the *Scylla*'s masthead, Reeves shouted out. 'Land to windward! Three points off the starboard bow! An island – a chain of them!'

Nightingale could not see the islands from the deck, not like Reeves could see them from the top. He only ordered for Smythe to hurry back to the main chains. 'Fourteen fathoms, sir!' the midshipman, armed for battle, counted.

They reduced more sail. The speed dipped but the *Ulysses* mimicked them, hauling in t'gallants and relentlessly trying to use her starboard broadside. The aft-most cannon fired with a sudden roar that made Nightingale's heart jump. The ball missed but reached off their stern before falling into the sea. If she succeeded in only some of her manoeuvre, she would be able to rake the *Scylla*.

'Starboard the helm, Barty,' Nightingale ordered. They could make the *Ulysses* move how they wanted her to.

Still keeping the weather gage, the *Scylla* crept out of the *Ulysses*'s eye. It was agonising – chess-pieces scraped over a board, getting closer and then retreating to a safe square. Nightingale clenched his fists, convincing himself to stay patient. To windward, he began to see the line of an island through the remaining fog. They were safe as long as the wind did not veer and blow them towards it.

But there were other dangers, too. And across the water, Nightingale could see what he had been waiting for.

The *Ulysses* had seen it too – and he realised that was why she was still manoeuvring. Finally, the *Ulysses* reefed and double-reefed more canvas. Her stern once again faced them, bowsprit turning away from the island. She had cost herself time and now the *Scylla* scythed into her wake.

The bow-chasers ripped through her taffrail, leaving nothing but scraps. One of the balls narrowly missed the helm, bouncing along the deck and sending the crew jumping aside. The man at the wheel – close enough now that Nightingale could see his dark hair flying free – yanked at the spokes in a scared spasm. The yards wailed as they tried to tack. Topmen scrambled, seemingly at random, on the masts, wrenching at sails.

The *Ulysses* moved strangely – a way no ship should move, jerking along her starboard side. Suddenly, she listed, as if a wave had struck her. Another bounce, this time coming along her bow and rippling to her stern. Cries erupted from the deck. The masts trembled; men clung to the shaking spars.

And then there was a terrible, deafening crunch.

Silence.

Reeves at the *Scylla*'s masthead broke it. 'She's grounded!' he shouted. 'She's on the reef!'

Wedged beneath the *Ulysses*'s bows, Nightingale saw the dappled, razor-sharp teeth of the coral. He had not expected her to go so close. But now, rising awkwardly from the water, bowsprit pointed unnaturally to the sky, she was trapped.

Caught between *Scylla* and the dangerous sea.

–

The afternoon watch turned to the first dog watch and the *Ulysses* remained lodged on the reef. No one had emerged from the ship, fearing the fire of the marines who were now posted along the *Scylla*'s bows. Captain Nightingale stood in the midst of them with Lieutenant Courtney at one side and Lieutenants Hargreaves and Charlston at the other. All sails had been hauled in, all movement drained, all guns quiet for now. The two vessels stared at each other in a stalemate.

And gradually, the tide lowered, exposing more and more of the *Ulysses*'s damaged timbers.

Nightingale clutched a speaking-trumpet in his hand. 'I am Captain Hiram Nightingale of the *Scylla*!' he called over the silent water. 'You have committed the crimes of mutiny against a king's ship, and murder! I am under orders to seize your ship and take her into port to face the justice of the courts! Surrender her and bring your papers across!'

Nothing. At one point, a pale face glanced above a hatch but then immediately retreated. There was no sign of anyone else, not even the dark-haired helmsman.

Nightingale took a breath and repeated the order. He knew they would not surrender.

'We cannot fire on her too severely,' he said to the assemblage around him – his officers and a handful of loitering deckhands, wanting to know the next move. 'Any serious damage and she'll be even more wounded than she is now – certainly as we don't know how far her hull has been breached. We still have to get her home. We cannot approach much closer, else we'll be stranded ourselves when the tide falls.'

'But we cannot wait for them to surrender, sir,' Hargreaves said. 'We do not know if they even will.'

'They might when they realise how hopeless their situation is,' Charlston suggested.

Nightingale could not wait that long. He knew it would be hours before the crew managed to get the *Ulysses* off the reef – if they at all managed it – and he had to secure the vessel. They were so close, so frustratingly close. He lowered the speaking-trumpet and resisted the temptation to smack it against the gunwales.

'We could go across the reef, sir,' Courtney said quietly.

Hargreaves turned to him. 'We cannot approach the reef.'

'We lower the boats,' Courtney continued, undeterred. He spoke to Nightingale, and no one else. 'Row as far as they will go and then walk across the reef. It is right beneath the *Ulysses*'s hull.'

'We will be cut to ribbons on the reef,' Hargreaves said.

'Only if we fall.'

Nightingale again looked out at the reef. Large chunks of it had been unveiled, and there were channels where they could get three men abreast at least. The rest could easily accommodate a single-file line of men. He sighed.

'Lower the boats,' he ordered. 'The boarding party will muster by their divisions. Lieutenant Courtney, you shall take the larboard side, and I the starboard. Lieutenant Hargreaves, you shall command the *Scylla* in my absence. Fire as you will with the great guns and muskets – enough to draw the *Ulysses*'s eyes away from us, but not enough to damage her excessively.'

It took no time for the men to gather on deck. The last time Nightingale had stood before them like this, they had been about to drill for the mock-boarding. Now, he could hear the patter of gunfire and the crying of the enemy crew: pretence no more. He swallowed, gripped and re-gripped the hilt of his sword, realised how dry his mouth was. Some of them would not survive.

'Over there is the *Ulysses*,' he said. 'I don't have to remind you of her crew's actions. They have mutinied and murdered and stolen a king's ship. As soon as they did that, they relinquished all protection. We have chased them across the sea to bring them to justice. Now is the moment to finish that. I shall be coming with you into the fray. I shall be right beside you.'

It sounded ridiculous, a hollow attempt to unite a crew who had been together since the very start. Nightingale had been the outsider; he had nearly lost them. Now, he was at one with them, and he could not find a way to express that.

Courtney, beside him, stepped in. 'Three cheers for the *Scylla*!' he cried.

'*Scylla*!' they shouted. '*Scylla*! *Scylla*!'

Nightingale swallowed the emotion. He could prepare them no more.

They still yelled as they swarmed for the boats. Nightingale accompanied them, all grief and pain discarded for now – living in this one moment.

'Sir.' Nightingale turned, one leg over the side. Courtney stood by him.

'Yes, Lieutenant?'

Courtney hesitated, glanced over at the waiting *Ulysses*. 'Take care, sir.'

Nightingale smiled, his chest tightening and loosening all at once. 'And you, Arthur.'

Courtney nodded. He seemed to want to say more, but only saluted and joined his division. Nightingale watched him a moment longer. Then he climbed over the side.

Fifteen men waited in the cutter, including Charlston and his marines, and Rylance, who gave a shaky smile. Sweat clung to his flushed cheeks.

'Out oars,' Nightingale ordered.

The first strokes cut the waters. The *Scylla* remained like a rock behind them, her shadow looming. Two other boats separated from their wake, one manned by Courtney, the other by Smythe.

The stern of the *Ulysses* rose, growing with each minute that passed. Men appeared at the taffrail. 'Surrender your ship!' Nightingale shouted again through cupped hands. 'Surrender, or we shall board you and take you by—'

A musket shot cracked. Water splashed not far from the cutter's bows. Nightingale gritted his teeth, determined to stay steady. Men had finally appeared on the *Ulysses*, but they remained faceless in Nightingale's vision.

'Give them an answering shot,' he said to Charlston, keeping his voice level.

The lieutenant's aim sent chips flying from the boom. For a blessed moment, the figures at the stern ducked beneath the rail. But then they were back and more shots flew.

'Pull, pull,' Nightingale urged and heard Courtney order the same thing. In the tight squeeze of the launches, the marines covered their heads with fire. The blast of the muskets, popping between the rhythmic pull of the oars, deafened Nightingale. He gripped his own flintlock, suddenly helpless. They were sitting ducks until they could reach the ship. They just had to reach the ship.

Courtney's boat rowed to larboard, forcing the *Ulysses*'s crew to separate their defence. Smythe went to follow, but the reef narrowed in that direction. They could not navigate side by side. 'The stern!' Nightingale called across to the midshipman. 'Go for her stern!'

'The stern, men!' Smythe shouted in response, his voice breaking. 'Put your backs into it!'

The ragged sheen of the coral rippled beneath the waves as the water rolled and swarmed through choking channels, then poured into deeper troughs. It was a tight matter to row through a reef in the best conditions, let alone with guns blasting over their heads.

'Sir!' Rylance suddenly shouted. Nightingale glanced up and saw the mouth of the *Ulysses*'s stern-chaser gaping at them. His heart clenched.

'Lieutenant Charlston,' he began, but was interrupted by a sickening boom.

A ball screamed above them. It slammed into the 'U' and 'L' of '*Ulysses*' and broke the glass of the stern gallery windows, jarring the men at the taffrail and making them lose their aim. Nightingale turned, saw a figure in the *Scylla*'s bows. Hargreaves waved his hat.

'Come on, men!' Nightingale urged, no time to breathe in relief. 'Pull for all you're worth! To the reef!'

Courtney had disappeared to larboard. Smythe had reached dry ground and was scrambling with his division out of the launch. They had split the *Ulysses*'s aim but the Scyllas had been lucky so far, too lucky. Nightingale waited for the shot that would snuff him, or one of his men, out. But he kept waiting and waiting, and still it did not come.

The boat nudged against the exposed coral. The *Ulysses*'s starboard side rose before them. There was damage to her naked hull, shattered timbers reaching deep into the keel. She was desperate, cornered like a wounded dog, snapping at them with all her teeth. Nightingale swallowed and manoeuvred through his boatsmen into the bows. 'Come on!' he cried. He had to lead; he had brought them here.

Ducking low, he stepped onto the coral. Immediately, he slipped, but managed to stop before he plunged onto the razor-sharp ground. He didn't have time to consider it, not with his men swarming behind him. Charlston and Rylance and Kieran hurried out along with the rest, weapons drawn. He didn't even realise the loud noise was their shouting voices until he joined in himself. They ran, faster than was sensible, driven on by anger and terror and the desire to finally finish this awful thing.

Musket and pistol fire burst into the coral and the waves. Charlston and the curtain of his marines kept stopping to shoot ahead. Men on the deck cried as bullets found their targets. Nightingale felt as though he were storming a castle, the fortress walls looming in front of him. He could not breathe, could not think, could only keep going forward

'Come on!' he screamed and suddenly his sword was in his hand, waving towards the open portholes.

One of those open portholes roared into life. The cannonball soared over their heads and the men ducked in fright. Nightingale heard someone fall into the sea. Another man yelled as he cut his hands on the jagged coral. Nightingale staggered on, stockings ripped and damp with blood. He did not feel it.

His division followed him as he diverted across a wider ridge of coral and leapt across a narrow channel. His foot slipped but Charlston grabbed him unceremoniously and shoved him forward. As he righted himself, he caught sight of Smythe and his men halfway up the stern gallery. They were succeeding. If Courtney had reached his side, they could take them.

'Fire!'

A scream echoed from the *Ulysses*'s deck, followed by a sudden chorus of shots. Nightingale saw the flashes and then Charlston fell. Uriah went down too, and Coleman. Nightingale slipped in the spray of blood and staggered over Charlston's body. He looked at his face, the expression frozen on it, and scrambled to his feet. Shock numbed his grief. He had to keep running.

The *Scylla*'s marines answered, knocking through the line of men on the *Ulysses*'s starboard side. Jennings was in charge now; he rushed to Nightingale's side, panting, streaked with someone's blood. Less than half a minute in command and his head snapped backwards in a halo of gore. Nightingale did not stop.

He fired blindly into the veil of smoke, gasping for breath. A bullet whistled past his ear; another shattered coral by his foot. He heard himself shouting, '*Scylla! Scylla!*' as if it were the only thing keeping him upright.

They reached below the range of the cannons. But the muskets were right above them and it was only the skilled aim of Nightingale's marines and the urgent speed of his men that kept them alive. He only looked ahead at the solid wall of the *Ulysses*'s starboard side. He was nearly there, weaving through the smoke and spluttering out the acrid taste when something barrelled into him.

He lost his feet, knees slamming into hard coral. His palms ripped on it as he tried to stop himself rolling into the water but his legs slipped below the surface, salt on his wound making him cry aloud. At the same time, a shot nearly shattered his eardrum. Whoever had smacked into his side was still falling. With a sickening thud, they landed almost on top of him.

The bullet meant for Nightingale had pierced Kieran's throat. He was alive for a few moments more – enough time to look at Nightingale and breathe, through gargled blood, 'I didn't blame you, Captain. Not for the lash.'

Sudden tears clouded Nightingale's vision, the relief of forgiveness for a punishment he knew too well.

'Thank you,' he managed, but the light had already left Kieran's eyes.

Grief surged in Nightingale. He dug his fingers into the reef and heaved himself back to his feet, dripping water and blood. Yelling, he covered the last distance in a few bounds. His mind detached from his body, primal instinct driving his muscles. It made him clamp on to the *Ulysses*'s side, grabbing at splintered timbers and climbing over the holes the *Scylla* had pierced in her hull. The five that remained of his division were right with him – Rylance, knife between his teeth, clambered up beside him.

Pikes and bayonets jabbed down. Nightingale ignored them until one came too close and he grabbed the pike's sheath and yanked it so the wielder tottered over the edge. Faces appeared in the open portholes; familiar accents screamed at them as dirks and pistols tried to find their marks. Nightingale kicked at an axe, bashed at a cutlass, and heard both fall into the water.

His legs and arms burnt. His lungs screamed with every rattling breath. Men younger than him overtook, nearly reaching the gunwales. He jammed his foot against the next porthole lid and forced himself up, with Rylance's hand roughly shoving him the final way.

Then, the deck. He shouted hoarsely as he vaulted the rail and was faced with a clump of pulsating, pushing, fighting bodies. Smythe had got over the stern and was swinging his blade, stopping only to fire into the gang of men around him. Courtney wrenched himself over the larboard side and for a moment, his gaze crossed with Nightingale's.

'Below!' Nightingale shouted across the heaving mass. 'Try to get below!'

They had to find the captain, or whoever was in command. Driven by that idea, Nightingale shoved his way through the horde. Voices screamed in his ear and he responded, thrusting his sword blindly, firing towards enemies. He felt the blade scrape on ribs; blood spurted over his uniform; nails clawed blindly for his face and neck. He did not know how he saw it all at once – something primordial, desperate for survival, possessed his limbs.

Courtney fought his way through to him. When they met, Nightingale grabbed his arm and pulled him close, panting, fingers digging into his muscle.

'Below!' he shouted again.

Side by side, they forced their way through anonymous bodies blocking their path to the hatches. Courtney's back pressed to Nightingale's, shielding him as he hurried into the pungent, metallic darkness of the gun deck. Nightingale's feet slipped on blood and he nearly plunged headfirst, only to catch himself on the ropes. The deck was not as crowded as above – many of the crew had hurried to defend the vulnerable sides.

Still, men came running. Nightingale's blade clashed with a steel point which snapped towards his eyes. He parried furiously, slashing the attacker back towards the cannon. The man tripped on the breech-rope, smacked his head on the iron gun. More took his place. Stained with gore and heaving in the smoke, Nightingale fought through. Close by, Courtney barrelled, screaming, into the assault. Nightingale saw him jam his elbow into a man's throat and kick his knee into his groin.

More of the Scyllas joined them now, driving the enemies back in an unstoppable tide. Those with sense went for the guns, spiking them, leaving them useless.

Nightingale met Courtney again at the stern. One fleeting moment passed. Nightingale rasped, 'You are unharmed.'

Courtney nodded, shivering with energy.

'Come on,' Nightingale urged. He could not stop or the emotion and fear would well over.

The partitions had been pulled up again around the great cabin. Two marines waited outside. They raised their muskets, but without hesitation Courtney fired and took one out at the knee. Pulling out his secondary pistol, Nightingale did the same to the other and threw the muskets aside.

'You can't go in,' one of the marines managed, grabbing his leg.

Nightingale kept his pistol trained on the man's head but said softly, 'I am Captain Hiram Nightingale of the *Scylla*. I have come to take your ship back to port for justice.'

Fearful eyes stared up from a young, bloodied face. Tears fell. 'I am not a mutineer,' he pleaded.

Nightingale looked away. 'Arthur,' he ordered, 'open the door.'

With a heave, Courtney snapped the lock and wrenched the cabin's door back. The bright light streaming through the broken gallery windows blinded Nightingale for a moment. When his vision returned, he found he was staring into the barrel of another musket. He froze.

A young woman stood at the other end of the gun. She wore men's clothing but her dark hair streamed down her back in wild curls: the figure Nightingale had seen at the helm.

And on her belt was Ransome's eagle-headed sword.

She blinked, breath heaving. Dirt and blood streaked her face. She looked at Nightingale, lips curled, eyes black with rage and terror.

Then her gaze shifted and she saw Courtney.

Her shoulders sagged. The musket dropped. 'Arthur?' she whispered.

Courtney pushed in front of Nightingale. He said one word.

'Jane.'

Chapter Twenty-Six: The Ferryman

The ship had been taken. After weeks and weeks across the ocean, leagues and leagues covered, it barely took twenty minutes.

As Nightingale walked over the ravaged quarterdeck, he had to avoid the pools of blood and fallen bodies. Nearly all were men of the *Ulysses*, cut down beneath the trained, determined assault of the Scyllas. He had pressed the young surgeon's mate of the *Ulysses* into service with Dr Archer and they both worked in the cockpit to dress wounds and revive anyone from the brink of death.

Around one hundred men remained. Nothing distinguished them from Scyllas. Many came from the same counties, perhaps the same hometowns, as his crew. Nightingale had tried not to consider them his countrymen anymore. Now they had surrendered, it was impossible. They had all been in the same service once; there was understanding and fear in their faces as he walked past the survivors. All of them brothers and sons and husbands and fathers.

He kept his face in a stony mask and did not meet their eyes.

Ferguson, acting lieutenant of the marines since both Charlston and Sergeant Jennings had fallen, watched over the prisoners with his men. He gripped his musket firmly but Nightingale saw his bloodied hands shaking. Smythe and Burrows walked beside him, noting down names and ranks and staring down men, some of whom were triple their ages. Smythe wore the bravest face of all. Finley, the youngest of the midshipmen, had been cut down in his division, a pistol shot piercing his thirteen-year-old heart, and Nightingale knew the lad would blame himself.

This was not how Nightingale had imagined the boarding. He had anticipated relief. But he searched himself and found that the cold coil of anxiety had grown again, blooming from some seed that would always exist.

He concentrated on his duties. Lieutenant Hargreaves had been sent for to come across. Over the sides, parties of Scyllas already worked to ease the *Ulysses* off the reef. The breach to the hull was not as ugly as Nightingale had feared: five inches of seawater sat in the hold, and Mr Parry and his mates hammered and caulked to stopper the break whilst men worked the pumps. They had to succeed before the tide rose again and flooded through.

All of that raced around Nightingale's mind – but always at the fore was what he had left in the great cabin.

Leaving Smythe and the marines in command, he descended into the slaughterhouse of the gun deck. His men threw water over the timbers to clean out the blood and gore, but nothing could be done about the smell other than leaving the gun ports open. Gaping wounds and decay sat heavily in Nightingale's lungs. Men looked up from their foul work as he passed and saluted him. Such abuse to this one ship, over and over.

Voices drifted from the great cabin. He entered to see Courtney at the windows, fists clenched behind his back. He turned sharply, unable to hide the grief painting his handsome but pale features.

Jane sat at the desk nearby. The musket still lay before her, along with Ransome's sword. A rust-coloured mark stained the blade: the American mutineer's blood. 'I am under arrest too, yes?' she asked without a quiver.

Nightingale picked up an overturned chair and sat, feeling the ache in his legs and back. 'Miss Courtney,' he began, only for her to shake her head.

'I was married, Captain. I am Mrs Howard.'

'Apologies, Mrs Howard. I appreciate you spreading the word to surrender. You saved many lives.'

'We had no choice, Captain. It was not our intention to run the *Ulysses* onto the reef. We were nothing more than target practice for you.'

'I trust you understand why I am here, and what happens now.'

Jane nodded.

'Mrs Howard,' Nightingale continued, 'I need to know exactly what occurred. From the moment of the mutiny to now.'

Jane watched him without blinking. Her eyes had the same striking defiance in them that Courtney's had, but beyond that and her wild curls, they did not look similar. She had soft features where Courtney had hard, angular ones; her cheeks still retained their pinkish puppy-fat, her mouth a downturned pout. And yet she wielded a sword and musket, and had fended for herself amongst these angry, bloodthirsty men.

'You shall have to tell someone, Mrs Howard,' Nightingale insisted. 'There is no use in—'

'I shall tell you.' She sighed. 'Arthur – please sit down. You shall think badly of me when you hear it.'

'No,' Courtney rasped. 'I could never do that.'

Jane raised her eyebrows as if she did not believe him. But with Courtney sitting down, she began.

'It was terrible from the moment we left port,' she said. 'Lieutenant Davidson ruled the ship like a tyrant. Even Captain Wheatley was afraid of him – he always did what Davidson wanted and pretended he didn't know what was happening. I don't know what possessed Davidson – I think there might have been some slight given to him before the ship set sail – but he had his favourites and men suffered if they were not one. Perhaps he was just evil, as some men are.

'There were floggings and beatings and harsh words. The men were frantic. They remembered the *Hermione* not a few years ago. Certain…talk was suggested. Ransome was the leader, and a handful of close companions agreed with him. They met in secret each night – it did not take long for them to make a decision.'

Jane leant forward, elbows on the desk, rubbing her thumb around her wedding ring. She looked down at it, avoiding Nightingale's eyes. 'One night when Davidson was not on watch, Valentine and Travers, two of Ransome's mates, feigned a fight. They argued and called each other names. Lieutenant Wainwright – poor Lieutenant Wainwright, he was so kind – went to break them up and Ransome knocked him over the head with a belaying pin. As soon as he fell that was it. It barely took ten minutes.'

Jane shook her head and paused, obviously still seeing that terrible event. 'The men grabbed Davidson first and brought him to the deck. He was still in his nightshirt when they hanged him from the yardarm. When Wainwright awoke, he tried to stop them and a few of the men argued, but they soon quietened under Ransome. I remember Davidson kicking and choking – they did not kill him quickly. I did not like him, but to kill a man that way…

'And then,' she sighed, 'it was the other officers. They imprisoned a couple, including Wainwright, as he'd never done a thing wrong to them. The rest they hacked their way through and tossed into the sea. My husband raised a hand to stop them. He did not last long.'

A single tear gathered in Jane's eye. She wiped it away. Courtney reached a hand to her, but she pushed him away.

'After that, they locked Captain Wheatley in the great cabin with them. Ransome planned to use him as a cover for what they had done. He was clever back then. He convinced the rest of the crew that they had acted rightly. He told them that this service would only bleed them dry and usurp their freedoms. He was an American pressed into the service a while back, I think. Those people have such bold ideas about liberty.

'I and Olivia – the gunner's wife – were eventually brought into the cabin. I knew about Wainwright's escape attempt but I did not tell them. I hope the man managed to get away with some people.'

'He did,' Nightingale remarked. 'I spoke to him in a hospital in Antigua.'

'I'm glad he escaped. He got out before it really became terrible. Oh—' Jane's breath trembled. 'I believe that it would have been better with Lieutenant Davidson. At first, after the mutiny, Ransome behaved well. We had heard rumours of the gold by then. Ransome promised to separate it between us and told us of all the wonderful things he would do. But he only shared his long-term plans with his favourite comrades, Valentine, Gardner, Nolan and Travers.

'I soon realised that Ransome's dreams of utopia did not include everyone aboard. Before, there had been a hierarchy of rank, of work. But when he took command, Ransome split everyone by their creed or their colour or their place of birth. We once had more freed men aboard than we do now, but he treated them as if they were still in chains. Liberty, to Ransome, had a clause which some people did not meet.

'And he was reckless. When we met a Spanish ship, he tried to bribe them with the gold so they would accompany us down the South American coast. They escorted us some of the way but then there was a storm. For three days and three nights, I thought we were going to be lost. And I think I welcomed it.'

'The Spanish ship was the *Fénix*,' Nightingale commented. 'We met her also.'

'I wished I had tried to stow away onboard. But more and more, I realised that someone had to act. Ransome would kill us with his carelessness, or we'd be captured. We had to stay in Salvador for weeks upon weeks for repairs. And whilst he was there, Ransome turned into even more of a monster.'

Jane shivered, her eyes filling with furious tears. 'He kept going into Salvador with Valentine. They went to the whipping post in the city – so much for rising up against cruelty – and I assume all the whorehouses and taverns, and Ransome had a sword made – paid for by the gold, gold that others could have easily recognised and traced us by. Every time they left, he and Valentine argued. It was about Captain Wheatley. Once they had paraded him in Salvador and the repairs were underway, they didn't need him. Valentine wanted to keep him alive. Ransome wanted him dead. Of course, Ransome won.'

More tears fell. 'But that wasn't what made me... That wasn't it. One night, when they came back drunk, they took Olivia away. They... they...'

'It's all right, I understand,' Nightingale said.

'No,' Jane spat. 'No. You have to know. They raped her again and again and again. I don't – I don't think it was the first time they had done it. It only stopped because Olivia slit her throat the next morning.'

Nightingale bowed his head. It was one evil atop another: a pyramid of cruelty worse than anything he had imagined.

'I couldn't stand it,' Jane wept. 'My – our – mother used to face the same terror from our father. I'm so very tired of men, of people, acting like – like… God, I couldn't stand it. I had to do something. Everyone else was too scared. So one day, when we were due to leave Salvador, I went to Ransome. He never suspected us women. I lied to him, I said I wanted to help him, that what he had done to Olivia was the final card and I did not want to end the same way… Then—'

'Jane,' Courtney whispered brokenly. 'Please.'

'Please what, Arthur?' She snapped her head around to face him. 'Please don't say it? I killed him, Arthur! I took his musket and I shot him, and then I stabbed his goddamned sword into his throat!'

Nightingale closed his eyes. He wanted to weep, not only for Jane and what she had experienced, but for what she had had to face. She had murdered a man, and she had taken possession of a mutinous ship. No matter if she had done it for good reasons, she was a pirate and a killer. Courtney knew it too.

'Jane,' Courtney breathed. 'I'm so sorry. I should have never put you aboard.'

'Mrs Howard,' Nightingale said. 'Why did you fire upon the *Scylla*? We could have helped you. You were free from Ransome.'

'Free from him, yes, and all his comrades. Once he fell, the others rose up and slaughtered them. I did not stop them. I wanted to see them suffer, I wanted to see them die. And I…' She stopped suddenly. For a while, she stared down at the weapons before her: the weapons that had saved her life, or perhaps condemned it. 'We still wanted to escape. We wanted to run away and take the gold. We knew we would be tarred with the same brush as Ransome and his mutineers, no matter what we did.'

'Jane.' Courtney finally moved. He knelt beside his sister, taking her hands away from the weapons and squeezing them in his own. 'You must not tell them this. Say that you were forced or—'

Shouting from above interrupted him. It wrenched Nightingale back to the present. He stood, instinctively gripping his sword as hurried footsteps echoed over the deck, running to the source of the yelling.

Jane let go of Courtney and reached for the gun. Courtney grabbed her again with a fierce, 'No.'

'Mrs Howard,' Nightingale ordered, 'stay here with Lieutenant Courtney. Do not move. I will return.'

Before they could respond, he raced from the cabin. Around, the sounds of the repairs and the men on the reef had stopped so everyone could listen to the din. Smythe's familiar, not-quite-broken voice suddenly pierced through. 'All of you!' he called. 'Stay where you are!'

Another man responded.

Lieutenant Hargreaves.

Nightingale scaled the ladders, sword banging against his legs. Without even knowing what was happening, fury surged. He had chased the *Ulysses*; he had boarded her; he had taken her and she had surrendered. But a single spark could still ignite the powder. The same cordage that had hung Lieutenant Davidson swayed above them all.

He burst onto the deck, and in a second, took in the view: Hargreaves in the middle of Smythe and Ferguson, Barty reaching to hold him back. The *Ulysses*'s men were on their feet again, bristling behind the curtain of marines, all of them shouting towards the *Scylla*'s lieutenant.

'Please!' Smythe begged, sounding like he might cry.

Nightingale didn't pause. He gripped his sword and bellowed, 'Everyone on your knees!'

The din continued. 'On your knees, now!' Nightingale repeated.

Faces turned to him. In a slow wave, the men dropped to the blood-soaked deck, tainting their knees in the detritus. The Scyllas glanced at each other, open-mouthed, then followed suit.

'And you, Mr Hargreaves!' Nightingale shouted.

Wide-eyed, the lieutenant bent down. His gaze affixed to Nightingale as he approached.

'What in God's name is this about?' Nightingale exclaimed. 'I ordered all men to stay at their stations and obey the orders of Mr Smythe!'

Smythe, at his feet, snivelled. Tears ran down his red face, making him look younger than his already youthful fifteen years.

'Stop that, Harry,' Barty hissed at Smythe's side. 'The captain ain't angry at you.'

'S-sir,' Smythe whimpered. 'Lieutenant Hargreaves, he came aboard, sir, and the men – the *Ulysses* men – they refused—'

'Refused?' Nightingale yelled at the assemblage. 'What right do they have to refuse? Lieutenant!' Hargreaves jerked. His knees shook where he was kneeling. 'Stand up. You shall accompany me to the cabin.'

'Captain Nightingale, sir!'

At first, Nightingale thought the voice was Hargreaves's – but it came from aft. Everyone turned towards an older man who shuffled awkwardly amidst the crew.

'You shan't address me!' Nightingale ordered. 'You shall have your time to speak.'

'I know the lieutenant, sir! He was in English Harbour. With a fancy gentleman in a blue coat and red hair.'

Nightingale stopped. Sweat had been dripping down his back at having to speak to the *Ulysses* crew like this. Now, ice flooded his veins.

'Sir,' Hargreaves whispered.

Nightingale held up a hand. A fancy red-haired gentleman in a blue coat. Lord Fairholme had been at the governor's house in Trinidad, bedecked in azure, laden with decoration, hair in distinctive auburn ringlets.

'What is your name, sailor?' Nightingale asked, quieter now.

'Will Canning, sir. Gunner's mate. I was not part of the mutineers, sir. Many of these boys were not.'

'Why do you so protest about Lieutenant Hargreaves being onboard, Mr Canning?'

Canning blinked. One of his eyes was milky-white, his skin almost brown with the sun. 'They were on the harbour before we set sail, sir, talking with the ordnance officials. I thought perhaps the lieutenant was one of ours but he never showed. All he did was talk to some of my crewmates onshore, him and this fancy gentleman. Then our stores came onboard.'

'Sir, it was to ensure the—' Hargreaves began.

'Quiet, Lieutenant. Mr Smythe, signal to the *Scylla* for Master Loom to come across with some of our men. I want as many hands as possible.'

Instinct festered inside of Nightingale. Something was wrong: something he could not quite pinpoint. He could not deny it – certainly not when he reached the cabin and Jane sprang to her feet.

'You!' she choked. 'You son of a bitch! You came aboard with that man in Antigua, you—'

'Mrs Howard!' Nightingale leapt between Jane and Hargreaves as she rushed at him. Courtney grabbed her arms, pulling her back against his chest. She still struggled, too close to the weapons for Nightingale's liking. 'Lieutenant Hargreaves, please sit! Mrs Howard, you know this man.'

'I do.' She was ashen. Anger pulsed behind her eyes, staring, accusing, at Hargreaves. 'He was at English Harbour before we set sail. Him and his lord spoke to some of the crew ashore, he spoke to Ransome! Ransome said they'd put the gold onboard!'

'Mrs Howard,' Nightingale said, 'I know why the gold was onboard the *Ulysses*.'

'That gold killed my husband! This crew killed each other over it, they raped my friend!'

'That was Ransome's choice,' Lieutenant Hargreaves said in a hushed voice. 'He did not have to take it so far.'

'Take what so far?' Nightingale asked.

Hargreaves shut his mouth. He was almost as pale as Jane, hands pressed between his knees, body tight and trembling.

'What did Ransome take too far?' Nightingale pressed.

'The mutiny.'

'Once you have raised one hand in mutiny, Lieutenant, that is already too far,' Courtney spat. He still held Jane, who was gripping his arms so hard her knuckles were white. 'My sister could have been killed!'

'Lord Fairholme did not intend for that!'

'That bastard and his bribe for Saint-Domingue. And you helped him!'

'Lieutenant Courtney!' Nightingale turned on the young lieutenant, though he was shouting exactly what was on his own mind. To Hargreaves, he said, as calmly as possible, 'I need to know what is happening here. My orders are to seize the gold and take it to port. I do not understand why it could not be left to me. I want to know what you are here for.' A sudden dread sparked inside of him. 'I want to know what the gold's purpose is.'

'It is Lord Fairholme's business, sir. Our role in the service is not to question. We... we obey, that is all.'

Nightingale stayed calm. 'What is the gold here for, Michael? Tell me, or I will ensure that it does not reach port.'

Cold silence fell. Nightingale was no stranger to adapting his schemes to fast events; wind and weather could never be predicted. But all those other times, there had been a constant: the ship and her crew, a sturdy deck to set his feet, men who he could trust. This was not war anymore, and this ship was crammed with hidden trapdoors. There were too many secrets, too many lies.

Hargreaves's eyes flashed at his threat. Nightingale was surprised to see frightened tears in them. 'Your orders,' he began. 'They are to deliver the gold. I am to ensure that happens.'

'Then tell me what it is for.'

'I can't!' Hargreaves swallowed convulsively. He was far from the secretive agent of Fairholme's that Nightingale had feared. 'Please, Captain.'

'Then this gold...' Nightingale marched to the false panel above them. He cracked it open, prayed there was still money left, and dragged one of the heavy cloth sacks out. Gold jangled inside. Hiding his sickness at being so close to it, he walked to the broken gallery window and held it out over the reef and the churning sea. 'It'll go to the depths this instant.'

'You wouldn't!'

Nightingale felt the heat of their eyes upon him. He flexed his fingers around the bag. In a heartbeat, Hargreaves rose to his feet and crossed the cabin – but Courtney released Jane and grasped his elbow. Suddenly, Jane clutched the gun again.

'No!' Nightingale cried.

'I want to know the truth!' she wailed. 'I want to know why so many people died! I want to know why I had to kill a man! I'll do it again!'

'No, please!' Hargreaves pleaded, shrinking towards Nightingale. 'It wasn't my fault! I only did what Lord Fairholme told me to do!'

'What did he tell you to do, Michael?' Nightingale tried to keep his voice steady, not wanting to fracture the tension in the cabin.

'The gold... It can't be lost. It was never—' Hargreaves gave a wretched sob and collapsed against the locker beneath the windows. 'It was never meant to reach Saint-Domingue.'

'What?'

Hargreaves's head sank into his hands. 'Don't make me say it,' he sobbed.

Heart thudding, Nightingale sat beside him. Jane slowly lowered the gun and Courtney hurried to draw her back into his arms.

'Tell me, Michael,' Nightingale urged.

Hargreaves sniffed, eyes and nose streaming. He resisted for only a few moments more. 'Lord Fairholme is in debt,' he said. 'He has money in the Caribbean islands, in Saint-Domingue. When the rebellion began, he lost much and then, out of fear, tried to withdraw his investments from other plantations. He can no longer pay off his agents or the debt that grew out of his failed attempt to raise a company for India.'

'And?' Nightingale prompted.

'He could not ask for more money,' Hargreaves relented, 'and he is too proud to sell his lands and estates. He needed a way that was unofficial – he knew that the government was scared about the slave uprisings and their potential to spread, and he knew that they would agree to a bribe for General Louverture.'

Nightingale cycled back through what Fairholme had told him in Trinidad: the revolution in Saint-Domingue, the terror of the violence unfurling and gutting the profits from the slave industry, how the gold was supposed to stop the risk. He had hated the furtive nature of it and had hated being so embroiled in the ugly topics, but it seemed these depths were fouler than he had feared. He had thought Fairholme had trusted him, had taken him into his confidence…

But he had used him as much as his father and Sir William had.

'You bastard,' Courtney spat. 'All of this – this violence, all of these lives lost…'

'This was not what Lord Fairholme intended!' Hargreaves insisted. 'When we spoke to Ransome, we told him to take the *Ulysses* into Georgetown and wait for an agent. We paid him, but he didn't know about all of the gold, and he was not supposed to kill Lieutenant Davidson nor all of those men. Lieutenant Davidson was there to observe things!'

Nightingale's head ached. Still gripping the gold, he rose, not wanting to be close to Hargreaves.

'You paid a man to mutiny,' he breathed.

'To mutiny, yes. Not murder! When he did not arrive in Georgetown, Lord Fairholme knew something was wrong. And when they were sighted off Salvador, days south from their destination, he regretted it.'

'Regretted losing out on his money,' Courtney hissed.

'When the *Scylla* lost her second lieutenant to fever, he knew I had to replace him. And he knew that you had to continue on the voyage as well, Captain.'

'That was why he insisted I kept my position,' Nightingale said. 'Because he did not want to tell anyone else about the gold.'

'He said that you would roll over and do whatever he required, and you'd shut your mouth about it. He knew things about you, and that if you refused, he would reveal you for what you are.'

Nightingale glanced at Courtney. Courtney looked away. All of those old terrors built again: the concerns that he was not ready for this voyage, that he would harm himself and others. Others had seen it. He could not run. He could strike off one head, and another would grow, and another, and another…

'But he knew that you would do worse, didn't he?' Courtney suddenly said. 'You knew exactly what he was like, and what the gold was for, and you still obeyed. You laid the powder, Lieutenant, and gave the match to another man, then pretended you were not to blame for the fire. How many have died for that? All for a handful of fucking gold.'

'Arthur, please.' Nightingale pushed himself away from the desk. Suddenly, he knew what he must do. It would not be easy, but it had to be done for the greater good. 'I have heard enough. Arthur, accompany Mrs Howard across to the *Scylla*. Give her Mr Hargreaves's cabin. The prisoners of the *Ulysses* shall be escorted across as well, but I want a handful to remain here to help with the ship.

'As for you, Mr Hargreaves… You shall be arrested and taken back to port to face trial.'

'Sir!' Hargreaves protested.

'I'll not hear anymore! Lieutenant Courtney – pass the word for Acting-Lieutenant Ferguson. My decision is final.'

Hargreaves opened his mouth to argue, but stopped when Courtney – instead of passing the word – simply yelled, 'Mr Ferguson!' outside the cabin. The marine ran down the ladder, musket in hand. Nightingale gave him his orders, and Hargreaves's fate was sealed.

As was all of theirs.

Chapter Twenty-Seven: Catharsis

For the next hour, the boats ran back and forth between the *Scylla* and the *Ulysses*, transporting the prisoners. It took many journeys to get them all across but Nightingale was adamant: he wanted them away from the ship which had been such a danger – and still was, lodged upon the jagged reef.

Each man that left took a chapter of the *Ulysses* with him. Her physical wounds remained: blood dripping from the scuppers, staining the bulkheads and timbers; scorch marks from pistol and round shot; discarded weapons in place of the crew. But all else was ghost-like. Everything Nightingale had thought about the *Ulysses* and this voyage was wrong.

All wrong.

Nightingale watched as Hargreaves was taken into a cutter by Ferguson and another marine. He was one of the last to go across. Nightingale hoped that his public arrest had allayed the *Ulysses* men's frets. Another two launches waited: one for Jane, Courtney and the other marines, and one for the remaining men upon the *Ulysses*.

Jane stood near, one of Courtney's hands around her arm. Her face betrayed nothing. The crew had continually looked towards her, and Nightingale was glad for how calm she had stayed.

'Mrs Howard, Lieutenant Courtney, if you please,' Nightingale said, and they came forward to the rail.

Courtney's face was still marred with streaked powder-burns, remnants of how he had furiously wiped away his tears before coming on deck. 'Sir,' he said, 'I can stay here and help with the *Ulysses*.'

'No. You should be with Jane. She needs you now more than ever. And in my absence, you shall command the *Scylla*.'

'You shall…' Courtney started, then paused. 'You shall come across soon – to the *Scylla*?'

'As soon as the *Ulysses* is secured, yes. That is why some men are staying behind with Mr Parry, Mr Loom and I.'

'You are not keeping many.'

Courtney was correct, but he could not know why. 'We shall be fine.'

Courtney nodded reluctantly. He glanced at the boat, looked down, and said, quietly, 'Please do not act as Ramirez did. This ship is not worth it, and neither is Lord Fairholme or your father.'

It was not advice that should have come from a subordinate officer, but many a time Courtney had gone beyond his duty, or perhaps stepped around the restrictions it set. Nightingale trusted him – trusted him even more now his faith had been shaken in others – so he smiled. 'Concentrate on the *Scylla*, Arthur.'

Now, he had to watch him leave. Courtney moved slowly, as if one of them would change their minds, and when he climbed over the side, he turned back. The *Scylla* bobbed behind him – the ship he deserved, the ship he might one day command. Nightingale wanted to give him what he could never give Leroy.

And that was why he had to do the next part alone.

As soon as he and Jane were gone, Nightingale climbed down to the orlop deck. Below, the *Ulysses* could have been the *Scylla*'s twin. He felt an uncanny familiarity as he entered the sickbay where Dr Archer and the *Ulysses*'s surgeon's mate prepared the final men. Some had died from their wounds in the last hour. Three had already been sewn into their shrouds and sent over the side with the other dead. Perhaps that fate was kinder than the hazy futures of their brothers.

'The next boat is here, Francis,' Nightingale said to Archer. 'Are you ready to leave?'

Archer wiped his forehead with the back of a bloody hand and nodded. 'Yes, sir. I've done what I can. It'll not be comfortable, but these men will make it across in one piece.'

Nightingale smiled meaninglessly at the *Ulysses* men. One was bandaged around his eyes, another with his arm wrapped in a reddened sling. The third could not move without help – his right foot had been crushed by a falling spar and his left leg cut dreadfully. Archer and Nightingale lifted him and carried him up into the bright afternoon. The sun had turned fierce through the last turn of the glass and now Nightingale had to squint.

'I'll have Obi help you and Mr…'

'Mr Ainsley.'

'Mr Ainsley across the reef,' Nightingale finished. 'Go carefully now, Francis.'

Just like Courtney, Archer looked at him sidelong. After a while, he reached out a hand. Nightingale took it and found it being shaken firmly. 'Congratulations on securing the *Ulysses*, Captain,' Archer said, as if he felt obliged to say something. 'She is yours now.'

Nightingale nodded. *Mine*, he thought. *My burden alone.*

Loom and Parry remained on the reef with the rest of the men. Nightingale climbed down onto that jagged, red-raw landscape. The tide washed in slowly, kissing the fringes of the island, but there was still time before it badly endangered the *Ulysses*. The main worry was the ship's hull. Her bows were arched, wedged solidly into the rock which had gashed her open below her waterline and bent her inwards. All the timber around the void was vulnerable.

Parry still had men inside, hammering away and working at the pumps, but now, he stood with Loom. Nightingale arrived at the end of their discussion.

'How does she fare, Mr Loom, Mr Parry?' he asked with a stoic smile.

'Not as miserable as we thought, sir,' Loom said with an answering smirk. 'I think we can have her off the reef. Once the waters rise, a kedging manoeuvre might see us right.'

Nightingale nodded and peered at the hole. He thought of all that still remained on the *Ulysses*, all that waited for them at port, all that he had done. He straightened again, squeezed his hands behind his back, and said, 'I want you all to return to the *Scylla*.'

The silence that followed was deafening. Loom frowned and glanced at Parry. 'Sir, this ship can still be rescued.'

'I don't doubt you. But I want you all to return.'

Others were stopping, turning towards them and this strange order. Nightingale wondered if Loom would refuse. He would be within his rights to question his superior officer. 'Sir,' Loom said. 'I don't understand.'

'It is not your place to understand, Josiah. I have made my decision. Please return to the *Scylla*.'

It was not fair to keep the reasons from them – but he had not told anyone for fear they would stop him, or tell him what would inevitably happen. He already knew the risk. And that was why they had to leave.

'Captain,' Loom tried once more. 'I can aid in whatever you wish.'

Nightingale stayed firm. He had refused Courtney; he could refuse Loom. 'I have ordered you to return to the *Scylla*,' he repeated. 'A boat is waiting. Board it and I shall follow.'

Perhaps they thought he had gone mad. Only their loyalty made them obey. Nightingale had come through hell with them to earn their respect. The idea that he was playing with it, pushing it too far, made his stomach turn.

But, watching them walk across the reef towards the cutter, he knew it was necessary. It was better to deceive them than drag them down with him.

'A captain should be the last to leave his ship,' he said, and with a nod at the men, he descended into the depths.

The *Ulysses* was utterly silent – no more hammering or caulking, no more shouts to pull her off the reef. Gone were the men who had trusted her and gone were the men who had mutilated her. Only the sea made any noise.

Too many times, he had placed deeper meaning onto his ships. They had been homes or places of escape or confinement. There had been the *Strabo*, his first ship as a midshipman; the *Lion*, the ship which had changed everything; the *Scylla*, the ship which had made him understand so much about his life.

The *Ulysses* was another. He had painted her as an image of hope, a way to alleviate what he had lost, proof he could still stand – but now her symbols were stripped away. She was a desolate, melancholy construction of wood and canvas and metal and hemp. Nightingale faced the very core.

In that kernel, he saw himself.

As he walked the gun deck, he thought of the Nile. Two years had passed since the *Orient* had erupted, taking Leroy and almost taking his own vision. He had lied to himself that he had recovered, but like the sun so often mocked his sight, moments like these reminded him that he would always bear his inner injuries. Always, the darkness crept in.

Even when he cut one thread from the web, another emerged to replace it. Sir William and his father had convinced him to travel to the West Indies. Sir William and his father had then tried to take his command away. Lord Fairholme had saved him, only to throw him into another quagmire, equally deep. So many people had lied to him, had taken his weaknesses and turned them into weapons.

Men had died for this deception, as men would always die for deceptions. The *Ulysses*'s men had been stirred to rebellion – doubtless they had behaved evilly, as all men could – yet there was evil around them too. He still wished to help those who had suffered – perhaps a common suffering existed amongst them all.

The more he thought of it, the more the disgust and regret grew. He had walked straight into his father's trap and Fairholme's snares.

From Tom to now, he had looked through the bars of a cage.

If he followed his orders and took the gold and the ship to port, he would hand those men a victory – not only over himself, but over the crew they had bribed and killed. This voyage had unveiled many terrors: the mutiny, the deaths, the loss of the *Fénix*, Richmond's injuries, the questioning in Trinidad, the crew he had opened fire on – and all the brothers and sisters, mothers, fathers and daughters who would suffer because of it.

Lieutenant Hargreaves had been right. He had always obeyed orders without question. His life had never been his own.

But he had one advantage over Lord Fairholme, over Sir William, over his father. They were not here. They could burrow into his mind like woodworm and they could try to command his thoughts, but they were not here.

They were not here to stop him dragging the gold into the magazine.

They were not here to stop him taking a keg and scattering powder over the decks.

They were not here to stop him throwing canvas onto the timbers.

They were not here to stop him standing back, taking a breath and letting fall a match.

They were not here to stop the flames.

Nightingale stood outside of the great cabin as the fire spread. The conflagration ate at the bulkheads and gouged holes in the deck. Wood cracked, metal hissed, glass shattered. Every inch of destruction was another seared memory, melting into black smoke. Nightingale sensed the intense heat and tasted the acridity, but he felt no more fear. As the ship shed her tragedies, so his own were scorched into dust. This was his pyre: the pyre of his trauma, of his guilt.

He closed his eyes, letting them stream. Choking sobs escaped his throat. His legs weakened in relief. His heart soared with the growing column of smoke and fire billowing through the portholes. He was here, suddenly starkly aware of his own self and his own thoughts.

This was his choice.

Finally, a way to stand taller than those who had hurt him.

The sobs turned into laughs. The flames made him delirious, the bars breaking on the cage at long last. The inferno tore along the deck, disembowelling the ship, turning it into the rubble and debris it had once been before men had moulded it.

He ascended onto the main deck to see the blaze raging up the ladders, approaching the mizzen mast. The sound was incredible, a roaring, furious storm that deafened everything else. He looked to starboard and saw Loom and Parry on their feet in the cutter, maniacally waving their arms. Across on the *Scylla*, another boat was being lowered. Nightingale raised a hand in acknowledgment, then calmly climbed down the side.

He did not look back as he moved over the reef. He only felt the relief throbbing in his chest – until Loom and Parry grasped him as he raised a foot to get into the boat. His knees were buckling.

Someone was shouting, 'Sir! Sir!' and a cloak was being pulled around his shoulders.

Tears flooded his cheeks.

'Give way,' he ordered in a rasp.

They obeyed, pulling off from the reef and rowing with all their might away from the inferno. Nightingale still did not turn. He kept staring ahead at the *Scylla* – even as the *Ulysses* screamed and burnt – even as she shuddered in anticipation – even as the flames gutted the powder store and she erupted with an almighty wail.

Nightingale heard the debris scatter astern of them. Those shards were the last fragments of his cage. They were the last of the *Fénix*, the last of the *Orient* finally coming to rest.

Part III

Chapter Twenty-Eight: Janus

9 August 1800

The weather bloomed into a fine, warm evening, a fresh breeze sweetly blowing one point abaft the beam, and the *Scylla* made eight knots with a course for Trinidad: the kindest conditions the ship had experienced for days. In the fair weather, she sailed under nearly full canvas, with only the royals missing. Her t'gallants filled like white wings, joining her topsails and courses on a larboard tack. Nightingale sat in the great cabin, listening to the kiss of the wind against the hull and the singing of the canvas high above him, interrupted by the bosun's whistle as Acting-Lieutenant Smythe gave the orders during his watch.

The routine of the ship was almost intolerably normal. But Nightingale would have been stupid, and reckless, to not see the approaching storm.

'I shall be court martialled, without a doubt,' he said to Courtney – the only person he had invited to dine with him. 'I lost the *Fénix*, and now the *Ulysses*. Every captain must answer when he loses a ship, no matter how it happened. And these circumstances will not look favourable for me.'

Courtney nodded. He had not said a word for or against what Nightingale had done. When Nightingale had boarded the *Scylla* again after the explosion, Courtney had pushed through the gawping crowd and helped his shaking body over the deck, all the while asking, 'Are you all right, sir? Are you all right?' and bellowing for the crew to return to their duties.

Prompted by the silence, Nightingale said, 'I had to do it. I could not let that ship see land again, not with the gold onboard. Everyone is free to call me mad when they are brought up to be questioned at the trial.'

'It's not my place to question what you did, sir,' Courtney replied. 'Even if it was, I think I may have done the same.'

Nightingale smiled dryly. 'Don't you ever do the same, Lieutenant. Don't you take that as a guide.'

Courtney huffed, winding his fork between his fingers. He had barely touched his pork and his glass was still almost full.

'I shall speak to Mr Hargreaves,' Nightingale continued. 'I don't entirely understand what passed between him and Lord Fairholme – whether he was as forced and duped as I was, or if his head was entirely in it. Whatever occurs, I shall tell the court martial the truth about Fairholme. Perhaps it will allow them to bestow some leniency on the innocent prisoners.'

'Do you think they deserve leniency, sir?'

Nightingale paused. He thought of the tyrannical Ransome and all his crimes against his fellow men, the women, the service... It was so simple to view that, and all his followers, as cruel and deserving of punishment. Nightingale did not mourn his death. But what had occurred afterwards had still been a crime. No matter if Jane had acted for the good of the crew, her actions were still mutinous, or piratical.

The intentions might not sway the cold heart of the court.

'Some, no,' he answered. 'Some... yes. I believe not all took part in the violence. Pardons may be granted.'

The alternative was without question. They would be condemned, and they would be executed.

Courtney knew that as well as he did. 'What shall happen to Jane?'

'Have you spoken to her since returning to the *Scylla*?'

'No, sir. She has been sleeping in Mr Hargreaves's cabin.'

'I would like to speak with her again. She can aid in identifying trustworthy prisoners. Come tomorrow, I would like to have them help on deck.'

Some – those who had spoken up on the *Ulysses* – had already been put to work under the observation of the officers and the uncertain crew. More would be welcome if Nightingale knew he could trust them.

Courtney nodded. He raised his glass to his lips and then put it down again without tasting a drop. With a sigh, he set down his fork as well, looking pale. 'You shall not... allow her to be hanged?' he managed. 'She murdered a man and helped to command a stolen ship with plans to sail it away and take the gold... I know what she has done. But I can't watch her hang.'

'I will do everything I can. But whether my word means anything depends on how the court martial accepts the information about Lord Fairholme and Lieutenant Hargreaves.'

'I can't watch her hang,' Courtney said again, voice tight with emotion. Tom appeared in Nightingale's mind again: that terrible October morning where his father had scratched the mental scars to accompany the physical. He wished that upon no one.

'I will do everything I can,' Nightingale said once more.

The *Ulysses* was gone, the gold was scattered on the terrible reef, the mutineers were en route to port, yet Nightingale still felt a heavy weight. He would take whatever waited for him. That had been a decision he had come to long before the first flames purified the *Ulysses*.

He was more concerned with the crew and their opinions of his actions. Only an unhinged man would do what he had done without justification. They would not see that he had acted for them, or at least for some fanciful idea of them.

Hargreaves had been confined below in the same place Ramirez and Allende had once been. Two marines stood watch outside the cramped cabin. With a nod at them, Nightingale stepped through the door they opened and kept it ajar as he entered into the warm darkness. The smell of the animals rose up from the hold, intermingled with sweat from the *Ulysses*'s crew, still confined nearby whilst information was gathered. Nightingale had been tempted to order Hargreaves's imprisonment with them, but he feared how they would treat him.

Hargreaves sat on a barrel, hands bound, staring into the shadows of the small space. He had been stripped of his uniform coat, sword, and anything signifying his rank. His cold blue eyes flicked up to Nightingale as he entered and he rose to his feet – not out of politeness, but to make himself tower over his captain.

'Sit down, please, Mr Hargreaves,' Nightingale said. He didn't, so Nightingale sat, calmly, upon another barrel. He looked up into the tall man's pinched face without reaction.

'I heard the explosion yesterday,' Hargreaves accused. His voice was ragged and raw, scoured by the sandpaper-like horror of the last day. 'Why did you do it?'

'I shall ask the questions, Mr Hargreaves.'

'I will answer to a court and to Lord Fairholme. I do not owe you any explanation.'

'Then I do not owe you one either, Mr Hargreaves.'

Hargreaves stared at him as if trying to identify his tone, before eventually relenting and sitting firmly upon the barrel. He crossed his legs, one foot shuddering as he moved it nervously.

'Mr Hargreaves,' Nightingale began. 'I won't hide what I have done, just as, when I'm asked, I won't hide why I did it. They shall all know that I acted because I did not deem the *Ulysses*, or what she carried, fit to return to port.'

'That was not your call to make,' Hargreaves snarled, a man pushed into the corner with no other choice but to bite and snap.

'Perhaps not,' Nightingale said slowly. 'And I know that I shall answer for it, just as I expect you to answer for what you fomented on the *Ulysses* with Lord Fairholme.'

'I was there to retrieve the gold and ensure the ship went to port. That was my priority. I followed my orders. Until you disobeyed and put it all to ruins.'

'You and Lord Fairholme believed I would not disobey, yes?'

Hargreaves nodded. 'He saw what you were like – how you'd submitted to your father and to Sir William to take the position in Trinidad, and then how you'd just as easily changed your plans and accepted command of the *Scylla*. He thought you would relent to anything.'

'Did you think the same?'

Hargreaves nodded again.

'Well, I am sorry to disappoint you and Lord Fairholme, Michael.'

'It was Lord Fairholme,' Hargreaves spat. 'Lord Fairholme was the one to foment the mutiny.'

'You are very willing to throw Lord Fairholme to the lions.'

Hargreaves trembled, his mouth full of things he wished to say. 'He will not be pleased. I had to retrieve the gold for him.'

The man clung to that idea like a lifeline. Perhaps he had convinced himself that, by following Lord Fairholme, he had acted correctly.

'That is why you were so eager to board the *Ulysses* with us, yes?' Nightingale asked.

Hargreaves stayed silent. His eyes shone with desperation, with fear, with anger. Nightingale bore his icy gaze; he had faced worse men than this misguided, confused lieutenant.

'Mr Hargreaves,' he said. 'I cannot see why you did it. You are a naval officer. You understand how evil mutiny is, how uncontrolled it can become once the match is set. And you understand the severe repercussions and punishments against it.' He paused. He couldn't help thinking of how Courtney had distrusted Hargreaves and accused him of inexperience. 'I am assuming that you are a naval officer?'

Hargreaves dropped his eyes to the ground. A thread of pain weaved across his face. By chance, Nightingale had hit upon something deeper.

Eventually, Hargreaves nodded. 'I am.'

'I spoke with Lord Fairholme in Trinidad. He has a penchant for men who are vulnerable and who have exploitable weaknesses. I know that he manipulated mine. And I have been acquainted with many awful men,' Nightingale admitted. 'My father, for one. I know how they act. I understand how it feels to be under their sway. That is how I know that you are not awful, Mr Hargreaves. So why tie yourself to someone as awful as Lord Fairholme?'

Hargreaves still had not looked up. 'Why obey your father?' he asked.

'Loyalty. Obedience. Because of what he held over me. Love. Fear.'

Hargreaves sighed. 'Then there is your answer.'

'I also disobeyed him for the same reasons. Loyalty to those who have lost their lives. Acknowledging what I have long held over myself. The fear of choosing the wrong path. The love for... many people, many ideas. If I had not done it, I would have regretted it even more intensely.'

273

'It was not your place,' Hargreaves repeated. 'Your regret will mean nothing to those who shall question you. You were ordered to retrieve the gold – I was ordered to retrieve the gold…'

'Well. There, you have my explanation. I believe that you have an explanation too. You say that they shall not care about my reasons, but I will listen to yours, Michael. I want to know.'

Hargreaves shook his head. Around them, Nightingale sensed the wind changing, a slight movement in the *Scylla*'s stable course. Within seconds, Courtney's distant voice shouted to set the royals. Hargreaves scowled. 'I did not lie,' he said quietly. 'I am a lieutenant. But my promotion is only dated to three months ago.'

'Three months?' Nightingale asked, frowning.

Hargreaves nodded. He gritted his teeth, swallowed convulsively, and continued, 'I have been – I was – a midshipman for twenty years. Now, I am thirty-four, I failed the examination so many times, countless times, I don't know how many. I gave up hope of promotion. Even as everybody around me was promoted. For years and years, I have been ordered around by boys half my age – boys of fifteen, sixteen, called "senior" midshipmen, and by lieutenants barely out of their teens. I hated them. I hated them all.'

Nightingale stayed silent. He had heard of ageing midshipmen and ageing lieutenants, trapped in their positions – sometimes by their own ineptitude, sometimes by the stagnant way the Admiralty worked, denying them their ascent.

'My ship – the *Galene* – conveyed Lord Fairholme across the Atlantic. You say that he seeks out men's weaknesses. He paid attention to me, the first attention I had felt that was not mocking. He told me about Saint-Domingue and about his problems. He kept speaking to me of Portugal, where I have family. I thought that he cared about them, but he only wanted more information. They have suffered through France's pressure on Portugal; Fairholme assured me that if I did not help him, they would suffer further. But by that point, I had already agreed to help him.'

A harsh mix of emotions churned in Nightingale's stomach. He hated Hargreaves's weakness and what he had done to the *Ulysses* with

Lord Fairholme. He hated that he had opened a door for Ransome and his fellows to brutalise the crew. And he hated the threads that had been pulled around them all. Each of them was a fly in the intricate web that unseen hands wove.

'I believed that you had been in Lord Fairholme's employment for some time,' Nightingale said. 'You seemed to know what you were doing in Salvador, finding the right man to contact and then locating Ransome's body.'

'Lord Fairholme fed me that information about Salvador before we left Trinidad. He knew the *Ulysses* had been sighted there, and he wondered how long Ransome would survive onboard. At that point, it did not matter. Ransome had already sailed past Georgetown, where he was supposed to guide the *Ulysses*. And I doubt that... I doubt that Lord Fairholme would have let him live had he obeyed him anyway.'

Too many secrets and too many loose ends. Nightingale wondered what Fairholme would do to Hargreaves.

Hargreaves's tears finally began to fall. He wept in convulsive sobs, but Nightingale felt nothing. He doubted he was crying for the lives that had been lost because of his patron's deception. He cried for himself, the small boy who had joined as a midshipman and had never grown up.

'When we reach Trinidad,' Nightingale uttered, 'we shall face questions, as you say. If you speak up and talk of Lord Fairholme's influence—'

'No.' Hargreaves's head snapped up, his cheeks shining with tears. 'No, I cannot. I know what he would do, what he will do now I've failed, let alone if I speak against him. No, I will not.'

'What do you plan to do, Mr Hargreaves?'

'I don't know. I thought we would succeed.'

Nightingale knew that if Hargreaves spoke up, it would add weight to his accusations against Fairholme. But, as events had shown, he was a dangerous man to rely upon. 'You have helped us before, Mr Hargreaves. It might have not been with the best intentions, but you guided us through Salvador and gave good counsel. I believe that you can help us again, and this time, with better motives.'

'Do you believe that your motives are good?' Hargreaves spat. 'Whatever happens, whatever you say, men shall be hanged. Someone shall have to bear the blame for the *Ulysses*. It could be any one of us.'

I will take that risk, Nightingale wanted to say – but in Hargreaves's sobbing, weakened figure, he saw himself. That was what he could have allowed himself to become. The temptation to give into self-pity and crumble under the awful shadows that lurked, dormant, would always be there. He would never be able to shed the scarred, abused skin he had worn in the past.

But there was a difference between picking at the wounds and letting them heal over.

Ignoring those wounds would make them fester. Running back to the same thorns, expecting them to curl back this time, would only lead to more pain.

Hargreaves had a choice to make. In the close, pungent confines of the lower deck, bound in chains, it might not have seemed that way. Yet, no matter how terrible, there was always a choice.

When he left him in the early hours of the approaching day, Nightingale could only hope he made the right one.

Chapter Twenty-Nine: Cuckoos in the Nest

Three days passed and they again cruised through the waters off Salvador. The pleasant weather and fresh breeze remained, and from the masthead the world was an orb of fragrant blue, the light azure of the sky mixing with the calm line of the cobalt sea. Nightingale clung to a brace, feet firmly planted on the main top yard. Miles stretched around this lofty pinnacle, and for a while, he enjoyed the scent of the water, the ruffling kiss of the wind, and the warm sun just passed its zenith.

Each afternoon, he climbed up as if he were a midshipman again. It was a departure from the close confines of the ship and her remaining troubles. Just a day previously, he had performed the final service for the Scyllas who had died in the attack on the *Ulysses*. He had read the rites, watched their shrouded bodies vanish into the waters, and thought that the last time he had led a funeral was for Leroy. As he said farewell to Kieran and Charlston and Jennings and Finley, he knew he never wished anyone to die under his orders again.

From this height, he could look down upon the deck and see the busy shipboard life. His eyes, scarred and blurred as they were, could still decipher the dashes of colour as the lower berth sailors flitted about, interspersed with the uniform hues of the officers.

They were all his crew now, no matter what ship they came from. Jane had offered names of *Ulysses* men who she thought could be trusted and, since she had spent so long trapped with them on the *Ulysses*, Nightingale believed in her judgement. There was a muted acceptance from the Scyllas; so far, there had been no outward conflict.

But Jane could not answer for some of the men below. They remained like an open powder-keg, either harmless or about to be struck and ignited. He would be happy to finally see Trinidad and remove the smoking match.

Ropes and spars creaked and Loom appeared, grasping his way through the rigging. 'You did not have to drag yourself all the way up here, Josiah,' Nightingale said, gripping his hand and steadying him on the yard.

'I can see why you come up here, sir,' Loom panted. 'There's peace and quiet, despite the drop.'

Nightingale smiled. 'They've behaved themselves so far,' he said in reference to the crew.

'More or less, sir.' Loom paused. 'I've just come from Mr Winthrop and the quartermaster. It's fortunate we were stocked for six months for rounding the Horn. It's keeping the new boys fed as well as ours. Seems we'll reach Trinidad without reducing to three-quarter rations, even.'

They'd have truly seen how the men behaved themselves if they had had to reduce. 'I did consider that,' Nightingale said, 'before... before the *Ulysses*.'

Loom hummed vaguely. Nightingale had sat his officers down the day before last and explained to them why he had condemned the *Ulysses* and the gold. No one could speak for or against him. Yet he felt lighter for revealing the truth, even if it turned into a one-man campaign against Lord Fairholme and his kind.

'Perhaps I am closing the stable door after the horse has bolted, but how do you think they are faring, Josiah? You say they are behaving themselves, "more or less".'

'It's hard to say what I think, sir. My opinion doesn't amount to much in the scheme of things, and despite it all, it's hard to read men even after being confined with them. It's why I keep myself to the ship.'

'But if I had to prompt you? As your captain.'

A small smile tugged at the corners of Loom's weathered lips. 'Can't judge them in a mass, sir. The *Ulysses* lot've been through hell.'

'I believe there are good men in there, just as much as the opposite,' Nightingale admitted, knowing he did not have to say such things before Loom. 'Ransome made sure to bring out their anger, though it's hard to tell if they only followed to stop their own deaths. The punishment for mutiny is hanging, and it seems the punishment for going against Ransome was just as harsh. I wonder if they all hate Mr Hargreaves and Lord Fairholme, or if some would have acted without the prompt.'

'It's hard to look into the mind of another man, sir. Hard enough to read your own, let alone another's. It's for the courts to decide. Meddling might stir the pot 'til it bubbles over.'

Perhaps it was a tacit warning from a man who had nearly twenty years on Nightingale. Nightingale knew, though, that he had already stuck his hand into that pit of vipers by setting fire to the *Ulysses*. It would be foolish to think he could take it out without getting bitten. He only hoped he could take the venom himself, and not harm any others.

As he descended to the deck with Loom, he noticed Jane sat at the taffrail. Before now, the only women Nightingale had conveyed on his ships had been the spouses of diplomats. Certainly, none of them had been guarded by marines, or dressed in trousers and a man's shirt.

Jane looked up as Nightingale approached. Barty, at the helm, lowered his eyes in respect. On instinct, Nightingale glanced at the binnacle and marked their progress.

'Seven knots and a fair wind,' Jane said. 'It shall be a few days until we reach Trinidad, yes?'

'That is correct, ma'am.'

'We had been long under Ransome's spell by then. I remember passing the island and hoping that a fleet of English ships would come and rescue us. My husband thought about sending off a signal to the port. Ransome and Valentine killed him shortly after.'

'I'm sorry for what you experienced, Mrs Howard.'

Jane did not react. 'I have already told you everything, Captain Nightingale. If you are here to ask me more, then I shall return to my cabin.'

'I needn't remind you that you are still our prisoner. I have been lenient with you because of the trust I have in your brother. But I cannot give you any more preferential treatment.'

Nightingale sat beside her. She glared at him with a tight mouth and a firm jaw. Though she had washed all the blood and grime from her skin and clothes, she still looked haggard, far older than her twenty years.

'I am not here to press for more details about what happened, Mrs Howard. I have heard all I need to, and I have acted accordingly.'

'By destroying the *Ulysses* and all the gold?'

Nightingale bowed his head.

'They shall have your head for that. Why not tell the courts that it was accidental? That the *Ulysses* caught fire in the fight?'

Such bold questions and astute comments: the same that had been plaguing Nightingale.

'I should hope it allows for more leniencies towards the men, and towards you, Mrs Howard.'

To his surprise, she laughed. Burrows, on watch, and the marines, glanced at her. 'With all respect, Captain Nightingale, you do not know yourself who the culprits are, or who still harbours mutinous thoughts. Even I do not know, and I was confined with them. Circumstances changed by the day on the *Ulysses*. One man may say he is not a mutineer at sunrise but by moonlight, he's a different person. The courts are not there to prise open a man's head and judge his goodness. We shall be condemned one way or another.'

'You are very sure of this.'

'I lived thirteen long years with my father. Never once did any justice come for him. Justice only came for Ransome because I was the one who delivered it.' She paused, looking up at the driver sail. A kind wind blew, and the sea flowed past them in gentle waves. It seemed obscene that she could talk so openly about such ugliness. 'I would kill Ransome again, Captain, and feel no remorse. And I cannot say I was not tempted to escape with the gold and sink the ship. We all wanted to vanish.'

'You do not have to tell the courts this.'

Another laugh. 'You are advising me to lie to the courts when you will tell them what you did and why? Why should I lie? We are the same, Captain Nightingale. We both acted against people's expectations, and did something we thought was morally justifiable in the moment. Others may not see it the same way, and I accepted that as soon as I picked up Ransome's gun.'

'Mrs Howard, the difference is that I may lose my rank and any hope of command. You shall face harsher punishments – for piracy, mutiny, murder.'

'I am a pirate, Captain. I am a mutineer. I am a murderer. Along with many of the men on this ship.' She sighed. 'Where is your confidence now? I thought you said that when you tell the court the truth about Hargreaves and Fairholme, they may be lenient.'

'Mrs Howard—'

'You have no confidence in your plan, do you? You know as well as anybody what the court will do. You have dug yourself into a hole and do not know how to crawl out.'

'That is not true.'

'You need evidence, Captain. Someone to verify your accusations. The word of a simple sailor saying that he saw Lord Fairholme and Mr Hargreaves in English Harbour, talking to the crew, will not suffice. Ransome is dead. Lord Fairholme ensured that all traces of his actions were cleaned away.'

'I have Mr Hargreaves. He shall speak out.'

Jane shook her head. 'My brother thinks you are pinning false hope on Mr Hargreaves. He believes he cannot be fixed, or does not deserve to be.'

Nightingale pushed down his disappointment at the comment about Courtney's views. 'And how about you, Mrs Howard?' he asked. 'Shall you speak out?'

'I will not return to Trinidad.'

The words did not connect for a moment. Nightingale mulled them over, turned them around, and they still made no sense coming from Jane's lips. 'I'm sorry?' he tried.

'I will not return to Trinidad. How can I? And nor do I want to return. I have had my fill of what men do to each other.'

'Where do you intend to go? The world will not be kind to a lone woman.'

'The world is not kind to anyone, Captain. And I have fared well on my own so far. Perhaps I shall marry again. Let me worry about that. I want to be set down in Salvador, or any other place nearby, and be granted freedom. You do not even need to know where I shall go, so you truly will be blameless.'

'Mrs Howard.' Nightingale did not know what to say. He was no stranger to women speaking their minds; in Jane, he saw a fragment of Louisa. But he fretted over the repercussions of what she desired. 'You know that I cannot allow that. You are our prisoner, for one. Moreover, I would never rest easily if I abandoned a woman to the world.'

'If I were a man, Captain—'

'Then I would act in the same way. I promised to keep you safe.'

'By returning me to Trinidad to be hanged?' She shook her head again. She had maintained command for these last weeks, and such a thing was hard to relinquish – just in the way of Courtney in the early days of Nightingale's captaincy of the *Scylla*. 'Who did you promise? Your orders were to take the *Ulysses* and the gold.'

'I promised your brother. What do you think he shall say when he finds out what you have planned?'

Jane sighed. She looked down at her hands and squeezed them in her lap. 'I know Arthur will not be happy. But the alternative is worse.'

'I shall not allow you to be hanged, Mrs Howard,' Nightingale insisted, laying his hand on hers. 'And Arthur has agonised over finding you. He shall not let you go.'

'How do you know my brother's feelings?'

'I care for him very much, Mrs Howard.'

Jane looked up and tilted her head. Whatever she had been about to say was interrupted by another voice.

'Sir.'

Courtney appeared by the companion-ladder and ascended onto the poop deck. He tipped his hat in salute to Nightingale then swept it off in Jane's presence. She revealed nothing about what they had been speaking of. Instead, she rose to leave – only for Courtney to hold out an arm to stop her.

'I think you should stay here, Jane,' he said. 'There's trouble below, sir. It's the *Ulysses* men.'

Nightingale was on his feet in an instant. 'What is happening?'

'If you please, sir.'

Nightingale was already following Courtney as the marines surrounded Jane again. They descended further and further into the darkness of the ship, delving through the different levels of scents. From the airy breeze of the upper deck, stirring up the salty tang of the sea and the sweetness of the pitch and tar, through the canvas, rope and iron miasma of the gun deck, and down into the rich, close odour of men forced to live and sleep on top of each other. After so many years at sea, Nightingale should have been accustomed to it, but it still rose, thick and cloying, in his lungs.

On the way he accosted two more marines. They went into the hold first, almost swallowed by the heavy darkness. In the shadows, Nightingale's ears attuned to any noise. The murmurings of the captive *Ulysses* men sounded louder and more vicious. He understood why captains ate themselves alive over the fear of mutiny. He could not let that show.

He stepped into the circle of Courtney's lantern light and ducked under the low beams. A young man rose from the remaining prisoners. His wrists were manacled and his back was bent beneath the timbers. Ferguson, the new commander of marines, gripped his musket and kept it positioned between Nightingale and the man.

Nightingale looked up as the shadows slowly unveiled his face. He remembered him on the deck after the capture of the *Ulysses*. Perhaps a little younger than himself, wiry hair curling over a sweat-soaked brow and large, piercing grey eyes.

The murmuring had stopped.

'I have come because I have been informed you are discontented,' Nightingale said, measured, trying not to accuse. 'Is that correct?'

'We feel there's been an injustice, sir,' the prisoner replied, voice raspy and hoarse.

'An injustice?' He frowned. 'What is your name?'

'I am Daniel Meyer. Forecastle man on the *Ulysses* in Lieutenant Davidson's division.'

'Very well. What injustice has befallen you, Mr Meyer?'

A sardonic smirk plucked at the corners of Meyer's mouth. 'Can you not see where we are, sir? Chained down here in the hold?'

'Be mindful who you're speaking to,' Courtney snapped from beside Nightingale.

'It's all right, Lieutenant,' Nightingale assured. 'Be mindful who you're speaking to, Mr Meyer. The *Ulysses* is gone, and you and the rest of her crew are under my command until we reach Trinidad. You shall speak to me as you spoke to Captain Wheatley.'

'Captain Wheatley did nothing, sir. Even after Ransome and his mates rebelled, he bent over and let them have him at will. Went along with every one of Ransome's tricks and disguises. He should've never been in command.'

'Then you would have risen up against the captain if given the chance?' Nightingale asked, and saw the smirk on Meyer's mouth slip.

'I admit,' he said, 'I did not stand against Ransome as some men tried to. But Ransome's actions were against Lieutenant Davidson, not Captain Wheatley. And that Yankee bastard pushed it too far. Murdering half the crew in the name of liberty. Even if that fancy lord and Lieutenant Hargreaves bribed him, like some're saying, he didn't have to do that.'

'Do you all feel this way?'

Meyer glanced over his shoulder at the assembled prisoners. Many eyes adhered to him and Nightingale.

'Reckon everyone has their own opinion, Captain, and everyone did what they thought was right.'

It sounded eerily familiar. 'If Lieutenant Hargreaves had not prompted Ransome and the others,' Nightingale said, knowing he was confirming Meyer's suspicions, 'would he have mutinied?'

Meyer shrugged, then, at a sharp look from Courtney, said, 'I don't know, sir. Ransome and his mates were eager for it. Perhaps they had good ideas, to a point. I doubt all of them were put in his head by Hargreaves and Fairholme. And after a while, it didn't matter who had bribed whom, or even if they had. We'd gone too far.'

'Are you willing to say such things in court? They will question everyone involved, you are aware of that.'

'Yes, sir.'

'"Yes" you shall speak up, "yes" you understand? You do not seem afraid. Mutiny is an ugly thing.'

'I know what I did, sir. I know what I didn't do.'

'Then what is this injustice you feel has befallen you?'

'This, sir.' Meyer looked around him at the crowded space. 'We are condemned like cattle down here whilst others work on deck.'

Nightingale sensed Courtney beside him, bristling at the question to his authority – a long way from the young man who had done the same at the start of this voyage.

'Mrs Howard provided me with names of men she trusts,' Nightingale said. 'I trust her judgement.'

'She is a mutineer as much as all of us. How can you know to trust her?'

'Be careful how you speak,' Courtney sniped again. This time, Meyer's gaze turned upon him. A knowing glint passed over his face.

'Yes, Mrs Howard said she had a brother in the navy. You have the same eyes and hair.'

Courtney fell silent.

'That is enough,' Nightingale ordered firmly. 'The status of the *Ulysses* and her crew is for the courts to decide. I am not the judge or the executioner.'

'You made your choice by destroying the ship, with all respect, Captain. You made your choice by listening to Mrs Howard.'

Nightingale turned away from Meyer's accusatory gaze, finding Ferguson in the low light.

'Keep them under watch, Mr Ferguson. They shall remain below until I see fit to allow them access to the deck.'

It was all he could say.

Rising again through the ship, the light increased but did not stir the shadows in Nightingale's chest. He had left Meyer on a weak note, scurrying away, trying to patch together the pieces of his authority over them. Much of that authority came from the manacles they wore and the fate that awaited them. He just had to keep them quiet until they made port.

'I shall be glad to reach Trinidad,' Nightingale sighed honestly. 'I shall be glad to see the back of this voyage, if you'll pardon my dourness, Lieutenant.'

'I'm sorry, sir.'

'What do you have to be sorry for?' Nightingale stopped. The world rushed for a moment, as if everything suddenly caught up with him. To think that Courtney reckoned he had anything to do with that burden was ridiculous.

But Courtney wore a dark and serious expression. 'If they know that Jane is my sister, sir – and I'd say Meyer made that connection – I don't know what they shall suppose. The ties I have to a mutineer, a murderer. Our bias towards her...'

'You bear no responsibility for Jane's actions, Arthur, and certainly no blame. I have only known her a few days, but do you truly think you could sway her mind into doing anything?'

With that comment, Jane's ominous request returned to Nightingale. There was a pile of grievances to sort through and each one kept clawing to the top.

Nightingale glanced over his shoulder, but the orlop was curiously lonely. 'Have you spoken to her?' he asked. 'Recently? Do you know of her wishes?'

He was not surprised to see the confusion in Courtney's face. 'No. I have barely had chance to see her. Aside from at the end of the day when she settles down for the night. Is she well?'

It broke Nightingale's heart to see the steadfast lieutenant laid low by the fear and guilt he felt for Jane. They were two people in a terrible circumstance, one which could have been completely avoidable. 'She asked me if she could leave, Arthur,' he said carefully, as if speaking to a frightened animal. 'She asked me to set her down in a boat bound for Salvador. And then to leave her there to fend for herself. She doesn't wish to return to Trinidad.'

'What?' Courtney's eyes widened. His mouth quivered with emotion. 'Wh-why? She could not... She needs to be with people. She needs to... to recover.'

'I agree with you. She needs company after what she has been through. I know as well as any other what it is like to...' He cut himself

286

off, but Courtney already knew his past and what he had suffered. 'I would like her to testify in Trinidad as well. She is a witness to all that happened. She and Mr Hargreaves are key players in all of this, and I need them.'

Courtney stayed mute for a while. The silence echoed, deafening, on the empty deck.

'I shall try to protect her,' Nightingale insisted, but knew that if he could not control the men below, there was precious little he could do to control the court. 'My offer still stands. I am willing to let her into my home if the trial goes in our favour.'

'Our favour? She is a mutineer, Captain. It does not matter what intentions she had. You shall be seen as a traitor if you accept her into your house, and she is my sister. My sister... a mutineer.'

'If they know the true circumstances of the mutiny, if they know how Lord Fairholme and Lieutenant Hargreaves acted...' It was an argument he had pushed time and time again, constantly pulling it apart in his head and insisting it was intact. But the more he thought and spoke about it, the more hollow it sounded. He decided it was better to shut his mouth.

'Thank you, sir,' Courtney eventually said. 'For the offer to protect her. I do appreciate it, I truthfully do. But...'

Nightingale saw that Courtney did not believe in him, just as Jane had suggested. He noted the loss which already swarmed in his eyes. He had two terrible paths before him – even more terrible because of how the directions were out of his hands.

The lesser of two evils, Nightingale thought. Once again.

Chapter Thirty: The Figurehead

Within a day, as if the weather understood, black clouds emerged. The temperature dropped into a cold shroud, and with the barometer falling, Nightingale ignored the need for sleep. He kept a lantern lit in his cabin, dashing off letters to Louisa and the Admiralty: obsessive reinforcements in case the trial did not go his way. Terrified he had missed something, he checked and rechecked the ship's logs, knowing the court would scour them more intensely than he could in his fogged mind.

Rain pattered against the windows and leaked through seams. Nightingale noted the need to close reef the canvas if it worsened, and began another letter.

His pen scraped the paper as blinding light ignited the cabin. For a moment, he thought the lantern had blown. The rumbling roar of thunder corrected him.

In a moment, he pulled on his heavy-weather coat and raced to the deck, almost slipping on the wet timber. The night sky was as black as pitch, not a star in sight. Moonlight struggled to illuminate the canvas: still too much aloft. He opened his mouth to give the order but choked as a sudden gust of wind stole his breath.

'Close reef all canvas!' Courtney's voice boomed. 'Storm sails only! Forecastle men, aloft, now!'

Men, cowering under the downpour in hooded oilskin coats, joined the topmen on the masts. The growing fury of the tempest eliminated all differences between the Scyllas and the *Ulysses* men. Nightingale expected the orders to be obeyed no matter who they were.

Clinging to belaying pins and stays, Nightingale groped his way to the helm where Barty and his mate grabbed the spokes. Above, the men on the yards planted their soles firmly on the foot ropes, having to lean their whole bodies onto the spar to tie up the sails. Looking up, Nightingale could see how much the masts already rolled in the waves. The next pitch had Barty's mate slipping when a blast of water poured over the rail.

'Steady!' Nightingale called as the man nearly smacked his head on the spinning spokes. He grabbed them, feeling the beleaguered soul of the ship through the helm. She bucked and jerked, making him and Barty strain as they held on.

'There's more than sixty men in the hold, sir!' Barty shouted. 'The balance is shot! That's extra ballast she doesn't need!'

'I'm aware! Brace!'

Proving Barty's point, another wave streamed from aft, lifting the stern, slamming it down to then raise the bows. The *Scylla* pitched unnaturally, buffeted by a blow from starboard.

'She'll founder!' Barty yelled.

It took the three of them, and two other men running from the *Scylla*'s waist, to try to control her. The canvas drew taut above them but the tempest wrenched at the *Scylla*'s masts and yards. She rebelled with every timber, every plunge of the sea against her hull. Each minute that passed added another struggle. Nightingale tried to bring her about, away from the broadsiding waves, but they were everywhere, frothing in the moonlight, rising ghost-like above the deck until they plunged everyone into frozen water.

Nightingale pushed the *Scylla*; she pushed back. As lightning illuminated the men's pale faces, he thought of the *Fénix*: the inferno from one freak strike.

Impossibly, the wind gained with a scream. The helm tugged. Ropes whipped and pulled taut.

Then, above the din, a sickening crack.

Nightingale peered up through the hail. In the confusion, he could not tell what was wrong, but something was out of place and so he stared, stricken, as the scattered moonlight caught the fore-topmast.

Unintelligible cries shouted through the night. Topmen leapt to the lower yards.

The wind had scoured the lifts. The upper-topsail yard dragged against them, straining out of position. It pulled and pulled and then, suddenly, the spar broke free. It arced in the darkness, lashed by the rain, and in one piece, toppled forward. Rigging, still attached to the mast, streamed behind it and tangled into the stays as it collided with the bowsprit.

The impact rippled through the ship. Nightingale ran, slipping down the companion-way and pushing through the deckhands. Some of his men dangled from the lower fore-topsail yard, held tightly by their mates who tried to pull them to safety. A wave slammed to starboard and Nightingale's back collided with the mainmast. One of the men above fell and landed, upside down, in the shrouds, and ahead, Nightingale saw the fallen spar jerk, embedding itself further into the mass of ropes and wood. The figurehead of *Scylla*, with her spear aloft, stopped it from toppling entirely into the water.

But the fearsome collision had wrecked the ship's balance. The spar tugged on the foremast like a sea anchor, bounced in the tempestuous waves.

One wave – it only had to be slightly worse than the last – and they could founder.

Nightingale staggered upright. He felt the back of his ringing head, surprised to find no blood. 'Cut it free!' he heard himself yell, hoping they could understand him above the storm. 'Cut it free!'

The men had watched, as aghast as he had been. But now they sprang to action again, energised by a tangible goal. Obi and Garrett clambered over bits of rain-soaked yard into the bows.

'I can go, sir, lash me into a sling and I can go!' Smythe materialised at Nightingale's side. His hat had blown free and his pale hair glowed in the moonlight. He pointed over the prow, down into the cat's cradle between the bowsprit and the topmast. 'I can go!' he repeated. 'I'm light enough!'

'You're an officer, Mr Smythe!' Nightingale shouted back. 'I cannot allow you to go! Supervise the men!'

A gang of men, small and lithe, quickly assembled under Smythe's direction. By that time, Courtney had pushed his way into the fray, accompanied by others wielding marlinspikes and boat-knives. They stood precariously on the wales and reached up to saw at the taut ropes. But even after loosening them, the topmast was still stuck fast.

And so the men under Smythe wreathed themselves in cordage and began the descent over the bows. Nightingale and his crew held on to the lines securing the vanishing sailors. 'Hold tightly!' he shouted as the waves dragged them.

It took extreme courage to climb down into the mouth of a raging sea and hack at a tangled spar, trusting in others to prevent a fall. Only when the ocean rose for a long, terrible moment, tilting the ship, could Nightingale look down at the men. They were assaulted by the foaming spray and the frozen teeth of the waves, furiously trying to relinquish the topmast from the figurehead. Her spear and tentacles still held it upright.

'Cut her away!' Nightingale screamed. 'Cut her away!'

It hurt to give the order. Every crew was attached to their figure-head: the symbol and heart of the ship. But now, there could be no hesitation. They hewed at her raised arms, cutting the spear from her grip. Chunks of timber dropped into the water, each monstrous head of the sea creature decapitated. Inch by inch, the snarled topmast shifted. A whine, a creak, and then the stem of it rolled and began to fall with the remnants of Scylla.

Nightingale and the men clung to the ropes when the mast hit the sea and shifted the balance again. A wave of water washed over the men, clinging to the bowsprit. No time to feel relieved. Smythe and Obi clambered to the rails, pulling people from the spar. The rain drenched their outstretched hands, turning the timbers into ice-like surfaces.

'Sir!' Courtney appeared behind him suddenly and grabbed his arm. Nightingale turned towards his horrified face, which stared out to port.

Nightingale barely had a moment to brace before a fearsome wave collided with the *Scylla*. It threw him off his feet and he fell into the mass of bodies. Courtney landed atop him. Nightingale blinked through the rain and the shock and pushed the tangle of Courtney's wet hair from his eyes. Obi had Smythe in his grip whilst Smythe clung to a man still dangling over the ship. For a long, dreadful moment, the *Scylla* rolled to starboard, water racing over the deck.

There was a crunch, the awful sound of timbers snapping.

The ship righted herself. Nightingale eased Courtney off of him and staggered to his feet. He stepped over men to reach the starboard side. His heart jumped as he looked over the wales, dreading what he might see.

The fore-topmast had jammed into the hull. A crevice gaped. Every time the waters rose, the sea drained into it.

'Find me Mr Parry and Mr Loom!' he shouted. 'Assemble a party of men for the hold to plug the breach!'

Courtney hurried alongside him as he rushed back to the helm. 'Lieutenant,' he panted, 'I need you to find Mr Ferguson. Tell him to gather a party of marines. If the breach is as bad as it seems, I will release the prisoners from the hold. They can work the deck. I cannot have them down there, frightened and penned in, during a crisis.'

'And Mr Hargreaves, sir?'

'And Mr Hargreaves. I shall confine him to my cabin until this is over.'

Courtney nodded. 'Yes, sir.'

By the sound of the crunch, Nightingale had imagined worse – but in this raging sea, the entire bows might have been ripped away. He hurried between the deck and Parry's team in the hold, each time seeing the water getting deeper, sloshing about the timbers.

The *Ulysses* men said nothing as the marines herded them away from danger. There was no fear, no awe, nothing. Out of confinement, there seemed so many of them. This would be the perfect moment if they were to act.

But Nightingale had no choice.

Still, he could not rid the feeling of being watched. The *Ulysses* haunted them all – and instinct, Nightingale knew, had saved many sailors' lives. So he hated to utter it but knew he must, when he turned to Courtney and said, 'I am going to fetch my pistol from the great cabin. I want you to arm yourself too. Be vigilant.'

Courtney's eyes widened. Nightingale wondered if he was jumping at shadows. Yet Courtney glanced at the marines and nodded.

Nightingale nearly slipped on the ladder as he clambered down to his cabin. Staggered moonlight forced its way through the gallery windows. By that light, and the flashes of lightning, he found the case for his flintlock. The weapon would only be good for one shot, but he prayed he would not even have to use that. He flipped the lid, reached in…

…and found it empty.

For a moment, he stopped, kneeling in the patch of grey light. He tried to think back to when he had last had it: it had been during the attack on the *Ulysses*, and he had returned it here afterwards where he always kept it. He could not think straight; these last hours had drained him. One hundred scattered possibilities ran through his head.

But none of them involved hearing a quiet footfall on the boards, then rising to meet Hargreaves's terrified, pale face across the room. In his hand, he held the missing flintlock. He aimed it directly at Nightingale's heart.

Nightingale looked at the barrel; Hargreaves's shaking grip; his former lieutenant's tear-filled eyes. He slowly held out a hand. 'Michael,' he said quietly. 'Give me the gun.'

Hargreaves did not move. 'I want to be let go,' he rasped, voice gruff with fear and desperation. 'I want to be set down in a boat with some of the *Ulysses* men and allowed to escape. I heard what you said about Mrs Howard, what she wanted to do… I cannot return to Trinidad.'

'Michael.' Nightingale said his name again, clinging to the seconds he needed to think. 'I cannot do that. You must return to Trinidad to stand trial, along with the men. And these seas… Even if you did get into a boat, you would not survive this storm.'

'I will not stand trial.' Hargreaves shook his head emphatically. His lip quivered and thick tears fell down his gaunt cheeks. 'I could hang, and even if I did not, Lord Fairholme would tear me to pieces for failing. I cannot return to how I was. My family… All that I have done. I've shamed them all.'

'Think of what you're doing, Michael. If you return, leniency may be granted. But if you kill me now, in cold blood, it'll be the noose for certain.'

'Then let me go,' Hargreaves spat. He pulled back the cock on the flintlock, the sound deafening in spite of the storm. A wave sliced alongside of the *Scylla*. Nightingale slammed a hand on the table to steady himself.

'You don't want to do this.'

'Let me go,' Hargreaves sobbed. 'If you do not, the boat shall be taken by force, and I do not know what the *Ulysses* men shall do if they rise up again.'

'You have spoken to them?'

'I've heard them. I know their feelings about you and what you've done.'

He could have been bluffing, but Nightingale did not want to underestimate a man with a gun in his hand. He thought of how he could defend himself: the sword at his belt would be too slow and he could not escape at this close range. So his mind turned to the ship. 'I cannot have them harm my crew, nor Mrs Howard. I promised I would protect them. Do as you will to me, but spare them.'

'It is your choice, Captain. Let me go, or there will be blood.'

As soon as he said it, a cry echoed above. Running footsteps hurried towards it. Nightingale heard the shouts of the marines and felt ice coat his stomach.

Mutiny.

'Michael, give me the gun, please. I can help you,' he pleaded, but knew there was little he could do.

'Captain!' Courtney's voice yelled from the main deck. A spark of hope burst in Nightingale's breast, quickly dashed. He could not pull Courtney into this. He would rather Hargreaves shoot him; he had had his day, had made enough mistakes and now he had to live, or die, by the consequences. 'Captain!' Courtney shouted again. 'Stay here, Lieutenant Ferguson! I shall fetch the captain!'

Nightingale wanted to shout for him to stay away. But he could not find his voice. He stared at Hargreaves and saw that, try as he had, he could not save everyone. Someone must always suffer.

'I'm so sorry, Captain,' Hargreaves managed.

Courtney skidded to a halt at the door. Another wave slammed against the *Scylla*. Hargreaves pulled the trigger.

'No!' Courtney screamed.

The bang deafened him. Nightingale's back hit the table. His legs gave beneath him. Pain, unlike any other, ignited inside him. He reached the floor, hands convulsively pressing to his side. Open-mouthed, he stared at the blood welling between his fingers, spouting through his shirt.

Courtney appeared through the haze of agony. He was shouting something over his shoulder, but Nightingale could not make his mouth respond. Hands pressed over his to stem the tide of blood. Hargreaves was trying to run. The soaked, red coats of marines emerged in the doorway.

'Arthur,' he managed. 'Don't let him get away. Save the ship.'

He did not hear the answer. Merciful, hot darkness rolled over him, turning his body to lead. To the sound of the raging storm, he drifted into shadow, almost grateful.

Then, nothing.

Chapter Thirty-One: Nostos

It was ironic how exquisite Louisa had looked that day in September 1783.

She was blooming in the late summer heat, graceful features illuminated by how she had been made up. She wore blue, of course: a fine, azure gown with golden brocade decorating her corset and skirts to match the colours that Nightingale stood at the altar in. Long, raven tresses were curled and drawn back beneath her bonnet, revealing the elegant lines of her neck and collarbones, glowing with a thin sheen of perspiration.

Her father, then the Right Honourable William Haywood, held her arm as he walked her down the aisle – but no one's eyes were on him.

Louisa smiled shyly at Nightingale as she joined him. She smelt of rosewater, heightened by the temperature in the cathedral. It made Nightingale dizzy. She was so perfect that he barely wanted to touch her – as if she were a precious doll that he was scared to break. They had only known one another for a few months, conversing mainly by letter over the Atlantic: Louisa in Bath, Nightingale in Virginia. It seemed cruel to marry a twenty-year-old woman like her to him. He recognised that she was beautiful but he could not give her the life she deserved.

He knew, when taking her hand and speaking their vows, that it would not only be the sea keeping them apart.

Yet in the eyes of their fathers, this was an ideal match. Even during those first months with her, Lieutenant Nightingale realised why his father proposed it with such enthusiasm. He, a young bachelor, should marry to preserve their family line. She, a young woman, should marry to fit with expectations. Nightingale accepted it. He went to his marriage like he went to his career on the ocean.

The wedding ceremony and the following event at Mr Haywood's Portsmouth estate were muted. Husband and wife flitted around one another like butterflies afraid of damaging the other's wings. Nightingale barely said a word to her. Everything had already been agreed: he would move into this fine estate with Louisa while Mr Haywood relocated to the family home in Bath. Soon, he would be at sea again and Louisa would be alone with the household in this grand manor. She said nothing for or against it.

Instead, both of them went through the motions of a newly married couple. They smiled at the toasts and blessings. Nightingale had been neither happy nor sad. The overwhelming emotion was one of relief as each moment passed and he soldiered through it without erring.

And relief, also, that Leroy Sawyer was still stationed in the colonies, awaiting transport home, and had been unable to attend. Nightingale missed him terribly since they had parted – and that was the problem.

Day turned to night over Nightingale's sumptuous new house. When the guests departed, the empty, quiet rooms pressed him and Louisa into ever-closer proximity. The vanishing of any audience – his and Louisa's fathers being the last to go – made Nightingale realise that the next part was only for them. A coil of fear tightened in his stomach, so much so that he stumbled over his words, calling Louisa 'Miss Haywood' as he had done these last months.

She smiled that rigid smile that had been plastered to her lips all day and only said, sympathetically, 'May I call you Hiram?'

It sounded terribly intimate on her tongue. He wanted to recoil from that intimacy, not knowing what to do with it, but in the confines of their bedroom, nothing could be hidden. She lay beside him, unbound hair over their pillow, and stared up with those wide green eyes, waiting, shaking on the edge of this boundary to be crossed. With trembling hands, Nightingale raised her nightdress and performed his duty.

Louisa closed her eyes. Neither of them made a sound; neither one acknowledged the other. He did not kiss her until afterwards, and it was cold and full of obligation.

Then she turned away, settled her clothes around her body again and stayed in the same, stoic position until morning. Nightingale remained sitting with his arms crossed over his chest, watching obsessively for the dawn light.

'Captain. Captain.'

A voice echoed at his ear. It came from nowhere, piercing through the darkness. Nightingale blinked. He tried to move but his limbs would not shift.

'Don't move, Captain. Stay there. You shall be all right.'

The memory of his bedroom faded, cast away by the scything light of a lantern above his head. Someone shifted in front of it: a woman with wild, unbound dark hair, faceless in the cast shadows. She pressed a hand to his forehead.

'He is not warm, Dr Archer,' she said. 'That is a good sign, yes?'

Nightingale attempted to open his mouth. It was as dry as dust.

'There is no fever,' a man, vaguely familiar, replied. 'The ball must be removed quickly, though. You do not have to watch this, Mrs Howard.'

'I have seen my fair share of blood, Doctor. I wish to help.'

Jane. His skin felt clammy and tight beneath her rough, warm palm. Her rolled-up sleeves were stained with blood.

His blood.

Hargreaves. The cabin. The gun.

The mutiny.

'The ship,' he croaked. 'Wh-what is happening to—'

'Lie back, Captain. My brother is seeing to the ship. You must stay here.'

Nightingale nearly choked on a sob. He had left Courtney to deal with the mutiny and the wreckage He vaguely remembered the foretopmast falling, tangling in the bowsprit and then gouging a hole in the hull.

'I have to,' he began, only for Jane to ease him down again.

'It is best for you to stay here,' Dr Archer said from somewhere else in the orlop.

Nightingale ignored him, as he had ignored his body and his health so many times before, but blinding pain forced him onto the cot. Fire surged in his side, his head swarmed, and he cried out.

'It'll be all right, Captain,' Jane repeated over and over, and over and over, as he drifted away once more.

The sea. Always the sea. Through the agony, slowly merging into merciful numbness, he could still hear it. Nearly everything of importance in his life had happened on the ocean. A hundred ghosts lingered in their watery graves, rising to meet him now he stood at death's door.

He was aboard the *Lion* again. She was the symbol he would always cling to – the prison where his grief remained locked up, immortalised in the miniature in his study. He remembered her intimately, down to the decoration of her great cabin. The span of it was painted airy blue, reflecting the azure Mediterranean waves. A portrait of Louisa hung near his cot. One of the checkerboard tiles was scuffed where a cannon had marred it during one of the ship's many battles.

That day in 1796, she had been docked in Gibraltar. He had been at his desk, quill in hand, writing to Lieutenant Lewis's family. The officer had recently been invalided back to England, one leg gone. His replacement was due to arrive within the week but Nightingale had not expected the knock upon the door – nor the man who entered.

Nightingale rose to his feet, the pen falling, forgotten, from his fingers. Despite the breeze through the open window, heat prickled his cheeks. For a moment, twenty years fell away and he felt sixteen again. That was when he and Leroy Sawyer had met for the first time on the *Strabo*, en route to the American colonies.

'Captain Nightingale,' Leroy said, as formal as any subordinate, but with a smile tugging his lips. 'I apologise for my lateness. I wanted to be here a day ago.'

'No, Lieutenant, you are not late in the slightest. I am glad to see you. Very glad.'

Nightingale moved around the desk and grasped Leroy's hand in his, shaking it vigorously. He was exceptionally handsome, fair hair pulled back into a short tail, blue eyes gleaming. His uniform was immaculate, just as he was.

'Please sit, Lieutenant Sawyer,' Nightingale offered. 'I shall have Vaughn fetch you something to drink. You must be weary after your journey.'

'I am well,' Leroy said, sitting elegantly, his hat neatly beneath his arm. 'I wished to secure the fastest packet and the quickest coach as soon as I knew who I would be serving under.'

Nightingale reddened. He covered it with a laugh. Leroy had always teased him, even as a young, precocious midshipman. 'It seems we were never in Portsmouth at the same time as each other. I did, however, see your sister before I left. She is growing very quickly.'

'She is, indeed. She wishes to join your crew.'

Nightingale smiled. 'I regret not writing to you more often. I should offer my apologies.'

'You are my captain, sir. You do not need to apologise.' Leroy's eyes sparkled. He looked down at his hat, brushed the dust off it, and then glanced up at him again. 'Perhaps now,' he said slowly, 'you can tell me how you truly feel.'

Nightingale froze. The memory had been entirely accurate so far. But that... That was not what Leroy had said. 'What?'

'Perhaps you can tell me how you truly feel.'

Suddenly, the cabin was wrong. The airy blue paint dripped into a muddy, dark bruise. The portraits and paintings on the bulkheads cracked. The timbers turned spongy and paper-thin. Nightingale looked around, then back to Leroy. His throat opened and blood spouted from the hole that would kill him. He blinked calmly, though tears swarmed in those beautiful eyes.

'You never told me, Hiram,' he choked, voice full of bubbling red. 'I know how you felt. What if I had felt the same way?'

'No.' Nightingale leant back. The desk was hot beneath his hands, just as the ship had felt when she had burnt at the Nile. 'No, that is not fair.'

'I will die in two years, Hiram. Even then, at the end, you could have told me.'

'No. Don't do this.'

'You know what you should have done. You regret it every day. And now, you might die. Why have you not been honest with anyone?'

'I am trying.' The wood smouldered, pockets of fire igniting through the great cabin. He thought he could hear the guns firing again, or perhaps they were the shouts of mutineers. 'I tried. I have always tried to take the right course.'

'You never told me that you loved me.' The colour drained from Leroy's face. He sat there, cold and weeping, blood staining his perfect uniform.

'I did not know... Not until you were gone. I'm sorry, Leroy.'

'The truth shall come out soon, Hiram.'

Walls of flame scratched at the *Lion*'s cabin like a great beast licking her wounds. Fragments of the *Ulysses* and *Strabo* burnt with her, more and more upon the pyre Nightingale had already built. His defences crackled hotly and turned to ashes. Leroy watched him through the conflagration, serene at the end as he had been when facing his death.

Why was he seeing this? Why did he have to torture himself? This obsession with his past was an anchor around his neck, constantly weighing him down. He had to move on. He had to accept it.

It would always burn and sting.

But he could not sit and abandon others.

He rose, fighting the choking flames, defying the ship which still held him captive. Leroy looked up at him expectantly.

'I loved you, Leroy,' Nightingale said.

Leroy smiled.

'The truth shall come out soon, Hiram,' he repeated.

The words echoed around the melting walls. They followed the *Lion* as she split and descended into the depths, the timbers bending and crumbling like wet paper. Nightingale climbed out of the cabin. He wanted to take Leroy's hand and drag him along, but there was no more he could do. The memory of him remained, peaceful and enduring, in his breast.

In the belly of another ship, Nightingale lay, bloodied and bruised. He slept, halfway between memory and reality, the two blending and merging with the to-and-fro of the lantern's swaying light.

Nightingale was aware that the motion of the sea had changed. It had pulled him from the wild chase of the storm to a strangely calm dance across smooth planes: the only constant through his dreams and the hazy reality he kept waking to. Now, days later, he was stirred by a gentle rising in the waves, an increase in the speed of the *Scylla*, almost imperceptible at first and then growing to a steady, respectable frolic across the ocean.

He blinked, wondering whether it was his imagination again. Tentatively, he felt the cot beneath him, searching for scorch marks or pockets of heat. It was sturdy against his aching back – and in the orange lantern light, he saw that the bulkheads were upright and solid, no longer melting like wax.

With every slow, syrupy minute that passed, reality remained firm – enough that he could see that this part of the orlop had been cordoned off with spare sail-cloth. Dr Archer's instruments and medicines lined the walls. Beside them, on a low bench, Nightingale's uniform had been laid out neatly: his undress coat, his white breeches and waistcoat. There was not a drop of blood on any of them.

Rylance, Nightingale thought, and smiled.

Carefully, he moved, his side aching. Unsure if he wanted to see, he lifted the sheets and looked down at a clean bandage wrapped around his middle. Relief washed over him, quickly followed by thoughts about the man who had caused that wound. What had happened to Lieutenant Hargreaves? The ship? The *Ulysses* prisoners?

He wanted to get out of the cot and rejoin the crew. Yet the more time stretched, the more he feared there was no crew to go to. The *Scylla* was silent above him. The usual trill of the bosun's pipe, the stamping of feet, the striking of the bell… He could hear none of them. Thoughts of the *Ulysses* crept over him, the ridiculous shame that he had gone to bring a mutinous ship to justice and had become the same thing he ventured to destroy.

The creaking of the timbers beyond the partition nearly made his pulse jump. He sat up, wincing at the soreness.

Dr Archer pulled the cloth back and glanced through. He paused, eyebrows rising. A smile pulled at his mouth. 'Captain Nightingale,' he sighed. 'How do you feel?'

Nightingale's shoulders loosened. He released the sheets he had been gripping in anticipation. 'I am well… I believe.'

'I trusted you would be, sir. One inch lower or higher and we might have had a different situation. You can count your blessings for that wave knocking off Mr Hargreaves's aim.'

So everyone had heard the story. 'Where is he?' Nightingale rasped. 'Why is my ship so quiet?'

'Lieutenant Courtney's orders, sir. Anything above the orlop from here to the main deck – quiet as a mouse to avoid disturbing you.'

'Lieutenant Courtney's orders' meant the Scyllas still held command. 'The ship has not been taken.'

'I should inform Lieutenant Courtney that you are awake. He wished to know as soon as you opened your eyes.'

'Don't have him hurry. That breeze is rising. He should think of those t'gallants.'

But Archer disappeared and, within minutes, hurrying footsteps echoed on the boards. Courtney ducked through the partition and Nightingale's heart swelled at the look on his face. The lieutenant sighed, sweeping off his hat and holding it to his chest. His tall form seemed to lose strength as he sank into a stool beside Nightingale's cot. Formality fought to still his expression, but his joy won over and he smiled beatifically, green eyes sparkling. He reached out and grasped Nightingale's hand.

'Captain,' he breathed. 'How are you?'

'All the better for seeing you, Lieutenant.'

Courtney reddened and laughed.

'I apologise for leaving you to deal with this tangle, Arthur. I pray that everything is well.'

'You did not leave us, sir. You were shot.' A momentary silence hung between them. 'I should have been more forceful about Mr Hargreaves,' Courtney went on, and then breathed out, as if a weight had suddenly lifted from his shoulders. Nightingale rubbed his thumb across his fingers, touched at his concern.

'There was nothing more you could have done,' he said softly. 'How is the *Scylla*, Arthur? I thought that the prisoners were going to rise up. And the fore-topmast…'

'The ship is patched up as best we could, sir. Mr Parry and his mates stopped the breach. The *Ulysses* men…' He paused. 'They tried to take the ship. Mr Hargreaves wanted to leave with a number of them, but the Scyllas and the other *Ulysses* men prevented them from getting to the boats. Between us, we managed to quell them for a time. But it was nip-and-tuck out there, sir, I'll admit it. If it weren't for Commodore Harrison's arrival, I dread to think what might have happened.'

'Commodore Harrison?'

'In the *Actium*. His passage crossed ours. The sight of a sixty-four-gun ship of the line soon turned the *Ulysses*'s men's minds. He is escorting us back to Trinidad, which we'll reach in two days. Many of the prisoners are held in his ship. Including Mr Hargreaves.'

Commodore Harrison – formerly Captain Harrison, who had nearly taken Nightingale's position as commander of the *Scylla*. He hadn't thought their paths would merge again, certainly not now in this fortuitous moment.

'The *Scylla* is safe?' he asked. 'All of our men? And Jane?'

'Yes, sir. Not a man or woman was lost in the storm or in the brief uprising.'

Nightingale sighed in relief. 'I am glad to hear that you are well,' he said. 'You have performed admirably, Arthur, to hold such a crew together, and such a ship.'

Courtney smiled. He swallowed and Nightingale realised there were tears in his eyes, the pressure of keeping strong and the fear of the last few days taking its toll. Without thinking, Nightingale lifted a hand and cupped his cheek. Courtney closed his eyes and leant into the touch. His skin was warm beneath Nightingale's palm, his hair soft where it brushed the backs of his fingers. Unfiltered affection raced through Nightingale. He caressed his thumb over Courtney's cheekbone, felt the fluttering of his lashes.

'Sir?'

A voice came from beyond the cloth. Courtney slowly, reluctantly, opened his eyes and straightened. Nightingale let his hand linger a moment longer, then dropped it to the sheets.

Smythe entered cautiously. His face glowed, breaking into a beaming smile when he saw Nightingale. Nightingale had not seen him smile since Finley's death on the *Ulysses*.

'Oh, sir!' he cried. 'Captain, sir, Lieutenant, sir! Sir, I am... sir!'

Nightingale laughed. Courtney rose and put his hat back on his head, unable to stop smirking. 'The captain is in command now, Mr Smythe,' he said. 'You shall address him.'

'I feel I shall be here a little while longer, Lieutenant. The *Scylla* is under your care.'

'Of course, sir.'

'Then, Lieutenant Courtney, sir,' Smythe said, still smiling. 'Commodore Harrison is signalling. I believe our fore-topmast is ready.'

'Apologies, sir,' Courtney said with a tilt of his head. 'I will not be long.'

Nightingale smiled as Courtney left. Already, knowing that the *Scylla* and her crew were in safe hands, his pain eased. He trusted Courtney, trusted them all: enough to feel that he could be a comfortable passenger in his own ship, not only her captain.

Within the next day, he felt well enough to leave the orlop. Rylance guided him through the ship, and all the way, he was greeted by his men saluting and saying, 'Sir,' with smiles. Nightingale had not realised the depth of their affection. He could not help thinking it was misplaced; they, alongside Courtney and Harrison, had been the ones to conquer the storm and the mutiny. He was only their figurehead.

But he relaxed as Rylance brushed down his coat and helped him into his uniform again. His cabin was spotless, not a drop of blood, not a spilled sheet of paper, not a crack in the timbers. 'Thank you, Rylance,' he said, and the young man blushed.

Helpful hands supported him up onto the main deck. The breeze, after the stale confines of the cockpit, made his colour rise in an instant. He breathed in the scent of the sea and the fresh air, glad to see the blue sky above the *Scylla*'s t'gallants. Gulls flew and called close by; land neared, and with it, all the uncertainty they would face. He pushed those thoughts down for a while and climbed to the poop deck where he could look down the length of the ship. Aside from the new fore-topmast and the wreckage of Scylla herself, she barely looked different. Storms and a near-mutiny had swept her deck, but she had returned from the brink. Her head rose confidently in the waves to then drop slowly and neatly down with barely a complaint from the yards and stays.

Love for the ship and her men pulsed in Nightingale's chest. He smiled, despite the stiffness down his body.

Commodore Harrison invited him to dine on the *Actium* that night. As much as Courtney and Smythe insisted they could hold the ship, Nightingale declined the invitation; he was not well enough to be jostled into a boat and climb the high sides of the *Actium*. Harrison, undeterred, made the crossing himself, bidding his boatsmen to carry bottles and baskets of food, and, after smoothly ascending onto the quarterdeck, gripped Nightingale's hand hard enough to hurt.

'What a journey you've made, Hiram!' he cried.

Nightingale reddened. 'Yes, sir,' he could only say.

'I am so pleased to see you up and about again.'

'My thanks for your support, Commodore. Lieutenant Courtney has told me how you helped us.'

'I do not need your thanks, Hiram. It is my duty to you as an officer and as a friend.' Harrison slapped Nightingale's arm boister-ously. Nightingale grimaced through the pain.

The commodore was just as ebullient when he sat in Nightingale's great cabin that evening, sharing stories and memories. Nightingale could not marry the image of this cheerful, red-cheeked, slightly drunken man with the idea of his firm and skilful treatment of the prisoners. Watching him sitting next to Courtney, Nightingale saw two men who would prosper in the King's Navy. He felt worn and broken – and yet for the first time, at peace with what would come.

Courtney caught his eye when Rylance and his mate brought out plum pudding from Harrison's stores. Nightingale nodded at him to show he was well. Courtney raised his eyebrows, glanced at Harrison, and smirked. Nightingale suppressed a laugh.

'He shall stand in your corner if it comes to it, sir,' Courtney said after Harrison was gone later and Nightingale had asked him his opinion. 'That, or he shall talk from dawn 'til dusk and we'll never hear the others' testimonies.'

Nightingale chuckled. 'There is that risk, yes.' He thanked Rylance as the boy hurried around, cleaning up the silverware. Courtney glanced at him expectantly. 'Is there something you need, Arthur?'

'Oh, no, sir, I only wondered if I should take some of the leftovers for Jane. Master Loom left a good deal.'

Nightingale nodded at Rylance. Though Courtney had his own steward, Rylance was happy to parcel up a selection of pies and pudding for him.

'How is Mrs Howard now?' Nightingale asked, once Rylance had hurried out.

Courtney smiled weakly. 'She is improving. To tell the truth, sir, I did not think she would help us when the *Ulysses* men tried to rise up again. But, as soon as she knew you had been hurt and Mr Hargreaves had been the one to do it, she went straight to Dr Archer.'

'I am glad that she is returning to Trinidad with us. I did not want to lose her – not as a witness, and not as... the remarkable young woman she is.'

'I am glad too. I shall be with her, no matter what happens.'

'You shall be asked questions also, Arthur,' Nightingale said.

'I know, sir. I am ready for that.'

'I shall not tell you how to speak, as I have said before. You should say the truth as it happened, and how you think.'

Courtney looked down. 'You do not need to tell me that, sir. I shall be with you, also, no matter what happens.'

The emotions, already buoyant through his exhaustion and pain and the port, churned in Nightingale's heart. 'I do not deserve your loyalty, Arthur.'

Courtney reddened, running his fingers over the rim of his glass. He picked it up, sank the rest of the liquid, and brushed down his uniform, rubbing at non-existent dust. 'Is there anything I can do for you, sir?' he asked. 'Can I help you to your night cabin?'

Nightingale chuckled. 'I am not that infirm yet, Arthur. But I appreciate the offer.'

Courtney's smile hesitated for a moment and then he gave a thin laugh. He set down his glass, blushing even deeper, and cleared his throat. 'Of course, sir. Well, if there is nothing else I can do for you…'

'I shall not keep you from Jane, Arthur. Send her my regards.'

'Yes, sir.'

Courtney lingered for a moment more before rising and giving a polite salute to Nightingale as he left.

Nightingale smiled. All the pieces felt as though they were in place now. It had not been entirely through his actions. There were other men, other forces, that he could not control. He only had to play his role now, and take what came his way.

Chapter Thirty-Two: Leviathan

The waters around the *Scylla* were familiar, as was the span of the port with its broad harbour and dry, dusty, crowded streets. It had been a little over a month since Nightingale had last seen the same sights.

But, aside from the landscape, everything else had changed. The *Scylla* was only one vessel in a fleet of others. Commodore Harrison's *Actium* was anchored further out, but even her sixty-four guns were dwarfed by the impressive three-decker *Leviathan*, freshly painted and gleaming in the sun. Harrison said she was Admiral Sir John Duckworth's flagship, new commander of the Leeward Islands Station. A tapestry of other ships accompanied her: frigates and sloops and brigs.

All waiting for Captain Nightingale and the *Ulysses* prisoners.

Harrison had sent a message ahead, advising Governor Picton to dispatch a contingent of marines to the port. Nightingale watched boat after boat deliver the prisoners to land. Hargreaves sat in one cutter, imprisoned between armed men. He had sobbed as he was guided down but Nightingale said nothing. That would come later.

Almost thirty men had risen up during the short mutiny on the *Scylla*, led by Daniel Meyer. Rebels or not, they all went to the same place to await trial. Beside them, the gallows and gibbets swayed in the afternoon breeze. Nightingale prayed his testimony would prevent some from filling those nooses.

The next boat rowed across to the *Scylla* now. Nightingale recognised the sour-faced marine lieutenant, Cavendish, as he and his marines ascended the *Scylla*'s flank.

Jane appeared at Nightingale's side. She carried all that remained of her possessions: a mirror that had been a gift from her husband

and a small brush for her hair, which hung in loose curls around her waist. She wore the same clothes from the *Ulysses*, although Rylance had insisted that he wash them for her. She still looked every inch the woman they had found in the great cabin of the *Ulysses* – angry, troubled… and now, fearful.

Courtney approached and laid a gentle hand upon her back. She jumped but did not turn to face him. Her eyes were locked on the approaching marines and their tall, dark-haired commander.

'You shall be all right,' Courtney whispered, just loud enough for Jane and Nightingale to hear. 'I shall see you very soon.'

Jane swallowed and said nothing.

'Mrs Howard,' Cavendish said, tipping the brim of his hat to her. 'I am under advisement to keep you separate from the rest of the prisoners. You shall be in confinement in the governor's house until you are called to the stand. Governor Picton has offered his maid to attend to you.'

It seemed a kind concession, perhaps a marker of Jane being a woman, but being placed in Governor Picton's own household would not be a pleasantry or a luxury. She would be watched at every corner. Yet she had no choice but to nod, lips quivering wordlessly.

'I trust she shall not be harmed,' Nightingale said.

Cavendish inclined his head. She was a prisoner, now at the mercy of the court and the king's justice. She did not look back as she was guided away.

Cavendish remained on the deck. He observed his men doing their duty and then turned to Nightingale. 'And you, Captain,' he said.

Nightingale frowned. 'Me?'

'Yes, sir. You, also. I am under orders to place you in close confinement. You are an essential witness in the coming trial – and a defendant also, you must understand.'

Of course he was – it was all he had thought about these last weeks. Yet hearing such a thing from Cavendish's lips, a man who represented the authority he must face, hardened it into cold reality. He looked away from the lieutenant, over the deck of his ship, and realised there were eyes on them – curious crew members who had watched the arrests and now would watch one more.

'Sir,' Courtney breathed.

'It is all right, Lieutenant. I entrust you to care for the *Scylla* for me.'

He didn't want to see the pain in Courtney's eyes. He had lost his sister and now his captain. But Nightingale glanced at him, anyway, and felt his heart throb.

'Y-yes, sir,' Courtney managed.

All the ships seemed to stare at them as they crossed the harbour: Captain Nightingale, in all the finery of his post-captain's uniform, reduced to sitting between two armed marines, and, before him, Jane. She wrapped her arms about herself, hair catching in the breeze – a young, seemingly unremarkable woman enmeshed in the heart of this ongoing trouble. Nightingale stayed firm for her and for his men, who pressed to the gunwales to watch. The next time he would see them would be during the trial: the moment he had pinned all his hopes on.

Jane separated from him when they reached land. Her legs, unsteady after being on the sea for so long, rocked so a marine had to grip her arm. Nightingale wanted to help her but she was whisked into a waiting carriage, and he was walked along the harbourside where more people had come to gawp.

They took him to the same inn he had been in before, where he had tried to sleep after losing command of the *Scylla*. It seemed fitting, somehow. Now, two marines were posted outside of his door. It was pointless, truthfully. The thought of escape never crossed his mind; he would go to trial.

He sat at the table where he had confessed to Courtney about Tom, and thought about what lay ahead. He had never sat on a court martial panel before, but he knew their rigorous nature. That diligence could either mean the trial lasted for hours or for days. With a crime such as mutiny, the punishment was death. Yet there were complications here, snags in the web, that meant it was not so simple.

Nightingale did not envy the men who had to judge this case.

Late afternoon – six bells in the afternoon watch – and the door opened. Nightingale did not know who he expected, but he rose to his feet.

His stomach twisted.

'Hello, Hiram.'

Lord Fairholme, in a flawless emerald coat and embroidered waistcoat, entered with a charming smile. Marines flanked him but with one wave of his hand, they let him be and shut the door behind him. Suddenly trapped in the room with the man who had ruined the *Ulysses* and good men with her, Nightingale could barely contain the surge of anger. He stepped forward but Fairholme held up his hand as he had done to the marines.

'I know what you want to ask, Hiram,' he said. 'If it was me who ordered you to be placed into confinement.'

Nightingale said nothing.

'You lost a king's ship… again. A captain who does so must answer for it.' He paused, seeing Nightingale was not responding, and then continued, 'I hear you had trouble with Lieutenant Hargreaves. I apologise that my man did not live up to standard. He was arrested for shooting you, yes?'

Fairholme said it as if it were the most natural thing in the world. Nightingale glanced down at his wound, bandaged beneath his waistcoat and shirt. When he looked up again, Fairholme had approached closer, like a ringmaster taunting an enraged bull. 'I said: he was arrested for shooting you, yes?'

'You cannot intimidate me,' Nightingale spat, punctuating every word with the grief Fairholme had put him and others through.

'Oh, I think I can,' Fairholme scoffed. 'I can make things very miserable for you, your lieutenant and his sister.'

'You shall not be making anyone's life miserable but your own, from the inside of a prison.'

'I cannot be imprisoned for debt, Hiram. Not with my status.'

'Debt shall not be the crime!'

'And who shall believe you? It shall be the word of a disgraced sea captain against mine, a peer of the realm.'

'All of the *Ulysses* men are willing to speak against you and what you did,' Nightingale threatened, praying it was true. 'Mrs Howard shall. Lieutenant Hargreaves shall.'

'Words of mutineers,' Fairholme dismissed. 'And I have already spoken to Lieutenant Hargreaves. He knows where his loyalties lie if he has any sense. All it shall take is one nudge.'

Nightingale shook his head. Hargreaves needed to go to trial. Lost cause or not, he could not stomach the thought of Fairholme harming him before a decision was made. 'You are a murderer. You bribed a man to rise up against his ship. He slaughtered men, drove a woman to suicide.'

'And you, *Captain* Nightingale, destroyed a king's ship. The property of the Crown.' Fairholme sighed, as if this conversation bored him. 'Do not stand here and tell me that I am a murderer – not when your own actions have led to countless deaths. Perhaps you convince yourself that it is war and they are rebels, but what of the widows and orphans whose husbands and fathers perish under your guns?'

So hypocritical of Fairholme; he did not really feel any sympathy for the men, women and children who died. 'I have never acted to benefit myself,' Nightingale said. 'Never for the sake of money.'

'That is very noble of you, Hiram. Very noble to deny how some of the sum of your beautiful house comes from prize money.' Fairholme shrugged. 'If that is how you justify it to yourself then who am I to tell you not to? If you are willing to lie to yourself—'

'Lying? Do not lecture me on lying, Lord Fairholme. You are—'

'I know what I am, Hiram. I may lie to others but at least I do not lie to myself. I know what I am. Who are you?'

Nightingale fell silent. Arguing with Fairholme was like trying to wrestle a snake; his coils constantly slipped through Nightingale's hands and every time he thought he had a good grasp, fangs would suddenly sink into him.

'You have lost your gold, no matter what I say,' Nightingale intoned. 'If you wish to claim it, it is at the bottom of the sea. I have stopped you from benefitting from this damned voyage.'

'Not necessarily.' Fairholme smirked. 'They shall not look favourably on you in the trial. Not for losing another ship. You shall face the consequences and remuneration shall be demanded, if I have any suggestions. You are not poor. There is so much money of yours, Sir

William's and dear Lou's in your house and estate. Someone of sounder mind should take possession of it. Not a mad molly sea captain, his long-suffering wife and an unrepentant abolitionist.'

The barbs of his words stung. Not for himself, but for what he might do to Louisa. 'You would not.'

'What is stopping me, Hiram?' Fairholme hissed, his voice suddenly dropping – the dangerous, scheming man behind the fragile mask. 'Who is stopping me? You? I don't think so. Not with the defence you have. Do not forget what I know about you, Hiram. And do not think I won't scream it aloud.'

'My lord—'

'No. I have heard enough. You brought this upon yourself. I am not the architect of your pain. I am merely using it to my own benefit, as men have done since the dawn of time. Farewell, Hiram. It is a shame to see you so low – but perhaps not a surprise.'

There was more Nightingale could have said, more hatred that he could have poured upon Lord Fairholme. But it was as though the younger man was impervious to it. Nothing stuck; he always wriggled out of the justice which should come for him. And it did not matter if Nightingale spat such things at him in a small room of an inn. The trial loomed, and then his truths and words would be aired to an entire court.

Before then, sometime in the late evening, another knock came at the door. Nightingale feared it was Fairholme back again. Instead, Sir William entered. His face was drawn with fatigue, lines crinkling around his eyes and mouth. Although he was dressed immaculately, as always, his greying hair frayed out of its tie and his dark frock coat was spattered with mud from the road. Nightingale jumped to his feet, unprepared for how Sir William hurried over and grasped him around the arms.

'Hiram!' he gasped. 'Hiram, I am so deeply sorry. I never wished to see you in this position. I never thought that this would be how it ended.'

'It has not ended yet,' Nightingale heard himself say.

'I did not know where you had been taken. I did not know you were off the ship until I heard the rumours that you were arrested. What on earth has happened? They are saying that you lost the *Ulysses*.'

'I shall explain it all in the court martial. It was Lord Fairholme. He and Lieutenant Hargreaves conspired to take the gold from the *Ulysses* to pay off Fairholme's debts. They bribed Ransome to mutiny and commandeer the ship into Georgetown. Listen.'

Sir William's eyes widened. His fingers gripped Nightingale's arms. 'I don't…' he began. 'I cannot—'

'You must listen to me,' Nightingale urged. 'Please. I have witnesses, but Lord Fairholme says they shall be discredited as mutineers. He is going to try to discredit us all. But it is Lieutenant Hargreaves… You must ensure Lieutenant Hargreaves gets to trial.'

'They are saying that he shot you.'

'Yes. Yes. You must help him. I fear that Lord Fairholme is going to harm him, or he is going to convince him to commit suicide. You must ensure that he gets to trial.'

'He shot you,' Sir William said again, as if he could not fathom Nightingale's charity towards a man who had nearly killed him. But, seeing Nightingale was earnest, he nodded. 'The trial begins the day after next. I shall do what I can.'

'My thanks. I apologise.' Nightingale was not sure what he was apologising for. He stepped away from Sir William and twisted his hands nervously. 'I only want justice for the men who died. And for Lord Fairholme, whom I should have seen as a villain from the start. Do you understand?'

'I shall try, Hiram.'

Nightingale nodded. 'Who is on the panel?' he asked with an undercurrent of trepidation. 'Where shall it be held?'

'It shall be onboard Admiral Duckworth's *Leviathan*. They wish to try the mutineers in batches, not separately. Only Mrs Howard is distinct from the rest – and you are in the strange position of being both a witness and a defendant. Admiral Duckworth is the president and the panel is already assembling. Captain Thomas Bridger is here from Antigua, Captain Rodney Clark, Captain Andrew Willoughby – he is one under Commodore Harrison – Captain David Morrison…'

'I only know Bridger. What of my father? Where is he?'

'I've seen nothing of him since Commodore Harrison's message arrived. But, Hiram...' Sir William came forward again and took Nightingale's arm. 'If what you say about Lord Fairholme is true, you should tread carefully. I am not sure what he is capable of, but I do not wish to find out.'

'I have trod carefully for too long. He has already threatened me. I believe he came to me to gauge what I knew. Perhaps I should have kept my mouth shut. But if he is threatening me, then it means I have frightened him. It means I am doing the right thing.'

Sir William watched him a moment longer. 'How has he threatened you, Hiram?'

Nightingale sighed. He sat at the small table and brushed his hair from his eyes. 'He knows things about me. And he will not keep them to himself.'

He did not wish to say more but in the pause, he felt the weight of Sir William's understanding. 'I know that I cannot stop you, Hiram. You have made your own path, and I was a fool to try to direct you. I do hope you shall forgive me for coercing you to make the journey out here.'

'What is done is done. I do not need your apologies. When you return home, it is Louisa who you shall have to explain yourself to.'

A flutter of a smile touched Sir William's mouth. 'Yes, I think you are correct about that. Do you know, Hiram, I suggested your marriage for convenience. Your father convinced me that you would be a proper match for her. I had my doubts. Yet I am happy to call you my son. She does so care for you.'

Nightingale felt a swell in his chest. 'I love her very much.'

'I am sure that you do.' Sir William drew his hands behind his back again and returned to the stiff, formal pose of a gentleman. He was like his daughter in his ability to appear cold and distant, but to hide such warmth and affection beneath the mask. 'Well, I wish you luck, Hiram. I must go – I've stayed too long already and I do not wish Lord Fairholme to know I have come.'

'Thank you, sir. Please, ensure Lieutenant Hargreaves is safe. Find Lieutenant Courtney and he shall help you. Tell him… tell him I am fine. And so is Mrs Howard.'

Sir William nodded. 'I shall do my best.'

He left and Nightingale was once again alone – although it did not feel that way. The marines still waited outside his door and all the eyes of Trinidad were upon him and the mutineers.

He was prepared.

Imprisoned and under watch, he finally felt a fragment of freedom.

Chapter Thirty-Three: Ithaca

On the morning of the day Sir William had indicated, Nightingale heard rumbling as the *Leviathan's* great guns sounded their salute. It meant that the trial had begun. Nightingale sat by the window of the inn's room and tried to see what was happening on the ship. Seventy-four-gun or not, she was still only a blur of black-and-white chequer. He wondered how many mutineers would be questioned before the witnesses came; Sir William said they were in batches, and he could only hope innocent men were not tangled amidst the guilty.

Whatever "innocent" and "guilty" meant in this wretched case.

All morning boats ferried men back and forth across the harbour. At first the people of Trinidad stared as marines accompanied chained gangs of sailors, but the novelty soon wore off. For Nightingale, it was a stage play. He watched through the glass with growing dread.

That tension transferred from his mind to his body. Towards noon, he had to rise from his place at the window and lie back down. The barely healed wound on his side throbbed. Dr Archer was called and Nightingale latched onto the chance to speak to someone from the outside.

'How is it?' he asked as Archer carefully inspected beneath the bandage.

'The wound is clean, sir. You'll make a full recovery if you do not exert yourself.'

'I meant the trial, Francis. Do you know anything of it?'

'All I know is what I've heard and seen. Many of the men return weeping. The court is not being kind to them, as expected.'

'Has Mrs Howard been called to speak yet?'

'Not that I know of.' He produced a vial of laudanum from his satchel. Nightingale shook his head as he tried to hand it over. 'I suspect I shall be a witness against you, sir,' Archer said carefully. 'They shall want to know of your… state of mind as the *Ulysses* was lost.'

'I understand, Francis.'

'Although I dislike feeling I am "against" you, sir. I simply have to follow orders.'

'I understand, Francis,' Nightingale said again.

The afternoon came and went and still no call materialised for Nightingale. He tried to eat, tried to drink, but feared that his appearance would suddenly be needed and he would stand there in court, feeling nauseous with the food. Instead, he let time consume him, his mind returning again and again to what he had to say. The *Ulysses*. Lord Fairholme. Lieutenant Hargreaves. The true purpose of the gold.

He only hoped he could state it before the nooses stretched over the yardarms.

The sky had long turned dark before they finished for the day. The captains of the panel returned to their ships or to land, and Nightingale watched them obsessively through the window. They wore the same uniforms as he did, a couple seemed the same age, but he could not have felt more different. Captain Bridger was the only one he recognised: the same man who had given Nightingale his orders all the way back in Antigua. Little had they known it would lead to this.

That night, Nightingale slept roughly, still attuned to the ways of the sea. Mercifully, he dreamt of nothing, though that did not stop him waking time and time again, jostled by his injury, pained by a migraine which began in the early hours. He wished he had accepted Dr Archer's offer of laudanum.

It was with a groggy, heavy head that he awoke the following morning. He forced himself to eat, walking to the inn's common room and struggling with egg and sausages. The cook lacked Rylance's talent and it made Nightingale ache to be back onboard the *Scylla*. He wondered how Courtney fared as temporary commander. His heart squeezed as he thought of the lieutenant, then squeezed again at the thought of how much he missed his presence.

With the marines close behind, Nightingale braved his wound's pain and wandered to the harbour. He had no spyglass anymore so he squinted through the bright sun to see the shadow of the *Scylla*, dwarfed by the gargantuan *Leviathan*.

The morning crowds passed by. Business continued as usual, unmarked by what happened on the ships. The normal bustle and trade, with its smell of fish and pitch and its sound of heckling voices and barking dogs, faded into the background. It was only when it stopped that Nightingale realised something had changed.

He turned as a carriage stopped by the makeshift stalls. A marine jumped from the front, musket in hand. He opened the door and Nightingale rose to his feet, stomach churning.

Jane stepped out. Her men's shirt and simple loose trousers were gone. Instead, she wore a plain, drably coloured dress, poorly fitting and bunched tightly around her waist. Curls of pitch-black hair fell from their pins. It was as though someone had attempted to imprint femininity onto her and she had failed to live up to it.

Whispers grew around her, only drowned by a snapping dog which tried to approach the strangers. Jane did not look at it, or the people craning to stare at her. Only when she raised her head for a moment and saw Nightingale did her eyes widen. For a moment, she faltered. Even her disturbingly rouged cheeks could not hide the whiteness beneath. 'Arthur?' she mouthed.

Nightingale subtly shook his head. Jane's face fell. She bit her bottom lip to stop it trembling but tears gathered in her eyes.

Nightingale could only watch as she was steered into a boat.

The dread sapped the sun's heat. Nightingale watched until the small vessel faded from his sight and then retired back inside. His migraine flared again, his side twinged, but he waited through the next hours, hoping Dr Archer would hear something of Jane's statements. When the doctor arrived, it was the first thing Nightingale asked.

'Do you know how she is? I do not suppose there have been any rumours from her testimony?'

Archer regretfully shook his head. 'I was called to check on her after she left the ship. She was shaking dreadfully. I do not think she was scared for herself, though, only Lieutenant Courtney.'

Nightingale prayed she had not stated her and the crew's true intentions to the court. If she had spoken of those plans – to take the gold and sink the ship – she would have been many steps closer to the noose. If she had lied, she would have helped herself and the other men, claiming they had not committed any further mutiny after Ransome's death.

But lying to a court martial…

Nightingale winced as Archer redid the bandage. 'Tell me there has been good news, Francis. I'm losing my mind sitting here alone.'

'The witnesses shall come forward now, sir. The former *Peregrine* captain has been called already. Poor soul, it looked as though he was going to the gallows himself. And I've heard talk that another lieutenant has arrived to give testimony.'

'Another lieutenant?'

'A Lieutenant Wainwright, formerly of the *Ulysses*.'

For the first time, Nightingale felt a tug of hope. Wainwright. Nightingale had assumed he had died in the hospital in English Harbour.

'He might help separate innocent from guilty,' Nightingale said.

Lord Fairholme believed, perhaps rightly, that the words of mutineers would be scrutinised and ignored because of what they'd done. He was confident that society's distaste for the men and their low backgrounds would save him. But Lieutenant Wainwright was an officer, a man untarnished by the mutiny as he had escaped it.

Wainwright needed to speak of Fairholme and Hargreaves at English Harbour, visiting the *Ulysses* crew. But he would think nothing of it, having not heard Hargreaves's admissions.

It meant Nightingale had to be even more forceful with his accusations; they would then bring Wainwright back to the stand, the mutineers, Jane, to ask them more.

'Let us hope he is well,' Nightingale said. 'And that he can identify the men who participated in that initial mutiny.'

This time, before Archer left him, Nightingale accepted the laudanum. Knowing that his call might come soon, he was intent upon sleeping that night.

They came for Nightingale on the third day. He wore his best dress uniform, but that drew attention as he was marched across the harbour and towards a waiting cutter. The gold lace on his sleeves and the polished buttons glittered in the blazing sun so he crossed his arms to hinder them.

Ahead, the *Leviathan* loomed. Nightingale kept his eyes on her: a beautiful but terrifying monolith that dominated the waters, her high sides like fortress walls, her masts scraping the sky. Silence covered her decks. When he climbed over and his name was shouted by a clerk, drawing him into the great cabin, it echoed humiliatingly.

Captain Hiram Nightingale, RN. It sounded so foreign.

The large space seemed small. Five post-captains gleamed in a wealth of shining medals and gold lace, history permeating the air. The jury all wore their best uniforms but Nightingale suddenly felt distinctly shabby, questioning the worth of his epaulettes and accolades. Surely, he thought, as their eyes roved over him, they wondered where his absent Nile medal was.

It was not a good start to have such thoughts – and not a good start to remember how the Nile medal was now somewhere at the bottom of the bay beneath them.

Admiral Duckworth addressed him. He had not been in the position of Commander-in-Chief long but he had much knowledge and experience of the West Indies. Nightingale shifted his hands nervously behind his back as he examined him.

'Captain Nightingale,' he began. 'We have already read your testimony from the informal court held on the thirteenth of July of this year that took place in Port of Spain. We know your words, and those of your crew, in regards to the *Fénix* and the conclusions that were drawn and overturned by Admiral Laurence Nightingale and the panel. We should like to hear your account of the pursuit of the *Ulysses* after leaving Trinidad in July.'

'Yes.' Nightingale opened his mouth, then quickly shut it when he realised Duckworth had not finished.

'We have already perused the *Scylla*'s logs. We understand that in your pursuit, you relied on intelligence from Salvador and from a Portuguese brig, the *Senhora da Graça*, as well as meeting with Captain Sallis, new commander of the *Peregrine*.'

Nightingale waited for more. Duckworth watched him expectantly. 'Yes, sir,' he rushed. 'Salvador was the final place where the *Ulysses* was spotted. We set a course for the Bay of All Saints. With help from Lieutenant Hargreaves, we discovered that the *Ulysses* had only been gone a week. After this, we travelled south, adhering to the coast, until we met the *Senhora* who stated that they had seen a ship – who stated that they had been in a fog-bank and seen a ship... acting erratically.'

'And you made the decision to enter the fog?'

'Yes, sir.' Duckworth still waited. 'I understood the dangers, sir. My officers made that plain. But with the *Ulysses* potentially so close, I did not want to give them another inch. We relied on dead reckoning and when it became too... When we were becalmed, I employed a kedge anchor to heave ourselves forward. It was then that we first saw the *Ulysses*. Her lights, sir. The fog cleared enough for us to pursue her more firmly.'

Duckworth nodded. The clerk's pen scratched loudly. 'Did you know of the reef that the *Ulysses* was eventually grounded upon?'

'I did, sir.'

'And?'

And what? Nightingale thought. 'And... It was not entirely my plan to allow her to ground. I knew of the reef and its dangers and I drove her close but I... Well, I then made the decision to attack directly.'

'Across the reef?'

'Yes. I drilled my crew on many occasions for many potential scenarios. I adapted one of our earlier schemes. Lieutenant Courtney led one party, Midshipman Smythe the other, and I led the starboard division across the reef.'

Duckworth glanced at Captain Bridger beside him. Bridger leant forward. 'Why did you not simply wait for the tide to turn, Captain Nightingale?'

'I did not think we had the time, sir. It was either approach on foot or continue firing at the *Ulysses*. I did not wish to unduly damage her, not when she was meant to return to port.' Meant to return to port. A bad choice of words, knowing how he had disobeyed that order later.

'When you boarded the *Ulysses*, Captain,' Duckworth spoke again, 'what was your impression of the crew?'

'They fought well, sir, but they had little choice but to surrender. Many claimed not to be mutineers.'

Duckworth paused. The pen continued scratching. 'And did you believe them, Captain, or did you believe it was merely a plea to save themselves?'

'I believed them, sir,' Nightingale replied with certainty. 'Once the ship had been taken, I listened to Mrs Jane Howard's story. She had gone through hell, sir, and was motivated by a desire to preserve herself and the rest of the crew after Ransome's—'

'We would ask you not to speculate, Captain Nightingale. It shall be for the court to decide.'

'Y–yes, sir. Apologies, sir.'

The clerk turned over a page. Duckworth did the same with the logs set out before the panel. 'You gathered the *Ulysses* prisoners on the *Scylla*. You state that some men were put to work whilst others were imprisoned below. What would you say the attitude of the *Ulysses* men was?'

'Their attitude? It was… well, there was no uniform attitude, sir. The men that I put to work, after Mrs Howard's suggestions, behaved admirably, especially when the *Scylla* was struck by a storm. The men in the hold, they believed that there had been some unfair treatment.'

'Perhaps an apt comment to make, considering their brothers were on deck,' another captain – Clark – remarked. Duckworth did not quieten him.

'So you relied on Mrs Howard's judgement of the prisoners, Captain?'

'I did, sir. She seemed in a good position to judge, having been around them for many weeks. And I believe her suggestions were sound. When the prisoners rose up during the storm, many of them were from amongst the men in the hold, the men she did not speak for.'

Duckworth nodded. 'Could you point these men out?'

'Perhaps some, sir. I understand they were led by Daniel Meyer.' He said the words, knew at once that he had spelt out the man's death sentence and felt a chill because of it. 'But the others, I am not certain. I could point out the men who claimed they were not mutineers, the men I relied on to work on deck. But the others in my crew – Lieutenant Courtney, Master Loom, Midshipman Smythe – could surely point out the men who rose. I believe that some men are innocent, sir. I believe they were pressed into the mutiny but did not feel right about it. They acted for their self-preservation and at the first chance to return to their duties, as I employed them on the *Scylla*, they behaved very well.'

This time, Duckworth allowed the speculation. 'Now, Captain,' he said after a pause, 'I wish to discuss the fate of the *Ulysses*. The logs are strikingly vague, simply saying the ship was lost. We are aware that one vessel has already been lost under your command, hence the hastily called trial in July. That was the *Fénix*, not officially condemned or brought into service. But the *Ulysses* was a king's ship. Please, enlighten us – and understand that because of the loss, your crew shall be questioned too.'

Nightingale felt the shift in the trial – the turn from his witness statements about the mutiny to a dive into his own conduct. He swallowed, squeezed his hands and looked out the gallery windows across the sun-drenched bay. God, it was warm in the cabin. 'To, ah, to do that, sir, I must tell you more about the mutiny. Aspects that I was not aware of until certain points in the voyage.'

'Go on, Captain.'

'Well. I…' Nightingale felt the wrath of Fairholme lingering around him, the potential for the destruction of everything he held dear. Yet he could not back down now. 'Lieutenant Hargreaves joined the *Scylla* in Antigua. He performed well, aiding us with the intelligence in Salvador but… Um. He…'

All eyes burnt holes in his body. Nightingale cleared his throat.

'After the capture of the *Ulysses*, he came aboard with the purpose of protecting the gold. After some... pressure, he claimed that he had been approached by Lord Fairholme when Fairholme sailed to the Caribbean. He claimed he was threatened by Lord Fairholme, that he was pressed into helping him steal the gold from the *Ulysses* to pay off Fairholme's debts. That they had bribed Ransome in English Harbour to mutiny, take the ship into Georgetown and deliver the gold to Fairholme. Not to be taken to Saint-Domingue as I... as we all were told. Fairholme spoke to Hargreaves in Trinidad as well and claimed I had been kept in my position because of their... agreements.

'Others recognised Hargreaves on the *Ulysses*, claimed to have seen him in English Harbour with Lord Fairholme and been approached by them but – Ransome took it further than intended. He stole the ship, schemed to take the gold himself. The loss of life was—'

'Captain Nightingale.' Duckworth held up a hand. The cabin was silent. Nightingale realised he had babbled the words out like a nervous child and had barely stopped for breath. He stood there, trembling. 'These are serious accusations.'

Nightingale said nothing.

'Captain, do you suggest that Lord Fairholme was the master of this mutiny? That a peer of the realm lied to divert government-sanctioned funds into his own possession?'

'I do, sir.' A long pause where Nightingale was sure they could hear his heart hammering. 'Lieutenant Hargreaves was prepared to kill me because of it. And Lord Fairholme himself recently admitted it to me. The mutiny was not entirely because of the men. Perhaps Ransome and his ringleaders. And the men who later rose. But... As I say, I believe many are innocent. They were manipulated terribly.'

The officers on the panel turned to one another. Nightingale could barely stand, his wound suddenly throbbing, his legs feeling like tar. He had said it now, had accused Fairholme, and there was no retracting it.

'Captain,' Duckworth continued, trying to retain control of the questions and panel, 'I do not fully understand how this relates to the loss of the *Ulysses*.'

'I destroyed her, sir.'

Murmurs rippled through the cabin. The clerk looked up at him. These admissions did not feel as powerful, as vindicating, as Nightingale had imagined. They felt utterly terrifying.

'You destroyed her?'

'I did. I set her ablaze and ensured that the gold sank.'

'I am waiting for your justification, Captain Nightingale.'

'That, sir, what I have said, was my justification. She was damaged anyway and to retrieve her from the reef would take effort and time – time I did not have with the *Scylla* full of prisoners. And I could not allow the gold to return, not after what I discovered. The *Ulysses* was…touched by it. I did not believe she could return either.'

Duckworth was silent, and that was all that Nightingale needed to hear. His admissions hung thick and palpable in the air. He looked at the captains, each individual in turn, and knew his fate lay in their hands.

Finally, Admiral Duckworth turned to the waiting clerk and said, 'Find Lieutenant Hargreaves and Lord Fairholme. Bring them to the cabin. Captain Nightingale—'

'Yes, sir.'

'Do not leave the *Leviathan*.'

Nightingale had no intention, even if it had been permitted. He stood in the wretched, scorching heat of the afternoon, the sun burning his neck and spine. And yet the shadow still hovered, falling upon the wrong people. They needed to find Lieutenant Hargreaves and Lord Fairholme – the men from whom the shadow might extend.

It would have been so simple to blame the mutineers, to cling to the ideas of mutiny being evil. Yet the only man who bore certain guilt was himself. He had confessed to his destruction of the *Ulysses*. Word would spread. He could never hide from that, as he'd known he could not.

The clerk returned within the half-hour. Nightingale, and everyone else, stared at his approaching boat. He was alone as he climbed up the ladder.

'Well?' Admiral Duckworth urged.

The clerk looked around at the expectant faces, twisting his hands and flushing. 'Lieutenant Hargreaves is nowhere to be found, sir. It seems he has fled.'

Nightingale closed his eyes. Lord Fairholme had once again piled the cards in his hands.

Chapter Thirty-Four: The Two Evils

Lord Fairholme climbed the high sides of the *Leviathan* as though he travelled to attend dinner with the captain. Accompanied by marines, he stepped onto the quarterdeck dressed in brocaded velvet and lace. With fine gloved hands, he smoothed down his red hair, some of which had flown free during his journey across the harbour. Absent-mindedly, he plucked at invisible dust on his waistcoat – the façade of a man untouched by his circumstance. He caught Nightingale's eye and inclined his head politely.

The port had been searched but Lieutenant Hargreaves had not been found. Only one half of this imbalanced duo was here to meet Nightingale's accusations. He was not foolish enough to think this meant they had ensnared Fairholme. They still had to keep his twisting coils from strangling them.

For the second time, Nightingale stood in the great cabin. It suddenly felt colder, though the sun still beat down on a sweltering day. Lord Fairholme adopted a frigid, stiff posture, a small smile upon his lips. Nightingale thought he might speak out of turn but Duckworth, staring sharply at Fairholme, opened the session again.

'Cornelius, Lord Fairholme,' he said once the formalities were done. 'Please inform us what you are doing in the Caribbean. Surely you have a wealth of men to do your bidding?'

Fairholme laughed. 'I am here on business for the king, Admiral, guarding assets for this country. I deemed myself the most worthy for such an important task. Sometimes, it is good to get out of England and see the empire first-hand.'

'Indeed. You have been in Trinidad since June, yes?'

'Yes, in Trinidad since June. Previous to that I visited Antigua – English Harbour.'

'We are aware, my lord. What was your business there?'

Fairholme sniffed as if these questions were not worth his time. 'I had to ensure the cargo's security upon the *Ulysses*.'

'Were you alone when you visited Antigua, my lord?'

'No,' Fairholme responded confidently. 'Lieutenant Hargreaves, of the *Galene* and later of the *Scylla*, accompanied me. We conversed onboard the *Galene* during my crossing to the West Indies. It was beneficial to have a Royal Navy man with me.'

'What was the purpose of the cargo on the *Ulysses*?'

'That is not for everyone's ears, Admiral. Political necessity deems that it is kept secretive.'

'Come now, Lord Fairholme.' Duckworth spread his hands. 'You are present in court. It cannot be a secret here – and certainly not when such an accusation as Captain Nightingale's has been made.'

Fairholme looked at Nightingale. Nightingale bore his amused gaze. There was not a shred of fear or doubt there. The lord had known that he would lay charges at his feet. He had lasted this long, weaving deception around them all. This trial was a small matter to him when he had already decided on his narrative.

'Captain Nightingale,' Fairholme said, eyes twinkling, 'has a softness, perhaps a commendable spirit, but not when it is turned to mutineers. It is surprising for a man of his station in the Royal Navy to so believe in the goodness of these men.'

'That is speculation, my lord. You are suggesting that Captain Nightingale has invented these claims to save the lives of the crew?'

'Save them. Grant them some leniency. Cover his own errors and lapses of judgement.'

'Then you are aware of the claims he has made against you?'

'I am. This case is hardly a secret any longer, as you say, Admiral.'

Duckworth ignored Fairholme's breezy dismissal. 'What is your answer to them, my lord? To clarify, Captain Nightingale suggests that the gold was to pay off a debt of yours. You bribed a seaman to mutiny and to take the *Ulysses* into Georgetown.'

Fairholme did not react. 'These are fancies from a man who is trying to justify his destruction of a king's ship. They have no worth. Through ineptitude, through malice, through an inflated sense of morality, Captain Nightingale lost the *Ulysses* and spat in the eye of the Admiralty. He has already lost the *Fénix*. I sat on the panel which judged him in July. I told him what I will say now: his command of the *Scylla* was a lifeline thrown to a drowning man. The court judged him unfit for captaincy.'

Nightingale could not restrain himself. 'You were the one who convinced the panel to let me retain my command. You overturned their conclusions.'

'For the sake of convenience, Hiram.' Nightingale hated hearing his given name on the man's lips, so outwardly friendly and so contrived. 'With the *Ulysses* seen in Salvador, no more time could be wasted.'

'No. It was to manipulate my position. You believed I would obey your wishes. Lieutenant Hargreaves will testify to that.'

'Lieutenant Hargreaves is a feeble-minded man who shall do anything to keep his position. Were you aware, Admiral, that he was a midshipman until three months ago? That he has family in Portugal of what stock I cannot tell?'

Nightingale opened his mouth to respond but Duckworth held up a hand. 'We are yet to locate Lieutenant Hargreaves, my lord. As you have been in such close acquaintance with him, have you any notion of where he might be found?'

'I do not know,' Fairholme replied. 'I have not seen him since the *Scylla* moored and he was arrested.'

'I see.' Duckworth waited for the clerk to finish scribbling and then concluded, 'We shall need to hear Lieutenant Hargreaves's testimony. Once the crews of both the *Scylla* and the *Ulysses* have been brought to the stand again, then we shall ask you to return here if we have any further questions. Until then, you shall be under guard as Captain Nightingale is.'

Fairholme nodded. 'As you wish,' he said airily.

But hour followed hour and there was still no trace of Lieutenant Hargreaves. Nightingale feared Fairholme had made good on his threat to harm the man. The lord was powerful and dangerous, certainly now when he was backed into a corner. He could drag them all down with him.

Waiting on deck, Nightingale shivered despite the heat. *You fool*, he thought again and again. *You have tried to save the* Ulysses *men and have condemned your own.*

The mutineers were herded by batches back to the cabin. Nightingale listened to their shuffling feet on the deck below. They would face further questions about English Harbour and Lord Fairholme and the gold. If any spoke up, their words would seem tenuous, pleas of men eager to save their own necks.

Soon, Nightingale's character and behaviour would be examined, and his chances would slip even more. What would be found? A man who failed to bring the *Ulysses* to port, who allowed his own feelings to rule him in the disobedience of his orders. A man who had had his day and should not have been recalled.

When his crew were first herded onto the *Leviathan*, Nightingale could barely meet their eyes. He retreated back to the frightened shell he had been when he had first boarded the *Scylla*, reading pity in their expressions. He looked for Courtney but the lieutenant did not appear. With rising anxiety, Nightingale caught the clerk and, fearing Courtney was in the same wretched place as Hargreaves, stated, 'My lieutenant must be called also.'

'He was not onboard the *Scylla*, sir,' the clerk said curtly. 'But the town is teeming with marines and Governor Picton's men. He shall be found.'

Nightingale could barely think plainly as the Scyllas were called to the cabin: Master Loom, Smythe, Parry and Archer in close succession. As the defendant now, Nightingale listened to their testimony. Smythe garbled his way through his answers, but Loom carefully and intimately discussed the ship's logs, strengthening what Nightingale had said.

Only Dr Archer was questioned about anything close to morals. 'In your judgement, Doctor,' Clark said, 'do you believe Captain Nightingale was in a fit state of mind when he destroyed the *Ulysses*?'

Archer paused. For a moment, Nightingale doubted what he might say, and he remembered his own wailing sobs as he had watched the ship burn. Then, 'Yes, sir. He was sound. Perhaps unnerved as any man would be, but in control of his capabilities.'

'In control' was not a feeling Nightingale had experienced for a while. This voyage had been a struggle to simply keep his head above the water. He could still sense the surface lapping at his throat, feet trying to touch a bottom that did not exist.

After Lieutenant Wainwright's interrogation, as the afternoon stretched into evening, the court adjourned. Nightingale, with directions not to leave the *Leviathan*, remained on the deck under watch. He leant at the taffrail, legs weak, head aching. Behind him, anchored in the bay, the *Scylla* bobbed. He turned to look at her. She had not been his most powerful ship, nor his fastest, not even his finest-looking, but her crew did her the greatest credit.

A surge of emotion crested. The sea, Nightingale had thought, was where he belonged, on ships where he could keep his mind on what existed between the wooden walls. He had been wrong. His past, these laws, would always catch up to him.

He could not expect the sea to grant him freedom when he would never allow himself to have it.

Perhaps an hour passed, when a boat suddenly appeared across the water. Nightingale glanced at it, thought nothing of it, until he realised it was being rowed strenuously towards the *Leviathan*. He stood – just as a figure in the stern stood too.

'Sirs!' a voice bellowed. 'Sirs! Permission to come aboard!'

Nightingale knew that voice. He had heard that voice shout through a hailstorm, scream across a beleaguered deck, softly speak to him through his misery.

'Sirs!'

Crewmen hurried to the side. Others emerged from below-decks. Captain Bridger appeared from the wardroom, trailed by the clerk. Nightingale rushed to them, heart in his mouth.

Lieutenant Hargreaves was shoved unceremoniously up the ladder. Ridiculous for this weather, a black cloak, done to the neck, swathed him. His legs swayed unsteadily, his head drooped. For the first few moments, as he stood there, Nightingale thought the man would collapse.

Then a hand gripped his arm.

Lieutenant Courtney, in full dress uniform, politely saluted the quarterdeck. He did not let go of Hargreaves. Nightingale stared, pulse thundering. He did not even try to connect the events that had led to this moment. He only revelled in seeing Courtney again, unharmed, smiling – and with him, the man he had urgently hoped for.

'Sir,' Courtney said in a clear voice to Bridger. 'I heard that you were searching for Lieutenant Hargreaves. I pray I am not too late.'

Bridger looked at him and Hargreaves, who was yet to meet anyone's eyes. 'This is most irregular, Lieutenant. But no. We would welcome Lieutenant Hargreaves's testimony.'

Marines took Courtney's place, grasping Hargreaves about the arms and steering him towards the great cabin. Nightingale felt the shadow rising for a moment. Across the deck, Lord Fairholme had risen to his feet. Hargreaves did not look at him, keeping his head low beneath his wide-brimmed hat.

In the clamour, Nightingale caught Courtney's eye. Courtney smiled and laid a hand over his heart.

A thousand questions ran through Nightingale's head, but now he was called to accompany Hargreaves to the cabin. Fairholme received no such call. Hargreaves refused to meet anyone's eyes. He was deathly pale, as if he had barely survived an illness, and his brows were in deep, dark shadow. As Admiral Duckworth opened the session again, Hargreaves seemed to be in a different place entirely, either buried inside of himself or pretending he was far, far away.

'Lieutenant Michael Hargreaves,' Duckworth said slowly, as though speaking to an invalid. 'We have already heard Captain Nightingale's testimony. He has suggested information that we were not previously aware of. We wished to bring you here to see through your eyes. Please tell the court how you came aboard the Scylla.'

Hargreaves did not look up. Nightingale noticed Duckworth glance at his companions. 'I was assigned to the Scylla to replace Lieutenant Pearson after he died from fever,' Hargreaves replied simply.

'Why were you assigned to the Scylla, Lieutenant? I've not heard your name mentioned before and you have not appeared in any navy list I am aware of.'

'My priority was to ensure the safety of the *Ulysses* and her assets.'

'So you were aware of the assets when you were assigned to the *Scylla*?'

Hargreaves looked up. His mouth moved wordlessly.

'Yes or no, Lieutenant?' Duckworth pressed.

'Yes, sir,' Hargreaves whispered.

'What is your acquaintance, if any, with Lord Fairholme?'

Nightingale almost expected Hargreaves to deny it. But he cleared his throat, shivering. 'I… I, um… I served on the *Galene* which transported him to the Caribbean. He attended a handful of dinners onboard. I met and spoke with him then.'

'What did you speak of, Lieutenant?'

'General matters. My family in Portugal. The ship.'

'Lord Fairholme is quite a character,' Clark suddenly said. 'He has a certain… reputation. He tends to leave an impression. What did you think of his manner?'

Hargreaves's eyes darted between the panel members, the cogs of his mind whirring to pull apart the implications of that question. 'I'm not sure. He was… an average man. Perhaps uncomfortable with the sea travel and the heat, but I'm not certain. I did not pay much attention to him.'

'Lord Fairholme is not, by any stretch, an average man, Lieutenant.' Clark smiled. No one else did. 'You say you did not pay much attention to him. Did he pay attention to you?'

'I—'

'Did you speak beyond the dinner table? The *Galene* is not a large ship. You must have come across the man whilst not in the captain's cabin.'

'I did not befriend him, if that is what you are asking. I barely knew him.'

Clark nodded slowly.

'Captain Nightingale has laid some serious accusations,' Duckworth continued. 'Against both you and Lord Fairholme, Lieutenant. He says that the assets onboard the *Ulysses* had an ulterior purpose. Crew members of the *Ulysses* have already identified you and Lord Fairholme as men who approached them at English Harbour. Did you visit Antigua with Lord Fairholme in May of this year, Lieutenant, before the *Ulysses* sailed with the *Peregrine*?'

Hargreaves blinked. He chewed the inside of his bottom lip. Ever so slightly, he shook his head.

'You shall have to speak, Lieutenant. Did you or did you not visit Antigua with Lord Fairholme and speak with the crew of the *Ulysses*?'

'Lord Fairholme wished to ensure the assets were safe onboard the *Ulysses*.'

'So yes, you visited Antigua with Lord Fairholme. Why did he speak to the crew of the *Ulysses* and not the captain?'

Hargreaves fell silent again. He looked down at his hands, irritating the edge of his cloak. Nightingale glanced between him and Duckworth.

'I would advise you to speak, Lieutenant Hargreaves,' Duckworth ordered. 'There are grave accusations before you. We would hear you address them. Why was Lord Fairholme so intent on ensuring the safety of the cargo? Why did he have you accompany him?'

Hargreaves shook his head again. His lips quivered. He looked like a boy, scolded by his father for something he knew he had done but did not want to admit to.

'Lieutenant Hargreaves. Please tell us why you were assigned to the *Scylla*, why Lord Fairholme kept you so close.'

A quiet moan escaped Hargreaves. He violently pressed his hands to his face. Something inside snapped. Shoulders shaking, he sobbed, great gasping cries that sent chills through Nightingale and made the panel shift uncomfortably.

'Lieutenant Hargreaves,' Duckworth said uselessly.

'I did not want to hurt Captain Nightingale!' Hargreaves suddenly bawled. He looked up, cheeks streaked with tears. 'Lord Fairholme told me that he would be easy to manipulate – that he would do what he wanted. He let him retain his command because of it. But he is a good man, he's worth a hundred of Lord Fairholme. I was forced into it! Lord Fairholme said he would break me and my family if I didn't help him to take the gold. He made me a lieutenant, he bribed

Ransome, made him rise up – all because he was in debt, and he...
he... It was never meant to go to Saint-Domingue.'

'Lieutenant, slow down.'

The clerk was writing frantically in the corner, trying to hear
through Hargreaves's weeping. Duckworth caught Nightingale's eye.
Nightingale swallowed. This did not feel like a victory, though
Hargreaves had said everything he wanted him to say.

'Lord Fairholme bribed Ransome to mutiny,' Hargreaves repeated.
'He didn't care who was hurt, as long as he received the gold. I didn't
know if he was right, but I had to obey. When Captain Nightingale
found out, I wanted to escape. I could not let Lord Fairholme punish
me. I didn't want to hurt Captain Nightingale, I didn't want to kill
him! Please, I—' Hargreaves turned to Nightingale. He shook like a
beaten dog. Nightingale wanted to look away but he made himself
face what he had done. 'I am glad Lord Fairholme failed. I'm sorry,
Captain, I am so sorry. Please, forgive me. Look at what he made me
do!'

Hargreaves tugged the collar of his cloak and revealed a bright,
angry bruise around his throat. Nightingale recognised the imprints
of a rope. Sickness rose in him.

'He pushed me, threatened me, and handed me the rope,'
Hargreaves sobbed, eyes and nose streaming. 'I would have done it.
I would have succeeded if Lieutenant Courtney had not found me.'

Nightingale could not respond.

'Lieutenant Hargreaves, please.' Duckworth rose from his chair. At
a subtle signal, marines appeared at the door. Hargreaves frantically
stared around at them. 'If there is nothing Captain Nightingale wishes
to ask, then I believe we have heard enough.'

Nightingale shook his head. 'No, there is nothing.'

'Please, Captain!' Hargreaves cried. 'Please, don't let them do this
to me! Please!'

'Take Lieutenant Hargreaves below,' Duckworth ordered. 'Chain
him if you must.'

'No! Captain, please!'

The marines grasped Hargreaves around the arms and dragged his
struggling body to the cabin door. Nightingale may not have been the

337

one to break the man entirely, but he had brought a hammer down atop him, smashing the fractures. If things had been different, he could have been the weeping, desperate man Hargreaves had turned into.

He would always recognise that rage and grief and trauma.

Hargreaves's cries echoed through the ship. Duckworth breathed out, sinking back into his seat. Nightingale could hear the racing of his heart. His thoughts collided with his ringing skull.

'Captain Nightingale.' Someone was saying his name. He blinked, trying to escape his head. 'Stay here whilst we question Lieutenant Courtney.'

Nightingale nodded. 'Yes, sir.'

Courtney's presence and his confident testimony soothed some of the ache in Nightingale's head. He spoke about the *Scylla*; about the *Ulysses*; about what he had heard from Hargreaves's own lips regarding the mutiny and bribes. When Duckworth questioned him about Hargreaves's attempted suicide, he nodded and said, 'Yes. I found him hanging last evening, but he had not sufficiently tied the rope. He was insensible, not dead. I had him taken to the hospital, where I did not leave his side, not until I knew Lord Fairholme had given testimony and could not return to harm him further.'

Nightingale had experienced all the emotions under the sun that day. In the dense warmth of the cabin, he nearly wept. The truth had finally been admitted, but at what cost? So many had died or been broken.

Yet, through the blood and destruction, ground had been gained. As he walked out into the hot night, lit by a sliver of moon and dotted with small stars, he felt closer to the justice he had clung to like a point of anchorage. Relief, exhaustion, bewilderment coursed through him. He caught Courtney's eye when he left the cabin and knew what a dangerous risk the lieutenant had taken for him and the good of the two crews.

If they won, it would not only be Nightingale's victory. It would be the victory of Courtney too, of the Scyllas and all the *Ulysses* men and women who had suffered.

Chapter Thirty-Five: Judgement

30 August 1800, Port of Spain, Trinidad

The morning bloomed warm and bright. On the deck of the *Leviathan*, elevated above the crystal-smooth waters of Port of Spain, Captain Nightingale felt the sun's heat dripping down his back but nevertheless kept his head raised into its rays. For the first time, he was glad for the blur in his vision and the way the burning solar halo merged everything into shadow.

Once again, the sixteen-pound cannon spat a blank blast from the *Leviathan*'s starboard flank and once again, the men at the mast repeated their grisly task.

Nightingale stood with the panel from the court and the invited *Scylla* officers. He knew that others would be watching from the cutters bobbing in the harbour and from the anchored vessels. This was what they had been waiting for.

Nightingale took a slow breath. It staggered in his chest. He tried not to let his thoughts break through the careful barrier he had constructed. He had made his choice, he had said his words, and this was a consequence he had to live with.

Again, names were read aloud. Mercifully, Nightingale was unable to attach them to men. It was easier that way. They were simply 'mutineers' and the Admiralty needed their deaths to be a warning to all who might follow. Anonymous and faceless in the bright sun, these crew members were symbols only.

Still, Nightingale wanted nothing more than to look away. In battle, there was no time to think of who he dispatched with sword and pistol. It was quick, and if he agonised over every man, he would surely go mad. Now, though, there were slow, dreadful minutes upon minutes.

Three bodies were raised above the waters. Nine had come before them, and eighteen would follow – thirty men in all, the remnants of the *Ulysses* and *Scylla* mutinies. Each one had been lashed to the yardarm, hoisted by the necks and left to dangle and kick over the bay. These men did so silently, the noose too tight to add any more to the final words they had been granted.

Eventually, the first man on the yard turned limp and began to swing in the breeze. It was not long before his two partners followed, but they would all be kept there until the next striking of the bell to ensure their deaths. And even as they hung, casting gruesome shadows across the waters, the next three men were shepherded on deck. They stared at their dead crewmates and waited to join them.

It took almost five hours to execute the mutineers. At first only one side of the spar was used, but during the afternoon, the main yard stretching to port was rigged too and six men were killed at once. After the first few deaths, anyone not obliged to watch was losing interest.

Nightingale was relieved when it finally ended – relieved and selfishly anxious, as after a late afternoon meal that tasted like dust, he and those remaining to be judged returned to the deck.

For possibly the last time, he stood by the ring-bolt and stared at the open doors of the great cabin. He could almost feel the rope about his throat, as it had been around Daniel Meyer's, as it had been around the *Ulysses* men's, as it had been around Tom's…

'Mrs Jane Howard and the *Ulysses* prisoners!'

In a slow, resigned way, they walked up from below-decks. None of them had watched their former crewmates killed by the noose, yet each man looked to the yardarm as if seeing their ghosts. Even Jane did, only to glance away quickly. Nightingale tried to catch her eye but she looked instead for Courtney, who waited for her. Courtney removed his hat and held it to his chest. She laid a trembling hand over her heart.

All testimony had now been given, defendants and witnesses shuffled back and forth to the cabin. So it was in silence that the eighty remaining crew stood before the judges. Nightingale listened to Admiral Duckworth's strong voice carry through them. He summarised their crimes and their testimony, placid and unmoved by the emotion that many stewed in. This was no time for sentimentality.

'It is of the court's decision,' he finally said, and Nightingale held his breath, 'that in the case of the mutiny on HMS *Ulysses* in the year 1800, the surviving crew—', a bird flew overhead, squalling and momentarily breaking Duckworth's speech, '—the surviving crew shall be recommended for a royal pardon. Until such pardon is granted, they shall remain in Trinidad under watch, reliant upon their good conduct.'

Nightingale's heart skipped. For a moment, all the tension in his muscles ceased. He had nearly sacrificed himself for the good of the *Ulysses* crew, had taken a risk greater than necessary, and at last, here were the words to show it had been worth it.

More than ever, he knew he had acted rightly when Courtney sobbed and put a hand to his streaming eyes. Loom, beside him, grasped his arm. Jane emerged from the cabin and immediately looked towards Courtney. In one moment, before she was steered away, their gazes crossed and she smiled. For a second, she looked her youthful age, unweighted by the trial.

'Cornelius, Lord Fairholme and Lieutenant Michael Hargreaves!'

Nightingale turned away as the next men were brought to the panel. Fairholme had been broken by the past two days of questioning. The control over his own narrative had slipped, perhaps for the first time. Though his coat was still elegant and his waistcoat still beautifully embroidered, the gold and silver brocade did not shine as brightly and his clothes appeared to belong to another man. He looked at no one as he was led across the deck, not even at Hargreaves, who walked with his head down. The tears had long dried on his gaunt cheeks, but his spirit was cracked and every slow step was as if he trudged through tar.

Duckworth spoke again, intoning solemnly.

'It is of the court's decision,' he repeated, 'that in the case of the mutiny on HMS *Ulysses* in the year 1800, for the crimes of corruption and bribery, the abetting of murder and mutiny, Cornelius, Lord Fairholme is to be transported back to England under imprisonment to await further trial. Lieutenant Michael Hargreaves will, after consideration of his health and state of mind, bear the same judgement.'

The words severed the bottoms from the two men's interconnected worlds. Further trial – embedding them in the harsh web of British law, not simply a military ruling. Fairholme would be delivered into the hands of the men whose money would have been diverted into his coffers, and Hargreaves would be ensnared with him. There was a small mercy in the reference to Hargreaves's wellness, although Nightingale could not feel relieved.

'After all I have done…' Fairholme began. 'You are standing on the side of mutineers? On the side of Captain Nightingale?'

Duckworth did not react. 'We shall hear no more, Lord Fairholme.'

'You cannot do this. I demand to be tried by—'

'And you shall, Lord Fairholme. In London, where you shall employ your defence and deliver your statements. I suggest, sir, that you do not say a word more, lest that is harmed.'

'After all that I have done,' Fairholme repeated, breathless with anger. 'After all my service to this country and—'

'Marines, please take Lord Fairholme and Lieutenant Hargreaves away. They shall be imprisoned until a suitable ship is found to transport them back to England.'

'Take your hands off of me!' Fairholme struggled but the captain of the marines grabbed him about the arms. He half-dragged him from the cabin, followed by a weeping and shaking Hargreaves. Nightingale stood near their path, yet he did not need to be close to hear Fairholme's furious shouts. 'You cannot do this! I have men, I have – I have—'

But the lord did not have money, and no true defences to fall upon. He fought in the grasp of the marines – only for his gaze to cross with Nightingale's. Fairholme paused, eyes wide, as if realising something, and suddenly yelled, 'I know what you are, Captain Nightingale! I know what you have done! You stand here and condemn me, but you are a criminal yourself!'

Nightingale stiffened. The memory of the hanging mutineers turned into Tom, swinging at the end of his father's rope. He and

Fairholme shared a sin; if Fairholme fell, he could drag him down too. He shook his head, desperate, begging.

'I know what you are!' Fairholme cried again. 'You are a mad so—'

'No!' Hargreaves's voice interrupted. 'No, please, don't do this to me! Captain, please!'

In surprise, Fairholme quietened, turning to his companion. Hargreaves once again took up his cry from the trial, writhing against the marines. Nightingale caught his eye. There was lucidity there, beneath the tears; he knew precisely what he was doing. He shouted and screamed and drowned out Fairholme.

'No! No!' he wailed as they were taken away. Nightingale watched in stunned silence, heart hammering. Nobody else seemed to mark that anything was wrong – nothing more than the desperate ramblings of a condemned criminal.

'Captain Nightingale.'

The clerk appeared at the cabin door again, ignoring the vanishing cries of Lieutenant Hargreaves. Nightingale blinked and stepped out of his rigid shock.

'If you will, Captain Nightingale.'

Once again, Nightingale nodded and entered the great cabin. He waited, trying to clear his mind.

Admiral Duckworth, the deliverer of such dramatic news in these last fifteen minutes, sighed and looked up from the papers before him. He no longer seemed so imperious and cold. Perhaps Duckworth took pity, or perhaps Nightingale was simply prepared for the judgement he spoke.

'Captain Nightingale,' Duckworth began. 'Your service to the king and to the country has been long and full of great deeds. Nobody here would doubt your bravery. The Naval Gazette and your fellow captains have previously attested to your good conduct and sound judgements over the years – at Chesapeake, the Glorious First of June, Cape St Vincent, to name but a few examples. You possess a Nile medal, which no one else here can claim. That is why it grieves me to see what I have seen these last few days.'

Nightingale waited in silence.

'Hiram,' Duckworth said, familiar now. 'You did not simply lose a king's ship – you, by your own admission, destroyed her. You disobeyed your orders in one of the most serious manners I have ever heard of. Your reasons, however, were driven by a sense of duty, and that is why I have suggested leniency for the *Ulysses* crew and punishment for Lord Fairholme and Lieutenant Hargreaves. But, Hiram, it remains that the loss of the *Ulysses* is your responsibility. I believe, by examining your actions and presuming their motivations, our judgement is the kindest for everyone involved.'

Nightingale nodded, agreeing, confirming what Duckworth was presuming. 'Yes, sir.'

'Captain Hiram Nightingale, we do not malign your previous sacrifices, but it is of the court's decision that, effective immediately, you shall be dismissed from the service.'

Nightingale had expected it, had prompted it as soon as he lit the fuses on the *Ulysses*. And it was not as terrible as he had imagined. This, at last, was a fate he had written.

'Hiram, I do not wish for you to be simply turned out onto the streets, so you shall be granted a disability pension. You and your wife shall be supported until you find employment, yet it shall not be with the Royal Navy. Do you understand and accept this judgement?'

Nightingale nodded. 'Yes, sir,' he said. 'I understand and accept the judgement.'

Nightingale felt strangely disconnected as he walked out onto the deck. There was a sudden, pleasant void where the threads of the web had once bound him. No longer did he tread water in the depths, trying to keep his head above the surface. He gazed upon it, free and untroubled.

It was done.

A cutter waited for him, Barty sitting in the bows. Aside from the shouted orders, Barty and all the oarsmen stayed silent as they rowed across the harbour. Nightingale tried to school his face into something neutral, not wanting them to think that he was hurt or shocked by the court's decision. His reaction was too complex to explain; it had no firm reasoning, only a feeling deep inside, a sense of control that he had never truly experienced since the *Orient* erupted.

He had thought before that this was not a victory. It did not have to be. No victory was ever complete, no victory was ever fully glorious. There was no shame in surrendering, not when the hardships of continuing were so harmful.

Barty helped him from the boat as they touched the pontoon. He took off his sennit hat, decorated with a ribbon saying '*Scylla*', and reached out a questioning hand. 'If I may, sir,' he said.

Nightingale smiled and allowed Barty to shake his hand firmly.

'It was an honour to serve with you, sir,' the large man said, voice choked. 'Those men were talking out of their arse getting rid of you.'

Nightingale laughed and shook his head. 'Thank you, Barty. But I feel they are right. It has been pleasant to have your services. I wish you well.'

'Thank you, sir. Until I see you again.'

'And you, Barty.'

Already, it had come to farewells. Nightingale supposed he should consider his next actions – he would have to surrender his effects and inform Louisa what had happened before rumour reached her. Yet he could not simply leave his former crew without a message of thanks. He could not simply leave Courtney.

As if emerging from his thoughts, a cry soon echoed across the harbour. Another cutter bumped against the docks and the lieutenant himself scrambled from the stern, stepping over the oarsmen. Jane, aided by Lieutenant Wainwright, followed more gingerly.

'Sir!'

Parting from his sister and Wainwright, Courtney ran through the staring onlookers on the harbour, sword banging against his legs.

'Sir!' he called again, though Nightingale had stopped dead in the dusty market. Courtney skidded to a stop. His chest heaved, unruly curls falling into his wide eyes as he gripped Nightingale's arm. 'They have made a mistake,' he panted. 'To discard you like that after all that you have done... It isn't fair. I heard all that Admiral Duckworth said about your previous victories, they should not have—'

'Arthur.' Nightingale slowly removed Courtney's hand from his elbow. 'Slow down. It is all right. I am fine. I agree with the decision.'

'You do?' Courtney frowned. 'But, after everything—'

'If they had not dismissed me, I would have resigned. Truly. I am fine.'

'Oh.' Courtney searched Nightingale's face as if wanting the confirmation that he was not lying. For once, Nightingale told the truth about himself. 'If you are certain. If you are not, I shall fight for you. I will do everything that I can.'

'I am certain. But, my thanks. It has been...' Nightingale fumbled for the right words. An honour to have you by my side? A joy? A pleasure? 'You are a good man, Arthur. I know you shall do well, and I wish you all the fortune in the world.'

Courtney smiled, his eyes shining. His hands twitched as he stood awkwardly. Nightingale would not have refused an embrace if so suggested.

'Thank you, Captain. I wish the same to you.'

'I am not your captain anymore, Arthur. You need not call me that.'

Courtney laughed. 'My apologies. It shall be so very strange. But I...' He cleared his throat. 'I hope that, though you might not be my commander, I could consider you my friend?'

Nightingale's emotions welled over in a bright smile. 'Of course. I would like that.'

'Then, as your friend, I would be honoured if you could join me and Jane for supper tonight. Lieutenant Wainwright is accompanying her.'

'Thank you, Arthur, but I am very weary. And I would not want to encroach upon you. Your sister would not want me there, not a dismissed captain shadowing her joy.'

'Captain,' Courtney sighed, then checked himself. 'Sir, we would be very happy to have you join us. You have cared for the crew and the *Scylla* for so long, but... You have friends here. Let them care for you. Let *me* care for you.'

Nightingale opened his mouth dumbly, searching for words as he felt the weight of Courtney's knowing gaze. He swallowed and knew that his cheeks were reddening.

'Yes. Of course. I shall attend.'

'Thank you, sir.'

As if nothing had occurred, the daily life of the market continued around them. Fish were sold, prices were called, boys and girls ran back and forth to herd patrons. Always nearby, the sea rolled against the shore, ebbing and flowing.

Nightingale did not know what to do. He stood there, free, unconnected, himself for the first time in so long and not a captain, not a commander, not a pawn for people to manipulate.

It had not been how he had intended it to happen.

But it was over.

Finally, it was over.

Chapter Thirty-Six: Surrender

Lieutenant Courtney was still wearing his full dress uniform when he collected Nightingale from the inn that evening. Nightingale had spent the last hour debating whether he should attend. A mess of emotions, exacerbated by exhaustion, rested upon his chest. Yet when Courtney arrived, smiling, looking as though he was going to an admiral's ball, he knew he could not refuse.

For the first time in months, Nightingale wore civilian dress: a simple, unadorned black coat and a navy-blue waistcoat. He kept reaching for the non-existent sword at his side; he had surrendered it earlier. His hands felt empty, just as the rest of him felt distinctly underdressed. He supposed he would not wear a uniform again.

And yet when he and Courtney reached the tavern, their companions greeted him with all the respect due a commander. Lieutenant Wainwright rose to his feet alongside Loom and Smythe who were, unexpectedly, there. Jane, bedecked in radiant blue and gold and with her hair curled and preened, gave a beaming smile. Her cheeks were still pale yet she appeared a different person from the cowed, frightened woman from the trial. She remained seated – as did another guest.

Midshipman Richmond, in a wheeled chair, removed his hat. The last time Nightingale had seen him, he had been sweating and weeping in a hospital bed. Now, his eyes gleamed and his face reddened healthily.

'I did not expect you all,' Nightingale could only think to say.

'They insisted, sir,' Courtney said, pulling out a chair for him. 'I could not order them away.'

Nightingale was glad that he had not. It was not a rich meal, nothing in the way of what had been served at the governor's house, yet it was all the better for it. He ate simple beef and drank port and forgot about everything else. Wainwright told them rambling stories about his home and his family which started one place and ended up somewhere quite different, but they all listened and laughed – Jane the loudest as Wainwright directed humorous asides to her, ensuring she was involved in the tales of farming and his seven sisters.

Loom and Smythe could not share much more than the events of the last months, and no one wished to talk of the time before Nightingale had taken command of the *Scylla*, yet the Bristol-born master and the Kensington-born midshipman found much in common. Smythe ate what seemed to be twice his weight, prompted by Loom buying him more. It was pleasant to see something other of them beyond the personas on the ship.

However, it was Richmond who told the most intriguing story. He had been sequestered in the hospital since July, slowly recovering from the loss of his limb. A young nurse had stayed at his side, and the midshipman had patiently taught her her letters. It had been that same young nurse who had aided in Courtney's hiding of Lieutenant Hargreaves amidst the patients.

As Richmond told the tale, Courtney lowered his head and blushed. He only looked up when Richmond said that Courtney had bid him to watch out for Hargreaves, keeping him hidden from sight and anyone who came looking for him.

Before Nightingale could respond, Courtney insisted, 'You told me to bring Lieutenant Hargreaves to trial, sir. When Sir William came to me after he'd visited you at the inn, I knew I had to act. I do wish I could have found Hargreaves before Lord Fairholme prompted him to go to such drastic measures.'

Nightingale smiled, again awed by Courtney's dedication. The risk had been monumental. He opened his mouth to speak, but Wainwright said, 'You did well, Lieutenant. Hargreaves's testimony turned the tide at the court martial.'

Nightingale shook his head. 'You do too much,' he said.

'You helped us, sir,' Courtney said softly. 'It was only right that I did the same.'

Nightingale reddened. He had always felt so alone as a captain, teetering at the top of a rigid pyramid, but truly, he could not stand there without those below. It was only when stepping down that he realised how much they had all done – and not only out of tradition or obligation. The balance was even now, and they would all move apart and on.

At the end of the night, with the bright moon high, fatigue sapped at Nightingale's bones. He sat there, the words and laughter drifting into a pleasant drone, but worried that given much longer, he would drift off with his head on his chest. He yawned, trying to stifle it. Courtney glanced at him.

'Well,' Courtney said as Wainwright's story about Norfolk's county show came to an amusing conclusion, 'I apologise, gentlemen, but the hour is late. We have our duties in the morning and we have all had a trying day. Perhaps we shall meet again like this when times are calmer?'

A ripple of agreement spread. Courtney smiled. 'Mr Nightingale, I shall accompany you back to the inn. You look as though you might drop down in the street.'

Nightingale chuckled, feeling more comfortable with the new lack of naval hierarchy between him and Courtney than he would have thought. 'My thanks, Arthur. And thank you all for a wonderful evening.'

Wainwright raised his glass to him, followed by Loom and Smythe, who was a little cross-eyed from the port. Before he left, Jane reached to touch his hand. 'Bless you, Hiram,' she said sweetly, though Nightingale did not need her thanks for what he had done – having her here, safe and happy, was enough.

Yet the warm words still settled nicely in Nightingale's chest as he and Courtney left the tavern. He felt not a shred of guilt for his joy.

Courtney walked at his side as they navigated the dense streets. He guided Nightingale around an overturned barrel in their path then kept his hand familiarly on his elbow. The night was warm but not uncomfortably so, a breeze rising from the sea which crashed in the distance. Nightingale breathed in the scent. He had not drunk enough to be inebriated, but he experienced an openness that drink could bring.

'I wager my sister and Lieutenant Wainwright shall be married within the year,' Courtney suddenly said.

Nightingale turned to him. 'Do you think so? How can you tell?'

'I see the looks he gives her, and the looks she gives in return. She looked at Bill that way too. Lieutenant Wainwright and Bill were close. I have no doubt he would approve of Wainwright caring for her now he is… Well, now he is gone.'

Nightingale nodded. He knew the complexities of marriage, knew that there could be many reasons and rationales. 'You can truly tell by a look?' he asked.

'Of course. Many a woman's given me those looks.'

Nightingale frowned, only for Courtney to laugh.

'I am jesting, sir. Not *many* a woman.'

Nightingale shook his head affectionately. Feeling looser with Courtney's easy attitude and with the quiet night around them, he sighed and said, 'As I am not your captain anymore, Arthur, can I say how disastrous this voyage has been? From the second I set foot in Antigua – no, far before that – I have felt so out of control. It was a failure. I made some terrible mistakes.'

'Come, sir. It was not a failure. You had your reasons for destroying the *Ulysses* and refusing to bring the gold back to port. The right people faced justice and the right people were spared.'

'All the same, many died. I endangered many others. Perhaps I was too hasty in coming out here and accepting command. My father and Sir William suggested me for the role in Trinidad, then for the *Scylla*, but I can see now that I was not ready. I did not always act well.'

'Nor did anyone else, sir. No man ever does the right thing all the time. And, whatever you think, it was not a failure. You saved Jane and kept her secure. For that, I am eternally grateful.'

Nightingale smiled. 'You are not obliged to me because of it, Arthur.'

'I'm not here because of obligation, sir.'

'For pity then, perhaps? To help out a man who should be careful at his old age?' Courtney blushed. Nightingale laughed. 'Now I am jesting, Arthur. I seem to remember that you said something similar to me shortly after I joined the *Scylla*.'

'I apologise, sir.'

'There is no need.'

They had reached the inn. It was still remarkably tranquil; perhaps the novelty of the trial had not worn away yet and many were at the docks to stare at the ships. A handful of snoozing drunks, and a maid scrubbing overturned mugs and plates, occupied the common room. No one marked Nightingale as he and Courtney stepped through. He kept expecting the lieutenant to return to Jane but he stayed at his side all the way to his room.

'You do not need to wait on me, Arthur,' Nightingale said at the door. 'You have done more than enough. If I need, I shall send for Rylance.'

'He shall be carousing into the early hours, sir. You'll not see him.' Courtney chuckled. 'I have no objections, sir. You've been wounded and it has been a wearying day. I wish to see you safe.'

Nightingale relented. He entered, held the door for Courtney, and lit a lantern to throw a struggling glow through the small room. With the closing of the door on everything, the exhaustion suddenly found him. His limbs felt heavy, his hands useless.

'Here, let me help you, sir,' Courtney said as he fumbled with the cuffs of his coat. The lieutenant stepped closer and as neatly as a steward, eased it down his arms.

'Thank you, Arthur.'

'Sit down, sir,' Courtney offered. 'I don't want you keeling over.'

'I am fine,' Nightingale insisted, but the world loosened as he sat at the edge of the bed, entire body thrumming with the pleasure of finally being off of his feet. Courtney smiled, set aside his sword and deftly dropped to a knee before him. 'Arthur, please, I am not that infirm,' Nightingale teased, yet Courtney was adamant on unbuckling his shoes and sliding them off. One hand cupped his calf. It was warm through his silken stockings. 'Come now,' Nightingale breathed.

'How is your wound, sir?' Courtney asked.

'It is… it is improving. Dr Archer is a skilled man.'

'Indeed he is. Tell me if this hurts.' Courtney slid the first button of his waistcoat through its loop. He leant up onto his knees as he did, and he seemed so near in the confines of the small room. His gaze lowered to what his fingers were doing; Nightingale took the chance to look at him, his handsome, youthful face, the lashes about emerald eyes, the soft bow-curve of his mouth. His thoughts travelled to what Fairholme had nearly screamed about him onboard the *Leviathan*, what had happened to Tom, what he had harboured about Leroy…

The old terror did not feel so awful any more.

Courtney looked up. He smiled. Carefully, he slipped Nightingale's waistcoat down his arms, close enough that his nose nearly brushed Nightingale's. Nimble fingers reached for the stock around his throat. He pulled it from its knot, glancing for a moment across Nightingale's skin. A shiver rippled through Nightingale.

Courtney paused. Silently, he glanced down at the way his touch rested intimately against Nightingale's neck – then back, up to his face. Their breath intermingled.

Courtney's lips touched his. It was the merest brush, a hesitant crossing of boundaries. But it was enough to make Nightingale know exactly what his place was.

When Courtney pulled away, questioning, Nightingale found himself reaching out. He brushed a shaking finger over the lieutenant's cheek, letting it dip, stroking over the softness of Courtney's bottom lip. Courtney sighed and for a second, his mouth pressed to his skin again.

Nightingale kissed him. This time, it was no minute caress. They lingered until the world seemed to stop, allowing these heady moments of courage. It was nothing but Courtney – Courtney leaning into him; Courtney gently cupping his jaw; Courtney so near and beautiful.

'Your wife, sir,' Courtney suddenly breathed, but barely retreated. 'You are married. I cannot – I do not wish to harm that.'

Nightingale leant his forehead against Courtney's. His heart was racing. It took a great effort to calm his voice.

'Come here, Arthur. Let me speak to you about my wife.'

Obediently, Courtney sat beside Nightingale on the bed. Nightingale took his hand and fondled it, drawing lines over his palm. 'My wife,' he started, 'is a remarkable woman. She knows where my heart lies. I could not hide such a thing from her, she is too clever. And she is not shocked or repulsed by it, as some women may be. Her own desires are… Well, she does not have them. She has no interest or need for physical love, so to speak, or the manner of romance you might find in books. When we first married, we tried to force traditions upon ourselves and we were so unhappy. It took many years to settle into our own frames.'

Nightingale paused, hoping he was phrasing himself correctly. 'I love her very much. She is my dearest friend – and how many men can say that about their wives? But there is nothing in our bond to hinder me following my wants. Just as I would never coerce her or prevent her from doing whatever she wished. Does that make any sense to you, Arthur? It is a difficult feeling to set words to.'

'No, no, I mean – yes, of course. It is not my part to say if it makes sense or not.' Courtney laid his other hand atop Nightingale's, tracing warm fingers over his knuckles. 'You told me about Tom, sir. I have not forgotten. Aside from him, has there – have you been… open with another man?'

Nightingale smiled, touched with the sadness of his past. 'I did not love Tom. I was intrigued by him and what he told me but I did not love him, not with the intensity that I loved Leroy.' It felt strange to say it aloud, but not unpleasant. He knew that he met no judgement from Courtney, and that was half of the battle. The other half was to dredge these emotions from the walls he put them behind. 'I never told Leroy. I never considered that such a man could think the same. The way I feel… Well, sometimes it is not so different from wanting a companion or a friend. I do not, I have never, ah, how can I word this?'

'You have never wished to bed anyone?'

Nightingale blushed deeply. 'No. The temptations that men feel have never found their way to me. That is not to say that I don't feel affection in other ways.'

'How do you feel about me?'

Courtney was searching the core of his most intimate self. Nightingale squeezed his hand, and said, 'I am very fond of you. From the

354

moment I saw you, I couldn't help noticing how… striking you are.'
Courtney smiled. 'My fondness was tested by your attitude. But it did
not fade. I learnt how good a man you are, how you command, and
how you hold yourself. Again, I never thought you would have the
inclination. I am fifteen years your senior.'

'You assumed so much about me, sir. I have no qualms about your
age. You say it as though you are eighty – you are barely forty, sir. And,
for what it is worth, I felt the same about you when you personally
rescued the *Fénix* survivors. When you spoke to me badly afterwards,
I was so galled.' He laughed softly. 'I knew for certain in Trinidad.
These feelings do not frighten me or surprise me anymore. Did you
truly not realise?'

'You never gave me any cause to realise.'

Courtney laughed again. 'Sir! I jeopardised my career when I spoke
against the decision to remove you from the *Scylla*. I nearly stood in
the way when Lieutenant Hargreaves turned a gun on you. I then
risked Fairholme's wrath because you asked me to bring Hargreaves
to trial. Did you – you truly did not realise?'

Clarity struck Nightingale like a squall. He scoured the last few
months, reinterpreting everything. 'I… No. No one has ever spoken
to me in that way before. At least, I do not think so.'

Courtney beamed. 'Well, tell me what you wish me to do. I won't
press for anything untoward.'

'This is pleasant,' Nightingale said truthfully.

'And this?' Courtney slowly raised Nightingale's hand to his mouth
and, without breaking eye contact, placed a soft kiss on his weather-
beaten knuckles.

'Yes, and that.'

'And this?' He glanced his lips across Nightingale's wrist where the
pulse skipped.

'Yes.'

'This?' Now, a chaste kiss upon his cheek. Nightingale could not
speak; he nodded. 'This?' Courtney whispered and reached his lips
again. Heat bloomed over Nightingale's skin. 'Would you like me to
continue?'

'Please,' Nightingale managed. 'I do not know… how long we have before…'

But Nightingale did not wish to think of leaving. He only focused on the moment as Courtney gently laid him down, careful not to upset his wound. He was vaguely aware of uttering a quiet, 'Yes,' when Courtney asked if he could remove some of his uniform. Nightingale wanted to raise his hands to help him but they were trembling violently. Instead, he watched Courtney take off his gorgeous coat and waistcoat. When he slipped the stock from his throat, Nightingale could not stop his eyes from wandering to his open collar and the sun-browned skin.

'You can touch me,' Courtney murmured. 'It is all right.'

Courtney joined him on the sheets and Nightingale obeyed the request. He stared in fascination at his own fingers against Courtney's collarbones, tracing up to his bare neck. Bumps erupted beneath his touch. Barely believing he caused it, Nightingale reached into the dark hair he had so admired. It was soft and unruly, even more so when he loosened the ribbon, letting curls fall around Courtney's shoulders.

Courtney smiled, cheeks flushed. He leant down, caressed Nightingale's upturned face, and captured his mouth. Nightingale's bravery surged as he kissed him back. It was exquisite, warm and tender and kind where his first encounter with Louisa had been cold and hostile and awkward. He found himself pulling Courtney closer, not wanting to let him go, wanting this to be his whole world.

They only broke for breath. Then Courtney, chest heaving, lips swollen, returned for more. Nightingale could feel how he wanted to move; he took his hand and guided it to his waist. His touch roamed and they shifted until they were almost chest-to-chest. Kisses upon kisses Courtney rained on his mouth before turning them upon his neck, tracing paths of delight over the quivering skin of his throat. Nightingale closed his eyes, trying to remember how to breathe.

Up his side Courtney's hand went, caressing where Nightingale was still bandaged. Before he realised what he was doing, Courtney's fingers found the ridges upon his back.

Nightingale broke away. For a moment, he had forgotten those scars. Now, the memories of how they were delivered rushed back like a cold wind.

'I'm sorry,' Courtney said. 'I didn't mean to—'

'No. It is all right. Sometimes, I can ignore them. They are very ugly.'

Courtney paused. 'I'm sure they are not.'

'Oh, they are. They are there for the ugliest of reasons. My father—'

'I know.' Courtney retreated, cradling Nightingale's hand in his again. He whispered, softly, 'Let me see.'

'I don't know.'

'You can trust me.'

'I know that. But...' He remembered the first time Louisa had seen them. It had been the morning after their wedding night, when he had risen to dress. She had looked and immediately turned away. Nightingale had had to live with the idea that she might decipher what they meant. Apparently, she had.

With infinite care, Courtney raised his shirt. Nightingale stared ahead at a patch of damp stone beneath the window, arms crossed about his chest. He could not see Courtney's reaction, and that made it worse.

'Oh,' Courtney intoned.

'They are ugly, yes?'

'No. Not at all.' Courtney's fingers touched the very top scar. They moved leisurely, drawing along the line that stretched across Nightingale's spine. It crossed with another and another and another, a whole terrible patchwork that may have healed physically but not inside. Nightingale had never truly looked at them, so very glad they were upon his back and nowhere else. He felt that freezing Hampshire winter again, the roughness of the oak's bark beneath his scrambling nails and the harsh grate of his father's orders.

Now, Courtney's warm breath tickled those memories. He pressed his lips to his spine where the wounds would always be. With a supportive hand on Nightingale's hip, he kissed them, slowly rising. Nightingale shivered – though not for that wintry tragedy anymore.

He closed his eyes as the tears gathered but eventually, could not withhold them. As Courtney soothed the underlying pain, he began to weep. It was not for agony or grief – only an upwelling of tension and everything that he had hidden before. Unashamed, unburdened, he sobbed, and Courtney did not stop until the entire tapestry of scars had been kissed.

Then, smiling and tender, he turned Nightingale back to his side and wrapped his arms about him. Nightingale buried his face into his neck, shaking and torn by the ecstasy of trauma laid bare.

Patiently, Courtney stroked his hair. When he was ready, Courtney softly lifted his head to face him. With his lips mere inches away, he asked, 'Would you like me to stay?'

Nightingale swallowed. He smiled.

'Please,' he whispered.

Chapter Thirty-Seven: Xenia

A bright sliver of sunlight split through the worn shutters. It fell across the threadbare rug and over Nightingale's sea-chest. He knelt and gently traced the designs painted on the outside. He had drawn the whorls of blue waves and painted shells when he was alone in his berth as a twelve-year-old midshipman, emblazoning them alongside the crest of his initials. Ever since that first cruise, the chest had accompanied him onto every vessel – as a junior officer, then a third lieutenant up to a senior lieutenant, and finally commander and captain and post-captain. On the back was a scratched record of each ship.

That list would end with HMS *Scylla*.

Nightingale opened the lid and gently pushed aside the neatly folded post-captain's uniform, alongside the spare shirts and stockings and unread books. At the bottom was a small journal which he tore a page from, then quietly crossed the room to the little desk.

For a while, with the sunlight warming his face, he sat there, twirling a pen in his fingers. Twenty-eight years of service wallowed inside him. He had hated it at first, forced there by his father, but he had grown to love it and his crews. Still, for all those decades, it was as if he was an imposter whose mask would suddenly be ripped off.

Now, it had been. And what was beneath was not as terrible as he had feared.

He dipped the pen's nib in ink and began to write a note he had stalled upon for too long. He didn't want to, but it was a necessity for his peace of mind – a closing of this chapter.

As he was about to sign his name, the bed behind him creaked softly and a small groan sounded from the sheets. 'You're awake,' Courtney's tired voice said.

Nightingale smiled and turned to face him. Stripped of his uniform, Courtney leant with unruly black curls against the headboard. They had slept snugly in each other's embrace all night, cupped as close as cutlery in a drawer. It had been a small token of serenity after such a long storm. 'I didn't want to disturb you,' Nightingale said.

'What're you doing?'

'I'm writing a note to my father. I wish to speak with him.'

The fatigue left Courtney's expression. 'Are you sure that is wise?'

'I have to talk to him before I leave for England.'

Courtney sat up and stood from the bed. He was still dressed in his loose shirt and drawers, and was warm from the sheets as he put his hands on Nightingale's shoulders. Nightingale let him read the note.

'You are going to leave for England so soon, sir?' he asked.

'You do not have to call me "sir" anymore, Arthur. You may call me "Hiram".' Nightingale smiled. 'And yes. There is not much for me here anymore. I have no commission. I am not even in the service. I need to return home and arrange things – and try to decide what it is I wish to do now.'

Courtney's eyes searched his face. He seemed to be about to say something, but then slowly nodded. 'I understand. Jane wishes to return once the pardon arrives. She and Lieutenant Wainwright. He wants to set her up in his house in Great Yarmouth where some of his sisters live. There are only bad memories for her here.'

'I wish her well.'

'I shall have to remain here,' Courtney continued. 'My place is with the Scylla. I highly doubt I'll be promoted, not so soon after this trial, whether we were acquitted or not. But somewhen, perhaps... And I don't wish to stay in the West Indies my entire career. I'd like to return to the Mediterranean stations.'

'I would say that I'd write a recommendation for you, but I don't think my word is worth very much anymore. You don't need my help, anyhow, Arthur. You'll do perfectly well on your own.'

'I don't wish to be entirely on my own.' Courtney's tone softened again. He rubbed his fingers down the collar of Nightingale's night-shirt and wrapped his arms about his shoulders. Nightingale touched his hand where it rested over his heart. 'I would very much like to see you,' he said, lips against his ear.

'I would like that too. I shall give you my address in Portsmouth. You are very free to write, and when you return home, visit me.'

Courtney gave a beaming grin. 'I shall count the days. Now, are you finished with the note?'

'Yes. I'll give it to Rylance to send on.'

'He'll be thrilled to visit Admiral Nightingale.' Courtney laughed. 'Come with me.'

With his hand still in Courtney's, Nightingale rose from the desk. They settled beneath the quilt again and Courtney shifted so his arms were crossed upon Nightingale's chest, faces close. Nightingale stroked his cheek and said, 'Thank you for staying with me, Arthur.'

Courtney answered by kissing his fingers as they caressed his mouth. 'I admire you for your reaction to your father. I was going to suggest that I duel him.'

Nightingale surprised himself by laughing. Courtney's smile grew and he joined in until tears were in their eyes.

Guilt shifted away from Nightingale's heart. He had come through hell to reach the ground where he stood. He would be foolish to think it was the end, but at last, he had his hands upon the course and the fog was vanishing.

Clear-eyed for the first time in an age, he cupped Courtney's cheek, leant in and easily, freely, kissed him. He let it linger, enjoying his warmth, enjoying his open affection, enjoying the idea that this was his – and damn everybody else.

—

Nightingale waited on the coastline. The sea lapped at the sand, leaving soft, muddy patches beneath his shoes. The gentle roll of the waves was the only sound other than the squawking of the gulls – far from the loud, busy bustle of the market along the shore. He had come to this cove alone, without his uniform, without his finery, simply as a man: forty years old and finally ready to face the tormentor of his childhood and adult life.

Three days had passed since the trial in slow, syrupy undefined chunks of time. Without the rigidity of naval structure, he felt as though he drifted above everything, unable to set it into a logical sequence. It wasn't frightening anymore. He was free to come and go without an eye on the sandglass or waiting for a bell to chime. More than once, he had visited the harbour and watched the *Scylla*, without a captain again, rocking gently at anchor, her future uncertain. He had seen the crew onshore a handful of times and tipped his hat to them, receiving friendly smiles in return. And he had fulfilled his promise to check in on Toby Warren, finding him resting his leg in a tavern, wooing a serving maid and no doubt on the verge of upsetting another father.

Throughout all of those days, Nightingale had not changed his mind about this meeting.

The sand crunched behind him. Nightingale turned to see his father, Laurence Nightingale, approaching. He was in civilian dress, a cane in one hand and Nightingale's note in the other. Nightingale had not met with him since leaving Trinidad for the first time – not since his father had come to the inn with Sir William and wrenched his command away from him like a child who had played with a toy too long. In his father's eyes, he doubted he had ever grown from a boy needing direction.

'Good afternoon,' Nightingale said placidly.

'Hiram,' his father answered with a nod.

'I wanted to speak to you,' Nightingale said, no longer caring about unnecessary pleasantries, 'before I leave for England.'

Admiral Nightingale remained silent.

'I shan't apologise for what I did. I shan't apologise for tarnishing our name, which I know has always been important to you. It was through your choice that I joined the navy and through your choice that I took the *Scylla* command. I am not certain what else I would have done with my life; I am not certain what I shall do now. But I do not need your suggestions any longer.'

'You have made that quite clear, Hiram.'

'Why treat me like this? What have I done to warrant it?'

Nightingale was not sure if he wanted, or needed, to know. No explanation could justify such neglect and hatred. Yet he still listened as his father sighed and said, 'You were always different, Hiram. I know how hard the world is on men. I simply showed you how you would be treated if you continued down that path. Do you know that your mother left for Portugal due to the strain?'

'She did not leave because of my actions.' Nightingale heard the bitterness in his voice, and hated it. He could not allow this man to dictate his emotions anymore. He shook his head and looked away. Long before coming to this shoreline, he had made his decision. 'I won't forgive you for what you did to me, or to others – as I know you will not forgive me. All I have to say is that I do not wish to see you any longer. You have played your role. Now let me be.'

Surprise crossed his father's face. Nightingale did not relish it.

'Goodbye, Father,' he only said.

He started to leave. As he climbed the banks, he heard Admiral Nightingale shout, 'I could have done worse, Hiram! I could have condemned you too. I pray you never have sons and realise what a sadness they can be!'

Nightingale did not turn. Strange relief washed through him: the knowledge that he had made the right decision. His father was unrepentant and would remain that way. Nightingale did not need such an anchor.

Ahead, waiting under the shelter of calabash trees, a figure stood in silhouette. Nightingale raised his hand into the sun to shield his eyes.

'You should be with the ship,' he said with a frown.

Courtney smiled and joined him in step.

'We have no orders yet. I'm half-expecting us to be paid off and the *Scylla* to be put into ordinary.'

'You shall be her captain one day.'

'Perhaps.' He glanced behind him. Nightingale didn't need to see if his father followed them. 'I have something I want to give you.'

'You don't need to give me anything, Arthur.'

'Come.'

They returned to the inn where Nightingale had already arranged his effects, anticipating a passage within days. Courtney closed the door behind him and revealed something from his inside pocket. A small box rested in his outstretched hand.

'What is this?' Nightingale asked.

'Open it. Please.' Courtney smiled, though a sudden nervousness touched his eyes. Nightingale relented and took the gift.

When he opened the lid, his heart jumped. Without thought, he found himself reaching in and tracing the familiar patterns of the token: the goddess Pax brandishing an olive branch, the bust of Lord Nelson on her shield, and on the reverse, the etched fleet at Aboukir Bay. His throat scratched as he asked, 'Where did you find this?'

'A couple of fishermen dredged it up whilst we were in Trinidad last time. I made them give it to me. I knew you had one, and I – well, I know it wasn't an accidental loss. Perhaps it wasn't my place to return it, but… I was waiting for the right moment.'

Nightingale held it up, looked deeply into its aureate glow, and realised that the feelings were still there: the shame, the guilt, the grief. They were seeded long before that night at the Nile, but what had happened there had inflamed them into a choking fiery grip. Such emotions would never truly leave him.

Yet the old pain did not last as long now. With his father gone, with his shackles beaten off, Nightingale was able to look away from the hypnotic trauma.

'Here.' Nightingale put it back in its box and handed it to Courtney. The lieutenant frowned. 'You keep it. I have no need for it anymore.'

'I cannot. You earned it. It's a medal from the Nile.'

'And now I am giving it to you. Please, I insist. I had one made for Leroy and… I want you to have it.'

Courtney slowly opened the lid again, as if expecting it to vanish before his eyes. He nodded, breathing out a long sigh. 'If you are certain.'

'More than anything.'

Courtney blinked, hurriedly stowed the box in his pocket, and then Nightingale found his arms full of the young lieutenant. Holding him tight enough to almost stop his breath, Courtney kissed him – a long, impassioned embrace that spoke what he did not need to say aloud. Nightingale gently cupped his neck, tangling his fingers into his curls and smiling, chest taut, when he pulled back.

'I shall miss you,' Courtney whispered.

'And I shall miss you too, my dear. I hope to see you soon.'

'I shall count the days,' Courtney repeated.

—

The journey across the harbour was bittersweet. With every pull of the oars, Nightingale separated himself from Trinidad and from the rigorous, painful venture of the past few months. The nights and days of fear and doubt slipped beneath the waves, leaving only a dull kernel of remorse.

And yet emptiness still pulsed inside of him. He had tried to carve out all of that fear and doubt and along with it, had to leave behind other emotions, just as potent – because every doubt and every fear had arisen because of love and loyalty to the Scyllas and to those he cared for. The sudden wrenching away of everything that had been firm left a confusion of what would fill the gap. It was intoxicating and new, but still, sitting in the stern of the cutter with Jane and Lieutenant Wainwright, he was aware of the thin wood beneath him, balancing above a deep sea.

Jane's hand rested close by Wainwright's. She was as silent as Nightingale, her face turned towards the sun and away from the island. Nightingale had been with her when the pardon for her and the remaining *Ulysses* men had arrived. He had watched as she embraced Courtney. But she had not wept or laughed. One pardon did not erase all that she had experienced.

Lieutenant Courtney would no doubt be watching from the *Scylla*. Around a cable-length away, she bobbed at anchor, neat and trim and shining in the golden light. To think that she had been Nightingale's home for so long, a witness to such tragedy and triumph, made his throat tighten. Over the years, he had placed too much importance on those wooden walls: the *Strabo*, the *Lion*, the *Scylla*, the *Ulysses*. But there was magic about her: the way that she still remained so strong and untouched by what she had been through. Nightingale knew she would continue under a new commander – and this time, the parting did not seem so painful.

Courtney and Smythe and Loom and Parry and all the rest would look after her, and she would sail in memory of all those who had died for her.

'She looks so like the *Ulysses*,' Wainwright remarked as he saw what his two partners were staring at. 'She sits nicer, though. A far prettier line with that new paint. It will not dry as easily with the gun ports open, though.'

Nightingale had not noticed, but now he saw that Wainwright was correct: three of the ports hung open and strangely, the guns were run out. 'Perhaps it is a minor repair,' he commented, then nearly jumped out of his skin as those mouths roared. Blank charges spat out, the sound rippling across the harbour and sending gulls racing into the sky. Jane gasped and clutched Wainwright's arm. She stared, half in concern, half in delight, as the *Scylla*'s marines raised their muskets and fired into the air.

'What is it?' she asked breathlessly.

'Ssh, it's quite all right,' Wainwright replied, beaming. 'They are saluting us. Well, I should say, you and Mr Nightingale.'

Upon the deck and on the yards and rigging, all hands on watch lifted their hats. In one voice, they cheered. At the waist, Courtney and Smythe stood on the gunwales and led the cry. Nightingale laughed. He mimicked them, sweeping off his hat and waving. Beside him, Jane raised a shy hand.

'I hope he does not get into trouble for that,' Nightingale said when the cheering was done.

'Arthur has a way of finding fortune,' Jane replied.

'Long may that last.'

Nightingale smiled. Breathing in the rich afternoon air, he was able to finally look ahead: out over the blue waters that led back to England and beyond.

Historical Note

In August 1798, the time of the Battle of the Nile, the French Revolutionary Wars had been sweeping the globe for the past six years. Battles on both land and sea raged. The Royal Navy was a formidable fighting force, defending Britain and her colonies. Fleet actions such as the Nile and, later, Trafalgar now define the public image of the 18th and 19th century navy but frigates of the Age of Sail also played significant roles. Admiral Nelson called them "his eyes", fast and nimble sailers that scouted for the fleet, harassed trade and could operate independently. Many captains, such as Pellew and Cochrane, gained fame through frigate command.

HMS *Hermione*, launched in 1782, was a frigate which would acquire a more ignominious reputation. After suffering cruel treatment from her captain, Hugh Pigot, the crew rose up in a bloody mutiny during September 1797, slaughtering many men aboard. The *Hermione* was then sailed to La Guaira and handed over to the Spanish authorities. It would not be until October 1799 before Captain Edward Hamilton, commanding HMS *Surprise*, would cut her out of Puerto Cabello's harbour and recapture her into British service.

In the meantime, revolution also swept across the island of Hispaniola which, at the time of *Leeward*, was split between the French Saint-Domingue and the Spanish Santo Domingo. From the early 1790s, factional conflict broke out in Saint-Domingue, influenced by French revolutionary ideals, the mistreatment of slaves, and class divisions between European colonists, slaves, and *affranchis* (free people of black or mixed descent). After slave uprisings and French attempts to appease all sides, slavery was abolished in the colony.

By the end of the century, Toussaint Louverture, a former slave, had risen to power as a significant military leader. His forces ousted the Spanish, later invading Santo Domingo, and he gave nominal allegiance to the French but dealt with others in pursuit of his own schemes, including the British forces that had been sent to the French West Indies. An agreement was signed that promised that, in exchange from British withdrawal from Saint-Domingue, no more uprisings would be fomented.

In the early years of the 19th century, Louverture was named governor-for-life and he called for a sovereign black state. This would eventually materialise as Haiti in 1804, but not before internal conflict, a French invasion and Louverture's own capture and imprisonment. French troops withdrew from the island and Napoleon's desires of re-establishing widespread French control in the Americas were at an end.

British influence in the Caribbean remained in areas such as Jamaica and the British Leeward Islands, whose base was at Antigua. In 1797, a British force led by Sir Ralph Abercromby invaded Trinidad, resulting in a Spanish capitulation. Under Thomas Picton, Trinidad became a British colony, something which was formalised in the 1802 Treaty of Amiens.

Acknowledgements

Thank you to everyone at Canelo for all their support and interest in *Leeward*. Especial thanks go to Kit and Miranda for their hard work and aid through *Leeward*'s journey. Their encouragement and editing talents helped to polish *Leeward* and bring it into the wider world.

I wish to also thank my readers from Wattpad who were there when *Leeward* was first serially posted online. I received valuable feedback from all of them, and they were a part of transforming *Leeward* during its early drafts. Reading their comments and positive reactions was endlessly entertaining!

There were multiple resources, both fiction and non-fiction, which provided very helpful research into this quite intimidating period and setting. Patrick O'Brian's *Aubrey–Maturin* series and CS Forester's *Hornblower* books (as well as the accompanying films and TV episodes) are without match for a sense of the genre. The online contemporary manuals from the Historic Naval Ships Association and Dean King's *A Sea of Words* guided me through the unfamiliar world of naval lexicon, terminology and ship life, while Angus Konstam's *Mutiny on the Spanish Main* was a book I returned to again and again for inspiration.

I wish to also acknowledge family and friends for their encouragement in all areas. Their support and love through both good and bad moments is something I can't thank them enough for.

Thank you for reading *Leeward*

Nightingale and Courtney will return for another
romantic, swashbuckling adventure in:

THE
DEVIL
TO PAY

Coming April 2024

Read on for an exclusive extract…

Chapter One

Fickle Fate

September 1801, the Mona Passage, between Santo Domingo and Puerto Rico

The *Scylla* had no time to react. Captain Robinson ordered for hands to the braces. Before the yards could be braced around, preventing the *Scylla* from careering onto the bars, her stern began to turn towards the French ship, *Cygne*. As the helm threatened to spin out of Barty and his mate's hands, Courtney hurried to them, grabbing on to steady the rudder.

At the same moment, Lieutenant Derby emerged from the hatch. His eyes widened as a shuddering succession of blasts resounded from the *Cygne*. Courtney's legs nearly buckled when the shots impacted. The mizzenmast lurched; chunks of timber exploded; Abbott cried aloud and fell into Courtney, taking them both down onto the deck. Pressed to the timber, Courtney could hear the cries and orders of the mids and gun crew below, preparing to return the shots. Smoke poured out the portholes.

Courtney scrambled to return to his feet, only to find his limbs and palms slipping in a pool of hot liquid. His stomach tightened. Red soaked through his coat and breeches. Frantically, he felt for the injury, mind racing to that letter he had never finished for Nightingale. But he felt no pain or loss.

Abbott. The coxswain was alive too, though sprayed with the same blood and gore which Courtney now felt dripping through his hair and over his skin. He stared aft, pale beneath the crimson.

Captain Robinson's death had been quick, and that was the only mercy. One of the *Cygne*'s shots had taken him through the waist, sundering him almost in two, snuffing all his years in a single second. Bile rose in Courtney's throat. He desperately swallowed it and rose to trembling legs. For a moment, he had no clue what to do. His life condensed to this one, bewildering, awful moment.

Then he saw Derby half-collapsed upon the companion-ladder, looking as though he was nearing hysteria; Abbott and his mate, stricken, upon the deck; the remaining topmen and Murray, in the chains, ashen with shock. Courtney wiped the blood from his cheeks and gripped the sword at his waist. 'Hands to the braces!' he shouted to the tops. 'Ready about! Lieutenant Derby, to the gun deck!'

It was a risk to try and tack in the rising wind, but Courtney trusted this crew and trusted this ship. In the heat of the *Cygne*'s fire, the canvas was shortened, the mainsail hauled and the yards ached about. With what felt like inches to spare, the foremast came around and they soared past the stuck *Meridian*. She signalled for aid, her bows jammed into the protruding sand. Men already climbed down her sides to assess the damage which Courtney could see was not serious. They could have her off at the turn of the tide. As long as the *Cygne* did not empty her guns into her vulnerable frame, she would sail for many years to come.

'Seventy fathoms, sir!' Murray cried. The *Scylla* had avoided the worst of the bar and now deeper water awaited her. Safely on the starboard tack, she left the *Meridian*, drawing the *Cygne*'s fire. Her progress was marked by the forward starboard guns blasting across the clear waters as the *Scylla* beat on towards the *Cygne*'s flank. Closer, Courtney noticed the previous damage done to her: a stern chaser off its carriage, rudder chipped, spanker-boom hanging on by its stays. The next shot cracked it entirely. The sail and timber fell with a resounding clatter, nearly crushing the man at the helm.

'A little nearer and she'll be in range of a broadside,' Courtney said.

Though she had just delivered devastating fire across the *Scylla*'s deck, Courtney knew the *Cygne* struggled. Troubled by the harm to her spars and rudder, she already floundered towards the island, trying to cross the *Scylla*'s bows and prevent the might of a thirteen-gun broadside which would cripple her. A minute adjustment to the course had the *Scylla*'s cannons maintain their targets along her hull, but the *Cygne* still turned, closer, ever closer to the rocky shore.

Courtney turned to stare at the unforgiving walls of Monito Island. The ragged cliffs vaulted high above the ships. He would not play the fool and chase the *Cygne* so close. She could lacerate herself on those rises.

A blast from the *Scylla* brought his attention back to the *Cygne*'s gun deck which had just been lacerated by shot. One of the portholes at the waist ripped wide open and a cannon's muzzle disappeared. Courtney thought it had overturned but then, violently, a hail of timber blasted from the *Cygne*'s flank. The force made him flinch. He ducked on instinct, seeing chunks of heated metal pinwheeling through the air and plummeting into the sea. A gaping hole remained, full of felled men pressed together in a gory mass.

'A cannon!' Courtney gasped to Loom who stared as aghast as him. 'A cannon has erupted!'

Flames suddenly flickered on the frigate's gun deck. It sputtered out of the void in the hull, before tearing back, igniting the dry wood. The *Cygne*'s other guns fell silent, the absence of sound strange and ominous. Dead bodies, struck down from the explosion, were heaved from the ship as crewmen scrambled to douse the blaze. Fire at sea was a sailor's worst fear; it could destroy a ship in minutes.

That was all it took for the *Cygne*'s waist to turn into a sparking beacon. With men drawn down to deal with the blaze, and the damage eating through the vessel, the frigate kept drifting, sailing towards the island, the wind fanning the danger. Little figures hurried past the shimmering heat, fire buckets at hand. But the deck was a keg, stuffed with gunpowder. Across the waters, Courtney could hear it popping and bursting.

'Good God,' Courtney muttered aloud. 'Mr Abbott, helm amidships. We'll not endanger ourselves. Lieutenant Derby!'

Courtney's shoes slipped in Robinson's blood as he ran to the hatch down to the gun deck. Gun smoke bled through the dingy space below, making the crew look like ghouls. Derby emerged, wraith-like, fair hair streaming out of its tie and plastered to his forehead. Smythe was not far behind 'Lieutenant Derby, avast firing.'

'Sir—' But then Derby turned to larboard where the *Cygne* burnt. The sunlight was choked with fire. 'Good God,' he swore. 'Did we do that?'

Within minutes, the conflagration had raced up one of the *Cygne*'s companion-ladders, reaching her quarterdeck. The foot of the main-mast became encircled with fire, cutting off the topmen's escape. Grey smoke started to churn, flooding over the sides. Courtney saw shadows falling through it, splashing into the waters.

'They're abandoning her,' he said. 'If that fire reaches the powder store...'

He did not finish. Courtney had seen two ships erupt before: the *Ulysses* and the *Fénix*. He had no desire to witness the deaths again.

With the smell of blazing timber covering his lungs, and the infernal heat swarming across the sea, he knew he had to make a decision. He could not simply stand there and watch the French frigate burn to the waterline.

'Mr Smythe,' Courtney said. 'You and I are going to attempt to rescue any survivors. Assemble a party of thirteen to man three of the launches. Quickly!'

Smythe disappeared without question but Derby's eyes widened, whether in prospect of temporarily captaining the *Scylla* or at the idea of Courtney saving the crew they had just been trying to kill. He did not have time to question it before Smythe reappeared, accom-panied by his men. Courtney was relieved to see Obi, one of their strongest and most dependable amongst them. He caught his breath and ordered, 'Pull anyone still alive from the water. Return them to the *Scylla*. If they reach the island, then let them. Do not approach the *Cygne* too closely. She does not have long.'

Courtney knew he should not accompany them – the danger was too great and Lieutenant Derby could not handle the *Scylla* – but he remembered how Nightingale had rescued the survivors from the *Fénix* when a lightning strike had ignited her. It had been the first time the man had inspired him.

With the animals removed from the launches, Courtney, Smythe and the men climbed down into the boats. Courtney perched in the starboard bank of the largest cutter, grasping an oar and ignoring the looks of the crew.

They did not set the cutter's sail, but pulled over the water, the heat growing the closer they approached the doomed *Cygne*. The masts had now turned into pyres, belching smoke and debris. Sails ignited and disintegrated into shreds of white canvas that flew in the wind until coming to smoulder in the sea. Bare heads bobbed above the surface, desperate arms protruding and splashing in an attempt to reach debris. Many sailors in the English Navy did not know how to swim, believing it to be tempting fate. Courtney wondered if French mariners were the same. He wanted to call out that they would be rescued, but knew no French. Thankfully, Smythe's voice shouted as he directed his launch towards the sandbars. *Cygne* men began to heave themselves towards them.

'Lay on your oars!' Courtney ordered and the cutter came to an unsteady halt. Men's chilled, wet hands pawed at the hull, slipping on the damp timber and trying to grope for the gunwales. He reached overboard and grabbed hold. With their water-logged clothes, he had to strain to haul them from the sea which sucked and dragged at them. Courtney helped a young, thin lad crawl into the cutter, followed by a man older than Master Loom. They all rested against the safety of the empty benches, shivering, coughing, some of them vomiting salt water. Courtney could see no officers.

The two other launches were becoming full. Smythe's boat sagged deeper into the sea, water lapping higher and higher. 'To the *Scylla*!' Courtney ordered in a harsh cry. The oarsmen had to labour to manoeuvre the heavy vessel and by the time they reached the *Scylla*, Courtney's arms and shoulders burnt. But he still grasped the French sailors and helped shove them up the ladder towards the waiting Scyllas on deck. An old seaman's legs trembled so vigorously that Courtney climbed halfway up with him, a hand constantly on his back. To his relief, Lieutenant Derby reached down and helped him up the last steps.

'We can save more men!' Courtney shouted up to him.

'The *Meridian*, sir—' Derby began but Courtney had already sat back down at the oars.

Fifteen more they heaved from the water. Courtney's back was in agony from leaning over the gunwales, and he was chilled to the bone despite the roaring conflagration. But he refused to let go of a man who flapped and twisted in the water. He shouted something in French, swallowing gouts of salt water every time he opened his mouth. Courtney caught him on the back of his shirt and dredged up his dwindling strength to scrape him over the side of the cutter.

'Sir!' Obi, at his side, suddenly shouted. Courtney glanced up, his arms still full of the struggling sailor. The *Cygne*'s mainmast blazed completely now, the yards resembling a forest consumed by a wildfire. Flames spat out of gun ports, untouched by the sea. For a moment, the ship and all her sailors held their breath.

'Down!' Courtney yelled. 'All hands, down!'

In case they did not understand, Courtney grabbed the nearest French crewmen and shoved them into the shell of the cutter. He felt Obi collapse close to him: the last thing he was aware of before the world erupted.